'I really loved it. Complex, unsettling and hard to put down, definitely not a book to read when you're alone.'

Jane Holland, bestselling author of *Girl Number One*

'An original, gripping read. A cast of well-drawn sympathetic characters lure the reader into their lives and there was a twist at the end that I did not see coming. I loved this book.'

Lesley Sanderson, author of *The Orchid Girls*

'Ambitious and intricately crafted, with a masterful cast of characters who instantly feel like old friends (and enemies). A deliciously dark and relatable tale of secrets, grudges and the long shadows cast by childhood cruelties.'

Kate Simants, author of *Lock Me In*

WHO
WE
WERE

WHO
WE
WERE

B.M. CARROLL

VIPER

First published in Great Britain in 2020 by
VIPER, part of Serpent's Tail,
an imprint of Profile Books Ltd
29 Cloth Fair
London
EC1A 7JQ
www.serpentstail.com

Copyright © B.M. Carroll, 2020

1 3 5 7 9 10 8 6 4 2

Printed and bound in Great Britain by
CPI Group (UK) Ltd, Croydon, CR0 4YY

The moral right of the author has been asserted.

A CIP catalogue record for this book is
available from the British Library.

ISBN 978 1 78816 417 7
Export ISBN 978 1 78816 418 4
eISBN 978 1 78283 647 6

For Rob, Conor and Ashling

The lock takes less than a minute, the fourth key a close enough fit, assisted with a few bumps from the handle of a screwdriver. The door pushes open into a hallway with off-white tiles laid on the diagonal. Next is an open-plan kitchen and living area, a study nook on the far side of the sofa: small desk, dated laptop, a printout of the invitation sitting atop a neat pile of paperwork.

You are invited to the twenty-year reunion of the Class of 2000

Deep breath. Don't get angry. Don't lose focus.

The laptop whirrs to life, its fan sounding inordinately loud in the silent apartment. No password required, stupidly trusting and naive. Insert the USB, click on install, twenty minutes to completion. Be calm. Be thorough. She won't be home for hours yet. Plenty of time to check her browsing history, her Facebook page and the rest of the paperwork on the desk. Glimpses into the construct of her life, the friends she holds close, her most secret desires.

Wander into the kitchen, opening and shutting cabinet doors, cataloguing the food she eats, the brand of coffee she prefers. The main bedroom is located down a short corridor. White cotton bedcovers, faux-fur cushions, the book she's reading – a bestselling thriller – open on the bedside table. Underneath it, another book, larger, sickeningly familiar.

1

Don't touch it, don't look at those hateful faces, don't fall for that fake innocence.

Back to the antiquated laptop. Glare at the screen as it reluctantly grinds through the final stages. Pocket the USB. Switch off the machine. Pause inside the front door, key poised, cap pushed low in case there's a security camera lurking somewhere. Listen. All clear. Bump, bump, bump goes the screwdriver.

It's happening. Their shallow lives will be blown apart.

And they'll be sorry. Finally.

Name: Annabel Moore (School captain)

What you will be remembered for: Not keeping a straight face when Miss Hicks fell up the stage steps on awards night.

Best memories of high school: Year 11 snow excursion.

Worst memories of high school: Double period maths on Fridays. Torture.

What will you be doing ten years from now: Marine biologist.

1
ANNABEL

The phone rings on the way to school pick-up. Annabel takes the call, even though she's almost outside the school and the conversation will have to be a short one.

'What happened to marine biology?' Grace's voice fills the car.

'What?'

'Our school yearbook. Apparently, you were going to be a marine biologist!'

'I was?' Annabel is astounded. She has no recollection of this.

'It's here in black and white.'

'What else does it say?'

'That you'll be remembered for not keeping a straight face at awards night!'

This she does remember. Miss Hicks catching the toe

of her shoe on the second step. Face-planting on the stage. Annabel trying, unsuccessfully, to quell the urge to laugh. Death stares from the principal, Mr Rowland.

She snorts. 'Well, they could hardly put in what I was *really* remembered for, could they?'

'No,' Grace agrees. 'That wouldn't have come across as well.'

Annabel Moore: the girl who was pregnant during the HSC. Her enlarged belly jutting against the exam desk. Her ankles swollen in her school shoes. No surprise that she and Jarrod got disappointing results. How could they study, concentrate, pretend that the Higher School Certificate mattered while their lives were imploding?

She flicks on her indicator and pulls into a space that isn't quite big enough. The rear end of her Ford Territory juts into a residential driveway. *It's okay*, she tells herself. *It's only for a few minutes.*

'Why are you looking at that stupid old thing anyway? Aren't your kids keeping you busy enough?'

Grace, like Annabel, is a stay-at-home mum. She has four children, all quite close in age. The strange thing is, she was never the maternal type.

'Katy Buckley wants to do an updated yearbook,' Grace explains. 'For the reunion.'

Katy Buckley. Plain and studious. Perennially mocked for being such a try-hard. Annabel feels a rush of that old derision, its resurgence taking her by surprise.

'Oh, for God's sake. What's wrong with just rocking

up on the night, getting drunk and making fools of ourselves on the dance floor? Who the fuck cares about yearbooks?'

'It's because Katy's a teacher. She's still caught up in that world. Where things like yearbooks actually matter … Having said that, I think it's a rather good idea …'

'And what did Katy Buckley want to be when she left school?'

Annabel can hear Grace turn the pages of the book.

'President of the Wilderness Society.'

Both women burst into laughter. Explosive, unstoppable laughter that reminds Annabel of when they were younger, and half the time didn't even know what they were laughing about. The school bell rings, the sound carrying through the open windows of Annabel's car, bringing a distinct feeling of nostalgia.

Some children, the quick ones, are already flying through the gates. The ones to whom being first means everything. First to get to school in the morning. First out the door to lunch. Their darting eyes able to establish where queues will be formed and their agile bodies manoeuvring so they're always at the front. Annabel used to be one of those kids.

'Gotta go,' she tells Grace. 'Mia will be out any second now.'

Mia is towards the back, a dreamy smile on her face. Dearest Mia. Such a gentle soul. Such a joy. If only her brother had a fraction of her affable nature.

'Hi, darling. Hop in quickly. We're going straight to

the mall. We're going to buy the most perfect pair of communion shoes.'

Annabel sees him in the food court, pushing up against some other boy with his shoulder. Guffawing in that annoying horsey way that teenage boys laugh.

'What the fuck?' It's out of her mouth before she can stop herself.

Mia's eyes widen in shock. 'You swore, Mummy. You said the F word.'

'It was an accident,' she counters weakly. 'Wait here, Mia. Don't move till I get back.'

Mia stands uncertainly, clutching the bag that contains her communion shoes in one hand, and her milkshake – the reason they are in the food court – in the other. Annabel marches towards Daniel, who is so absorbed in his friends he hasn't noticed her approach. It's a mistake, she knows, to confront him like this, to publicly humiliate him, but he has obviously dodged school – again! – and if he's not going to keep to the rules, then neither is she.

'What the hell are you doing here?'

His head jerks up at the sound of her voice. Surprise registers before he holds up a McDonald's bag as though it's vital evidence. 'Just having a burger … What's the problem?'

'You should be at school. *That's the problem.*'

'We had a free period for our last lesson.'

'Don't lie to me!'

'Ask anyone.' He looks carefully at his friends, as though she can't interpret what that silent look is really saying. 'Tell her, Jez. She'll believe you.'

Jez is the most sensible of a bad lot. His face reddens till it blends into his strawberry-blond hair.

'It's true … We were meant to have … maths …'

'You're a terrible liar, Jeremy Hughes.'

Daniel quickly resorts to anger. 'Just go away, Mum. *Leave us alone.*'

'You're coming with me.' She grabs his arm.

He shrugs her off. 'Go away. You're embarrassing yourself.'

'Do you think I care? You're coming home with me and Mia. *Right now.*'

'You can't make me!' He's shouting at her. In the middle of the food court. For everyone to see and hear.

'I *can* make you. Have some respect, for God's sake!'

Now she's being no better, shouting back at him. But she's so angry, and he does this to her, turns her into this demented stranger who people are staring at and will talk about when they get home from the mall. *Remember that woman screaming at her son?* If he would only listen. If he would only do what he's told. When she thinks of all the things she has sacrificed for him, for all three of them. She might have laughed about it with Grace earlier, but she will never forget the humiliation of sitting in that exam hall, her ballooned belly the talk of the school, the grave disappointment of the teachers, the disgust of the other parents, the shocked fascination of the students who once looked up to her. She didn't go to university because of the baby, because of Jemma. She never had a proper career. She got married too young – eighteen, for God's sake! – and while her friends were partying and travelling, she was stuck at home, lost in a haze of nappies, feeding and constant crying. Jemma is at college now and doing all the things Annabel herself missed out on: getting a degree, going to wild parties and travelling during the holidays. But Annabel's work is far from done. She still has Daniel and Mia to see through, and Daniel is proving to be the toughest.

'You come with me right now or I'll drag you all the way to the car, and then we'll see what's embarrassing!'

The email arrives a couple of days later.

From: admin1@yearbook.com.au
Subject: Updated Yearbook

Annabel clicks on it without much thought. That is not strictly true. If she is honest, there is a brief, quite vicious desire to topple Katy Buckley from her self-appointed role as reunion organiser.

The first thing Annabel sees is a grainy, unflattering photo of herself. Directly below there's text typed in an old-fashioned font.

Name: Annabel Harris (Née Moore)

Highest achievement at school: School captain.

What you do now: Stay-at-home mother.

Highlights of last twenty years: Nothing remarkable. Peaked at school.

Lowlights: Finding out your son smokes dope. Initially not telling your husband.

Deepest fears: That weed is a gateway drug for Daniel.

Her first reaction is horror, to the point where she actually feels sick. Then she recovers herself. This is someone's idea of a joke. The cruellest, most despicable joke. The kind of thing they'd have done twenty years ago, back when they'd time to waste, unlimited imagination, and the lines between humour and outright nastiness were blurred.

So, who sent this? Someone who knows about their struggles with Daniel, even though Annabel and Jarrod resolved to keep it within the family. Someone who wants the upcoming reunion to have a hint of mystery, and perhaps shock factor?

The photo – one she's never seen before – is fairly recent. Her hair is in its usual style – layered, blonde, shoulder-length. There are tell-tale lines around her mouth and purple shadows under her eyes: was it taken the morning after a night when she'd lain awake, listening hard to see if Daniel was moving around, sneaking out of the house? There are so many Facebook photos she's been 'tagged' in, so many casual shots in restaurants and other gatherings, who knows where this one came from.

Will everyone else get one of these 'updates' in their inbox? Yes, that must be the plan, otherwise there'd be no joke. Annabel can't fathom who would have the time or energy for something this elaborate. Hardly Katy Buckley. Not imaginative enough. Not cruel enough. Definitely not ballsy enough. Besides, Katy would be up to her eyes compiling the real updated yearbook.

Melissa Andrews? Co-editor of the original yearbook, so maybe possessing a vested interest in the revised one? Melissa and Annabel used to be friends, before everything turned toxic during those last few months of school. Now, as Annabel allows herself to think about Melissa, the jealousy returns. It was never an ordinary jealousy; it was obsessive, powerful, insanely out of proportion. But regardless of how Annabel might feel, then or now, she knows that Melissa wouldn't be so juvenile as to do something like this. Too busy with her high-flying career.

Zach Latham? Another co-editor. Zach would do anything for a laugh and did have the propensity for cruelty. Is he still the same today?

Luke Willis? God, she hasn't thought about *him* in years. Whatever became of Luke Willis?

Annabel is shutting the upstairs curtains when Jarrod's van pulls into the driveway. COASTAL CURRENTS is painted on the sides and rear of the van: they came up with the business name together. Annabel watches him sit there, probably listening to the end of something interesting on the radio. The fact that he clearly isn't in a rush to get inside to see his family bothers her.

A few minutes later, as Annabel is coming down the stairs, the front door swings open.

'Daddy, Daddy!'

Jarrod picks Mia up, hoisting her on to his hip like a much younger child. Mia loves it. This is the first time she has seen her father today; he was gone when she got up for school this morning.

Annabel notices two things in quick succession: at the end of Mia's dangling legs are her brand-new communion shoes; and one of them looks like it is already scuffed.

'Mia, why have you got those shoes on?'

'I'm getting used to them, Mummy.'

'You've already marked them! Take them off this instant.'

Jarrod gives Annabel a look that says he thinks she's being too harsh but he would never contradict her in front of the children. United front: that's been their parenting motto. It feels like a long time since they've put their heads together to come up with parenting mottos, business names or anything else. The last time she remembers genuine collaboration was when they built this house, four years ago, but even that was more Annabel's project than Jarrod's. Tweaking the architect's plans. Visiting the site to check progress. Making decisions about door handles, skirting boards, wall colours.

'Where's Daniel?' Jarrod asks, setting Mia down so she can follow her mother's instructions.

The need to check Daniel's whereabouts has become the underlying beat to their lives. It's always one of the first things Jarrod asks when he comes in.

'At Jeremy's house, working on a project for school. Some video they need to do for PE. I'm picking him up in half an hour.'

'I can get him if you like,' he offers, exhaustion etched in his face. He tends to go pale when he's overtired. Annabel knows that on an average day he deals with a series of irate inconvenienced homeowners, outdated and treacherous wiring, claustrophobic ceiling cavities, not to mention alarmingly regular electric shocks caused by ditzy apprentices who keep forgetting to follow the correct protocols.

'No, it's fine. Have your dinner. Here, I'll warm it up for you.'

Much later, when Daniel has been picked up and it has been confirmed that the PE project was all that he was up to, when Mia's maths homework has been extensively corrected and she's tucked up in bed, when Annabel has done her level best to remove the scuff from the communion shoe, she finally sits down next to her husband on the sofa. Jarrod is watching the cricket; Australia appear to be in trouble.

'This popped up in my email today.'

Jarrod takes the sheet of paper from her outstretched hand and skims it. 'What the fuck is this?'

She shrugs. 'I don't really know. Some kind of joke, I presume.'

He jabs it with his finger. 'How do they know about Daniel?'

Good question. Jarrod was livid when he found out about the bong. She had to tell him in the end, because although she confiscated it, Daniel lost no time finding both a replacement and a better hiding spot. Jarrod was equally livid with Annabel (for not telling him about it upfront) and Daniel (who point-blank refused to stop). The irony is, once Jarrod calmed down, his instincts were exactly the same as hers: to cover it up.

'I don't want anyone to know. I don't want people making judgements, writing Daniel off as a no-hoper,' he said at the time. 'Let's try to sort this out ourselves the best we can.'

They haven't been able to sort it out, though. They've tried the calm and forthright approach, reasoning with Daniel about house rules, his health and his future. When that didn't work, they came down heavier: limiting access to his bank account, keeping tabs on who he is with, enforcing curfews and a few sessions with the school counsellor. Daniel has responded by lying about his whereabouts, escaping from his room at night, and becoming increasingly disconnected from his family. His desire to get high, practically on a daily basis, suggests an inability to self-regulate and the possibility of a lifetime struggle with illicit substances.

So how has the author of this email found this information? The school counsellor? Unlikely. Maybe Jarrod broke his own rules and confided in someone. Or maybe Annabel accidentally let something slip, even though she's pretty sure she didn't. For God's sake, she hasn't even mentioned it to Grace.

Now she sighs. 'I have no idea. Did you tell someone?'

'Jesus, Annie, why the hell would I do that?' His voice is loud enough to carry to the kids' bedrooms. 'Didn't we agree that we'd keep it in the family?'

'Well, I haven't told anyone either.' She shrugs wearily. 'Unless I'm losing my memory …. Maybe I *am* losing my mind.'

'I'm going to find out who sent this and smash their face in.'

Jarrod was known for his short temper at school, especially at sporting fixtures. On-field grievances spiralling into tussles and swinging fists. Other team members pulling him back, talking him down. Minutes later he would be laughing and joking around. These days his anger is more entrenched.

Annabel stands up, pats him on the arm. 'It's a joke, Jarrod. Just a joke.'

He roars back at her. 'Stop saying that! Do you see either of us fucking laughing?'

Name: Luke Willis

What you will be remembered for: Playing the role of Danny in *Grease*. 'Summer loving had me a blast …'

Best memories of high school: Mrs Romford's face when I told her I didn't want to kiss 'Sandy' because I was gay.

Worst memories of high school: The mud and leeches during cross country in Year 10.

What will you be doing ten years from now: Famous Broadway actor (with at least five sports cars).

2
LUKE

'Ladies and gentlemen, this is the cabin crew speaking. We have a medical emergency on board and our plane will be met on the ground by an ambulance. On landing, please stay in your seats while the paramedics attend to the patient. We apologise in advance for any inconvenience and will notify the transfers department of possible delays.'

Luke's announcement is met with mutterings of frustration and sighs of inconvenience. Selfish bastards. A woman – fifty-something, extremely overweight – uses her bejewelled hand to beckon him over.

'I must get off this plane. I have a flight to catch.' Her accent is Eastern European, her tone accusing. 'You were already late taking off. It's your fault I have so little time to connect.'

Luke masks his irritation behind a slight, ultra-polite smile. 'I'm afraid the announcement applies to everyone, ma'am. You all need to stay in your seats. The paramedics will stabilise the patient and we'll do our best to have you off the aircraft as soon as possible.'

'Where is this patient?' She swings around in her seat. 'Tell me, which row?'

Jesus Christ. What is she planning to do? March down there and berate the man – who appears to be in the throes of a serious allergic reaction – for causing such inconvenience? Or declare that she could merely slip past the seat in question, and be on her merry way?

'I need to get back to my duties, ma'am. Excuse me.'

A flash of colour from the rings before her fingers bite into his arm. 'Listen to me, you *faggot*. I have a *right* to get off this plane as *soon* as it lands. I have no travel insurance to cover missed flights. *Do you understand me?*'

It always takes him by surprise. Invariably, it's the respectable-looking passengers, rather than the rough ones; the middle-aged women and harmless old men, as opposed to the supposedly mannerless youth.

He looks down pointedly at the fingers pressed into the white cotton of his sleeve. 'What did you just call me?'

She is not going to fall into the trap of repeating herself, not when there are other passengers listening now. She removes her hand quickly. Pats her hair.

Let it go, he tells himself. Fatima is waving at him

18

from the galley. They need to prepare for landing. He has bigger concerns, a procedure to go through to get this plane on the ground, a man whose life may be relying on their efficiency. She is a nothing. A bigoted, selfish, nasty nothing.

It's that word, though. *Faggot*. It reminds him of his father.

Luke forces himself to walk away. After a few moments he has even resumed the slight smile – it's almost part of his uniform, that smile – proof that he is above people like her.

'Rubbish, anyone? Just pop it in here. Thank you.'

Back to the intercom. 'Ladies and gentlemen, please make sure your seat backs and tray tables are in their full upright position …' He sounds as competent and calm as ever. Not at all rattled. 'Cabin crew, please prepare for landing.'

Nerida, his most experienced crew member, is assisting the man with the allergic reaction. It's unfortunate, and quite unusual, not to have an off-duty doctor or nurse aboard the aircraft. Nerida has administered oxygen and adrenalin and is on the phone to paramedics. Soon she will have to leave the man and belt herself in, as per procedure. Hopefully his blood pressure won't drop too low during the final stages of descent. In his twenty years of flying, Luke's had six passengers die on board, mostly from heart attacks. Life is short. He's always known this fact and it's why he's never been a time waster. He couldn't wait to leave school, to get out into the world, to be independent. He loves his work. He loves his life with Aaron. He loves calling London home. If he doesn't love something, or someone, he doesn't do it, or them. It's simple really.

The plane lurches downwards. A baby wails.

'Cabin crew, take your seats.'

Luke sits in his seat, flanked by Fatima and, at the very last minute, Nerida.

'His bloody EpiPen was past its expiry.' Her voice has a tell-tale wobble. 'When will people learn?'

Luke takes her hand and squeezes it. She is a good friend. Later on, when they've dealt with the ambulance and all the paperwork, they'll go for a drink and she'll have a cry, let it all out. As the plane descends through the rain clouds over Heathrow, he thinks about another friend, from another lifetime: Katy. He must respond to her email as soon as he gets home. It's been sitting there for over a week now.

From: admin@yearbook.com.au
Subject: RSVP

Still waiting on your RSVP for the reunion. I know you can get back to Sydney if you really wanted to, so no excuses. Also, thought it would be fun to compile a new yearbook, showing where everyone is at today. Questions are below. Can you send me replies as soon as possible? Xxx Katy

Where is he at? One of his passengers could be about to die, and if he does, Luke will be filling in paperwork for the next few hours. He has just been called a faggot, and it's made him angrier than it should have. Nerida will undoubtedly want to get drunk as soon as they escape the airport, and Aaron will be annoyed if he doesn't come straight home. A day in the life of Luke Willis.

Luke catches up with Katy whenever he deigns to visit Sydney, and she has dropped in on him in London a handful of times over the years. In between visits, they text, FaceTime and share funny jokes and videos. Their friendship has lasted twenty-plus years; not bad, considering his intentions at the start were less than pure. Luke – trying to get through exams on a minimum-effort policy – sat next to her in class, hoping to short-cut a difficult chemistry unit. Not only was she helpful – summing up the unit much more concisely than the teacher – Katy Buckley was other things, too: foolishly big-hearted, always believing the best of people, including him; so eager and perennially positive that it was actually hard to be cynical (Luke's speciality) in her presence. Something softens in him whenever he thinks about her. Their friendship was viewed suspiciously, incredulously, by his other more popular friends, but that didn't bother Luke; he never gave a shit about what other people thought. Katy was too nerdy to become part of that group. Neither was she pretty enough, but she's had the last laugh there. Years ago, she dyed her carrot-coloured hair a rich shade of brown and the effect was transformative. More recently she's got into fitness and developed a unique sense of fashion. The last time Luke saw her, she was unrecognisable.

Luke hasn't stayed in contact with any of the others. As soon as the HSC was done, that was it: he was out of their group, out of Sydney, out of Australia. He landed his first job with a budget airline, jetting around Europe and having the time of his life. He never looked back, never regretted not furthering his education. Who needed university when there was real life waiting to be lived? Who needed to be dependent on your parents and subject to their rules when you could call the shots yourself? Who needed school friends who – when it came down to it – you had absolutely nothing in common with, other than the shared experience – torture, more like – of class after boring class, exam after pointless exam, teacher after detested teacher?

Now, just thinking about that core gang – Annabel, Grace, Zach, Jarrod – makes Luke feel a surge of loathing. He can't understand why. He didn't hate them at school, far from it. It's not as if they victimised him for being gay. If anything, it was the opposite: his sexuality made him more popular, at least with the girls.

The plane breaks through the cloud cover and suddenly there is a close-range view of London. Grey on grey on grey: the sky, the buildings, the Thames. The greyness is the ultimate understatement, a clever disguise for the excitement, diversity and pulse of the city. History and modernity, classiness and grit, flourishing side by side. Luke has travelled the world. This is his favourite place.

He'll do an updated page for Katy's yearbook but there's no fucking way he's going to the reunion. Why waste time looking back? Look forward, people. Look *ahead*. Grab life by the balls and live it. Forget about the past. The man struggling for breath on row fifteen is not thinking about the past. He's thinking about the things he still wants to do.

The plane bumps against the runway and bumps again, then screams forward at a ferocious speed. Luke always holds his breath at this point, thinking: *Is this the one where we won't be able to stop?*

But they stop. They always do.

As soon as it's permitted, Nerida unclicks herself. Luke folds away both their seats. When he turns back to face the aisle, he sees two things: Nerida manoeuvring the man so he is lying flat on the floor, and the overweight woman hoisting herself up from her seat. She reaches for the overhead locker and has her bag out before Fatima gets there to berate her.

'Please sit down, ma'am. The plane is still moving and we must make way for the paramedics.'

The woman looks her up and down. 'I'm not having a *Muslim* tell me what to do!'

Luke picks up the phone to greet the ground staff. 'This is Luke Willis, cabin supervisor. Can I please request police as well as the ambulance? We have an abusive passenger who's refusing to follow directions.'

23

She'll be first off the plane all right, but not in the way she expected. The police will detain her and she'll be charged and fined. There goes her connecting flight and whatever money she was trying to save by not taking out travel insurance. Serve her right. Fuck her.

Luke's never been one to take shit, and he's not going to start now. When he cares enough to exact revenge, he does so in spectacular fashion.

Name: Grace McCrae

What you will be remembered for: Probably for being Annabel Moore's best friend!

Best memories of high school: The Year 10 formal.

Worst memories of high school: Food technology.

What will you be doing ten years from now: No friggin' idea.

3
GRACE

Grace can't stop looking at it: *Yearbook of Macquarie High, Class of 2000.* Ninety-odd pages that depict another lifetime, one that feels so very strange it could belong to someone else. All the girls wearing similar hairstyles – layered at the front, highlighted – and the frumpy uniforms that they'd hated, with good reason. The boys with hunched shoulders and sneakers instead of the proper school shoes. The self-conscious quotes speckled throughout, not remotely as meaningful or humorous as they'd believed at the time. God, they all looked so gauche. And so terribly, terribly young.

'We thought we were hot,' she comments to Tom as he emerges from the en suite, dressed for bed in a pair of old soccer shorts and singlet. 'But we were just babies, really.'

'Are you still looking at that old thing?' he asks, sliding into bed next to her.

'I can't seem to put it away,' she laughs. 'I've become fixated on it.'

He sidles over, rests his head hopefully against her chest. 'I could give you something else to be fixated on … if you like.'

Grace is considering his proposition when, with impeccable timing, the bedroom door creaks open.

'Mummy, Daddy,' whispers a voice.

Tom sighs and smiles at the same time. 'Yes, Lauren?'

It's nearly always Lauren who pays the after-hours visits. Their third child suffers anxiety about school, social occasions, nightfall, and a long list of other things.

'I heard a noise in my room. I'm scared.'

'Right.' Tom dramatically throws back the covers. 'Daddy's coming and we'll have a full-scale search. There'll be no escaping the eagle eye of Tom Coleman.'

He bounds out of the room, giving a great impression that this – a hunt for would-be intruders – is exactly what he'd like to do at this precise moment.

Grace goes back to the yearbook, flicking once again to her own entry.

Why did she say that the Year 10 formal was her best memory? Why not the Year 12 one? Was it because it was all coming to an end, and she felt sad that they were about to go their separate ways? Or was it because Annabel, seven months' pregnant, didn't attend the

Year 12 formal, and because her best friend hadn't been there, it didn't hold the same importance?

Probably, pathetically, the latter. For this reason, Grace is watchful of the friendships that her children form and, whenever she can, veers them away from relationships that compromise their own identity.

Don't have one friend, she tells them regularly. *Have lots and lots of them. Be your own person, not just a mimic of your friends.*

Sometimes she is more forthright: *When I was in high school, I had only one friend. If she was in a good mood, I was in a good mood. If she was in a bad mood, I was in a bad mood. I think I missed out on a lot of fun because of her.*

Grace is brimming with things to tell her children, lessons she herself had to learn the hard way. She even has a notebook where she writes things down, practical advice and nuggets of wisdom to be imparted when the timing is right. Tom calls it the Mother Manual, although he's been known to write a thing or two in there as well. They laugh about it – 'That's definitely one for the manual' – but beneath it all they're deadly serious. Tom was always one of those men who was going to make a great father. It's Grace who's the surprise. Being a mother is her calling in life, even though she never knew it until she held Tahlia – her eldest – in her arms. Grace plans to be proud about it at the upcoming reunion. *No, I don't have a paid job at the moment, because I have four fabulous kids – the best in the world – and I put all my time, energy and imagination into them.*

Grace waitressed when she first left school. An over-priced understaffed beachfront café that was always frantically busy. After a year of being paid a pittance and having an aching back at the end of each day, she landed a job in a travel agency. It was there she met Tom. He came into the office early one morning, his blue eyes fixing on Grace first and then her client.

'Does anyone here own registration UPL55T?'

'I do,' the client, a glamorous woman in her forties, admitted.

'Can you please move your car? I don't want to have to give you a ticket.'

Grace was instantly attracted to him. Those glittering blue eyes. The rugged tan of his face. The way his mouth twitched with a smile. But more than anything, his decency. How many rangers sought out car owners so they could avoid giving them a ticket? How did he even manage to keep his job?

Her client, immensely grateful that she'd avoided a 200-dollar fine, found him just as attractive.

'What a gorgeous-looking man,' she exclaimed when she came back from moving her car, presumably to a legal spot. 'I hope you got his number.'

Grace had. And here they are, sixteen years and four children later. She is looking forward to showing him off at the reunion. It will be his first time meeting her extended cohort: nothing was organised for the five-year or ten-year anniversary, too many people were overseas or interstate or unable to commit for one reason or another. The dress code is formal: black tie for the men, gowns for the women. Tom has a tuxedo that gets dragged out for occasions like these; he always looks particularly handsome in black tie. It will be hard not to feel smug. *Take a look at him.* Not just at how drop-dead gorgeous he is. This is a good man, inside and out. Grace Coleman is the luckiest woman in the world.

The question is what should Grace herself wear? Options from her existing wardrobe are limited – most things are a size or two too small – and there simply isn't the budget to buy something new. Plenty of time to work it out. As she tells her children, it's not about how you look, it's how you feel. And Grace feels great. She couldn't be happier with her life.

Tom is standing in the doorway.

'All good?' she asks.

He rolls his eyes, the ones she fell in love with, indicating that the only baddies in Lauren's room are those from her imagination.

'Okay to turn out the light?' he asks with a yawn.

'Yeah.' She closes the yearbook, pops it on the bedside table. No doubt she'll pick it up again tomorrow.

Twenty years. Grace's life is completely different and, presumably, so is everyone else's. She is genuinely excited about reconnecting with the guys from school. Seeing what they look like now, how their lives have turned out. For her own part, she's looking forward to proving to everyone that she has well and truly come out of Annabel Moore's shadow. Yes, they are still friends.

The truth is, she likes Annabel more now than she did in school. Maybe because their friendship is on more of an equal footing. Or maybe because Grace is her own person, driven by her own moods and thoughts and not those of Annabel.

Tom clicks off the bedside lamp. Maybe they could book a hotel room for the night of the reunion? Maybe, with some creative budgeting, there would be enough money?

Grace cuddles up to him. 'What was that thing you wanted me to fixate on again?'

He takes her hand, slides it under the band of his soccer shorts. 'It's this.'

Then he rolls on top of her, his lips – warm with a faint taste of toothpaste – seeking hers.

The email comes the next morning.

From: admin1@yearbook.com.au
Subject: Updated Yearbook

Name: Grace Coleman (née McCrae)

Highest achievement at school: Being Annabel Moore's best friend.

What you do now: Mum to four children (three girls, one boy). Keen gardener.

Highlights of last twenty years: Getting married. Giving birth to your children.

31

Lowlights: The miscarriage between number 2 and 3.

Deepest fears: That something bad will happen to one of your children. Lauren in particular.

Grace recoils from her laptop. What is this? Something relating to the reunion? She reads it again, more slowly, and realises it's set out in a format similar to the original yearbook. There's even a photo that's recent and quite familiar: Grace's curly brown hair lifted by an invisible breeze, her eyes – the same colour as her hair – squinting at the camera. Did Katy send this? No, Katy wouldn't know about either the miscarriage or her worries about Lauren, and would hardly be so insensitive. The miscarriage happened at eleven weeks, before her baby bump became noticeable. Not a lot of people knew she was pregnant, which made the grieving process both easier and more difficult.

Even so, Katy seems to be the obvious person to contact. The call goes straight to voicemail. Of course, it's mid-morning and Katy would be in class. Katy's a science teacher at a high school in the inner west. Grace knows the school: it attracts 'creative' types and has an ethos of encouraging the students' individuality. Grace and Tom are seriously considering it for Tahlia.

Grace decides not to leave a voicemail and calls Annabel instead. Annabel picks up straight away. It's rare she doesn't; she's one of those women whose phone is like one of her limbs.

'Hey, Annabel. I got this weird email just now … Like a fake yearbook entry.'

There's a noticeable pause at the end of the line. Then: 'Me too. A few days ago.'

Grace is perplexed. 'Why didn't you say something?'

Another pause. Then an embarrassed sigh. 'There was something in there that nobody knows. Some trouble we're having with Daniel.'

Grace wants to ask what the trouble is but senses that Annabel's failure to elaborate is deliberate. She has always been a selective confidante.

'Mine mentioned Lauren and my miscarriage. It was really quite upsetting.'

'Look, I think it's someone trying to be funny and missing the mark,' Annabel states with her signature curtness.

Missing the mark by a goddam mile, Grace thinks. Then a guilty niggle. 'Hey, you don't think it's Melissa, do you?'

Annabel snorts. 'She wouldn't lower herself. Luke Willis came into my head. I have no idea why.'

Luke Willis. The one who did his own thing, never cared what people thought and defied all the rules when it came to popularity.

Grace frowns. 'Didn't he and Katy used to be friends?'

'Yeah.' Annabel's laugh is unkind. 'I still don't understand what he saw in her!'

Grace casts her mind back. She sees Luke singing and dancing in the *Grease* musical, totally at home centre stage. She sees him standing near the locker room, smirking after delivering a retort that had everyone falling around with laughter. She remembers the excitement that built in him as Year 12 drew to a close, the blatant impatience to leave school behind and strike out in the real world.

She has a moment of clarity. 'Annabel, I'm pretty sure that Luke Willis hasn't thought about you or me since the day he left high school.'

Grace keeps busy for the rest of the day. She vacuums the entire house, sews a button on to Tahlia's school shirt and scrubs some mould from the bathroom wall. The shower is leaking; the entire bathroom needs to be gutted and replaced. The roof also needs replacing, as does the kitchen, but there's no money, not even for minor renovations. Just another couple of years of scraping by. Just another couple of years of full-time parenting to ensure that all the children are on track, to ensure that they're independent, resilient and responsible for their own behaviour. Then Grace will get a paid job. Something with short hours. Something she can fit around school. Maybe something involving children.

After lunch Grace puts on a sunhat and goes outside to do some gardening. The weeds are thriving but, on the positive side, so is her vegetable patch. While she's down on her hands and knees, perspiration dripping into her eyes, she thinks again about Annabel and Daniel. She hopes that the trouble isn't something serious or irredeemable. Teenage boys are such a difficult species.

Just don't let it be drugs.

Grace hears horrific stories from Tom, shocking things seen while doing his rounds of the local parks and beaches. Kids as young as twelve drinking alcohol. Teenagers unconscious in pools of vomit. The unforgettable morning he found a drug addict's body hanging from the monkey bars at one of the playgrounds.

The heat of the sun eventually drives Grace back inside, where she turns her attention to dinner. She deftly chops vegetables – some of which are home-grown – that she'll stir-fry later on. According to the yearbook, food technology was her worst memory of high school. Really? She quite likes cooking now. Finds it therapeutic. At least on the days when there's enough time to relax while she's doing it.

What was so bad about food technology? Why did she hate it so much?

Suddenly, she's back there, in the food tech room, wearing the compulsory blue apron, Melissa's face flushed and scornful.

'What do you mean I can't be your partner? We're always partners.'

'Sorry.' Grace shrugged helplessly. 'Annabel—'

'*What?* Annabel isn't even in this class, for God's sake. Do you care who her partner is in chemistry?'

'She … I … Sorry.'

'You're pathetic, Grace. She says, "Jump," and you

say, "How high?" Have some fucking backbone for a change.'

Melissa flounced off and found herself another partner. Grace got stuck with one of the boys, who was even more clueless than she was. She remembers glancing intermittently at Melissa, looking for signs of forgiveness, or even some level of understanding of the predicament she was in because of Annabel. Melissa's eyes were firmly trained on her chopping knife, which she was using in a furious manner much beyond her level of skill. Grace had turned her attention to her own dish when she heard Melissa's cry. She looked up to see blood dripping down her friend's hand, blooming on the sleeve of her white shirt. There was blood on the blade of the abandoned knife, the plastic chopping board and even the food itself, celery and onion splattered with red. Grace stepped forward to help, but the teacher was already there, pressing a clean cloth to the wound, muttering about hospital and stitches.

Now Grace cringes at the memory of that day. Her role in causing Melissa to be so uncharacteristically upset and therefore careless. How she was prepared to ostracise her purely on Annabel's say-so. Her lack of 'fucking backbone'.

Thankfully, she is not the same person as she was back then.

Is anyone?

As is always the case, Grace never quite achieves everything on her to-do list. Almost 2.30 p.m.: time to pick up Billy from preschool. She's on her way out the door when it comes to her. The photograph. She knows where it came from. In fact, she sees it a dozen times a day. It's from a group shot of the family, but everyone else has been cropped out. The photo was taken in the back garden on a sunny day in the lead-up to last Christmas. Grace had multiple copies printed so it could be popped into Christmas cards.

Grace backtracks to the kitchen. There's a gap on the fridge door where the photo should be. Where on earth has it gone to? Then a paralysing thought.

Has someone been in the house and taken it?

Name: Katy Buckley

What you will be remembered for: Probably, unfortunately, my hair.

Best memories of high school: Decorating lockers on birthdays.

Worst memories of high school: PE class. Especially on the really hot days, when my face would end up the same colour as my hair.

What will you be doing ten years from now: President of the Wilderness Society.

4
KATY

'Someone took that photograph from my fridge, Katy. And the other night my daughter said she heard noises … I thought she was imagining things but now I'm not so sure … What if someone's been in my house?'

Recess is a mere twenty minutes. Barely enough time to go to the bathroom, make a cup of tea, take stock before her next class. Katy regrets answering her phone. She should've waited until lunchtime. Now, despite the potential gravity of what Grace is saying, Katy has no choice but to cut her short.

'Look, Grace, that all sounds extremely serious and disturbing. The problem is that I'm due in class in five minutes. I'll call you back later, okay?'

'Yes, of course. We'll talk later.'

Grace's practicality throws Katy a little bit. Being

reasonable is not one of the things she remembers about her. Maybe because she was always in the vicinity of Annabel who could be so *unreasonable* (and caustic, her speciality). The truth is she doesn't know Grace any more than Grace knows her, either today or back then.

Katy gathers her notes for her next class and powers down the hallway, the walls of which are covered in colourful graffiti art.

'Hey, Miss Buckley.'

'Hello, Georgia.'

Katy is relatively popular among the students, despite the fact that the subject she teaches – science – isn't popular at all. Music, drama and visual arts are the favoured subjects at the school, followed by history and English. Bottom of the pile are science and maths. This doesn't bother Katy too much. There are always enough enthusiastic students to make up for the ones who are bored out of their minds.

'Hi, Miss Buckley.'

'Having a good day, Leo?'

'Absolutely, Miss.' She's treated to a flirtatious smile.

Katy is particularly popular with the boys. If only they knew that she'd been one of the most nondescript girls at school. This is precisely what she wants to get across to the current Year 12s. As soon as they walk out the door into the world, everything can – and should – change. They can reinvent themselves, if they want to. They can leave behind the fact that they were the quiet one, or the socially awkward one, or the silly one.

Katy reaches her class just as the bell sounds. This class is a particularly eclectic group, with plentiful body piercings and hair colour ranging from hot pink to electric blue. The school's policy is to foster the students' individuality and sense of self, helping them to experiment and have fun in a safe environment.

'Good morning, everyone. Today we are going to start a new unit – the chemical earth. The earth's biosphere, lithosphere, hydrosphere and atmosphere are mixtures of thousands and thousands of substances ...'

Katy pretends not to hear their groans.

She is on supervising duty at lunchtime – something that had completely slipped her mind – and there is no opportunity to call Grace. The grounds of the school are quite extensive, as are opportunities to get into mischief. Katy changes her shoes so she can walk the perimeter comfortably.

'Hey, Miss Buckley.'

'Good afternoon, Dylan.'

Dylan is easy to imagine twenty years from now. He'll work in sales or real estate, where his easy charm will make him lots of money. He'll wear trendy suits, drive a flashy car, and will be one of those men who walk around with their hands in their pockets.

Katy comes across a group of Year 9s clustered together at the edge of the perimeter.

'What are you doing there, girls?'

'Charlotte lost her jumper,' one of them replies, slightly out of breath.

'Yeah, we thought she left it here before school,' another adds, cheeks pink.

Charlotte herself looks bemused. The lost jumper is obviously news to her.

'Better try lost property, then,' Katy says chirpily. 'Move along.'

She waits until they've headed in the right direction, although she very much doubts that lost property is where they'll end up. Charlotte looks over her shoulder a few times. There's something arrogant about those backward glances. Charlotte has always reminded her of Annabel Moore. Katy loves all her students. She loves Charlotte a little bit less than the others because of this similarity.

Katy's thoughts turn to Grace. Has there really been an intruder in her house? No, there must be some other, less sinister explanation for the missing photograph. But someone is certainly up to mischief, sending those joke yearbook entries to both Grace and Annabel. Who would do such a thing? Someone who knows them well enough to guess at what might be bothering them? Should Katy expect a similar email? Good thing she has no major secrets or fears. The untold advantages of being a school teacher: a squeaky-clean private life and nerves of steel from day-to-day dealings with the most brutal of species: teenagers.

The music pounds in Katy's ears, propelling her up the final hill, towards home. Shorter stride on the incline, careful not to lean forward too much. This is what she'll be citing as her greatest achievement in the updated yearbook. The fact that she has transformed herself from an inactive, self-conscious girl to an athletic, confident woman.

I am a runner. I run ten kilometres a couple of times a week, and on weekends I run twenty: just because I can. I am fitter than I've ever been in my entire life.

Katy is looking forward to hearing about everyone's achievements, but the replies have been disappointingly slow coming in. She has managed to track down seventy-two of the eighty-odd students and has more than fifty RSVPs for the sit-down dinner at a city-centre hotel. Overall, pretty good and hopefully more to come. It's the information for the updated yearbook that seems to be the sticking point: only a dozen responses so far.

At home – a two-bedroom apartment that Katy is planning to renovate as soon as she gets enough money together – she peels off her sweaty clothes and steps into the shower. The water cascades over her face and she remembers Grace. Damn it. She must call her back before she forgets again.

'Hi, Grace. It's Katy. I'm so sorry, the school day is always busier than I think it will be.'

Grace laughs, as though she knows about days that simply slip away from you. 'No problem. Look, I feel quite sheepish now … Tom, my husband, found the missing photograph down the side of the fridge.'

Katy smiles with relief. 'Phew. I was beginning to think that maybe the police should be called.'

'I'm so sorry to have alarmed you. I feel like such an idiot.'

'Don't be sorry. No harm done. Let's not forget that there's still someone who's having a laugh at your expense. You said Annabel got one, too?'

'Yes … I found it creepy rather than something to laugh about … But creeping someone out isn't exactly a crime, is it?'

True. But Katy feels uneasy about the whole thing. 'Is having a new yearbook a bad idea, Grace? Should I scrap it? I must say, the responses so far have been underwhelming.'

'No, no, I love the idea. I can't wait to see how people have changed, how their lives have turned out. I'm really enjoying reading back over the original yearbook.'

'Me too.'

'We were so, so young.'

'Yes, we were.'

Katy hangs up shortly afterwards. That's the longest conversation she's had with Grace McCrae in her life.

Dinner is poached salmon and greens. Katy tries to be as good with her diet as her exercise regime. Afterwards, she sits in her study nook – a small alcove in the living area with just enough room for a desk and some shelving – and starts work on what she calls 'Project Reunion'. She works on it most nights of the week: it's startling how much time it sucks up.

Tonight, she has two new messages, the first on Facebook.

Thank you for your message to my wife's Facebook account. Unfortunately, Brigette recently passed away after a long illness. She always had happy memories of school. I hope you enjoy your night. Mike

Oh, how terribly sad. Katy barely remembers Brigette, and this makes her feel guilty and even more sad. She hits reply.

Dear Mike, I am so sorry for your loss. With your consent, I would still like to include Brigette in the new yearbook, with some photos and details of her life. Please let me know what you think. Deepest condolences, Katy Buckley

The second message is an email from someone called Samantha Rankin. Katy has no recollection of any Samantha in the year.

From: samantharankin@pharmacorp.com.au
Subject: RSVP

Dear Katy, please be advised that Melissa Andrews will be attending the reunion. Melissa will be accompanied by her partner, Henry Kent. Both Melissa and Henry have special dietary requirements. Details will be sent at a later date. Information for the updated yearbook will also follow. Samantha Rankin on behalf of Melissa Andrews.

Ah, Samantha works for Melissa. Katy remembers Melissa for her perfectionism: perfect hair, perfect marks, perfect focus. Does she still maintain such impossibly high standards? Is she demanding of Samantha and other staff? Katy chides herself. It's been twenty years: of course Melissa will have changed. She tries to imagine an older, less-perfect version of Melissa.

Next, she types an email to the Class of 2000, a mailing list compiled from the RSVPs received to date.

From: admin@yearbook.com.au
Subject: Fake yearbook entries

Someone naughty has been sending joke yearbook entries. Please stop. You've creeped out Annabel and Grace. If you have time on your hands, you can help me with the real thing. Thanks, Katy.

There. Short and to the point. Katy has learned, through her teaching career, to be direct.

She spends the next hour or so trying to find two students – David Hooper and Robbie McGrath – who nobody seems to have seen or heard of since graduation. She tries Facebook, Google and online phone directories, to no avail. Maybe they went overseas.

She types another email to the Class of 2000.

From: admin@yearbook.com.au
Subject: Missing classmates

Continuing to have trouble finding David Hooper and Robbie McGrath. Did either have brothers or sisters? Maybe we could track them down through their families. Anyone know their old addresses? Parents or family might still live there. Thanks, K

That's enough for tonight. Katy stands up from the desk, stretches. Her eye catches the original yearbook sitting towards the back of the desk, looking rather yellowed and older than it actually is. She is incredibly tired, the run starting to take its toll. She should go to bed immediately and yet she can't resist. She sits back down, pulls the book closer, 2000 emblazoned across the front. The millennium. The Harbour Bridge exploding with New Year fireworks. Surviving the Y2K bug and warnings that the world was about to end. The excitement of the Sydney Olympics.

The first page Katy looks at is Brigette's. Her face – freckled, smiling – is vaguely familiar. Best remembered for being in the unbeatable girls' netball team. Hoping to be a sports instructor when she left school. Did Brigette achieve her dreams? What was the illness she suffered from? Did she leave children behind?

Next Katy turns to her own page. There she is, so young, so vulnerable, so dreadfully plain. Who would have thought that a change in hair colour would make such a drastic difference? Plus all the exercise, of course, and not to underestimate the difference that self-confidence makes. Katy is as different as can be to that girl in the photo.

President of The Wilderness Society. She laughs out loud. Where on earth did that come from? Yes, she liked animals, but she was hardly a warrior for animal welfare. Was she afraid to say that what she really wanted was a science degree? That Annabel Moore and her gang would mock her for being such a try-hard? Katy can't fathom why she used to care so much about Annabel Moore.

Last of all, Katy turns to *his* page. Her heart lurches the way it used to lurch when she was seventeen. It's almost painful to look at him. To relive that intense feeling, that vulnerability, that heartbreak. A part of her will always love him. A *big* part of her, if she's honest. This is one of the things she *won't* tell her graduating students. The ones who've been in love or had their hearts broken. The ones whose feelings have been blithely dismissed as crushes or puppy love or something temporary and inconsequential.

The truth is they may never again love as intensely as they do now.

Katy hasn't.

Name: Robbie McGrath

What you will be remembered for: Just forget me.

Best memories of high school: None.

Worst memories of high school: Everything.

What will you be doing ten years from now: Living far away from here.

5
ROBBIE

It's been three or four weeks since Robbie checked his email. His phone got stolen a while back, swiped from his pocket while he was sleeping rough. The one before that got smashed when he fell over. Another one got water damaged. Every now and then he's offered a new phone – second-hand, of course – which he accepts and tries to keep from harm. In between, he can use the computer facilities at drop-in centres like this. He doesn't really mind: half the time he isn't in the right headspace to check his messages anyway.

'Hey, Robbie. How are you? Haven't seen you in a while.'

The fact that they like to remember his name is intensely annoying. There's an unofficial dress code: jeans and check shirts, male and female volunteers wearing more or less the same clothes. Most of them are Christians, their gormless smiles designed to reel you in, to save your soul. No fucking chance of that.

'Yeah, fine,' he eventually answers. Better be civil because he needs stuff done. For a start, there's his laundry: it's been building up and now everything's rank. He also needs a good feed: he's been living off noodles and tinned soup since he was last here. He has the mindset to check his emails today, so he needs one of their computers too. 'Bit hungry, though.'

The volunteer is excited to hear this. That's exactly why he's here. To feed and nourish the less fortunate, the strugglers, the *down and out*. To slap some food on a plate and think he's exonerated from all other responsibility.

'Is that all your laundry?' Another volunteer, a girl, twenties, too old to carry off the pigtails resting on her shoulders. And another gormless smile as she relieves him of the refuse bag packed with dirty clothes. Good luck to her. She'll gag on opening it.

Robbie lines up at the canteen. There's a sour smell coming off the old man in front of him. A woman of indeterminate age – mottled, bloated face – slides in behind him and she doesn't smell great either. The truth is, it's impossible not to smell. You can wash your face and hands at public toilets as much as you like, and occasionally scrounge a cold shower, but nothing can substitute for a long hot shower, morning and night.

The meal on offer today is beef casserole and rice. Robbie is disgruntled. He was hoping for roast chicken and mash, the last meal he had at this facility, the reason why he returned today. He had an appetite – he doesn't always have an appetite – and couldn't get the thought of the roast chicken out of his head.

The laundry will take a couple of hours to run through the washing machine and dryer. In the meantime, Robbie can avail himself of the facilities: hot shower, fresh razor for a shave, a rummage through the clothes bin, and internet access – the biggest draw card because most of the patrons, like him, have trouble hanging on to phones.

He has eight new emails. Six are junk. Two are from his sister.

From: celiamc@optusnet.com.au
Subject: Hello

Hi Robbie,

Hope you will read this at some stage. Just letting you know that Dad is in hospital. Nothing too serious: just some clotting on his leg that they're a bit concerned about. He'd love to hear from you. Even better if you came to see him and Mum. You have no idea how happy that would make them.

I think of you every single day. Hope you think about me, too.

Xxx Celia

Celia sends a message every couple of weeks. She never falters in her efforts to stay in touch. The births of her children, the break-up of her marriage, various illnesses and busy periods, nothing has deterred her from thinking of him and sitting down to type a few lines. He's grateful for the effort she puts in, for keeping him up to date with what's happening in the family, for always letting him know that he's loved, but he never sends a response. He has nothing to say. No words to explain his failure, his embarrassment, his self-loathing, his stubbornness, his defectivity, his utter inability to change himself.

From: celiamc@optusnet.com.au
Subject: Dad

Hi Robbie,

Dad's out of hospital and doing well. Mum is fussing over him and they're bickering like crazy, which is a sign that everything's back to normal. We've had some contact from old school friends of yours. There's a reunion coming up. Twenty years, imagine. The organiser, Katy Buckley, said that she'd love it if you can come. The details are below, along with some questions she wants answered for an updated yearbook. That's a nice idea, isn't it? Finding out what everyone is doing and where they are in life. Maybe the reunion is the incentive you need to finally come home?

Where are you these days? I assume you're not in Sydney. I look for you everywhere I go. Can't stop myself. I hope you're somewhere safe.

53

We love you and miss you and hope that you come home soon.

Celia

Twenty years! It slams into him. Robbie stands up, sits down, stands up again. Twenty years. *Twenty fucking years.* It's confronting, seeing it in type. Those years have been a haze of nothingness, a void in which he has managed to exist and little else. What's weird is that he can still see their smug, superior faces clear as day.

Annabel Moore: pretty, popular, poisonous.

Grace McCrae: couldn't go to the toilet without Annabel.

Zach Latham: thought he was so fucking funny, the idiot.

Melissa Andrews: stuck-up bitch.

Luke Willis: gay as Christmas.

Katy Buckley: always trying to be everyone's friend.

Jarrod Harris: Annabel's on-and-off boyfriend till he got her up the duff and became full-time 'on'. Jarrod is the one he despises the most. Robbie still dreams about him. Recurring nightmares of Jarrod chasing him across the uneven grass, his voice a shout from behind. Jarrod gaining ground, his yells coming fearfully closer. Jarrod tackling him to the ground, Robbie's face crashing into the turf, the taste of dew and dirt in his mouth.

Maybe Celia is right. Maybe it *is* time to finally go home. Maybe he'll turn up at the reunion, surprise them all. He could scrub up, get a suit from the clothing bin, convince them he's a successful businessman now. Then, when they've had a few drinks and their guard is down, he could settle a score or two.

Robbie stands up again. Clenches his fists. Jabs one forward. Undercuts with the other. Long time no see, Jarrod. Take that and that and that. *You fucking bastard. You ruined my life.* Hey, Zach, come to say hello? How's a nice punch between the eyes, you shitbag!

'Are you all right there, chum?' It's yet another volunteer. The place is teeming with them. This one's a pale nerdy-looking bloke. His job is to watch over the antiquated laptops in the 'technology room'. As if anyone could be bothered stealing these old heaps of shit.

'Yeah. Fine.' Robbie forces himself down, grinding his backside to the seat. He tries to distract himself with football news and other headlines. He tries to quell the feelings of inadequacy, self-hatred and bitterness that go hand in hand with even the most random thoughts about his schooldays. He tries a breathing technique some doctor taught him that's supposed to help him feel less agitated. He tries to convince himself that Jarrod, Zach and the rest of them don't matter a fuck.

But as with most things in life, he fails.

Name: Melissa Andrews (aka Snow White)

What you will be remembered for: Being smart. Maybe being a bit too serious.

Best memories of high school: Awards night. I like celebrating everyone's achievements.

Worst memories of high school: Slicing my finger instead of the celery in food tech.

What will you be doing ten years from now: Working my way up the corporate ladder.

6
MELISSA

The air-conditioning is broken and a temporary mobile unit has been placed in the corner of the boardroom. Melissa is sitting closest to the unit. It's blowing her normally immaculate hair all over the place.

'I feel like I'm in a nineteen eighties music video,' she mutters to Cassie, the head of HR. 'The wind machine is lifting my hair while I sing about my heart going on.'

'That was the nineties,' Cassie points out.

'Whatever.'

The finance director has to raise his voice to be heard above the motor of the unit. 'Next year's budget is almost final. We're just waiting on sales forecasts ...' He directs a meaningful look at Melissa.

'By the end of the week,' she says. 'As you know, it's not something that can be rushed.'

Melissa is resolute. She will not pluck sales figures from the air; they're too important for that. Commission is affected. Family incomes. Performance ratings. There is a protocol to go through: a review of the pipeline, a discussion about probability, an estimation process that is neither too bullish nor too cautious. This all takes time.

He turns his attention to Cassie. 'The headcount numbers and employee costs still need tweaking.'

Melissa and Cassie are the only two females sitting around the oblong table. The testosterone can be over-whelming at times.

'The headcount numbers are final,' Cassie retorts. 'You think they need tweaking only because you don't like them.'

Go Cassie! Melissa is well known for her activism in the industry, constantly campaigning for female advancement and representation around tables like this one. She also mentors a few young women who are starting out in their careers. She has a lot of advice to give them. *Work hard. Stand up for yourself. Be confident even though you might be shaking inside.* Unfortunately, she can't offer guidance when it comes to matters such as maternity leave and work-life balance. Melissa thought she'd have children by now. She expected to be juggling work and daycare, manoeuvring sticky fingers away from her business suits and small bodies in and out of car seats. But the prospect of children is looking increasingly unlikely. Henry – already father to two teenage children – is decidedly unenthusiastic. Melissa's ambivalence has been another factor; she has not issued an ultimatum or put any priority on the matter. And if that weren't enough, there's the added, insurmountable, problem of living arrangements.

The meeting comes to its conclusion and Melissa escapes the icy gusts of the air-conditioning unit. She detours to the bathroom on the way back to her office. As suspected, her hair is in complete disarray. She pulls a comb from her handbag and roughly runs it through. She is a striking-looking woman. Near-black hair. Flawless white skin. When she was in her final year at school, she had a holiday job as Snow White in a theme park. Some of her old school friends still call her Snow White.

OK, Snow White. Enough prettying yourself. Back to work.

This morning's meeting feels like a lifetime ago. A few things have gone wrong, souring the rest of the day. A potential client changing his mind at the very last minute. Another client being put on credit hold and threatening to walk away. Sales can be hard, thankless work. It's all or nothing; there's no middle ground. Either you clinch the deal or you don't.

Now, all Melissa wants to do is go home and put her feet up. Tomorrow she'll start again with renewed verve.

'I'm calling it a day,' she says to Samantha, her assistant. Samantha is one of the young women she mentors.

Next year Melissa will promote her into a junior sales role and recruit another exceptionally bright personal assistant, who will also – if she works hard and proves herself capable – be promoted in due course.

Melissa's apartment is cool and welcoming, a haven after a frustrating day. In the bedroom, she swaps her business suit for pyjamas and her stilettos for a pair of fluffy slippers. If only the executive could see her now!

Dinner is Weight Watchers' chicken pasta. She likes the convenience and portion control, even though she's fortunate enough not to have to watch her weight. She burns a lot of energy at work. Zooming from meeting to meeting at a hundred miles an hour. Taking the fire stairs instead of waiting for lifts.

She's fed and settled in front of the TV when Henry calls.

'How was your day?' he asks politely.

'Don't ask … You?'

'Christopher missed his bus so I had to do an emergency trip to school. The traffic was horrendous.'

Henry's children live with him most days of the week. The initial arrangement was meant to be Sunday to Tuesday but Henry's house is closer to their schools than their mother's. Melissa tries to put it down to less commuting time. Tries not to think of herself as a factor and the fact that the more *they're* in his house, the less *she* is.

'Am I going to see you tomorrow?' she asks carefully.

'Yeah, I'll drop in after I've taken Tessa to dance.'

That means they'll have an hour at most. Henry will want sex. He can think again.

'Will I make dinner?' she asks, even though she already knows the answer.

'No need. I'll eat early with the kids.'

'Whatever.' She knows this will annoy him – it's the favoured retort of his children – but says it anyway.

'Now you sound like a fifteen-year-old.'

'"Whatever" is a good word for *all* age groups,' she argues, picking a piece of fluff from her pyjama pants. 'It's the perfect balance between indifference and frustration. It's not as blunt as "Who cares" or as rude as "Fuck off".'

'Do you want to tell me "fuck off"?'

'What I want is more than a stolen hour between dance drop-off and pick-up.'

'Sorry.' He sighs. 'I'll make it up to you on the weekend.'

She says nothing. There is no making up the missed time together. There's too much of it. It's lost for ever.

'What are you doing now?' he asks in a softer tone.

'Just watching TV. One of those hospital emergency shows. After this I'm going to rouse myself to answer the questions for the new yearbook.'

'Okay. You do that … Goodnight, then. Love you.'

'Love you too,' she says automatically.

The truth is, she is not entirely sure.

She *did* love him. Couldn't believe how lucky she was to have met him, how well matched they were.

She was still deliriously happy on their wedding day, a year later, even though his children were digging in their heels and they both decided that it would be best if she held off moving in for a few months. Now here they are. Three years later. Still living apart. And she is not deliriously happy. Not remotely.

Melissa reaches for her iPad and opens Katy's email. Good on Katy for organising this. Tracking down eighty or so ex-students is no mean feat and should not be taken for granted. They should all chip in and present her with a bouquet and their thanks on the night of the reunion.

What are you doing now?

Where do you live?

Do you have a partner/family?

What has been your greatest achievement since leaving school?

Straightforward questions, really. Melissa can't fathom why it has taken her this long – over a fortnight – to answer.

Melissa is sales director for a multinational pharmaceuticals company. She lives in a modern apartment that has corridor views of Bondi Beach. The apartment cost a small fortune but is well within her means because her on-target salary would make some of her old classmates' jaws drop. Henry is her husband. She doesn't have children of her own, and can't count Christopher and Tessa because they've refused to accept her. It seemed easier at the time not to force the issue, not to foist herself upon them. Now she realises it was a big mistake. She and Henry have grown distant. They have become set in their ways. They have not learned how to be with each other for long periods of time. And the children are no more welcoming now than they were three years ago.

Melissa turns off the television. She is finding it hard to think. What is her greatest achievement since leaving school?

Her career? Is that a little too predictable? Too boring?

Melissa imagines that she'll be one of the few who followed the career path she set out to follow.

What will you be doing ten years from now: Working my way up the corporate ladder.

She's proud of her success. Proud of the fact that she helps other women climb the ladder too. Her work life has been anything but predictable or boring.

It's her marriage that's the sticking point. She is not proud of it, not at all, and has just realised that's what caused her to stall, to procrastinate rather than type an immediate response to Katy, which would be her usual style. Melissa's marriage is tripping her up. It feels fake. Like it doesn't deserve mention in her updated status.

Living in separate houses to keep the peace; well, that was even dumber than eating the poisoned apple, Snow White.

Now that she thinks about it, marriage is a bit like sales. It's all or nothing. There is no middle ground.

Name: Zach Latham

What you will be remembered for: Being the class idiot.

Best memories of high school: The day the frogs escaped captivity and were bouncing all around the science lab. (It wasn't an accident. Sorry, Mr Collins.)

Worst memories of high school: Getting a three-day in-school suspension in Year 10 and having to spend those days in Miss Hicks's office doing classwork while she kept her beady eye on me.

What will you be doing ten years from now: Trying to stay out of trouble.

7
ZACH

It all seems pointless to Zach. Both the reunion and the notion of an updated yearbook. He has neither the time nor the interest. He has more important matters to think about. Matters of life and death.

'Hop up on the bed, Mrs Carey. I'll pull the curtain and you can take your top off for me. You can use the sheet. Let me know when you're ready.'

Zach reads through his patient's medical history while he waits for her to de-robe. She's in her fifties, younger than she looks. Used to smoke, gave up a couple of years ago. Today she is complaining of a persistent cough, shortness of breath and chest pain. He has a bad feeling about this one.

'Ready?'

'Yes.' Even her one-word response is breathless.

He starts with percussion on her back, establishing a dull area at the base of the lung, suggesting fluid. He uses the stethoscope to listen. She winces at the coldness of the metal, then laughs at herself, a raspy laugh that turns into a hacking cough.

'Deep breaths through the mouth.' He can't hear any breathing sounds from that area. 'Have you been experiencing any back pain?'

She looks surprised. 'Yes, at night.'

That means it has probably spread to the bones. At least stage 3. What's frustrating is that smoking is becoming popular again, despite all the health warnings. Some people just don't value their lives until it's too late.

'Let's listen to your front now.' She turns, with another wince, to give him a better angle.

He moves the stethoscope around her freckled chest, listening carefully. 'All done.'

Zach fills in paperwork for a chest X-ray and pleural aspiration while she buttons up her top.

'Should I be worried?' she asks tremulously.

He pauses. He can't lie outright. Nothing is ever gained by lying.

'Try not to worry too much until we see the results. Then we'll deal with it together.'

His next patient is a toddler with a raging ear infection. The child screams and squirms in his mother's arms. Zach smiles, says hello, and hands him a spare stethoscope to play with. The child is immediately transfixed.

'That's the first time he's stopped crying today,' the mother says.

Zach is good with children. All the mothers say so.

'That woman – Katy – sent another reminder today. You should reply to her.'

Zach shares everything with Isabel, including a joint email address. She sees all his messages, he sees all hers, they have nothing to hide from each other. It's late at night and they've finally sat down to relax. Carson is asleep upstairs.

'Nah, Izzy. Not interested.'

'Why not?'

'I was a different person back then. A bit of a dick-head, if I'm honest.'

Isabel laughs, her dark eyes crinkling at the sides. She is almost nine years older than him. 'You were the class clown. I found that interesting.' Seeing his confusion, she explains further. 'Katy scanned a copy of your original entry, obviously hoping to prompt you to respond. Were you the one who let the frogs escape?'

His smile is sheepish. 'Yep.'

'So, when did you start to become more serious about life?'

'You know when.'

He's told her this story. His turning point, his epiphany. It happened when he was eighteen, a few months out of school, having started a degree in computer technology and discovering that he had zero interest in it.

Then, one night before dinner, his father had a heart attack. He didn't clutch at his chest, as one might have expected, or cry out in pain. He burped, as though he'd eaten too much, even though he hadn't yet sat down to eat. Then he grabbed hold of the kitchen counter in an attempt to keep himself upright and Zach had to lunge forward to catch him before he hit the ground. His mother called an ambulance and something happened while Zach watched the paramedics in action. He wanted what they had. A job that made a difference. A job that involved saving lives or making them better. Of course, this late decision meant having to do bridging courses in chemistry, biology and maths. It meant doing a six-year degree instead of a three-year one. He initially saw himself as a paramedic, but later decided that the long-lasting doctor–patient relationships in general practice were more for him.

Izzy tilts her head to one side as she regards him. She wears her hair long, over one shoulder. Its natural colour is brown-black. These days she dyes it to disguise the grey. 'Don't you want to tell this Katy what you're doing with your life? Are you not proud of who you are, who *we* are?'

Zach feels that a few trite sentences can't possibly summarise all the wondrous and tragic things he has experienced, or the wisdom he has accumulated about humanity and what is truly important in life.

'You know I'm proud,' he says, reaching for her hand. 'Our son is being made school captain tomorrow, a day

I thought I'd never see. I'll be the proudest man in that school hall.'

'Well, answer her then. Tell her about me and Carson and your job. Shout it out to the world.'

As is often the case, Isabel has helped him see things differently. He leans closer to give her a kiss of gratitude.

The school hall is half full. It's a small school, only sixty-odd students in total. Zach and Isabel have reserved seats in the front row. Carson is up on the stage, kicking his legs as he waits, a shoelace undone. He jumps up when he sees them. A teacher fondly returns him to his seat.

'Morning.' Barry, Zach's father, sits down next to them, looking the picture of health. Having the heart attack all those years ago changed his life, too.

'I thought I was gone,' he said when he was well enough to reflect on what had happened. 'And all I could think was, give me another chance. Please, God, give me one more chance and I promise I won't blow it.'

Barry hasn't blown it. He exercises, eats and drinks in moderation, and goes for regular check-ups. Sadly, Zach's mother passed away a few years ago and Barry is now on his own. Isabel's parents are more elderly and live in Buenos Aires. They visit Sydney once a year, staying for a couple of months at a time. They help with Carson. All the grandparents adore Carson.

The headmaster clears his throat and waits a few beats for silence to descend.

'Good morning, everyone. A very big welcome to St Kevin's School for Special Education.'

They knew beforehand, at the twelve-week scan. The baby had a tell-tale amount of fluid at the back of its neck. Both Zach and Isabel, who is also a doctor, saw the increased nuchal translucency on the screen. They both understood the ramifications.

'The baby might have Down's syndrome,' Isabel murmured when the sonographer left the room to fetch her supervisor.

They were offered further – more intrusive – tests, which they declined. They both agreed: the tests wouldn't change the outcome, there would be no termination. Of course, the increased fluid didn't automatically mean Down's syndrome but Isabel's age – thirty-five – was another damning factor. They knew. Deep down they both knew, and further tests, with their associated risks of miscarriage, seemed pointless.

Izzy grieved. It took time to adjust her expectations of the baby that would be born, to realign her hopes and dreams for the child and their family life. Then, with acceptance, came ferocity. 'Regardless of what happens, this baby has been given to us for a reason … He has been sent on earth to teach us to be worthy of him.'

Zach was just as resolute. He was disappointed and sad but he wasn't frightened of having a disabled child. He'd seen enough to know there is no such thing as perfect, and indeed no guarantees at any stage of parenthood. Robust babies can be struck down with leukaemia or other serious illnesses. Happy-go-lucky children can become mentally unstable during their teens. If you approached parenthood expecting no major challenges, then you were in for a shock.

The headmaster announces the new captains and Carson and his female counterpart stand up to boisterous applause. Their badges are pinned to their polo shirts and then there's a short speech from each.

Carson stands too close to the microphone. 'Thank you, Mumma, Dadda, Pops,' he booms. A teacher moves him back. 'Thanks, Mr Summers and Mrs McKay.' Now he is barely audible. The teacher tries again to put him in the right position. 'Thanks, friends, for voting me. You're best friends ever.'

Carson's speech is thick-tongued due to his low muscle tone. He makes up for it with authenticity, enthusiasm and an enormous grin. Izzy takes a thousand photos. Zach blinks away tears of pride.

Afterwards, there is tea and cake and even more photos. Barry says goodbye, and Isabel and Zach stroll back to the car hand in hand. A teen – ripped jeans, tattooed arms, a cloud of cigarette smoke in front of his face – eyes Isabel up and down. She is one of those classically beautiful women who appeal to men of all ages.

Zach stops dead. Stares at the cigarette between the teen's fingers.

'Yesterday I had a woman in my surgery who has lung cancer. She'll be lucky to last six weeks.'

'That's your fucking business.'

Izzy takes a turn. 'The people who love you – your mum and dad and maybe your girlfriend – won't want you to die young.'

After a few long moments, the boy grinds the cigarette against the wall behind him. It was only a matter of time before he capitulated. Izzy has this effect on people. Bringing out the best in them. Including Zach.

She gives the boy a dazzling smile. 'Well done, you.'

The truth is, Zach doesn't deserve Isabel. She is beautiful, inside and out. He is not.

8
ROBBIE

Robbie knocks on the door aggressively. Bang, bang, bang. *Open up. I'm back.* He hears voices, then light, quick footsteps. The door opens cautiously. Tangled dark hair, pink cheeks; she's the picture of her mother.

'Hello,' she states.

'Hello,' he responds, adopting her serious tone.

'Are you looking for my mum?'

'Yes, I am.'

'Who are you?'

'My name is Robbie.'

She tilts her head to one side. 'I have an uncle called Robbie. He lives in another city.'

'That's me. I'm your uncle.'

Her eyes widen. 'Really? Are you *really*?'

'Really.'

The little girl calls over her shoulder. Her voice is loud and strong, at odds with her size. 'Mum, Mum, it's Uncle Robbie, it's Uncle Robbie!'

There's a cry from the back of the house. Then Celia is barging towards him, her hair coming loose from its bun, a look of utter incredulity on her face.

'Robbie? Robbie?'

She stops up close to double-check. Then squeals, 'It's you! It's you,' and flings her arms around him. 'I don't believe it! It's *really* you. Oh, my God.'

Her arms are warm and strong. Her scent gets caught in the back of his throat. He can't remember the last time he was this close to someone. He likes it and hates it in equal measure.

'Sienna, this is your Uncle Robbie. Where's Charlie? Charlie, get down here!'

Charlie is already halfway down the stairs. He's older than his sister. Nine? Ten? Robbie should know his age. Celia is always talking about the two of them in her emails.

'Come in, come in,' his sister urges. 'Is that your bag?'

His 'bag' is a battered rucksack. She probably doesn't remember that it's the same one he left with all those years ago. She takes it, deposits it into one of the rooms off the hall. Then she ushers him into the kitchen-dining area. His first impressions are bright, homely, nothing flash. There's the smell of dinner in the air. His stomach twinges. He hasn't eaten since he got on the bus in Newcastle.

'I have a pasta bake in the oven. Are you hungry?'

He nods in a casual manner that he hopes doesn't betray how ravenous he is.

'I must ring Mum and Dad. Sit down. I won't be long, I promise. Sienna, get your uncle a glass of water. Charlie, put out some cheese and crackers.'

Celia disappears into the hallway with her phone. He is left alone with the children, his niece and nephew. He should have bought them presents. Children of their age would expect something from visiting relatives.

Sienna and Charlie deliver the water and food, clearing some school books from the table to make room. They sit down across from him.

'Where have you been?' his niece asks.

'Travelling.'

Charlie looks excited at this. 'Have you been to Paris?'

Robbie shakes his head. 'Nope.'

'New York?'

'Only cities around New South Wales – Newcastle, Wollongong, and smaller places like Byron Bay and Nowra.'

'So why haven't you come to see us before now?' Sienna crosses her arms accusingly. 'Those places aren't very far from here.'

The truth is complex and he doesn't fully understand it himself. Seeing the same people day after day makes him feel cornered and exposed instead of loved and secure. Being anonymous makes him steadier, more in control, and if something goes wrong, he can simply move on without having to cut any ties or provide a thousand explanations. How to rationalise all that to children? He could lie and say he was just too busy, but a few more questions would reveal that he doesn't even have a job.

Celia returns and saves him from having to answer. 'They're on their way over. They're so excited, Robbie. They didn't believe me at first.'

'I'm not staying with them,' he says bluntly. 'I'm not putting a foot in that house.'

She is visibly taken aback. Glances at the children, who are transfixed at this development. 'Sienna, take your handwriting homework upstairs. Charlie, go and tidy your room.'

Sienna – very unenthusiastically – reaches for one of the homework books on the table. Charlie has a staring contest with his mother before scraping back his chair. They trudge out of the room with such exaggerated reluctance that Robbie almost laughs.

Celia crouches down next to him. 'Why don't you want to go back to the house? Did something specific happen there? You must tell me, Robbie.'

Her scrutiny makes him squirm in his seat. 'Too many bad memories, that's all.'

She looks at him even more closely, if that's possible. 'But not of Mum and Dad, surely?'

'No, not them. The problem is me. The problem has always been *me*.'

Tears and confusion mingle in her pale blue eyes,

the exact same shade as his own. She can't comprehend either his motives for staying away or this abrupt reappearance. He wants to explain: hate is more powerful than love. Self-hatred kept him away. A different kind of hatred prompted his return. Love should have played a part – love for his ageing parents, and for her, his faithful sister – but it didn't. Hate alone has propelled him to this point.

She takes both his hands in hers, squeezes tightly as though she is never going to let him go. 'Robbie, I am so happy to see you. I am so incredibly happy that you've finally met your niece and nephew. You can stay here, with us, for as long as you like.'

The next day Robbie is feeling tired, overwrought and dangerously off-kilter. Seeing his mother and father after all these years. So much older, more fragile and shrunken. The tears and recriminations for not staying in touch. The questions he couldn't really answer. His mother wouldn't stop touching him. Squeezing his hand. Stroking his face or arm. She couldn't keep her hands off him. At some point a phone was pressed against his ear, his brother Nick hollering on the other end, promising to come up from Melbourne. Later, in Celia's spare room, sensory overload and the inability to settle down to sleep.

'I wish I could stay at home and be with you,' Celia said this morning. 'But I've already had too many sick days. The last thing I need is to lose my job.'

His sister works in an office in Brookvale. The pay is bad but the location is convenient for school. She split up from her husband last year. She claims the split was mutual but Robbie has his doubts. She winces whenever she says her ex-husband's name.

The children left the house with Celia.

'Will you be here when we get home?' Sienna asked suspiciously.

'Yes, of course.'

Robbie took a deep breath when they left. He made himself a cup of tea and worked out how to operate the TV. The walls started closing in on him so he went for a walk to the local shops, sat on the wall outside the pharmacy, loitered in the newsagent's until he was asked to leave. Celia had said a few of his old year group still lived in the area but he didn't see any familiar faces.

Now he's at his old school, Macquarie High, except it's gone. Bulldozed to make way for a new housing development. The demolition was more than ten years ago and the houses have established gardens out the front. Celia said that the locals are still angry about it.

'The kids have to travel two suburbs to the closest high school now. We don't understand why the government did this. *It was such a good school.*'

Her memories are obviously different to his. As he recalls it, it was a terrible school. Nobody cared, neither teachers nor students. Celia was two years younger than him; maybe her year group had some genuinely nice people instead of a pack of fucking arseholes.

Robbie leaves the housing estate and strides back towards the shops. It's rush hour now. People are stopping on their way home for milk, bread and take-away dinners. No sign of Jarrod, Annabel, Grace or any of the others. He can't explain this sudden fixation with seeing them.

Five p.m. He needs to go home. Celia will be worrying that he's not coming back. The children will be annoying her with questions. That reminds him. He has some loose change in his pocket. Enough for two bars of chocolate. Not the most extravagant present in the world but all he has to offer.

The next day he's beset with the same claustrophobic feeling as soon as Celia and the children leave in the morning. The same urge to get out, to distance himself from the cloying walls of the house. He decides to catch a bus into the city. Sydney hasn't changed much. Some of the roads have been widened. New blocks of flats have been built along Military Road. The bus rattles over the bridge, and Robbie has his first view of the harbour in twenty years.

He hops off the bus and walks towards Town Hall. Almost everyone is dressed in office attire, holding a phone or a coffee cup or both. The ones who aren't distracted meet Robbie's eyes before giving him a wide berth. It's funny how they can sense that he's different, that he isn't one of them. It must be his clothing, or perhaps his grooming, even though today he's shaved and wearing perfectly good clothes belonging to Celia's ex-husband.

Town Hall is a popular meeting spot. The greetings are effusive: girls squealing and kissing cheeks, men clapping each other on the shoulder before exchanging hugs. When did everyone become so touchy-feely? Robbie keeps walking. This part of the city is more interesting. Chinese convenience stores, organic health food shops, the homeless sitting on corners with signs: *Down on my luck* and *Grateful for anything you can give*. He ambles through the buskers and heavy crowds at Central Station. Then he spots a bus with Newtown on its banner. He jumps aboard, barely making it through the closing doors. Katy Buckley works in a school in Newtown. Her contact details were on the email forwarded by Celia.

Katy's school looks like any other public school: red-brick buildings, concrete footpaths, overgrown grass. It's lunchtime. Students swarm the grounds, sandwiches being eaten on the go, boys tussling with each other. Short skirts, board shorts, ripped T-shirts; there doesn't appear to be a uniform or indeed any prohibition of bold hairstyles, body piercings or even tattoos.

Robbie notices an abandoned wheelbarrow under one of the trees. Without really thinking, he slips inside the gates and wheels it around, nodding at the students, not getting too close to the supervising teachers, and stopping every now and then to pick up litter. He is keeping a keen eye out for Katy. A woman rather than the soft-faced girl of his memories. A teacher in place of the earnest student who always had books clutched to her chest. At least her hair colour should be recognisable.

'Miss Buckley!'

Robbie turns as soon as he hears it. The student is running towards a teacher with dark brown hair and tight-fitting jeans. The teacher is toned – she obviously works out – and has a nose piercing. It couldn't possibly be Katy.

'Miss, I've left my lunch at home and I don't have any money. Can I have a pass for the canteen … please?'

'How many times have you left your lunch at home this term?'

Her voice is familiar even if her appearance is not. Robbie recognises the wry undertones.

'Too many times,' the student replies.

'Exactly.' Katy, trying to hide a smile, pulls out a notebook from the pocket of her jeans. 'Here. Make sure you bring in the money tomorrow.'

'I will, I will. Thank you, Miss.'

The student belts off. Katy is still smiling. It's obvious that the student sought her out because she is more sympathetic than other teachers. Robbie remembers now. Katy *is* kind. She was always the one who ran to get his brother Nick, while the others stood around, watching his torment, never once stepping in to help. Yes, Katy is kind and good and lovely. It's the rest of them he hates.

The house is strangely quiet when Robbie gets home. That's right, they're at gymnastics. They'll be back by six. He goes into his room to change his shirt: all the walking around has made him sweaty. There's something on his bed, a sheet of paper propped against one of the pillows. It's a picture, a crude drawing of a red bus, coloured in with vigour rather than accuracy. Below, a message in wobbly handwriting: *Dear Uncle Robbie. I love you. From Sienna.*

It's not long before they burst into the house, an instant infusion of noise and activity.

'Sienna, don't dump your bag in the hall. Put it in your room. Charlie, close the door, for goodness' sake.'

Then the commencement of the panel interview, Charlie and Sienna lined up on one side of the table, Robbie on the other.

'Where did you go today, Uncle Robbie? What did you do?'

'I got the bus into the city. Did some people watching at Town Hall. Listened to the buskers at Central Station. It was a good day.'

It *was* a good day. The best in a long time. He mentions nothing about going all the way to Newtown. Nothing about Katy.

Robbie already knows that he'll go back to the school tomorrow.

9
LUKE

Luke is rostered on a charter flight every few weeks. He enjoys them; sometimes the passengers are celebrities. He's had his photo taken with Katy Perry, the English rugby team and Graham Norton. He only asks if he thinks the celebrity genuinely doesn't mind. Luke doesn't like to grovel.

There's nobody famous on today's flight, just a group of car manufacturing engineers going to Sweden to test their latest models against brutal winter conditions. Luke shivers: he is not a fan of extreme weather, be it cold or hot.

'We like coming here,' one of the engineers says chattily. 'You can achieve way more than you can with simulators or wind tunnels. You know, traction control was refined in Arjeplog.'

Luke doesn't know. He has only a vague idea of what traction control is. He doesn't drive, never learned how. His father was too angry to teach him when everyone else was learning. *If you'll stop being such a faggot, I might teach you.* Once Luke left home and moved overseas, it never felt necessary to learn. Who needs a car in central London?

The engineers are staying in Sweden for five days and the aircraft and cabin crew are staying too. Apparently, it's cheaper than flying home and back again with an empty aircraft. Luke doesn't mind. It's the chance to catch up on some sleep, and he'll be getting paid in full while doing so. Nerida, who's also on the flight, has done some research on the area. Temperatures that can drop below 40 degrees Fahrenheit. Frozen lakes that can be configured as motor tracks. Limited restaurants. Practically non-existent nightlife. On the plus side there are reindeer forests, the opportunity to go ice-skating or skiing and some stunning scenery. Nerida is hoping they'll get a glimpse of the Northern Lights.

'I know absolutely nothing about cars,' Luke says to the friendly engineer.

'Anything you need to know …' The engineer smiles. He has a cute smile. He's a few years younger than Luke. 'I might see you in the bar later on.'

Luke wakes the next morning with a dreadful headache and the relief that he's in his own room. Fragments of yesterday flash behind his eyes. Flirting with the engineer on the flight. Meeting at the hotel bar later on. Throwing back beers, then wine, then shots of bourbon. The only saving grace is that when the engineer – Sebastian – asked him back to his room he said no. Yet more shots as he told Sebastian about how much he loved Aaron, and Sebastian drunkenly recounted his latest break-up. Poor Sebastian, having to get up at the crack of dawn this morning. Trying to apply his hungover brain to complex problems involving speed, physics and traction. Possibly behind the wheel of one of the skidding cars.

Speaking of skidding, that's exactly what the room is doing when Luke sits up in the bed. Christ, he needs a glass of water. He goes to the bathroom, finds a glass. The water is so cold it gives him a different kind of headache; the kind you get from eating an ice cream too fast. He uses the toilet and then forces himself into the shower, in the hope that it will make him feel better. It doesn't. A strong wave of nausea hits and he throws up against the walls of the cubicle. The vomit, yellow and watery, runs down the tiles: bile and water. Now he feels insanely hot. He bursts out of the cubicle, gulps in some air. Jesus Christ. This happens every now and then. He drinks too much, and the next morning it feels like he has poisoned himself. Truth is, it happens more often than he'd like. Aaron is always begging him to show more restraint.

The walk back to bed is shaky. He's like an old man, stopping every few steps to rest and lean against the wall. His phone beeps just as he sits down. It's from Nerida.

Going to breakfast now. C U there?

The thought of breakfast has him rushing for the bathroom again. This time the vomit has more substance. It gets clogged in the plughole of the basin, sticks to the back of his throat. Disgusting. Disgusting. Disgusting.

Another shaky walk back to bed. He lies down, reaches for his phone again. He feels marginally better but doesn't trust that it's going to last. He'll give it another ten minutes before answering Nerida. In the meantime, he checks his emails. A message from work regarding a change to his roster next week. A few SPAM messages, offering him Viagra and fake prizes. One of Katy's reunion messages nestled in the middle of the SPAM.

From: admin11@yearbook.com.au
Subject: New Yearbook

Name: Luke Willis

Highest achievement at school: Being the first openly gay student.

What you do now: Flight Attendant.

Highlights of last twenty years: Travelling the world. Meeting your boyfriend, who is far too good for you.

Lowlights: Drinking too much. You're pathetic, Luke. Then and now.

Deepest fears: That Katy will ask you to father a child. Hold tight, it's coming. Pity she hasn't better taste.

What the fuck?

Luke reads the message again. Is Katy on drugs or something? What's she doing sending out shit like this? His outrage causes his hangover to momentarily recede. He FaceTimes her immediately. Doesn't care to check the time in Sydney. Serves her right if he disturbs her at work.

'Luke?' Her face, looking concerned, appears on the screen of his phone. 'What's up? Is everything all right?'

She's at home, eating a meal. Yes, now that he thinks about it, it's dinnertime in Sydney.

'Everything is *not* all right,' he tells her crossly. 'I just got your crazy message. Have you gone mad? Jesus Christ, there's no chance, no fucking way on earth.'

Now she looks confused. 'What are you talking about? What message?'

'Stop playing games, Katy. I have the worst headache imaginable.'

'I didn't send a message. I swear I didn't. I haven't emailed you for a few weeks at least.' She tucks her hair behind one ear. 'And you haven't answered my last message, I might add.'

'Well, *someone* sent me a message. A fucked-up message about this fucked-up yearbook of yours.'

'Forward it on to me. I want to read it.'

He does what she asks. He's deteriorating again.

His stomach is clenching and his head is going to split open. He's too old for this: getting into drinking competitions with strangers, vomiting in hotel bathrooms, waking up with that horrible mix of guilt, shame and self-disgust.

Thanks to the instantaneous wonders of technology, even here in the most remote place on the planet, it is only a matter of moments before Katy has received and read the offending email.

She is definitive. 'I didn't send this, Luke. The email address is similar to the special one I set up for the reunion, but it's not exactly the same. Annabel and Grace got messages too. More nasty than funny, just like yours. Remember, I sent an email asking whoever it was to stop?'

Luke doesn't remember; he's been barely skimming the reunion stuff. Why bother with the details when he has no intention of going?

'Is it true that you want me to be a fucking *sperm donor*?'

Silence. *Jesus Christ, it's true, then.*

'The thought had crossed my mind,' she eventually admits.

'Fuck it, Katy, it's a terrible idea.'

Now she's indignant. 'I'm thirty-seven, Luke, and I don't have a partner. What's wrong with asking an old friend?'

'A *gay* friend?'

'Being gay and being a father aren't mutually exclusive, you know.'

He groans. This is not the kind of conversation to be having right now. He can't seem to hold on to any thoughts. Nothing is sticking, only the fact that it's a bad, bad idea. 'I can't answer that. My head is too sore.'

She gives him a knowing look. 'Big night out?'

'Yep.'

For a moment, he thinks she's going to lecture him. But she returns to the matter at hand. 'Who is sending these messages? Who would even *know* I was thinking of asking you that question? I haven't discussed it with anyone.'

'Fucked if I know … Look, I have to go. I feel horrible.'

'Okay. Take care.' Then a friendly warning more than a lecture: 'Don't drink so much, hey?'

Luke hangs up, feels another intense wave of nausea and has to run for the bathroom again. He promised Nerida they'd go to the reindeer forests today. There's clearly no chance of that. He knows his body. Three vomits means that he needs to go back to bed, sleep it off.

He sends Nerida his apologies. *Feel ill. Sorry, love. Reindeers tomorrow, promise. Turning my phone off now so I can sleep. xxx*

Then he sends Aaron a message. *Miss you. Wish you were here.*

The response is instantaneous: *Me, too. What's Sweden like?*

Can't really tell. We're in the middle of fucking nowhere. Ha, ha. Hope you're being good.

Luke thinks hard about his response, then types: *Let's get married.*

He stares at the words for what feels like a long time. Then presses delete until each letter and then word disappears and the screen is blank. He turns off his phone, burrows down under the covers and is asleep within minutes.

10
KATY

Katy is rattled. Who sent Luke that message? How on earth do they know she was working up the courage to ask him to father a child with her?

Katy has a few different circles of friends. Her colleagues from work, including her best friend, Nina. The women from her running club, who she sees on Tuesday and Thursday nights. The old gang from university, who're scattered across Sydney's suburbia and manage a night out – usually of epic proportions – three or four times a year. It's no news to most of her friends that she would like to meet someone and start a family; she hasn't kept it secret. But she *has* kept quiet the idea of asking Luke. Because it didn't make sense to discuss it with her girlfriends before discussing it with him. Because she's still at the exploration phase and has lots to consider before asking such a momentous question.

Yet someone, *somehow*, knows, and thanks to their interference Luke has declared it a terrible idea. She never imagined his reaction would be so unequivocally negative. He is one of her dearest and oldest friends, as well as holding the dubious honour of being her first love. At school, she adored everything about him: his lightning-fast wit, his brutal honesty, his fearlessness. The fact that he did his own thing, never followed the crowd, but people still liked him. The fact that he saw something in her that she couldn't see at the time. In his eyes, boring carrot-haired Katy Buckley was just as worthwhile as the beautiful ultra-popular Annabel Moore.

Luke announced that he was gay when he turned sixteen and Katy was broken-hearted at the news. They had never kissed or been together romantically but she'd been secretly in love with him for months. She cried herself to sleep for nights on end. She actually prayed (proper prayers, with her hands joined and eyes closed) that he would 'change his mind', which makes her laugh now. It took months to shut off her romantic feelings for him. Now he is one of her closest friends and confidantes. Someone who knows her of old. She's still in love with him, an emotional love, not a physical one. What's so terrible about him being the father of her child?

Katy finishes her dinner, washes the dishes, and then

sits down at her laptop. Three new emails waiting in the reunion account. The first one is from Robbie McGrath. Hooray, he's been found.

My sister sent me the details of the reunion. I am coming. Robbie.

Well, Robbie won't win any prizes for eloquence, but never mind that. At least she can put a tick next to his name. She shoots back a message.

From: admin@yearbook.com.au
Subject: RSVP

That's great, Robbie. I am still searching for David Hooper. I think you both did French together. Any idea where he is these days? And don't forget to answer the questions for the new yearbook. Everyone will be very interested to hear what you've been doing.

The next unread email is from Mike, Brigette's husband. More success: Mike has attached the information for Brigette's memorial entry.

From: Mike1010@gmail.com
Subject: Yearbook

Sorry if the attached file is too long. I've realised how much I want Brigette to be remembered at your reunion. I want everyone to know how worthwhile her life was and how much she is missed by her family and friends.

Katy opens the file. Mike's response *is* long: three full pages. There are photos interspersed in the text. Brigette on her wedding day. Brigette cradling a newborn baby. Brigette, arms raised in victory, coming across a finish line. Brigette and a group of women holding up champagne flutes.

Brigette Saunders: 1982–2018

Greatest Achievements: Brigette was a semi-professional marathon runner as well as a volunteer running coach. She ran a total of fourteen marathons, including a few overseas in London, Boston and Hawaii. Brigette found it incredibly hard to give up running when she was ill. She would do shorter races or – if undergoing treatment – would convince someone (usually me) to push her wheelchair, so she could still be involved and soak up the race-day atmosphere. Even before she became ill, Brigette was an enthusiastic supporter of the Breast Cancer Foundation and other cancer charities. She raised more than $10,000 for breast cancer and almost the same again for ovarian cancer, which was the cancer that beat her in the end. There's a race named in her honour: The Brigette Saunders Classic. The running community lobbied for this race. Hopefully, it will exist many years into the future and will be her greatest legacy of all.

Tears smart in Katy's eyes. What a remarkable woman. What courage, determination and defiance she showed.

How wonderful to be so deeply loved and admired by her husband.

She thinks for a while, then sends a response.

This is beautiful, Mike. It made me cry. What a special woman your wife was. I'll send a copy of the yearbook when complete.

The last unread email in the inbox is from Zach Latham.

From: zachandisabel@optusnet.com.au
Subject: RSVP

Dear Katy,

Hope you are well. Please count me and my wife Isabel in for the reunion. Thank you for organising.

Zach

PS: answers for the yearbook are attached.

Once again, Katy is surprised when she opens the attachment. Zach Latham is a doctor. *A GP*. Well, she didn't see that coming. For a start, she doesn't remember him as being particularly smart, and medicine requires top marks. Neither does she remember him as being all that caring. All that mattered to Zach was being the centre of attention, getting a laugh, usually at someone else's expense: all too often, Robbie McGrath's expense. The Zach Katy remembers wasn't caring. He was cruel.

Katy is going out tonight. Damien, one of her colleagues,

is turning forty and has invited half the school. She has one final email to send before getting ready.

From: admin@yearbook.com.au
Subject: Not funny

To the naughty person who is STILL sending fake yearbook updates:

Please stop. Joke is well and truly over. People are getting upset.

Thanks, K

Then a left-field thought: *It's not Luke, is it?* Could he have intuitively known what she was planning – he does read her mind at times – and forced the issue? Highly unlikely. Luke has no trouble speaking his mind, no hesitation in saying the word 'no', in telling her outright when he thinks she's off her rocker. Besides, it doesn't explain the messages to Grace and Annabel, both of whom wouldn't cross his mind.

Which brings her right back to where she started. Who sent that message to Luke? How did they know what she was contemplating? And if she can't ask Luke to father a baby with her, *then who can she ask?*

The party is in a private function room off the main bar. There are a lot of familiar faces.

Damien greets her with arms wide open. 'Katy, you made it.'

She gives him the expected hug. 'Happy birthday, Damo.' Then hands him a bottle of red wine in a gift bag. 'Something to ease the pain.'

'What pain? I'm in my prime.' He pulls on his wife's arm. 'Tell her, Suzy.'

'Yeah, sure you are.'

Suzy is a regular face at staff nights out, as are all the spouses. The vast majority of Katy's colleagues are married.

'He's so pissed,' Suzy whispers in Katy's ear. 'Everyone's been buying him drinks. Any minute now, he'll be on the dance floor.'

Katy runs into Nina at the bar. Her best friend is wearing a figure-hugging dress and very high heels.

'Need a drink,' she gasps, before Katy can issue a compliment on her outfit. 'Barely arrived and already a call from the babysitter.'

Nina's little girls are aged four and six. When Katy visits, they fight to take turns to sit on her lap, stubby fingers exploring her hair and jewellery, peppering her with questions: have you got a boyfriend; what's your favourite colour; which do you like the best: dogs or cats, ice cream or chocolate, winter or summer?

'What's up with the babysitter?' Katy asks.

'The girls are hyper. Playing dress-up instead of getting into pyjamas. Dragging out toys that haven't been played with for years. Why does having a night out have to be so bloody hard?' Nina catches the attention of the barman. 'A bottle of the Sauvignon Blanc with three glasses, please.'

The wine comes in a stainless-steel cooler bucket. Nina shoves a glass into Katy's hand and pours far too generously.

'Let's hope you're not as liberal as this with your chemistry measurements,' Katy says drily.

'My test tubes are the envy of the department,' she retorts.

Nina's husband Philip appears, taking one of Nina's overfull glasses and clinking it with Katy's.

'Hey, Katy. How've you been?'

'Great. What's this I hear about your little angels?'

Philip has a slightly harried look that belies the fact that he is generally hard to ruffle. He's a good father; he and Nina make a great team.

He rolls his eyes. 'Little devils, more like. It's meant to get easier as they get older, not harder.'

Katy's stomach squeezes. Nina and Philip have each other, as well as their extended family. If Katy becomes a parent, she'll be all on her own. Her parents retired up the coast a few years ago and her sister lives in Adelaide. Putting geographical distance to one side, Katy can't imagine them approving: their ideas of family are too traditional. Night shifts, childcare logistics, babysitter problems, everything would rest on Katy's shoulders alone.

Is Luke right? Is it a crazy idea?

One of the technology teachers comes over and

strikes up a conversation with Nina and Philip. Katy half-listens as she sips her wine. Damien has made it on to the dance floor and is performing some kind of robot-inspired routine.

'Hello, Katy.'

The voice is behind her but she doesn't need to turn around to identify who it is. She'd recognise those nasal tones anywhere.

'Hello, William.'

William teaches geography and commerce. He's one of the few male teachers without a partner and it's not hard to establish why. For a start, there's his atrocious dress sense. There's also the fact that he has the charisma of wet clay, a topic that features regularly in his geography classes.

He nods at Katy's still-full glass of wine. 'Would you like another?'

'No, thanks. I'm fine for now.'

Then, after a long obvious look in the direction of the dance floor, 'Would you like to dance?'

'Maybe later.'

He shifts uncomfortably from one foot to the other, then starts talking at length about some changes to the syllabus.

She fantasises about putting her hand up, stopping him mid-track to ask, 'Would you like to father a child with me?'

It would almost be worth it to see the look of shock on his face. Here's the sad thing: he'd probably consider it.

He's made no secret of the fact that he likes her or that he's on the lookout for a serious girlfriend. Maybe she could buy him an entire new wardrobe and the prospect would become more palatable. She tries to imagine what he would look like after an extreme make-over. But the problem is that you can't make-over someone's personality. You can't make them more vibrant, more interesting, more compelling. You can't create chemistry when there's nothing to start with ... She's a science teacher, she knows this for a fact.

In the end, Katy dances with William. Because it makes him happy. Because she is essentially kind. Because Nina is talking on the phone and there is no one else to dance with. They dance to a DJ mix that has a strong rhythm. Her arms are in the air, fingers clicking. She knows some of the lyrics, shouts them out, and stays for another song, and then another.

It's the end of the party. The music has stopped. The lights have turned on. Nina and Philip are long gone. Damien is pissed and singing happy birthday to himself.

'Happy birthday to ME. Happy birthday to ME. Happy birthday to ME-EE ...'

William is hovering. Katy says a quick goodbye and shoots away, before he gets it into his head to follow her.

She gets home in record time, the taxi driver dismissive of speed limits. The flat is dark and lonely. She grabs her laptop and takes it into bed with her. No new messages. She'd been hoping for something from Luke. Something like: *Sorry for being so blunt*. Or even better: *I am actually thinking about this*.

She types a message to him.

Why is it such a bad idea?

Then presses SEND before she can think the better of it.

Who sent Luke that message? How did they know what she was planning to ask of him? She hasn't confided in anyone, not even Nina.

Think. Think. Someone who went to Macquarie High, who went to school with both her and Luke. Did they spot her somewhere? At a doctor's surgery? Looking at pamphlets or something like that? But she's never picked up a pamphlet, never gone as far as being examined by a doctor or a specialist. All she has done – so far – is search the internet.

Katy's breath catches in her throat. She moves her mouse across the screen, clicks on browsing history, and it's all there: fertility clinics, sperm donation, gay dad and single parent websites. Someone could easily piece two and two together if they were to see this.

Has someone been in her flat? On her laptop?

She shivers. Chides herself for being overly dramatic. But she's spooked, because didn't Grace think the exact same thing? That someone had been in her house and taken that photograph from her fridge? She changed her mind later on, when her husband found the photo. Still, what are the chances? Of someone breaking into

Grace's house and now Katy's, on some weird crusade to upset everyone?

Katy scrambles out of bed. Turns on all the lights. Double-checks that the front door, the balcony doors and all the windows are locked. Checks inside the wardrobe, the bathroom, the laundry.

Five minutes later she's back in bed. Her heart is beating erratically. Her mind's racing.

Who? How? *Why?*

It takes a long, long time to fall asleep.

11
ROBBIE

Robbie is seeing Nick today. His brother is flying up from Melbourne, and is expected to arrive any moment now.

'He's over the moon,' Celia says. 'Can't wait to see you.'

Nick, eighteen months older, was always a step ahead in school or sport or whatever they were into at the time. He's a lot more than a step ahead now. He has a job in some big telecommunications company, although Celia can't remember which one. There's a wife and three teenage children in Melbourne. They're nice kids, according to Celia. Well brought up and smart – they all do well in school.

'Do you keep in touch much?' Robbie asks with detached curiosity.

'Nick's in Sydney a few times a year with work. Sometimes he stays with Mum and Dad. Megan and the kids usually come in December or January, during the holidays.'

'Has he changed?' Robbie visualises his brother as a teenager: tall, gangly, gregarious.

'Well, he's *bigger* … But aren't we all?'

Bigger? Does she mean fatter? Nick always liked his food; he ate as voraciously as he did everything else in life. Nick and Robbie were close as young children. They engaged in long extremely competitive games of back-yard cricket, tore around the neighbourhood on their bikes, and traded football cards with each other before anyone else. Nick pulled away as soon as he started high school. Overnight he became more independent, more confident, more out of reach. A year later, when Robbie started at Macquarie High, he thought the same would apply for him. New friends. New experiences. A whole new life. But it wasn't like that at all. Robbie didn't grow; he regressed.

There's a pounding on the door.

'He's here,' Celia exclaims unnecessarily and races to answer it.

Robbie waits in the kitchen. He examines his feelings one by one. Various psychologists have recommended this strategy to him. To look inward. To put a label on whatever he is feeling. Apparently, it helps to process things, to come to terms with whatever is happening, or about to change. Apparently, it prevents a blow-out

or an extreme reaction. This morning he feels apprehensive, guilty and overwhelmed. Apprehensive about
the man at the door and how he may be received by
him. Guilty at the long-term upset he has caused Nick,
Celia and his parents. But he has learned that it's the
last feeling – being overwhelmed – that is the most dangerous one.

'Where is he hiding?' a voice, a man's voice, booms
down the hall. The timbre, the resonance, are only
vaguely familiar.

A figure bursts into the kitchen. A big, burly figure
to match the big voice. Nick stands at over six feet tall.
His belly protrudes, straining the buttons of his business shirt. His face is quite boyish and his hair is darker
than Robbie remembers. He envelops Robbie in a hug
and Robbie fights a wave of claustrophobia. Nick pulls
away before Robbie has to push him away.

'Look at you.' He has tears rolling down his face and
doesn't seem the slightest bit bothered by it. 'Just look
at you.'

Robbie doesn't know what to say in response. His
conversational skills are poor at the best of times.

'Jeez, it's so good to see you.' Nick pulls out a chair,
plonks himself down. 'Twenty years is a lot to catch up
on. You better start talking, mate.'

Robbie tosses and turns in bed. Nick is sleeping in the
room next door – Charlie is in with Sienna – and his
snores can be heard through the plasterboard wall, and

105

probably the entire house. Nick was a heavy snorer even as a kid. Robbie recalls throwing things at his brother in the dead of night, prompting him to turn on his side, from which position the snoring was never quite as bad. It was one of the downsides of sharing a bedroom. That and the fact that Nick could come crashing through the door at any minute; Robbie could never be sure how long he'd have on his own. He used to love and hate hearing the door crash open; love and hate the commotion that followed Nick around; love and hate his snoring, because even though it was irritating, at least it was there, like a one-way conversation he could listen to. Now Robbie wonders how one brother can be so vital and present (even when sound asleep), and the other so insipid and unessential. How one can be so engaged with life, and the other so adrift.

Robbie is desperately tired but unable to sleep. Nick talked late into the night. Telling Robbie about his kids, his wife and his job. Finding photos on his phone of the children, his house and Megan, who is dark-haired, attractive and works as a dental nurse. Of course, he asked questions of Robbie. What places he's lived. If there's anyone special in his life. How he spends his time. But when Robbie's replies were bare, Nick filled the gaps with even more information about himself.

At some point after dinner, when Charlie and Sienna were in bed, Celia opened some bottles of beer. Robbie sipped on one – he is cautious with alcohol – while Nick knocked back several. Drinking, drinking, drinking.

Talking, talking, talking. The more he drank, the more sentimental he became.

'I missed you, bro. I missed you every single day. I looked for your face everywhere I went.' He started crying again. Crying and laughing at himself. 'Look at me … I'm a big sook.'

As the night progressed, and more alcohol was consumed, Nick's sentimentality turned into self-recrimination.

'I should have been watching out for you. I was your big brother, it was my job to see that you were struggling, it was my job to give you a helping hand … I'm sorry that I didn't do my job, that I let you down. I'm sorrier than you can ever know.'

Nick is more subdued this morning. Hungover, not quite as talkative, but still able to laugh at himself.

'Jeez, the old head isn't good. Have you got anything I can take, Celia?'

Celia gives him some Panadol, a glass of water and a telling-off. 'You're old enough to know better.'

Nick grimaces. 'That's what Megan would say, too.'

Robbie is mildly curious about Megan. Is she loud and unselfconscious too? Or a quieter personality, a foil to Nick's brashness?

'I've got to leave for work,' Celia declares. 'How long are you hanging around for, Nick?'

'A few days. I can bunk down at Mum and Dad's if Charlie wants his bedroom back.'

'Never mind Charlie ... I'll be home around five thirty.'

Celia rounds up the children, there's a flurry of good-byes and hugs, and the bustle progresses down the hall and out the front door.

The two brothers are left alone, sitting across from each other at the table. Nick leans forward, clears his throat.

'Celia said there's a school reunion. Is that why you came back?'

'Don't know. Maybe.'

Nick is obviously perplexed. 'I thought you'd never want to set eyes on that lot again.'

Robbie averts his gaze from his brother to the window. For some reason this makes it easier to talk. 'Might be the chance to put some ghosts to rest.'

An extended silence. Nick is noticeably less frenetic this morning, less inclined to rush in with anecdotes to fill the pauses. Maybe some of yesterday's bluster was due to nerves.

'I suppose all teenagers can be cruel at times – my three are no angels by any stretch of the imagination. But to drive you away from home, away from your family for all this time ...'

There's a bird perched on the fence outside the window. Grey, nondescript, insubstantial, maybe a finch. It jerks its head from left to right, as though on the lookout for a companion, before staring straight ahead, obviously resigned to being alone.

I've got more in common with that fucking bird than any human.

'Nah, Nick, I can't keep blaming them. There was something amiss in me, something not right. It's still that way … I'm as fucked up as ever.'

12
ANNABEL

Annabel is wearing a knee-length floral dress. Her legs, tanned and bare, feel slightly chilly. She's had her hair styled and her make-up done professionally. She's the only one of the family who's made an effort, except for Mia, of course, who looks adorable in her white lace dress and glittery, albeit slightly scuffed, communion shoes. Jarrod is noticeably underdressed in a polo shirt and chinos – most of the other fathers are wearing suits and ties! Jemma is wearing a hippie-style maxi dress and large white-rimmed sunglasses, and Daniel is wearing jeans, T-shirt and a scathing expression.

'Why do I have to go?' he had the audacity to ask when she went into his room this morning to rouse him.

'Because it's an important day for Mia.'

'It's a heap of bollocks. The bread of Christ … How do you believe in that *shit*?'

She sucked in her breath. She would not be taunted into losing her temper and then having him laugh in her face. Not today.

'Come on, get up. Goodness, I remember your communion day like it was yesterday.'

Daniel had worn a cute pinstripe suit and a white shirt. He'd looked so solemn and handsome, and she'd been so proud of him. The suit jacket was discarded straight after mass. She remembers him climbing the fig tree in the churchyard.

In the end, due to Daniel's lack of urgency getting ready and then the car keys becoming temporarily lost – causing Jarrod to swear, Annabel to admonish him, Mia to be upset and Daniel to snigger – they were slightly late to the church. Thankfully, Grace realised they were running behind and kept seats.

Now, the formal proceedings are over and they're standing in the churchyard for another set of photos. Mia with the priest. Mia with her classmates. Mia with both sets of grandparents. Mia with her brother and sister, Daniel unable to disguise his contempt, Jemma looking dreamy, lost behind those ridiculously enormous sunglasses. Mia and Grace, god-daughter and godmother beaming at the camera. Mia and her most favourite person in the world: her dad. Jarrod rests his hands on her shoulders, his smile reaching all the way to his eyes. It feels like a long time since Annabel has seen him smile like that.

*

They go for lunch at a nearby restaurant, a Mediterranean place that used to be a family favourite, before Jemma moved out and Daniel started refusing to be seen with his parents. Annabel orders huge bowls of salad, and platters crammed with meat and garlicky potatoes.

'I think you've ordered too much food, dear,' her mother says.

Her mother likes to find fault. If it wasn't too much, it would be too little. Nothing is ever good enough.

Grace laughs. 'Oh, you haven't seen how much my four eat.'

It's true. Grace's children *do* eat a lot. Annabel sometimes wonders if they get enough at home. Now she is being downright mean.

Annabel's mother smiles at Grace. 'Your children are just delightful. Isn't it great they have healthy appetites?'

Grace's children *are* delightful. The four of them chat and giggle among themselves, as though they genuinely enjoy each other's company. The older ones look after the younger ones, and they're all protective of Lauren, who is such a skittish little thing. Tom, Grace's husband, is very attentive; in fact, he converses more with the children than the adults at the table. Annabel finds this both admirable and slightly irritating. It occurs to her that perhaps Tom is using the children as a means to avoid conversation with her and Jarrod. Jarrod was reluctant about inviting the whole Coleman clan. 'Do they all need to come to the restaurant? There are more of them than us!'

'Of course they have to come,' Annabel exclaimed. 'Grace is Mia's godmother. And I can't leave out Tom or the children.'

Jarrod's father, Bernard, clinks a teaspoon against his glass and stands up: speech time. Bernard enjoys occasions like these: plenty of food, drink and family, and a bit of religion to balance things out. Annabel likes Jarrod's parents; they've always been supportive and kind to her. In their minds, there was no question their son was going to marry the girl he 'got in trouble'. Given recent events, Annabel has wondered if they made a mistake. What if they'd advised Jarrod *not* to rush into a commitment? What if she and Jarrod had only Jemma, and Mia and Daniel and their whole married life didn't exist? How can she even ask herself these questions? She loves her children. All of them. And she loves Jarrod. Somewhere beneath the terseness and the stress, there is still some love, she is sure of it.

Bernard clears his throat. 'We're gathered here today to celebrate Mia's communion. A very special day for a very special girl, whom her family love very much indeed.' He raises his glass to Mia and she raises hers in return, with a flourish and a giggle. 'God bless you, Mia.'

Annabel's own upbringing was lacking when it came to formal religion. There was no weekly mass, and not even Christmas or Easter were religious celebrations.

She is happy to have her children ensconced in the Catholic faith. She likes a lot of things about it, especially the idea of there being a clear line between right and wrong.

'Don't even think about it,' Jarrod hisses next to her.

Daniel has his hand on one of the wine bottles. 'Why?'

How can he manage to inject so much insolence into just one word?

'As if you don't know,' Jarrod shoots back.

Conversation has petered out at the other end of the table, where Grace and her family are sitting. Everyone is listening intently and Daniel isn't shy about giving them a show.

'It's only a glass. What's the big deal?'

Annabel hears Jarrod take a deep breath. He is trying, very hard, to remain calm. 'The big deal is that you're underage. Take your hands off it.'

'Fuck you. You just enjoy telling me what to do.'

Oh God, the F word, as Mia calls it. Annabel throws an apologetic glance towards the Colemans. What must they think? Tom is watching closely. Grace's husband is a strict disciplinarian. Grace, too, is uninhibited about reprimanding children who are not her own: Daniel, Mia and even Jemma scolded for misbehaviour in the past. *Just don't say anything now*, Annabel implores silently. *Let Jarrod deal with this.*

'Watch your language, there are young children here. Now move your hand ... or I'll move it for you.'

A few seconds tick by. Finally, Daniel puts his hand

back on his lap, defiance and hatred emanating from every pore. Bernard, bless him, starts a new conversation. Jemma, who has been quite disengaged until now, joins in with fervour. Everyone gets down to the business of eating and exclaiming how delicious the food is. Annabel sips her wine and tries to regain her equilibrium, tries to recover some enjoyment in the occasion, but she can't seem to stop herself from analysing how they've got to this point. Tom's firm yet close relationship with his children leads her to question whether Jarrod was close enough to Daniel when he started high school and began to form the toxic friendships that have led him into nothing but trouble. And what about her own part in this sorry state of affairs? She's the one who played down the bong in Daniel's bedroom, who failed to involve her husband at a crucial point. She knew Jarrod would go ballistic but what kind of lame excuse was that?

The restaurant staff clear away the plates and it's time for the special cake: lemon and raspberry with meringue topping. The cake designer delivered it directly to the restaurant, for a fee, of course. Jarrod would explode if he knew how much it cost. When did she start hiding the true cost of things from Jarrod? When did she start hiding *anything* from Jarrod? She regrets not telling him about the bong. Will regret it until the day she knows that Daniel is going to be okay. The day that he has a good job, a family of his own and a healthy lifestyle. She prays for that day; a heathen bargaining with God.

There's another toast to Mia – Annabel's father does the honours this time – and the cake is cut and put on plates, which are then passed down the table. Lauren is the only one who doesn't want any. So unusual for a child not to like cake. But then, there are lots of things Lauren doesn't like: ice cream, pasta, balloons, loud noises and being apart from her mother. The restaurant has become quite busy, and the increasing noise levels are making her agitated. Her hands are over her ears and she's rocking in her chair.

'I want to go home.' Despite the noise, Lauren can be clearly heard.

Grace looks embarrassed. She catches Annabel's eye and shrugs, as though to say, *What can I do with her*? Annabel shrugs back sympathetically. Lauren is a difficult child to get close to, to feel affection for. Annabel's not sure if the anxiety is something she'll grow out of or if it will become more pronounced as she gets older.

Grace's smile is resigned. 'I think it's time for us to go home. Thank you so much for inviting us. It was such a beautiful day.'

Annabel's mother and father also make their excuses, and that spurs Jarrod's parents to stand up from their chairs too. Hugs and kisses and goodbyes are exchanged. Jarrod asks for the bill as soon as everyone is gone. He taps his VISA card against the table while he waits for the waiter to enter the correct amount in the machine. He looks like he can't get home quickly enough. The transaction done, he pockets the receipt, and that's when Annabel turns her eyes to her son and realises that Daniel is slugging back a glass of red wine.

Her mouth opens and closes in shock. Somehow, in the flurry of departures and the settling of the bill, Daniel saw his opportunity and took it.

'You little bastard,' Jarrod roars, jumping up from his seat and knocking against the table in the process.

Daniel smirks. 'What's the big deal?'

Jarrod lunges for the glass in his hand. 'Give it to me. Give it to me *now*.'

Daniel manoeuvres it so it's out of reach. 'Fuck off.'

'Daniel used the F word again,' Mia gasps.

Annabel finds herself strangely devoid of words. She knows she should be saying something, chastising Daniel, beseeching Jarrod to calm down, asking Mia to cover her ears. But the right words are not forming.

'What is *wrong* with you?' Jarrod shakes his head in disbelief.

'*You're* wrong with me,' Daniel says, getting slowly to his feet. Then he casts a scathing look at Annabel. 'And *she's* wrong with me. She's been topping up her glass every few minutes. Fucking hypocrite.'

At least he's put the glass down.

Jarrod takes a step closer to his son. Their faces are centimetres apart. 'Don't you dare talk to your mother like that.'

Daniel pushes him in the chest. 'Get away from me. Fuck the both of you.'

'I've already told you to watch your language!'

Daniel pushes his father again. Jarrod pushes him back. Who throws the first punch? Annabel can't tell. Only that her husband and her son are suddenly trying to hit each other. Flying arms. Curled fists. Faces pulsing with fury. Finally, too late, she finds her voice.

'Stop it!' she screams.

Jemma and Mia are screaming too. 'Stop ... Don't ... Dad ... Daniel ... Stop ... Stop!'

A glass has been smashed. A chair knocked over. This is her family, brawling in a public place, in front of young children and other appalled spectators. This *nightmare* is her family. Then she has an insane thought – at least Grace is gone, at least her friend hasn't borne witness to this, what must be the lowest moment of her life. For God's sake, why is it so fucking important to save face in front of Grace?

'Stop it!' Mia cries. 'Stop it, Daddy! Stop it, Daniel!'

Annabel still isn't sure who threw the first punch, but the last one comes from Daniel. He strikes his father on the jaw, pushing his lip into his teeth, blood spurting instantly. Annabel hears herself gasp. Someone starts bawling ... Mia? Daniel turns on his heel, charges out of the restaurant.

'Go after him,' Annabel shouts at Jemma. 'Don't let him out of your sight.'

Jarrod sits on a chair, puts his head in his hands. The restaurant staff, with surprising calm, start putting furniture back in place. Their quiet efficiency implies that this isn't the first time something like this has happened, which is both depressing and faintly consoling.

'Daniel is out of control,' Mia declares, a phrase she has heard her parents say far too often.

Annabel turns on her angrily – it is not helpful to point out the obvious – then sees the white dress and is reminded that this is Mia's *communion day*. A day that should have been a celebration, a joyous family occasion, a memory for everyone to fondly look back on. Instead it feels catastrophic, like they've hit rock bottom, because what could be worse than seeing your son punching his own father?

'Come on, love. Let's get Daddy home, and let's try really, really hard not to let this ruin your special day.'

13
GRACE

Grace doesn't recognise Katy. Her hair is glossy brown; it's impossible to tell that she's naturally a redhead. She's wearing tight jeans, a fitted T-shirt and a diamond stud in her nose. She looks young, fit, trendy. Grace feels frumpy by comparison.

'Grace?' Katy asks uncertainly as she catches her eye.

Katy must not recognise her either. The reasons are probably less complimentary, but Grace is not going to dwell on that.

'Yes, it's me. Wow, Katy, you look fabulous!'

Katy blushes and Grace remembers the blush. Annabel used to enjoy mocking it: *Katy Buckley, your face is as hot as your hair.*

'Thanks for offering to come along today,' Katy says, sounding slightly breathless. 'I can't believe the hotel double-booked.'

Grace can't believe it either. The venue for the reunion was decided months ago: a boutique city-centre hotel. A deposit was paid, which evidently didn't guarantee anything. Given the short notice and the busy run-up to Christmas, Katy was lucky to find this alternative: a function room on the third floor of a pub in Manly.

Grace sees a man coming in their direction. 'I think this must be the manager.'

The man is very attractive: early thirties, dark hair and skin. He sticks out his hand. 'I'm Stan. The function room is upstairs. Come and have a look.'

They follow Stan up a narrow staircase. He's nicely proportioned from behind and Grace has the sudden urge to nudge Katy, to whisper something like, 'Check him out.' She averts her eyes to take in the framed photographs on the stairwell.

The function room is a good size: a platform for the DJ, a generous dance floor, plenty of tables and chairs, and what appears to be a well-stocked bar. Stan gives them some brochures outlining the different drinks and food packages on offer.

'Let's have a coffee downstairs and talk it through,' Grace hears herself suggesting.

'Good idea.' Katy's smile comes readily and Grace experiences an inexplicable liking for her; inexplicable only because she recalls being so derisive of her at school.

Downstairs, they settle into one of the nooks and order coffees from the gorgeous Stan.

'He's all right, isn't he?' Grace comments. Then she laughs at herself. Here she is, acting like a swoony teenage girl instead of a happily married mother of four.

'Yep, but I bet he's taken.' Katy sighs deeply. 'All the good ones are.'

'Are they?' Grace asks, intrigued.

'Only the dregs left,' Katy says with a roll of her eyes.

'I know someone!' Grace exclaims, one of Tom's colleagues suddenly coming to mind. 'He's just come out of a long-term relationship.'

'Oh no, not a rebound!'

'Rickie's nice-looking, a hard worker. I'm going to set you two up so you can see for yourself … You'll have to name your first child after me.'

'Ha, ha, steady on.'

Stan returns with the drinks. Grace contemplates starting a conversation with him but Katy shoots her a warning look. There's obviously a limit to how much matchmaking she's willing to tolerate. Grace pulls over the brochures and at the same time notices some soil under her fingernails. Spending so much time in the garden is wonderful for her soul but brutal for her hands. She doesn't think Katy is the type to notice such things.

She starts to read the brochures. 'Should we go food only, or drinks and food?'

Katy chews her lip. 'The original venue was food only. I want to make sure it's affordable for everyone.'

Grace appreciates her thoughtfulness. This time of the year is particularly tight in her own household with Christmas looming on the horizon.

'Food only, then,' Grace says decisively. 'I like option two, the antipasto platters …'

'Me too. Motion passed.'

Grace laughs. 'What's next on the agenda?'

'Dress code. Formal attire isn't really appropriate for a function room above a pub.'

'Casual wear it is, then.' Grace mentally says goodbye to Tom's tuxedo. On the positive side, she won't need to buy something new for herself.

Katy sips her coffee, her expression clouding over. 'Luke got one of those emails. Very similar to yours …'

'Luke Willis?'

She nods. 'It really shook him up … Me, too … Parts of it were very personal … I can't understand how this person is getting their information.'

Grace recalls her own email, which also felt very personal. Her worries about Lauren, her heartbreak about the miscarriage. The only person who knows any of it is Annabel. She bawled in Annabel's kitchen after the miscarriage, and has expressed her concerns about Lauren numerous times. Maybe that means Jarrod knows too, although Grace isn't sure how much information Annabel shares with her husband. Certainly not as much as she shares with Tom.

'Who is doing this?' she asks in exasperation. Has Annabel or Jarrod been indiscreet? Has Tom?

Katy shrugs. 'I don't know, I really don't know … I got this crazy idea that someone might have been in my flat, on my laptop, looking at my Google history.' She laughs sheepishly. 'I actually jumped out of bed the other night to double-check the locks.'

'Oh my God. Do you really think—'

Katy shakes her head. 'No, it was just my imagination running wild … But should I take it as a sign? Call off the reunion and drop the whole idea of a new yearbook? Claim there's not enough interest? I could take advantage of the fact that the venue has fallen through.'

'All because of some immature idiot who's trying to freak us out? It would be such a shame … Have you reported the email address as malicious?'

Once again, Katy shakes her head. 'There's nothing threatening or pornographic or anything that might qualify as malicious.'

'I suppose so.' Grace sighs. 'Except when you're standing in our shoes and wondering how on earth this person knows what he, or she, knows!'

Who could it be? Someone at the core of the old group or someone on the outside? Her instincts say it's the latter: someone who was overlooked, who faded into the background and is now ready to command everyone's attention.

'So, what to do?' Katy asks, worry filling her eyes.

'Do nothing.' Grace is suddenly decisive. 'They'll get bored. All they want is a reaction from us.'

She glances at her watch. It's later than she thought

it was. Tahlia has a party this afternoon and Tom has to work; weekend shifts are a downside of his job, along with the woeful pay.

'Sorry, I have to go.'

'No problem. I'll sort out the booking.'

'I'll send on Rickie's details,' Grace promises.

Katy pulls a face. 'What if he isn't keen?'

Grace snorts. 'Oh, he'll be keen all right. He'll be thanking his lucky stars.'

Now Katy's blushing again. Does she always get embarrassed when someone pays her a compliment?

'Remember, first child is to be named after me,' Grace calls over her shoulder as she hurries towards the exit.

'Of course.' Katy's giggle is somewhere behind. 'Even if it's a boy.'

Grace is smiling as she emerges into the bright, blue-skied afternoon. She is smiling all the way home in the car.

The birthday party is at the aquatic centre. Twenty-odd preteens squealing, splashing and diving. Grace takes the other children swimming in the public lanes while they wait for Tahlia. Lauren likes the water and everyone is happy at first. But, as with all outings, there comes a point when Lauren's had enough and insists on going home. It's as though some sort of alarm goes off inside her head.

'I want to go home.'

'We need to wait for Tahlia.'

'Why can't Tahlia come now?'

'Because the party isn't over. Would you like to leave a party before it's finished?'

Stupid question. Lauren doesn't get invited to parties.

Lauren is quite distraught by the time they get home. It takes over an hour to settle her down. A tight hug. A quiet chat. Some alone time in her room. Grace is late putting on the dinner. She feels tired and uncharacteristically out of sorts by the time she gets everyone fed, washed and off to bed. She pours herself a drink from the open bottle of wine in the fridge. Her thoughts are skittish.

Lauren. What is she going to do about Lauren? Is it time to seek intervention? How much is intervention going to *cost*?

Katy. Lovely Katy, so considerate, humble and utterly likeable. Why weren't they friends at school?

Rickie. Grace must remember to ask Tom if Rickie is still single when he gets home.

Tom … Shouldn't he be home by now?

She picks up her phone to text him but for some reason she texts Annabel instead.

Saw Katy today. We've picked another venue for the reunion.

The reply comes so fast that Annabel must be doing the exact same thing as Grace: sitting down with a glass of wine in one hand and her phone in the other.

Not sure if we can go. Can't leave Daniel on his own. Just can't trust him at the moment.

Can't trust him, why? But Grace learned a long time ago to tread carefully and not ask such questions outright.

Quite suddenly, she recalls why she wasn't friends with Katy Buckley at school. At some stage, pretty early on in their school life, Annabel decreed that Katy was beneath them. Most of the time she blanked Katy out, pretended she wasn't there. Except for the time when Katy – for some foolish, naive reason – left a birthday card in Annabel's locker. Grace remembers Annabel smiling as she opened the card, her face transforming when she realised who it was from.

'Don't send me birthday cards,' she hissed, ripping the card into a flutter of tiny pieces. 'I am *not* your fucking friend.'

Grace is appalled by the memory, appalled that she would mutely stand by and allow Annabel to behave so viciously, birthday or not. Maybe instead of ogling Stan today, she should have been issuing an apology for being complicit in Annabel's meanness. Looking back, it is hard to fathom why she remained friends with her. She can only hope that her children are more discerning with their friendships, and braver about speaking up when someone is out of order.

She hears the rumble of the garage door: Tom. Almost an hour late. He must have got caught up with something. He often finds it hard to walk away.

He comes through the door, tiredness imprinted on his face, smelling of hard work and the night air.

'Annabel and Jarrod might not be coming to the reunion,' she tells him in greeting. 'They're worried about leaving Daniel alone.'

He goes to get a clean glass from the cupboard and turns on the tap. He drinks thirstily before replying. 'His behaviour at Mia's communion was disgraceful. No respect for his parents, no sense of responsibility towards the younger kids. He needs to be taught a lesson or two.'

'Oh, Tom, don't be so harsh.'

Her husband doesn't understand people who don't have the same parenting instincts as he does. From the moment the children were born, he seemed to know exactly what to do. When to be firm, when to be soft. When to be protective or to step back and allow them to make their mistakes. How to coax them to do something they did not want to do. How to command respect and the understanding that his word is final. Grace learned from watching Tom.

He rinses the glass, turns it upside down to drain. 'The truth can be harsh.'

Grace loves her husband dearly. She wouldn't change anything about him except this one thing: sometimes she wishes he was less judgemental.

14
MELISSA

Melissa is having dinner with Henry at the new place on Bronte Beach. The food is fresh and zesty in contrast to the conversation, which is decidedly stale. As she looks across the candlelit table at her husband, she can't help feeling irritable and dissatisfied with their life together.

'So what's been happening at work?' Henry enquires, adjusting his glasses so they sit higher up his nose.

'Oh, we're doing budgets for next year. Some of it is crystal-ball stuff.'

They're being ultra-polite with each other, cautious with their words and even their facial expressions. They could be distant acquaintances rather than husband and wife. The politeness is to cover up the tension. One wrong word or look and that would be it: an argument of epic proportions. The odd thing is, they don't argue frequently, and when they do it's usually over quickly with apologies all round. For some reason, she feels that the argument brewing is nothing like the ones of the past. It won't be over quickly, and she, for one, won't be saying sorry. How can they go on like this? Living apart, a few hours of togetherness snatched here and there?

'Do you think you can reach the targets?' he asks benignly.

She shrugs. 'I'm not going to sign off on them unless I think they're achievable. We're still in negotiations.'

He laughs. 'You're scary when you're in negotiating mode.'

She laughs too, but without any mirth. She's been talking about forecasts and budgets all week at work. She and Henry should be talking about something else.

'I've told you about the school reunion coming up? You've kept that night free, haven't you?'

'The eleventh, isn't it? It's in the diary.'

Would he need to rely on his diary so much if they lived together? Why does every aspect of their relation- ship feel so forced and unnatural? And why does she feel so critical of everything tonight?

She makes another effort. 'It'll be interesting to see everyone. Find out where they've ended up in life.'

'Any old boyfriends I should be watching out for?'

Melissa had a couple of boyfriends in high school. Short, intense relationships that were over in a matter of weeks. The one that meant the most, that cut the deepest, never really got off the ground: Jarrod Harris.

'Dozens,' she jokes. 'I was the school slut.'

Henry laughs. 'Snow White meets School Slut, now there's a paradox if I ever heard one!'

It wasn't funny at the time: being dropped by Jarrod and at the same time ostracised by Annabel and Grace. For the first time in her school life, Melissa found herself on the outside, having no one to sit with or talk to. Her self-esteem took a dent, as did her focus on her studies. But it was character building in the end.

Henry is asking a question. 'How long is it since you've all got together?'

'A proper reunion? This is the first, actually. Someone tried to organise a five-year one but everyone was off travelling. At the ten-year mark they were all in the throes of new parenthood.'

Melissa feels a stab of something when she thinks that most of her old school friends are parents many times over by now. It's not quite jealousy. A sense of missing out? Or perhaps resentment that the decision has been made for her – by virtue of Henry's reluctance as well as their bizarre living arrangements. Melissa has always made her own decisions, forged her own path. The logical part of her brain tells her that she may have ended up here anyway: it's not as though reproducing was high on her list of priorities. But that doesn't stop it from rankling and contributing to her general irritability of late.

'Katy Buckley seems to be doing a better job of mustering everyone this time round. Good on Katy!'

'Is that sarcasm?'

'Not at all.' She frowns at him. He can't seem to get it right tonight. 'You know I admire a job well done.'

Henry comes back to the apartment after dinner. His children are with their mother, for once, and he can stay the night and most of tomorrow. Melissa feels more daunted than pleased at the thought of all this uninterrupted time together.

'Want a nightcap?' she asks. Maybe another drink will make her less brittle.

'Go on, then.'

She pours two glasses of white wine – Henry doesn't drink red – and they sit out on the balcony with a rug across their knees. The apartment has an ocean view but all that can be seen at this time of night is blackness. The ocean can be heard, though, waves crashing one after another on to the beach, the rhythm having a massage-like effect on Melissa's tension. At last she relaxes. Henry does too. His fingers lace through hers. She rests her head on his shoulder. They talk very little. She much prefers this companionable silence to the polite small talk of earlier. It feels more natural. More like what a married couple would do.

Her thoughts revert to those last few months of school, when she ended up learning less about the syllabus and more about life. She learned that female friendship doesn't have to be hard – another group of girls accepted her into their circle without any sign of reticence or schoolyard politics. She learned that loyalty is something she values above everything else. And she learned to recognise the power and destructiveness of fear. The blood that spurted from her finger that day in food tech could be traced back to her own carelessness, to Grace's lack of backbone and ultimately back to Annabel: barely eighteen, pregnant, petrified out of her mind.

Henry yawns, so does she, and by mutual agreement they decide to go to bed. Henry rinses the wine glasses while she locks up. They take turns in the en suite, switch off the bedside lamps, and then they have urgent, frantic sex. Strange that the controlled tension over dinner and the restrained truce on the balcony should culminate in this abandoned coupling: ripping their clothes off, fumbling in the dark, panting and grunting and gasping, with undertones of something forbidden and doomed yet deeply thrilling.

Melissa is sad afterwards, strangely vulnerable and unsure of herself as she lies in the dark. It's like she's eighteen again and it's Jarrod Harris who's in the bed beside her. Jarrod Harris who has blown her mind and senses with what he has just done to her body. Jarrod Harris, with whom she has this insane connection, while at the same time knowing that she can never keep him. Annabel hasn't yet dropped her bombshell, but Melissa is intuitively aware that there are too many things mounted against them.

Not that different to how things are with Henry today. It must be the sense of doom that's reminding her of Jarrod, sucking her back in time.

Henry is fast asleep, breathing heavily, oblivious to her turmoil. What is going to happen with them? Has she wasted the last three years of her life? If she was faced with this situation at work – a client who couldn't or wouldn't fully commit – she would cut her losses and walk away. It's always incredibly frustrating when something you've been working on dissolves to nothing but there's no choice but to rally oneself and move on. Right?

Melissa throws back the sheet and slips out of bed. She feels around the floor for her pyjamas, which were discarded during their lovemaking. In the kitchen she pours herself a glass of water and drinks it standing at the sink. Her phone is where she left it on the counter. No, she will not give in to the temptation to check work emails at this hour of night. Yet her hand, of its own volition, reaches for the phone. She quickly checks the news headlines: floods across Europe at the same time as water restrictions are threatened in Sydney; a celebrity chef who's in trouble for being politically incorrect. Next thing she's clicking on Facebook. Photos of friends, old and new, scroll in front of her eyes. Like, like, like. Marcus, a colleague on holiday in Vietnam, has posted so many photos over the past week Melissa feels like she's been in Vietnam too. Like, like, like. Then her breath catches. Jarrod and Annabel and one of their children are staring back at her. The little girl is wearing a white dress; it must be her communion day. Melissa savours Jarrod's strong features and jaw, his smile for the camera, the muscular shoulders that used to be such an asset in rugby scrums. Still an attractive man, still capable of provoking the same reaction from her: an instant flare of lust. She routinely squashes it, which is what she got used to doing in school, after they broke up. How odd that she should come across this tonight, when he has been so much on her mind. She and Jarrod have been Facebook friends for years but he rarely pops up in her feed. She thinks for a while, then types.

Lovely photo. Hope you are all well. Xx Melissa

Then she shuts down the phone and goes back to bed. Henry is still oblivious.

15
ZACH

People stare. They always do. Zach doesn't mind. There's nothing wrong with curiosity.

'How much longer?' Carson pants, his face red and disgruntled.

'Four more laps.'

Carson groans. He doesn't enjoy training or anything that involves hard graft. Kids with Down's syndrome have low muscle tone and poor coordination; exercise is hard for them, and therefore so is motivation. There is greater prevalence of obesity and congenital heart disease, which is why Zach and Izzy insist on at least forty minutes' physical activity a day. Their number-one desire is for their son to have a long and healthy life.

'How much longer, Dadda?'

'Stop asking the same question. Step it up and it'll go quicker.'

Carson's running technique is far from optimal. Heavy feet, clenched fists, head lolling to one side, tongue hanging out. Sometimes Zach runs backwards, which is good for encouraging his son as well as matching his slower pace.

'I'm tired.'

'Come on, keep going.'

The last eleven years have been an enormous learning curve, with ups and downs, triumphs and failures, and many instances of two steps forward followed by one step back. Isabel is always scouring for opportunities to broaden Carson's horizons. Thanks to her endeavours, he has modelled for a department-store catalogue, participated in various Special Olympic competitions, and even landed a short-term acting role in a TV hospital series.

But Carson's greatest achievement is his endless capacity for love. He loves his parents, his grandparents, his teachers and his friends. He loves animals, buses and aeroplanes. His kisses are slobbery, his hugs are a force of nature, and his face lights up as soon as you walk into the room.

'Track,' another runner calls out from behind.

This is a warning to stay on the outer lanes and not veer in front of the runner.

'Track,' Carson calls back cheerfully, which is not the protocol. The runner casts him a closer look as he overtakes. Sees. Understands. Gives Zach a nod.

'Good job, there.'

It's condescending but Zach doesn't care. Condescension and curiosity, he can take. Even wariness and fear, to a certain degree. Pity isn't so easy. It evokes memories of when Carson was a baby, their pride and love for him swamped by the overwhelming sympathy of others. Even worse than pity is the act of ignoring. The people who avert their eyes as though Carson weren't standing there. The people who don't speak or engage with him. The people who dismiss him as unimportant, inferior, when in fact he is the complete opposite.

'The waiting time is more than an hour,' Gloria informs him with a grimace. 'Sorry we had to call you in.'

'What happened?'

'One of Sandy's patients collapsed. We called an ambulance and waited a very long time for its arrival ... That was before Catrina started feeling sick and had to go home early.'

Sandy and Catrina have been Zach's partners for more than ten years now, and Gloria's been in reception half that long. They make a good team. It's not often he gets called in on his day off.

'Have you prioritised who's waiting?'

Needless question because Gloria excels in prioritisation. 'I don't like the colour of the woman over there – she looks like she's going to keel over any minute. Then I'll send in the gentleman who's been waiting the longest. The one with the cranky face.'

The patients usually forget their frustration as soon as their name is called. They're happy to see him, to sit down and finally say what's wrong. Poor Gloria bears the brunt of their impatience and bad temper.

The next four hours are long and busy. Zach processes the patients as efficiently as he can. He is polite and thorough, but can't afford time for niceties like making the children giggle or chatting with the elderly patients, who come in for human contact more than any ailment. His last appointment of the day, a little girl with red-hot cheeks and a precariously high temperature, vomits on the surgery floor.

Zach cleans up with paper towels. Gloria arrives with a mop and a bucket smelling of strong chemicals.

She scrunches her face. 'Do I get paid enough for this?'

'Probably not,' he says sympathetically.

In the bathroom, Zach washes his hands scrupulously. His reflection in the mirror shows blond-brown hair that's slightly too long, lightly tanned skin, green eyes that he's passed down to Carson.

You don't look like a GP, he has been told quite often. They never say why.

He pops his head in on Sandy, who's finishing some paperwork before she calls an end to the day. Sandy, at fifty-two, is the oldest partner. She's the one Zach goes to for professional advice. He goes to Catrina if he wants a laugh or to let off steam. Izzy is close friends with both women.

'I'm done here, Sandy. Any update on the patient who collapsed?'

Her expression is equal parts weary and relieved. 'Pulmonary embolism. He's in a critical condition but expected to make it through.'

'That's good news. See you tomorrow.'

Zach's car is parked a few streets away. A flyer has been left tucked under the wiper. He takes it off, chucks it on the passenger seat. He is in a hurry to get home. To see Carson's delight when he walks through the door. To see Izzy's quiet smile.

'What this?'

It's Thursday morning. They're on their way to school; Carson and the other school leaders are hosting their first school assembly. Izzy has her camera ready. She looks especially chic this morning in a navy and white dress. Carson has earphones in and is humming loudly. He doesn't seem to be at all nervous; he rarely thinks about things until they're actually happening.

'What?' Zach glances across at his wife. She has the flyer in her hand. 'Just something that was left on the car yesterday.'

She frowns. 'Not just something, Zach. Pull in and I'll show you.'

He takes the next turn off the main road. Pulls up a safe distance from the corner. Tries to read her face before he takes the piece of paper from her hand.

Name: Zach Latham

What you do now: General practitioner.

Highlights of last twenty years: Meeting Izzy. The birth of your son.

Lowlights: Carson being Down's syndrome.

Deepest fears: Lots of things. What will happen to Carson when you and Izzy aren't around to take care of him. Being sued by one of your patients. Izzy finding out the truth about you.

Izzy is looking at him suspiciously. 'What does it mean "the truth about you"? What truth?'

He scrunches the flyer into ball. The urge to swear is overwhelming. No, not with Carson in the car.

'Nothing. You know everything there is to know. It's just some silly prank.'

It's the first time he's lied to her in … he doesn't know how long.

16
ANNABEL

'Come on, Mia. Hurry up.'

Annabel checks her watch. She hoped to be out the door half an hour ago. Now they're going to get stuck in Saturday-afternoon traffic.

'Mia, what's taking you so long?'

Her daughter finally appears. She's biting her lip. 'Sorry, Mummy, but I can't find my money. It's gone.'

Annabel smothers a sigh, sets down her bag and car keys on the hall table, and proceeds to Mia's room to find the 'missing money'.

'Where did you last see it?'

'In my communion handbag.'

'Did you move it to a different handbag? Or into one of your drawers?'

Mia shakes her head. 'I didn't move it. I really didn't.'

Despite Mia's assurances, Annabel searches the other handbags – Mia has quite a collection – and rifles through her drawers. Then she checks her jewellery boxes, the pockets of various items of clothing, and every other conceivable place a nine-year-old might stash money.

'Are you sure you didn't hide it somewhere?'

'I didn't, Mummy, I swear I didn't. Someone must have taken it.'

Annabel experiences a plummeting sensation in her stomach. *Daniel wouldn't, would he?* No, he would never stoop so low. Besides, he has money of his own from working shifts at the local pizzeria. She dropped him to work only an hour ago.

'How much did you have exactly?'

'Three hundred and eighty-five dollars.'

Mia's grandparents, godparents and various other relatives were very generous. 'Buy yourself something nice,' they said, putting crisp new notes inside embossed communion cards. Mia is going to spend the windfall on a new bike.

'When did you last see the money?'

'Yesterday. I counted it again because I knew we were getting the bike today.'

'Are you sure you didn't put it somewhere unusual?'

'I didn't, I swear. I put it back in the handbag. Then I put the handbag in my cupboard.'

Annabel believes her daughter. She is generally reliable with both her belongings and with the truth. It is looking increasingly likely that the money was taken … stolen. And the prime suspect would have to be Daniel. The thought that he would be so dishonest – so lacking in scruples and basic decency – makes her feel ill. The thought of how he might spend the money makes her feel more than ill; she can hardly breathe.

'It's okay … We'll find the money.' Fake confidence. Can Mia detect the shake in her mother's voice? 'Now let's go, before it gets too late. We'll put the bike on my credit card and you can pay me back later. Okay?'

Mia gives her a trusting smile. 'Okay, Mummy.'

Mia chooses a vintage-style bike, complete with pale green paint, cream tyres and an adorable front basket. She spends the rest of the evening cycling up and down the street. Annabel watches for a while, making sure she is steady – it's quite a large bike – and warning her about road safety. Then she comes inside and gives the kitchen a quick tidy-up before making a start on dinner.

She's undecided on whether to tell Jarrod about the missing money. She doesn't want to upset him until she has her facts straight – what if they find the money in some forgotten hiding place? But hasn't she learned not to keep secrets from her husband? The fact that he'll go ballistic is no excuse. Plus, it's likely that Mia will blurt it out anyway.

She sends him a text.

What time can we expect you?

Jarrod used to answer only emergency calls on weekends. Now Saturdays have become like any other workday, complete with an early start and late finish. He looks worn out, older than his years. He needs rest, less work, more play … It's no wonder he's so short-tempered.

Truth is, when she's not worrying about Daniel she's worrying about Jarrod. Her husband is not coping. He has become introverted, antisocial, explosive. God, everything's such a mess, such an awful, awful mess. They've had their ups and downs over the years but she can't remember a time when things were as bleak as they are right now.

Jarrod's response flashes on her phone: *Be another hour or two.*

Annabel opens and closes cupboard doors, assembling cooking utensils and ingredients. The kitchen, with its sleek white units and aqua-coloured splashback, is only four years old but she's already itching to renovate.

'I've created a monster,' Jarrod joked when she admitted that she was bored of the splashback and wouldn't mind replacing it.

Is she a monster? Should she have been concentrating more on her children and less on her house? Should she be more like Grace? If there was ever a house that needed knocking down and rebuilding, it's Grace's. Yet her friend doesn't seem fazed by her leaky bathroom and antiquated kitchen. Her focus seems to be on things that are harder to see. Things like family unity and respect.

Annabel dices some chicken and vegetables and throws them in the pot with a ready-made sauce base. Chicken curry, a family favourite. The chicken is simmering away. She doesn't need to put on the rice just yet. There's time to sit down at the kitchen table, bury her face in her hands, and allow herself the luxury of weeping.

'We're going to search your room from top to bottom,' Annabel informs Mia after dinner. 'I don't want to worry Daddy until we are absolutely sure the money is gone.'

Mia nods gravely, and Annabel is left wondering what effect these recent events are having on her. Watching her brother and her father fighting in the restaurant. Witnessing Daniel's scorn for his parents and their house rules. Seeing him staggering through the door, stoned, his eyes rolling back in his head. Jarrod being so down on himself, Annabel being so tense all the time, the lack of trust in the household, the fraught atmosphere. What effect is all this going to have on Mia? Will she end up desensitised to drugs, family arguments, violence and deceit?

Jarrod gets home at eight thirty and pops his head around the bedroom door. 'There you are. I'll have a quick bite before getting Daniel from work.'

Mia scrambles to her feet to give her father a hug.

'What're you two doing in here?' he asks, noticing the upturned drawers.

Annabel fields the question. 'Mia has lost something. We're taking the opportunity to have a good clean-out.'

He accepts her explanation and extracts himself from Mia. The door closes and they resume the search. Annabel hears the far-off ping of the microwave as Jarrod reheats his dinner. Then the scrape of cutlery against ceramic; a plaintive, lonely sound. About fifteen minutes later, the slam of the front door, followed by the growl of the van's engine.

'Mummy, the money isn't here,' Mia says quietly.

Annabel sighs in defeat. They've turned the room upside down. Pulled the bed out from the wall. Checked down behind the chest of drawers. They've even taken the books from the bookshelf. She's going to have to tell Jarrod and confront Daniel. She is dreading one as much as the other.

She sighs again. She'll tell Jarrod tomorrow. He looks too shattered tonight.

'Let's put the last of this stuff away. Then straight to bed.'

Annabel pours herself a large glass of red wine as soon as Mia is tucked in for the night. After the debacle at the restaurant, they decided to avoid drinking alcohol in their son's presence.

'It's too much temptation,' Jarrod said. 'He sees us drinking and he wants to do the same.'

Annabel agreed. They would try to be perfect role

models. It's hard, though, because some nights – like now – the only thing that makes her feel better is a drink.

She swirls the wine around in her mouth, then closes her eyes so she can fully concentrate on its velvety taste. Her phone rings. It's Jarrod. Her face flushes with guilt, as though he can actually see what she's doing. They agreed they wouldn't drink *in front* of Daniel, not that they wouldn't drink at all.

'What's up?' she asks, trying to sound casual.

'Daniel's not here.'

Their son usually waits outside the front of the pizzeria when his shift is over. They pull up, he jumps in, and there's an attempt at conversation on the way home. The routine, other than the conversation part, is pretty seamless.

'He must have got delayed. Go in and see if he's doing something out the back.'

Jarrod hangs up. Annabel has another mouthful or two of wine. She's anxious and then chides herself; she must stop expecting the worst.

Jarrod rings again. 'He's not here, Annie.' Her husband's voice is unusually high-pitched. 'Apparently, Daniel doesn't work here any more. He got fired a couple of weeks ago.'

'*He what?*' The wine has left her mouth feeling parched. 'If he's not there, then where is he? Where has he been all the times he was meant to be at work? *What has he been doing?*'

148

Jarrod doesn't know the answers any more than she does.

'I'll go and look for him, Annie. You ring his friends.'

She has to tell him now. There's no waiting until tomorrow.

'He has Mia's communion money,' she wails. 'He has nearly four hundred dollars on him. It's gone from her room. It must be Daniel. Who else could it be? Now he's buying God-knows-what with it. *Oh, fuck!* Please find him before he spends all that money. *Please, Jarrod. Please.*'

17
ANNABEL

Annabel calls Jez, Adam and Dougie. Then she calls Liam, James and the two Matthews. The confusion and concern in their voices makes it evident: they've no idea where Daniel is either. She leaves messages for the ones who don't pick up.

'This is Annabel, Daniel's mum. We're worried about him. Please call us back if you know where he is.'

It takes all her self-control to make it sound like she's only mildly worried when she's actually beside herself. Exactly how much – and what kind of – drugs can $400 buy? Will Daniel blow it all at once? They've tried to limit his access to cash; his wages from the pizzeria are – were! – lodged directly into his bank account, and Annabel keeps his ATM card so he can't make withdrawals without her involvement. It didn't occur to her that he might steal from his family, *from his little sister.* But isn't that what drug addicts do? Lie, manipulate and thieve so they can get what they crave so badly? Now she feels stupid for not predicting that this might happen, and for not ensuring that Mia kept her money in a safer place.

Jarrod has driven the length and breadth of Manly, Daniel's usual haunt. Having no success from the driver's seat, he parked and went on foot up and down the Corso, checking the laneways and darkened doorways, calling Daniel's name. He gave up, came home, and now they're standing in the kitchen, unsure what to do next. It's after 11 p.m. *Where is he?*

Annabel's phone rings. It's an unknown number.

'Mrs Harris?'

Just from the way the woman says her name, the overly professional tone, she knows immediately that it's a police officer, or a social worker, or someone else of that ilk.

Don't let this be bad news. Don't let this be a phone call that I'll replay over and over for the rest of my life.

'Yes.' A lump of dread is wedged in her throat.

'This is Janine Egan. I'm a nurse at Northern Beaches Hospital. Your son's been admitted to Accident and Emergency. Don't worry, he's not in any immediate danger …'

She clasps a hand over her mouth. 'Oh my God. Oh my God.'

'What is it, Annie?' Jarrod asks frantically. 'Where is he? Is he all right?'

'He's in A&E … They said he'll be okay.' Then she asks the woman, whose name she's already forgotten, *'What happened to him?'*

'He's taken a combination of amphetamines and cannabis.' The woman's tone is unsurprised, implying she's seen it all before. 'Then he got beaten up by a gang of youths.'

Annabel's mind is spinning, finding it hard to keep up. *'What?'*

'It happens more often than you think. When you're in that state, you're vulnerable to crime – assault, in particular.'

'We'll be there in ten minutes,' Annabel promises hurriedly. 'We live quite close by.'

She passes on the details to Jarrod: amphetamines, cannabis, assault. They look at each other, stricken, for what feels like an eternity. How did they get here? How do they navigate this? Their suspicions have been unequivocally confirmed: Daniel *is* experimenting with other drugs.

'I'll go,' she decides, because Jarrod's face is a worrying shade of grey. 'You stay here with Mia.'

'I'll wake her up. We'll all go. The three of us.'

His voice is faint, lacking in authority. The last few months have sapped him.

'No. Mia sees enough. She doesn't need to be exposed to what happens on Saturday nights in Accident and Emergency.'

Annabel briefly thinks of Grace. She could ask her

or Tom to come over and watch Mia while she and Jarrod present a united front at the hospital. Grace is probably in bed by now, but Annabel knows that won't matter. Her friend would be here in an instant, given the chance.

For some reason, Annabel doesn't give her that chance.

She pecks Jarrod on the cheek. 'I'll ring you as soon as I get there. It'll be okay … They said he's not in any immediate danger … We'll get through this, Jarrod. I know we will.'

Where has that bullshit come from? She knows no such thing.

This is what she finds at the hospital.

Her sixteen-year-old son with a swollen face, a couple of cracked ribs and a bandaged hand – apparently, a deep laceration on his palm required stitches. Her sixteen-year-old son compulsively scratching himself, swearing under his breath, his pupils so enlarged he looks like a stranger. Her sixteen-year-old son unremorseful for his actions, blaming his woes on the 'gang', bridling with hostility as soon as he sees her.

'Look at what you've done to yourself,' she says sadly.

'It wasn't fucking me. It was *them*.'

'You made yourself a target.'

'I was going along, doing nothing, and this guy

153

pushed into me. He said, "This is him," and next thing five or six of them were on top of me.'

She sits down then. Takes a moment to collect herself. 'Are you saying you knew them?'

'No, I'm saying someone set me up.'

'More like they saw what state you were in and took advantage.'

'Fuck's sake, you never take my side.'

In the next cubicle, there's a man groaning in pain. Somewhere else there's a baby crying, a mother crooning in response. These people have a right to be here – it is through no fault of their own that they're not feeling well. Unlike Daniel, whose pain is completely self-inflicted. She is angry with him for doing this to himself, for directing precious resources away from legitimate patients, for being so selfish and self-destructive.

'You took Mia's communion money … That was pretty low.'

He shrugs. Then scratches his neck. He has a cut there. From the beating or the constant scratching, she's not sure.

'Did you spend all of it? So you could end up like this?'

Once again, he doesn't answer and she has to accept that she isn't going to see any remorse from him, at least not tonight. Maybe tomorrow when he's sober and has had some time to dwell on things and face up to his little sister.

She tries a different tack. 'What happened with your job?'

At least this time he answers. 'The boss was a dickhead.'

'Why didn't you tell us that they'd let you go?'

She knows exactly why he didn't tell them. It suited him. They thought he was at work when he was really somewhere else, doing something that he shouldn't be doing, something that was destroying him and destroying their family.

A nurse – young, pretty – pops her head around the curtain. 'So, you found us, Mrs Harris. I'm Janine.'

'Yes, thanks. Hello, Janine.' Annabel has no idea what to say to this young woman. Other than apologise for her son. 'I'm sorry about this.'

Janine gives her a gentle smile. 'It's nothing you've done.'

How can she be so sure about that? They could've been more vigilant, attentive, strict. They could've said no to the job at the pizzeria, locked him in his room at night.

Janine takes Daniel's pulse, moves her stethoscope around his chest, writes on his chart.

'Can I have a word?' Annabel asks, awkwardly getting to her feet.

'Sure.' A flash of that pretty smile. 'The tea room is usually quiet.'

Annabel follows Janine, trying not to stare at some of the Saturday-night 'clientele'. A girl, not much older than Daniel, screeching uncontrollably. A young man in handcuffs, flanked by police officers.

'Come in. Sit down … What can I help you with?'

Annabel gets straight to the point. 'We're at the end of our tether with him.'

Janine walks towards the back of the room, where there is a large brochure holder mounted on the wall. 'There's information here. Out-reach programmes. Counselling services. Contact details for social workers …'

Annabel nods, clutching Janine's selection of pamphlets in her hand. She and Jarrod have tried to deal with this themselves. They've tried reasoning with Daniel. They've tried pleading with him. They've tried being tough. Nothing has worked. Their son is in A&E. He has graduated from cannabis to speed. He is angry at the gang, not at himself. It's time to throw more resources at the problem.

'You look like you could do with a cuppa,' Janine says kindly. 'Daniel won't be going anywhere for the next few hours, there's plenty of time to have one.'

Annabel makes a strong cup of tea. Helps herself to a packet of the complimentary biscuits. Sends a quick update to Jarrod.

Battered and bruised. Some stitches on his hand. Not the slightest bit sorry.

Then she settles down with the pamphlets. In the middle of them she finds a flyer for a parents' support group.

Is your teen taking drugs? Do you feel helpless, ashamed, frightened and unable to cope?

She feels all of the above. A sob escapes, then another. She thought they'd hit rock bottom at the restaurant. She was wrong. Receiving that call tonight. Seeing Daniel so bashed up yet so unrepentant. Holding this flyer in her hand. Knowing she'll be calling some of these numbers on Monday morning. This is what rock bottom is.

18
KATY

'Auntie Katy, can you give us our bath?'

Nina's youngest gives Katy an imploring smile. Her older sister tries a more forceful approach, tugging on Katy's arm.

Katy stares from one to the other and uses her witch's voice. 'Ah, ha, ha, ha … You filthy creatures … I'm going to scrub, scrub, scrub until you're clean … Ah, ha, ha, ha.'

The little girls shriek and bolt towards the bathroom.

Philip, Nina's husband, winces and gulps some wine. He is preparing dinner for the adults. He does most of the cooking. Nina, excellent at scientific measurements, is conveniently dyslexic when it comes to recipe measurements.

Katy follows the girls and 'the witch' game continues

in the bathroom. She towers over them, washcloth in hand.

'You are mine … all *mine*!' she cackles. 'And I will not eat you until you're squeaky clean.'

'Don't eat us,' the youngest pleads. 'Don't eat us, please.'

'Eat us, eat us,' the older one challenges. 'Go on, eat us.'

She holds out her arm for consumption. Katy smacks her lips. The youngest lets out an ear-piercing scream and Katy can imagine Philip's grimace, followed by another slug of wine.

'Can we keep it down in here?' Nina comes in with towels and fresh pyjamas. 'Daddy has a headache.'

'She's going to eat us! She's going to eat us!'

Katy bares her teeth, the girls scramble to get away and a big splash of water hits her full in the face.

She laughs. 'Well, there goes my mascara. Now I look more like a ghoul than a witch.'

'What's a ghoul?'

'It's a ghost.'

'Can we play ghosts instead of witches?'

Nina takes charge. 'Come on, bath time is over. Time to get out.'

'We don't want to get out. We want to stay in. We want to play witches.'

'And ghosts.'

'Out,' Nina commands. It's the same tone that pulls teenage students immediately into line; the girls don't stand a chance. They stand up and meekly get out of the bath.

'Great way to spend Saturday night, eh?' Nina comments as she dries one child and Katy dries the other.

'Well, it's not as if I've had any other offers,' Katy says wryly.

'There's always William,' Nina points out.

Katy laughs and shakes her head. 'Still not that desperate.'

'Auntie Katy, can you read us a story?'

Katy cuddles up with the kids in bed while Nina goes to help Philip, or at least drink wine while she watches him do all the work.

'*The Cat in the Hat*, by Dr Seuss—'

'Why is he a doctor? Can doctors write stories?'

'Shush. The sun did not shine. It was too wet to play. So we sat in the house all that cold, cold wet day …'

Katy pauses to drink in their rapt expressions. Their tousled, towel-dried hair. Their plump cheeks and sparkling eyes. The smell of them: soap and shampoo. This is what she wants more than anything in the world. To have children. To be a mother.

Why is it so impossible to achieve?

Katy is driving home when her phone rings. It's unusually late for a phone call: 10.30 p.m. The number is unfamiliar.

'Hello?'

'Hi … Is that Katy?' The voice is male, and also unfamiliar.

'Yes … who is this?'

'It's Rickie. Tom's friend.'

Now he calls. Late on Saturday night. Why couldn't he have called earlier today? Or even yesterday?

'Oh, yes. Hello, Rickie.'

'Hello, Katy …'

There's an awkward silence. She scrambles for something to say, but thankfully he fills the void.

'I was wondering if you'd like to meet up …' His voice is slightly slurred. Has he been drinking?

Stop being critical. He rang. See what happens.

She stops the car at a red light. 'Sure. When were you thinking?'

'Well, I'm free now and not that far from where you live … Grace said you're in Neutral Bay?'

The light changes to green. Katy puts her foot too heavily on the accelerator and the wheels skid as she takes off.

'You want to meet up *now*?' she asks incredulously.

'Yeah. I'm in this pub but I could drop around—'

She's furious. So angry she can hardly concentrate on her driving. 'What is this? Some kind of booty call?'

'No, not at all. I just—'

'Fuck off, Rickie. Don't bother ringing me again.'

Her face is wet. She's crying. Is this the best she can hope for on a Saturday night? Hijacking Nina's family and getting a booty call on her way home? Is William, with his old-man clothes and prattle about the geography syllabus, the best she can hope for?

She pulls into the driveway of the apartment block a little too aggressively and her tyres protest once again.

Calm down. Rickie's not worth it. You haven't even met him. He's nothing to you.

Her hand searches for the remote control to open the security gate leading to the car park in the basement. She locates a tissue and blows her nose while the gate rolls upwards, creaking and groaning. This time she makes sure she takes off slowly.

The car park is desolate and poorly lit: some of the light bulbs need replacing. Katy hurries to the stairwell, her heels clicking loudly against the concrete. Four flights to the first floor, her breath caught in her throat. She has an irrational fear of being trapped in the stairwell, the fire doors locking from the other side. Not being able to get out or call for help. There's no phone reception in this part of the building.

The fire door bursts open when she pushes it. She proceeds down the hall: her apartment is the last one on the right-hand side. She knows all her neighbours by name. She knows the children the best because they're the friendliest and always want to talk. Her door key is ready in her hand. She slips it into the lock and she's inside within a matter of seconds.

She goes around the apartment turning on lights. Her heart rate is slightly up; she never enjoys the walk from the car park when it's late at night. She pours herself a glass of wine and is on her way to the bedroom, to fetch her slippers, when she sees something on the hall floor. A piece of paper, right inside the door. Something that dropped out of her handbag as she was coming in? Or perhaps a note from Jim, her next-door neighbour, that she failed to spot? Wine glass in hand, she bends down to pick it up. Unfolds it awkwardly with one hand.

You need a boyfriend, Katy, and better security in your apartment block. Great idea to have a new yearbook, though. Hope you're enjoying my contributions!

19
GRACE

Grace is woken by the sound of her phone ringing, and then Tom saying hello.

'Who is it?' she asks groggily. She and Tom were watching a movie together. She must have nodded off. She was tired: she'd been gardening all afternoon.

'It's Katy.'

'Who?' Her brain is still muddled with sleep. Her skin feels hot. Sunburn?

Tom hands her the phone. 'Katy, your friend from school.'

Oh yes, *that Katy*. But they weren't friends, that's the perplexing thing.

She pulls herself into a more upright position. It's late: almost eleven. 'Katy ... Hello ... What is it?'

'I'm so sorry for disturbing you ... I just didn't know

who else to call, who else would understand the implications …'

Grace is instantly more alert. 'What is it? What's happened?'

Tom catches her eye and mouths, *What's wrong*?

'Someone slipped a note under my door. This is what it says …' Katy's voice trembles as she reads the note. 'How did this person get inside the apartment block? How do they know where I live?'

Grace thinks for a moment. 'I would imagine they slipped inside while someone else was exiting. Didn't you include your address for RSVPs?'

'Oh, God, yes. Stupid me. My email was all that was really needed.'

'You weren't to know … You did nothing I wouldn't do.'

'What am I meant to make of the boyfriend comment? Whoever this is obviously knows that I live alone. I'm *so creeped out* …'

Poor Katy. Grace remembers those few hours of crippling fear when she thought someone had been in her house and taken the photo from the fridge.

'Do you have anyone who can come over and stay with you?'

'Jim, one of my neighbours, came around and checked all the rooms with me. Gave me some reassurance that there's nobody actually *in here*. But I'm scared, Grace. This person was *at my door*. What if they're still around, lurking in the building somewhere, waiting their chance?'

'Do you want Tom to come over?'

Tom's eyebrows shoot up. Grace ignores him.

Katy's laugh sounds strangulated. 'I haven't even met Tom.'

'There's always a first time.'

'Thank you, but no. I just needed to tell you. Because you get it. When Jim looked at the note, he couldn't see the menace in it. I'm much calmer now that we've spoken.'

'You're sure you don't want Tom to call around?'

'Yes, sure.'

'How about the police?'

'It's not a crime to put a note under someone's door … Is it?'

'Assuming the person doesn't live in your apartment block, then they were trespassing at the very least … Look, Tom knows a lot of police officers through work. I'll ask him to talk it over with one of them, see what they say.'

'Thanks, Grace, I'd appreciate that. I'm sorry, I shouldn't have called so late.'

'Don't be silly. I'm here any time, day or night. Goodnight, Katy. Talk to you tomorrow.'

'Goodnight, Grace.'

Grace hangs up the phone. Rests her forehead against her hand. It's burning; she definitely got sunburnt when she was in the garden this afternoon.

Tom is standing, waiting for an explanation. '*Where* were you planning to send me?'

'To Katy's place. In Neutral Bay.'

'Is she in some kind of danger?'

'I don't think so. She got a weird note about the year-book. She's upset and frightened more than anything.'

'*Should* I go there?'

'She said no need. But can you talk to one of your cop friends and see if anything can be done to stop this?'

They give up on the movie and go to bed.

Grace sleeps fitfully. She dreams that she's in a strange apartment and someone is repeatedly knocking on the walls and doors. She keeps running from room to room, trying to see who it is.

'Who's there?' she shrieks frantically. 'Who is it? Why are you doing this?'

Suddenly, she comes face to face with a corpse-like Katy Buckley: translucent skin, dilated eyes, unkempt hair.

'It's me,' she breathes. 'It's been me all along.'

Grace screams until she's awake.

Tom reaches out in the dark. 'Shush. It's just a nightmare.'

Grace has a quick shower and surveys herself in the mirror. Her forehead and nose are sunburnt, her hair is in need of a trim, and her face is drawn from last night's restless sleep. She puts on some foundation, one of her best tops, and rubs some cream into her hands, which are tattered from the garden. She always makes a special effort when she sees Annabel. She suspects that

167

at some deep-down level she's still trying to impress her. She laughs at the thought.

Grace dispenses chores before she goes out. 'Tahlia and Poppy, I want you two to change the sheets on all the beds. Lauren, honey, you're to help Daddy with the gardening. Billy, your job is to tidy away all the toys.'

The children groan half-heartedly. They know by now it's better to get the chores over and done with; moaning, as well as being ineffective, is a waste of time. Grace and Tom are firm believers in natural consequences as well as chores. If the kids forget their homework or sports uniform, Grace does not rush to school with the forgotten item; instead, they're expected to deal with their irate teacher, possible detention and other consequences of their forgetfulness. If they don't put their dirty clothes in the wash, they have to wear the item in a less-than-clean state – although this doesn't bother Billy in the slightest.

Manly is a short drive down the hill. Seven minutes later, Grace has transitioned from suburbia to beachside. It's a stunning morning: cloudless sky, piercing sun, barely a breeze.

Annabel is waiting at the café where they agreed to meet. She's wearing large sunglasses and a white sundress that shows off her golden shoulders. Grace kisses her cheek and gets a whiff of the scent she associates with her friend: a sophisticated, expensive smell.

Grace smiles and gestures towards the blue sky and sparkling ocean. 'What a glorious morning!'

Annabel grimaces. 'Shall we order?'

This response is abrupt even for Annabel, who specialises in being curt. It's obvious something serious is afoot. Grace knew this from the minute she received Annabel's text, asking if she was free for an impromptu coffee. Their catch-ups, while regular, are rarely of the impromptu kind.

Annabel raises her hand and a waitress – blonde, tanned, like a young Annabel, in fact – appears with astonishing speed.

'What's up?' Grace asks once the waitress has taken their orders.

'I don't know where to start …'

'Start wherever you like,' Grace says, reaching out to give her hand a squeeze.

'It's Daniel—' Annabel's voice breaks. Is she about to start crying? Here in the middle of the café? Grace is thrown. Annabel doesn't cry easily.

'He was assaulted last night, here in Manly—' Annabel chokes on a sob, tries to compose herself, fails miserably. Now she is crying openly and attracting glances from the other patrons.

Grace, who was half-expecting to hear that Daniel had been expelled from school or perhaps had got into trouble with the police, is shocked. 'Is he okay? Was he badly hurt?'

'He has cuts and bruises and a few cracked ribs. But it's not the assault that's the problem, it's the drugs …' Annabel pushes her sunglasses back on her head and roughly wipes her tears away with the back of her hand. Her eyes are bloodshot. 'He was so off his face he made himself a target. And not even this – ending up in hospital – has made him see the light.'

'What kind of drugs?' Grace asks with dread.

'Amphetamines … Speed …'

Grace could burst into tears too but that would be of no help to Annabel. 'Tom says that's the most prevalent at the moment. Seems to be everywhere.'

'I'm at my wits' end.' Annabel slides her sunglasses back in place. Her mouth is trembling and it's obvious she's trying to hold back another bout of tears. 'I don't know what to do or where to turn. Jarrod is too distraught to think straight. I need your help, Grace. I need your support, because Jarrod is as good as useless right now.'

Grace has never seen her friend this vulnerable. 'I'll help you and Jarrod any way I can … Do you mind if I tell Tom? The council provides some really worthwhile services. They're often badly advertised, but that doesn't mean they aren't good …'

'Tell whoever you like. Jarrod and I tried to keep it quiet, and look where that's got us.'

'You'll need to get Daniel on some kind of rehabilitation programme …'

Annabel nods. Then she crumples in her seat and begins crying again. 'Something this devastating hasn't happened since I found out I was pregnant with Jemma.'

Grace takes the opportunity to be positive. 'Jemma worked out okay, didn't she? This will too, honey. You'll get through it.'

Annabel uses some serviettes to dab her eyes and blow her nose. They both turn to their coffees, which arrived some time ago and are already half cold. Grace looks out at the ocean, her mug poised at her lips. There are dozens of surfers bobbing out at the break. A wave rolls in, they all paddle furiously and rise up on their boards, one managing to ride inside the curve of the water – a feat of timing and skill – while the rest topple and get wiped out. Life goes on, some people thriving at the same time that others are falling apart.

Her phone beeps with an incoming text.

Thanks for listening last night. Sorry I woke you up and alarmed you. I'm much calmer this morning. By the way, Rickie phoned. Drunk as a skunk and obviously looking for sex. First child will not be your namesake after all. xx Katy.

'Excuse me a minute,' Grace says to Annabel as she hits the reply button. 'I just need to answer this. It's from Katy Buckley.'

Glad to hear you're feeling better this morning. So sorry about Rickie. Can't believe he did that. What a jerk! We should catch up soon. Xx Grace.

'Why is Katy Buckley sending you texts?' Annabel asks, sounding more like her usual self.

'She received one of those messages last night, about the yearbook. She was totally freaked out by it.'

'But why text *you*?'

'Because I went to look at the venue with her. We had coffee and talked about the emails …'

Annabel snorts. 'All these years later and she's still trying.'

'Trying what?'

'Don't you remember? She was always trying to get into our group. Being all friendly and annoying. I guess she's finally got to you.'

The spitefulness in Annabel's voice propels Grace back through the years. The snow excursion: Annabel eyeing Katy's duffel coat as they waited to get on the bus.

'Oh my God. Where did she get it? The fucking army? It looks like a sack on her.'

Another flashback: Annabel sneering from the checkout counter as Katy, her arm hooked through Luke's, disappeared down one of the library aisles.

'She *still* thinks she has a chance with him. Wake up, Katy. He's fucking gay and you're fucking pathetic.'

But worse than anything was that scene with the birthday card. Its fragments floating to the floor, Annabel's inexplicable hatred, Katy's face puce with mortification.

'Get your own friends, Katy Buckley. Stop acting like you're one of us because you're *not*.'

Grace comes back to the present, guilt mingling with the taste of coffee in her mouth. She's tempted to tell Annabel to stop being such a bitch. She would, if it weren't for Annabel being so upset about Daniel.

'As a matter of fact, I really like Katy Buckley. I guess she *has* finally got to me.'

20
LUKE

Luke's schedule has been horrendous. Six trips to Paris this week, four to Amsterdam; he's lost count of the domestic flights. There's a staff shortage at the airline, along with a spate of sicknesses caused by London's nasty weather.

'Jesus, my feet are killing me,' Nerida groans as they emerge from the aircraft on to the gangway. They're greeted by a blast of cold air – a warning of the weather waiting outside – before the heating kicks in.

'Me, too.'

'Shut up. You're not allowed to complain.'

True. He shares her outrage that female flight attendants are still required to wear heels of a certain height and skirts instead of trousers. So much for equality.

'Let's find a warm bar and get pissed,' Nerida suggests, linking her arm through his.

Nerida is the perpetual party girl. No matter how tired or dispirited she feels, a glass of wine is all she needs to be instantly revived. Her social life is non-stop – four or five nights a week – and astonishingly eventful: Luke usually gets a blow-by-blow account when they're rostered on together.

This is where Luke should say no. This is where he should explain that he's bone tired and has barely seen Aaron all week. This is where he should show some self-awareness and willpower; after all, he knows he drinks too much. Some of the problem traces all the way back to high school. Competing with Zach Latham to be the funniest and get the most laughs. Then competing to see who could get the drunkest; Luke always won that competition hands down.

Nerida pulls on his arm. 'Ah, go on.'

'Okay, just a quick one,' he says, hating himself for being so weak.

It's after midnight when Luke fumbles his key into the lock, pushes open the door and lurches inside. The hallway is pitch-black. He tries to turn on his phone light, somehow loses his balance and bumps against the door frame. The phone goes flying into the blackness, clattering as it hits the ground.

'Shit.'

He sweeps his palms across the floorboards. Where the fuck has it gone?

This is how Aaron finds him – on his hands and knees – when he turns on the hall light.

'Jesus, Luke. What are you doing?'

Luke squints into the sudden brightness. 'Dropped my phone.' He spots it a few metres away – how the fuck did it travel so far? – and crawls towards it.

'Gotcha.' The screen isn't smashed, everything seems to be working. 'Ladies and gentlemen, I am happy to announce that the missing item has been located.'

He's tired now. Incredibly tired and incredibly drunk. Bloody Nerida. She was still going hard when he left. How does she do it?

'How does who do what?' Aaron asks.

Must have been thinking aloud. Luke is too jaded to elaborate. He thinks he might as well stay down here, on the floor, and have a little nap. He props himself against the wall, closes his eyes, immediately feels himself drifting off.

'You're pissed,' Aaron declares from somewhere above.

Luke snuggles against the wall. He is so happy to be home … even though he hasn't made it past the hallway. He's drifting, drifting … There's something cold touching his lips. It knocks against his teeth: a glass. Aaron is crouched down next to him.

'Drink some water, for God's sake.'

The water is delicious. Exactly what he needs. Relieves the stale taste in his mouth, the dull ache in his head.

'This is why I love you.'

'I love you too, you moron.'

The water is gone. Now Luke can sleep. Finally. All day he has been waiting for this moment.

'Up you get.'

'Ah, I'm fine here.'

'You're too pissed to know the difference between a soft bed and the cold, hard floor. But you'll thank me in the morning. Come on.'

Aaron hoists him to his feet. Props his shoulder under his armpit. Half carries, half drags him to the bedroom. The mattress sinks beneath his weight. Luke is vaguely aware of his shoes coming off, then his trousers, finally his shirt. Then the weight of the bedclothes over his bare skin. He is cocooned, safe, home at last.

Aaron gets in the other side of the bed, turns off the lamp.

Let's get married.

The words are on the tip of Luke's tongue but they won't come out. They refuse to formulate into anything beyond a thought. They never do. Why is that?

Aaron is a professor of sociology at University College London. He teaches as well as researches; as part of his position he's expected to publish regular articles on his area of expertise. Luke met Aaron in a pub. His first impressions were intelligent, cultured and self-possessed, as well as cute-looking. Four years later those impressions hold true, in addition to some other admirable attributes: Aaron never has more than three or four drinks at a time, he doesn't say yes when he means no, and he doesn't have a self-destructive bone in his body.

'You're burnt out, Luke. This is what you do when you're tired. You get filthy drunk and make things even worse for yourself.'

Luke groans. His head is aching. Waves of nausea rise and recede. He feels unbalanced, as though he could topple off the kitchen stool and crack his head on the floor tiles. He grips the counter. Steadies himself. 'I know, I know, I'm a fool.'

'You can't go on like this,' Aaron declares. He moves around the kitchen as he speaks, tidying away dishes, wiping surfaces. The movement is making Luke feel dizzy. 'You need a holiday. Three or four weeks at least.'

'I can't—'

'Look at yourself in the mirror. If you can see past the hangover, you'll notice a perilously tired man.' Aaron grins, and Luke knows he is about to say something harsh and wants to soften it. 'Being haggard is *not* attractive, you know.'

Luke laughs, which makes his head feel significantly worse. 'Jeez, thanks … And there was I, thinking I was hot …'

There's a small silence. Luke sips from a glass of coconut water. Aaron swears by it for hangovers … not that he suffers from many of them. 'I suppose I could take a week …'

Aaron rolls his eyes. 'That's not enough, and you know it isn't. You've never taken more than a week's holiday since the day we met. What are you scared of?'

Good question. Is he scared of something? That his job and livelihood will somehow disappear while he's vacationing? In the early days it *was* a money thing. Being on leave meant not being paid overtime, and the basic wage simply wasn't enough to live on. But money hasn't been a problem for years. Is it more to do with having time to stop and reflect on all the things in his life that are shit?

'It's a busy time of year.'

'So?' Aaron is being uncharacteristically obtuse.

'It's not really a convenient time to be taking extended leave.'

'You could be back on the job the week before Christmas. Surely, the airline would be happy with that?'

Actually, the airline would be thrilled with that. Finding people willing to work over Christmas is never easy.

Aaron rinses some coffee cups, then tries a different angle. 'Look, it'd be an opportunity to go to Australia. You're overdue a visit, and I've never been. I want to see the opera house, the bridge, Bondi Beach … More than that, I want to meet your family—' Luke snorts at this but Aaron continues nevertheless. 'I want to see where you grew up. You've met *my* family, seen *my* childhood house …'

Aaron's parents live in Wales, in the same three-bed

semi they purchased when they first got married. Luke and Aaron visit several times a year and are pampered for the entirety of their stay.

'You know how *difficult* my father is,' Luke says.

Difficult being the understatement of the century. Belligerent. Scathing. Bigoted. And more. His roar on seeing Luke's outfit for a Mardi Gras party. *Take it off before I tear it off ya.*

The scuff across the head when Luke got blond highlights. *Bloody hell, next you'll be wearing make-up.*

Luke's earrings and other jewellery gathered up and deposited in the garbage. *Where did I go wrong with you?*

'I know,' Aaron says gently, bringing Luke back to the here and now. 'But I still want to meet him at some point.'

Luke takes another sip from his glass. He doesn't think the coconut water is helping. Neither did the Panadol he took as soon as he woke up. The only thing that will help is another twelve hours in bed – and no further thoughts about his father.

'There's a reunion coming up,' he admits huskily; even his voice is not working properly. 'I don't want to go.'

'Why not? I thought you liked school?'

'What's the point in looking back? "Look forward" has always been my motto.'

'Might be time for a new motto.'

Luke closes his eyes and he's back in time again. Katy grinning as she brought her car to a jerky stop outside his house. 'Your taxi is here.'

Singing loudly to Backstreet Boys on the way to school, a bubble of happiness before the drudgery of class.

One particular morning, Annabel sidling up as they walked across the oval. 'I hardly see you any more. Why do you hang out with that nerd?'

Luke would have said 'shut up' or something to that effect but not before the damage was done. Annabel's intention was for Katy to hear, for Katy to blush, for Katy to feel miserable for the rest of the day.

Which leads him to question why Katy is the one who's driving this reunion. What does she want from it? The chance to reveal her new self? An opportunity to come face to face with Annabel as an adult, an equal? Katy is far from that blushing schoolgirl; she has learned how to stand up for herself. Although knowing Katy, her motives are more likely to be purely altruistic and nothing to do with Annabel.

Oh God, that reminds him. He hasn't answered her email about being a bloody sperm donor.

Why is it such a bad idea?

Where does he start?

His headache goes up another notch.

'Katy wants me to have a baby with her.'

'Whoa … Really?' Aaron is visibly taken aback. Stops his buzzing around the kitchen. Puts down the tea towel, pulls out the stool next to Luke.

'Yeah, really … Can you imagine me as a dad?'

Even though he feels like shit, it's good to be here

180

with Aaron. At home, for once. Talking about stuff. Important stuff.

Aaron takes his hand. Squeezes it. His look is one of pure love and belief.

'Yes, actually, I can.'

ROBBIE

21
ROBBIE

Nick went home this morning. Back to Melbourne, back to his photogenic family and his big job. He stayed longer than anyone expected. In the end, Robbie was counting down the hours to his brother's departure, wrung out from all the talking, the overload of emotion. Now that Nick is gone, he feels ashamed and guilty. His brother came all the way from Melbourne, tried to bridge twenty years of estrangement by wearing his heart on his sleeve, and this is how he responds? Delighted to see the back of him?

What the fuck is wrong with you, Robbie?

'Will we see Megan and the kids over Christmas?' Celia asked as they sat around waiting for Nick's taxi to arrive.

Her eyes met Robbie's, and she blinked and looked

down at her hands. Robbie left home the week before Christmas. He remembers the overwhelming need to get out, to be far away, to be on his own. It was a snap decision. Don't some people say that the best decisions in your life are the quick ones? All he took was his rucksack, some clothes, the book he was reading at the time and the money left over from his eighteenth birthday. He left the house in the early hours of the morning, about 4 a.m. He'd been awake all night, thoughts racing, but as soon as he made the decision he felt strangely calm and in control. Nick didn't stir as he clicked the bedroom door shut behind him. The bus stop was a ten-minute walk from the house. Of course, there were no buses running at that hour of the morning. He waited in the dark, and then in the muted light of dawn and early morning. Plenty of time to change his mind and trudge back home to bed. He waited, and the more he waited the more right it felt. He got on that first bus, empty except for him and the driver, threadbare tinsel twirled around some of the handrails. *Merry fucking Christmas.*

'Not sure,' Nick replied to Celia with a shrug. 'The kids are at that age now where they have their own plans for the holidays. I'll let you know.'

Celia went to check on Sienna and Charlie, who had been sent upstairs to get dressed for school. 'Hurry up! Uncle Nick wants a hug before he goes.'

Nick sat forward in his seat. Robbie braced himself.

'It doesn't sound fun, Robbie. Going from shelter to

shelter. Scraping by on the dole. You could come back here, to Sydney. Stay with Mum and Dad or Celia. Have the support of your family … Wouldn't that be an easier life?'

Robbie looked around the kitchen, cereal boxes still on the counter, smells of coffee and toast, Celia and the kids' voices babbling from upstairs. 'I can't live like this. I'm better on my own. I know myself.'

'Jeez, do you really mean that?'

'I know myself,' Robbie repeats. 'After all these years, I know what I can take, and what I can't.'

Nick nodded, and Robbie felt that his brother was at least on the way to understanding. Then the kids and Celia came flying down the stairs and – mercifully – there was no more time for talking.

There she is. A large tote bag over her shoulder. Head bent forward. Svelte in a short skirt and striped top. Wearing earphones. She could be a student rather than a teacher. Robbie is sitting on a low wall across the street. He's been waiting here more than an hour. Katy stayed long after the bell. She probably had a staff meeting or some paperwork to get through. Conscientious to a fault.

Katy looks in both directions before crossing the road. Any moment now she'll pass where he is sitting. Will she glance his way? Recognise him?

She walks straight past. He waits until she is further down the street, then he stands up and begins to follow.

What the fuck is wrong with you, Robbie? What are you doing?

He doesn't know what he is doing, or why. All he knows is that this is the fourth time he has done this: followed her all the way home to her first-floor apartment in Neutral Bay. She takes two buses, both packed to capacity. There's barely standing room; it's easy to go unnoticed.

Robbie hangs on to one of the overhead rails and his thoughts flit between Katy and Nick.

'I'll be back in a couple of weeks,' Nick said as he gave Robbie a final suffocating hug. 'Don't go anywhere between now and then. Promise me.'

Robbie promised but now he's not sure he can keep the promise. He's been told that his urge to run away is in fact a stress response: his body senses danger and wants to escape. It's triggered by fear, which is triggered by anxiety, which is triggered by depression. Shame plays a big part in it, too.

The bus hurtles over the Harbour Bridge. Then it hits traffic and comes to an abrupt halt. The rest of the journey is stop-start along Military Road. Katy's stop is a popular one; Robbie blends in with the crowd. She takes a detour into the 7-Eleven to buy some bread. Through the shop window, Robbie sees the attendant – a bearded twenty-something male – say something that makes her laugh. He feels a negative response within himself. Jealousy? Longing? Loneliness? She is still smiling as she leaves the shop. Shortly afterwards, she turns down the side street that leads to her apartment block. He hangs back further; there are fewer people around now, it would be easy to get caught.

Not once does she turn around and notice the man who's following her. A man who exists in the margins of society. A man who feels perilously overwrought and on edge, besieged with memories of twenty years ago. Annabel Moore gagging and crying within earshot, 'He's *disgusting*. I'm going to be *sick*.' Melissa Andrews standing up and moving seats when he sat down next to her. Zach Latham mimicking his walk of shame, to hysterical laughter. Jarrod Harris calling at his house day after day, jabbing the bell button, a knowing smirk on his face.

Katy was his only reprieve. She still is.

22
MELISSA

Melissa is having lunch with Cassie, something they try to manage at least once a week. They have a lot in common: the only two women on the board; both in their late thirties; ambitious, at the peak of their careers; married. Their only point of difference is children: Cassie has a three-year-old boy and is trying for another.

'It's a disaster,' Melissa says between mouthfuls. 'Henry and I should have stood our ground at the start. Here we are, three years later, and the kids still detest me.'

Cassie nods, swallows. 'Hindsight's a great thing, eh?'

Cassie is sympathetic and gives good advice but sometimes Melissa wonders how her friend can possibly understand. Cassie lived with her husband for several years before they got married. She sees him first thing in the morning, last thing at night, and all weekend long. It's a genuine partnership, an authentic sharing of lives. Melissa's marriage is more like 'dating' than anything else and she has the overwhelming sense that everything is about to come to a skidding halt. She feels the change happening inside her and welcomes it as much as she dreads it. Another concerning matter is the almost daily messages she's been exchanging with Jarrod Harris.

Melissa Andrews: How are things in the world of volts? xx

Jarrod Harris: Electric. How about the board table?

Melissa Andrews: Dull, dull, dull. Yawn.

Jarrod Harris: Nice photo at industry awards, Snow White.

Brief messages, jokey, nothing untoward. At the same time, a reopened connection and dangerous because of all those old, unresolved feelings. They shared something intense, albeit short-lived. At the time Jarrod said he felt different around her: more focused, more ambitious about the future. Melissa felt different, too: more adventurous, distinctly more sexual. Jarrod seemed like another species to the other boys: a man's face combined with an athlete's body, an innate knowledge of what to do with his hands and mouth, eliciting a sexual response Melissa never imagined herself capable of.

Their relationship lasted two incredibly vivid, lustful months. It ended via a taut conversation by the basket-ball courts. 'Annabel is pregnant. I'm sticking by her. I'm sorry, Melissa.'

Such loyalty. Annabel didn't deserve it; she'd been the very opposite of loyal with Melissa. Initially main-taining that she didn't mind about Melissa and Jarrod dating; her subsequent actions proving that she minded very much indeed. *It was fear*, Melissa keeps telling herself. *Annabel was scared.*

Now Melissa has the distinct impression that Jarrod is floundering, just like she is. Is he unhappy with Annabel? Is the marriage in trouble? Why else open up dialogue with someone from the far-distant past? When your present life is not working out, it's all too tempting to look back. She knows this first-hand.

'What are you wearing tomorrow night?' she asks Cassie, forcibly directing her thoughts away from Jarrod.

Tomorrow night is a female-only industry event. A gathering of pharmaceutical researchers, scientists and everyone from the production line to executive man-agement. Melissa is sponsoring the event and will be speaking about female empowerment. She's delivered many similar speeches in the past, but that won't make her complacent. Tonight, she'll practise in front of the mirror, delivering the speech over and over again, until it sounds completely unrehearsed and the audience laughs in all the right places, as well as listening when she's being deadly serious.

Cassie pulls a face. 'Whatever fits me. What about you?'

'Maybe the dress I wore to Steve and Anna's wedding.'

Steve is a fellow board member. The wedding was his third. It was a great day out but the pervading feeling was that this marriage wouldn't last any longer than the other two.

'The royal blue? Yeah, that's lovely on you.'

The conversation moves on to Cassie's little boy, who's starting preschool in the new year. Melissa listens intently. She is careful not to become one of those childless women who resent it when mothers talk about their kids.

Just before the hour mark, Cassie calls for the bill – it's her turn to pay. As they're walking out of the café, she links her arm through Melissa's, making them present more like conspiring teenage girls than board executives.

'You know what I think you should do?' Cassie says.

'About tomorrow night?'

'No … About Henry, stupid.'

Melissa is bemused. 'What should I do?'

'You should get a dog.'

'A *dog*? Are you kidding?'

'Nope. I'm being perfectly serious. Dogs are glue. They bring families together.'

A dog? Melissa is intermittently incredulous for the rest of the afternoon – whenever she has the time to stop and think about it. Henry is ill at ease with dogs. She doesn't exactly love them herself. A dog means more responsibility, more constraints on her time, and is just about the last thing that would solve her problems. Cassie has taken leave of her senses.

It's seven thirty before Melissa calls it a night. Her car – metallic blue, easy to pick out – is parked in the staff car park. The air is thick and claustrophobic in the basement. Melissa gets inside the car and turns on the air-conditioning full blast. As soon as she exits the car park, she phones Henry and they have a perfunctory discussion. She tells him she had lunch with Cassie but doesn't mention the dog. He reminds her that he's attending a school concert and won't be able to talk later on. This incites yet another flare of dissatisfaction with their situation.

The air inside her apartment is muggy with trapped heat and she flings open the balcony doors so the breeze can run through.

'There. That's better.'

She detests it when she talks aloud, as though there is someone here to listen.

Dinner is a toasted ham and cheese sandwich, which she takes outside. Someone from one of the other apartments is playing loud rap music. She can hear voices from the balcony below, as well as the background sound of a television. Most of what she hears is silence; this is what she hates about coming home to an empty apartment. She finishes her sandwich, brings the plate inside and swaps it for her laptop. A dozen unread messages since she left the office, over an hour ago. Her eyes skim over them. One stands out.

From: admin11@yearbook.com.au
Subject: Year Book Macquarie High

Name: Melissa Andrews (aka Snow White)

What you do now: Sales Director for pharmaceuticals company.

Highlights of last twenty years: Being promoted more than you deserve.

Lowlights: Henry refusing to live together because his kids hate you.

Deepest fears: Dying alone. And you will.

Ouch! Melissa reads it again, scrupulously, finding its accuracy even more alarming than its venom. A simple Google search would throw up information about her career, but not her living arrangements with Henry, or the ongoing friction with his children. Who sent this? How do they have access to this information? Has someone been spying on her? Watching Henry's car come and go and reaching the obvious conclusion? That seems too dramatic. Maybe it's a double connection, someone who knows her from the old days and also knows Henry, or perhaps his kids, through some other avenue? Sydney can be a small place. Whatever the connection, she's rattled and freshly angry with Henry. He should be *here*. Helping her make sense of this, even to laugh it off. Instead she feels strangely insecure and vulnerable. She goes back inside, locks the balcony doors and pulls the blinds. She's not the only one who's had these messages. They're an annoyance, yes, but no one has suggested danger of any kind. She reads the email yet again. Nothing overtly threatening. Except for the gross invasion of her privacy. Except for the unnerving accuracy. Except for the venom, which feels oddly familiar. Could it be Annabel? Dredging up old grudges after finding out that Melissa and Jarrod have resumed contact? But Annabel herself was one of the first to get an email, so how can that possibly make sense?

She forwards the email to Katy Buckley.

This came today. I'm a little unsettled by it … Who is sending these? Where is it all leading?

Melissa works through the other messages in her inbox, sending quick responses where she can. She is about to finish up when a response comes from Katy.

Have no idea. It's creeping me out. Starting to think I should call the whole thing off.

Is that the end game here? A simple desire to have the reunion called off? Or is the motive more elaborate? Elaborate enough for Annabel to send herself an email and thereby throw everyone off the scent? Maybe she can't bear the thought of everyone being reinvented, her old position as queen bee under threat. Or maybe she is insecure about the idea of Melissa and Jarrod coming face to face after all these years. Or maybe she has found out about their recent contact and is livid. Or scared. Annabel can be frightening when she's scared.

However, it does seem a rather long bow to draw for a mother of three who must have many other things to obsess about. Would she really go to such lengths?

Melissa stands up. Stretches. Yawns. Then sighs as she remembers that she still needs to rehearse her speech for tomorrow night. A copy in hand, she stations herself in front of the bedroom mirror. Her voice is quivery. She doesn't know if it's due to nervous tension or exhaustion. She clears her throat, injects more power, but now she sounds too harsh. Her voice rings through the apartment, hard and unanswered.

Here I am, talking to myself again.

Annabel's face materialises alongside her own in the mirror. Tanned skin, blonde hair, in stark contrast to her own looks. Her mouth contorts, words forming. Melissa hears them, resurrecting Annabel's acidic tones of long ago.

Dying alone. And you will.

23
GRACE

Tom doesn't like Annabel. Grace has always known this fact at an intuitive level, although her husband has never outwardly criticised her closest friend. It's obvious from the set of his mouth, how it tightens at the mention of Annabel's name. It's obvious from his reservedness around her, and around Jarrod too: he seems to hold himself back in their presence, not chatting or being engaged to his usual extent. But Tom would never allow his personal opinions to get in the way of helping Annabel. Nothing would give him greater pleasure than seeing Daniel come out of this phase unscathed. Her husband always wants the best for everyone.

'It's so upsetting to think of Daniel in hospital,' Grace sighs. The children have gone to bed and she and Tom have just sat down together. The television is turned down low. 'Annabel's confused about what to do next. I promised I'd ask you about what services she can access through the council.'

Tom's blue eyes are solemn as he turns to look at her. 'She should start with the drug and alcohol centre. There's also youth mental health and a support group that meets in one of the local high schools some week nights ... I'll find out which nights.'

'Thanks. The difficult thing is that Daniel is not being cooperative. He doesn't seem to want to be helped.'

There it is again. The tell-tale tightening around Tom's mouth. The sense that he has to work hard to keep his true opinions to himself. This time he can't seem to help himself. 'There's no point in locking the stable after the horse has bolted.'

'Oh, Tom.'

'It's true.' Her husband is unrepentant. 'Daniel's been given far too much freedom. Nothing good comes from kids his age being out late at night.'

'How do you know he's been out late? Have you seen him?'

Tom pauses before admitting, 'I've come across him on my night patrol. At one of the parks with a group of boys. Obviously up to no good.'

Grace blinks. 'You *have*? Why didn't you say?'

'I phoned Annabel straight away. She sent Jarrod to fetch him and specifically asked me not to mention it to you. Honestly, she seemed more concerned about keeping face than Daniel's safety … I presume, now that everything's out in the open, it's okay to tell you.'

Grace is lost for words. What was Annabel thinking? Why put Tom in such an awkward position? Why the secrecy? Did she think Grace would be judgemental, unsupportive or prone to gossip? Grace feels a familiar stab of hurt. All these years, and Annabel can still make her feel like this: as though she is inferior, a step behind; as though she is not worthy of trust.

'When was this?'

'About six weeks ago. The October school holidays.'

'Did you speak to Daniel at the time?'

'Just said a friendly hello. Asked him if he was going home soon.'

'And what did he say?'

'Told me it was none of my effing business.'

Grace can picture the scene. Tom meaning well. Daniel being horrifically disrespectful. Tom not being impressed with Annabel's handling of the matter. His dislike becoming more entrenched.

'So you knew Daniel was dabbling with drugs?'

'I could smell weed. I was hoping it was the friends, not Daniel, but that seemed unlikely.'

'Did you tell Annabel that part? What they were actually *doing* at the park?'

'I couldn't accuse Daniel outright, but I told her what I smelt.' Tom stands up abruptly and stretches. 'Are you coming to bed?'

'Not yet.' Grace feels deeply unsettled. How could

she not have known about this incident? 'I have a few things to do.'

He leans down, kisses her on the forehead, and she wonders what other things her husband has not told her.

Grace has another nightmare about Katy Buckley. Tom and Katy have become a couple. She finds them entwined together in the park down the road. Katy's hair and clothes are dishevelled. Tom's eyes are cold.

'What are you doing with her?' Grace wails.

'I forgot to tell you,' he replies emotionlessly.

She pushes Katy as hard as she can. 'Get away from him.'

Katy throws back her head and cackles.

Something tugs at her arm. There's a voice in her ear. 'Mummy, Mummy.'

Grace has to fight to surface from the dream. Katy's cackling is mingling with 'Mummy, Mummy'. She opens her eyes and sees a white face hovering over her. She almost screams. Then realises it's Lauren.

'I'm scared, Mummy. There's someone outside my window.'

Grace glances at the digital clock next to the bed: 2 a.m.

'It's okay, honey. I had a nightmare too.'

'It's not a nightmare. It's *real*.'

'Oh, honey. It's probably a possum. Or Mrs Vaughan's cat.'

Mrs Vaughan lives down the street. Her cat seems to

have free rein and its night-time antics are the bane of the neighbourhood.

'I'm really scared … Can you come?'

Grace groans as she hauls herself out of bed. This is usually Tom's job. Lauren mustn't have been able to rouse him tonight.

The curtains are wide open in her daughter's bedroom, and Grace is alarmed when she sees that the window has been slid across.

'Lauren, honey, why did you open the window?'

'I was trying to see what was out there. I was trying to be brave.'

Tom and Grace have been talking to Lauren about 'being brave', about challenging herself in little ways, but this is far from what they intended. Lauren could have climbed out of the window and they would have been none the wiser. Even worse, someone passing on the street could have spotted the lapse in security and climbed *in*. Grace's heart skips a beat. She pulls the window shut. It closes with a clang, causing both of them to jump.

'Okay, honey. Hop back into bed.'

'Don't go. Please don't go. There's someone *out there*.'

'Shush. You're being silly.' Grace gives her daughter a hug and is dismayed to feel her small body quivering with fear. 'There's absolutely nothing to be afraid of, do you hear? There is nobody outside, not even that dratted cat … But I'll stay until you fall asleep.'

Lauren is satisfied with this. She climbs into bed and

curls up on her side. Grace tucks the duvet around her and strokes her hair.

What is she going to do with this child? Is it foolish to hope she'll outgrow the anxiety and develop into a confident young woman? What if these are the early signs of a lifelong debilitating condition? Is it time to see a GP or a psychologist? Why has she delayed? Is she as bad as Annabel, turning a blind eye to an obvious problem within her household?

If only money wasn't such a problem. Paediatric psychologists don't come cheap. Maybe Tom should stop being so damn nice and distribute more parking tickets; bringing in more revenue might make him eligible for promotion. Or maybe Grace should bite the bullet, compromise on her ideals about child-rearing, and return to the workforce sooner rather than later.

Lauren has fallen off to sleep, already snoring softly. Grace tiptoes back to her room. The nightmare comes rushing back as soon as her head hits the pillow. Tom and Katy writhing together on the grass. Logically, it should have been Tom and Annabel together in her subconscious. The two of them in cahoots, keeping secrets from her. No, she is being unfair and melodramatic. Annabel would have spoken instinctively, her prime concern protecting Daniel's reputation. Tom just did as he was asked. He is not obliged to tell his wife every single thing that happens on patrol.

Grace's mind has skipped elsewhere. Something's jarring, not adding up. The yearbook entry that Annabel received. What were her exact words when they spoke about it on the phone?

There was something in there that nobody knows. Some trouble we're having with Daniel.

Annabel lied, or else she simply forgot. Somebody *did* know about Daniel.

Tom knew.

24
ANNABEL

'Annabel, is that you?'

It's a man's voice. Annabel takes a few moments to process that she's being spoken to. She was lost in her thoughts, in her despair. The man is good-looking: light tan, longish brown-blond hair, green eyes from long ago.

'It's Zach,' he prompts. 'Zach Latham.'

Good grief. Zach Latham. *Here.* In the drug and alcohol centre.

Annabel blinks. Tries to compose herself. To pretend that everything is fine, like they're meeting at the supermarket, or on the street, or anywhere less confronting than this waiting room with its beige walls and shattered lives.

'Hello, Zach,' she manages. 'It's been a while.'

Jarrod and Zach were good friends at school but their friendship petered away within months of the HSC exams. Jarrod was launched into parenthood, a world with broken sleep and dizzying levels of responsibility. Zach started a degree in computer technology, and that was the last they'd heard of him … until Grace recently mentioned that he became a GP.

'Do you work here?' she asks, glancing around the waiting room, plastic chairs lining the perimeter, a handful of people – hard faces, missing teeth – slouched in the chairs. In the half-hour she's been sitting here – they obviously don't run to schedule – various doctors and other professionals have emerged, looked down at the file in their hand, and called a name. Her name hasn't been called. She's dreading it being called. What can she say to these people? What will they say to her?

Zach shakes his head. 'My wife works here, she's one of the supervising doctors.'

What about you? What are you doing here? Zach doesn't ask the question but it hangs between them.

Annabel decides to answer anyway. 'I'm here because of my son—' She loses it then, her voice breaking with tears. 'He's only sixteen.'

Zach sits down next to her. Puts a hand on her shoulder. Jerks his head in the direction of the treatment rooms. 'Is he inside?'

'No, he refused to come today. Insists he doesn't need help.' She digs the heels of her hands into her eyes. There's no point in crying. It's not going to fix anything.

'That's common. Being uncooperative, I mean. You're in the right place.' Zach stands up again. 'Look, I need to see Isabel quickly and then check on a patient who lives nearby. There's a café a few doors down. Wait for me when your appointment is finished ... Unless you're rushing off somewhere?'

It's midday. Annabel doesn't have to be anywhere until school pick-up at three.

'The café,' she agrees, her voice leaden.

Annabel is mildly curious about Zach's wife and wonders if she's the person she'll be seeing today. But it's a man who calls her name. He looks thin and malnourished, like he could be on drugs himself.

'My name's Patrick. I'm one of the counsellors here.'

She follows him to a small room that has similar décor to the waiting room: beige walls and cheap furniture. There's a lingering odour that makes her question the personal hygiene of whoever was here before her.

'Take a seat, Mrs Harris, and tell me why you're here today.'

She sits down, positioning herself on the edge of the seat. 'I'm here because of my son, Daniel ... He's only sixteen.'

The exact same words she said to Zach, and once again she has to fight the urge to cry. Patrick begins to ask questions, writing down her answers with a pen that has its cap chewed. Daniel's medical history, all the way back to his birth. His siblings and home life.

His grades and attitude to school. His friendships and social life. When this all started. How it has escalated in recent months. She talks and talks and talks, and Patrick writes and writes and writes. Then, when she has told him everything there is to tell, her self-control cracks and she starts crying in loud gulping sobs.

'I'm sorry. I'm sorry.' She is barely coherent.

Patrick slides a box of tissues across the table. 'Don't apologise. Take your time.'

She dabs her eyes, blows her nose and tries to pull herself together.

'I don't know what to do. I'm at a loss. My husband too. We've tried talking to Daniel, using reason and cold hard facts. We've tried being tough, punishing him, limiting his social activities. We've tried kindness and understanding, and – for a short while – turning a blind eye. We've tried everything, short of locking him up. You would think that getting beaten up would make him see sense, but there wasn't a shred of self-reflection at the hospital. How do we get through to him? How can we make him stop taking drugs and tearing our family apart?'

Patrick rests his elbows on the scratched surface of the desk. 'The truth is you can't make Daniel do any-thing. It sounds like he's not ready to give up. You can't force him, however hard that is to accept.'

'So what should we do? Sit and watch him ruin his life? Expect phone calls from the hospital or the police as a matter of course?'

'In these circumstances, we sometimes recommend harm minimisation.'

'What does *that* mean?'

'Reducing the harm Daniel can potentially do to himself. If he's intent on using drugs, then at least making it safer.'

'What's safe about using drugs?' she wails.

'Nothing. But he can improve his chances by taking little amounts at a time. Being careful not to mix with other drugs or alcohol. Using around people he trusts, rather than being on his own ...'

'You mean other drug addicts?'

Patrick's voice is measured and calm: the opposite of hers. 'Just because they're drug users doesn't mean they don't look out for each other.'

He slides back his chair and opens one of the desk drawers. He puts some pamphlets down in front of her. She reads one of the titles: *Safe Snorting. Safe Injecting. Safe Smoking.*

'I can't believe this,' she wails again. 'It's giving him advice on how to do it.'

Annabel leaves the small, airless room almost an hour after she entered it. The pamphlets are stuffed in her handbag – she can add them to her collection from the hospital – along with all the scrunched-up tissues she went through. The last thing she wants right now is a catch-up with Zach Latham. She wants to be alone, so she can cry and cry and cry, so she can empty herself of the disappointment, the helplessness and the severe frustration.

Vanity forces her into the bathroom before leaving the centre. Her face is blotchy, her eyes swollen. She looks old, broken, miserable. She finds some eyeliner and lipstick in her handbag and tries to do some repairs. Why bother? Surely, she's not trying to impress Zach Latham?

The café is busy and noisy. Her eyes skim from table to table, hoping that Zach gave up waiting. No such luck. He's over by the window, engrossed in his phone.

He stands up when he sees her approach, pulling out a seat for her. She doesn't remember him being so gallant. 'I was beginning to think you weren't coming.'

'Sorry. It was a long session … Not that we achieved much.'

'The first meeting is often like that. They need to know a detailed history before they can give any advice.'

'The young man being present would also be helpful.'

'Yes.' He smiles at her wry tone. 'So what's been happening? Is this problem a recent one?'

She relays everything for the second time in the day, adding more detail about the impact on Jarrod because he and Zach used to be close.

'Jarrod is devastated. He has a great relationship with Jemma and Mia and desperately wants the same with Daniel. But Daniel acts like he hates us both. He has no work ethic, no desire for responsibility, no respect for rules or boundaries … Jarrod can't begin to understand him …'

'It's a difficult age,' Zach says sympathetically. 'They

see their parents as impediments to their freedom. They want to live their own lives, do their own thing, and don't have the maturity to understand the value of rules.'

Annabel sips her coffee. It's surprisingly good. 'Do you see many teenagers in your practice?'

'Some. Even the ones in their early twenties seem incredibly young and error prone. They're still working things out … aren't we all?'

Annabel puts down her coffee cup too abruptly and it clatters against the saucer. 'So, your wife is a doctor too?'

Not a very subtle change of subject, but she is drained from talking, and thinking, about Daniel.

'A better doctor than I'll ever be.'

There is genuine pride and love in Zach's smile. Would Jarrod look like that at the mention of her name? And what expression would *she* adopt if someone asked her about Jarrod? She can't even think about Jarrod without grimacing.

'Where did you meet? How long have you been married?'

'We met overseas, in South Sudan. Have you heard of Doctors Without Borders?'

'Yes, of course. How interesting.'

He laughs. He has a nice laugh. Warm. Throaty. 'Interesting is one way of describing it. It's a great initiative – doctors coming together from all over the world to provide healthcare for those less fortunate. But it was incredibly dangerous – the war going on around us, buildings getting blown to smithereens, rampant cholera and malaria. We settled back in Australia when Isabel became pregnant. Sudan is no place for bringing up a child.'

'She's Australian, too?'

'Argentinian.'

'How many children now?'

'Carson is our only one ...' Zach pauses briefly. 'He has Down's syndrome.'

'Oh, I'm sorry.'

'Don't be. Carson is a joy to us. He surprises us every single day with his achievements. He competes in athletics and swimming, and he's the school captain at his special-needs school. It's all down to Izzy. She works in the drugs centre a few hours a day, and the rest of her time is spent supporting Carson. She's determined that his disability is not going to hold him back.'

Hearing about Carson makes Annabel even more furious with Daniel, who is squandering away his talents and health. Every conversation and every thought seem to lead back to her son.

'Are you going to the reunion?' she asks, draining the last of her coffee.

'Izzy persuaded me to. Are you?'

Annabel sighs. 'I really don't know. Neither Jarrod nor I want to leave Daniel unsupervised for any length of time.'

Zach shifts in his seat. 'What do you make of the

person who's been sending the emails? You got one, didn't you?'

'Yes … Did you?'

'They left a note under my windscreen wiper. I don't like the idea of them knowing where I park my car … Are you worried about it?'

She laughs humorously. 'Oh, Zach, my son is addicted to drugs. All I can think about and worry about is him. I've no brain space for the reunion, or the new yearbook, or whoever is behind this childish fucking prank.'

He glances out of the window. A group of high-school students are meandering along the footpath, sipping from drinks, jostling each other, laughing.

'Do you think about school much?' he asks quietly.

'No, not really. Do you?'

'Sometimes.' He turns his gaze back to her. She is startled by the intensity in his grey-green eyes. 'I think about Robbie. I often wonder what happened to him. I'm hoping he'll be at the reunion. I want to shake his hand and say sorry.'

25
KATY

Katy's breath is loud and ragged in her ears. Her legs lack their usual spring. She's finding this difficult. Can't seem to get into the zone. There is too much on her mind: end-of-year school reports; the upsetting year-book messages; last night's drunken phone call from Luke.

'I'm coming home,' he said, sounding bemused. 'Aaron talked me into it.'

She's thrilled. It'll be wonderful to see him – it's been almost three years. She fully expects that his RSVP will prompt a string of others. Luke is very influential like that, without even trying to be. She didn't mention that she'd been on the verge of cancelling the whole thing, or that Melissa Andrews, of all people, talked her around.

'I've been thinking about this,' Melissa said when

she phoned. 'Don't call it off, Katy. That's exactly what this person wants you to do. Hold tight. They'll either give up or reveal their hand.'

Grace's advice was of the same ilk. 'We don't know for sure if any law has been broken. Just a nasty prank, by a nasty person. I always tell my kids not to let nastiness succeed over niceness. But, Katy, you must do what you feel is right.'

Katy doesn't really know what is right. Dusk is closing in and, even though her body is protesting, she steps up the pace. Two more laps of the park before the twists and turns of Kurraba Road. She doesn't enjoy running in the park at this time of night. It's more or less deserted, with poor visibility where the grass melds into the bushland.

She breathes a sigh of relief as she completes the last lap. The streetlights have turned on, and there is traffic along Kurraba Road; she feels safer now. She has become much more alert to her surroundings and the potential for danger. She's also become more scrupulous about double-checking locks, and not holding the door open for anyone else on their way into the apartment block.

The route home is uphill from here. Katy slows down. It's a slog. Sweat drips from her forehead into her eyes. She flicks it away and forges forward. It's fully dark now, a cloudy night with neither stars nor moon.

Home. She's proud of herself. For having the self-discipline and grit to go for her run, despite being late home from school. For putting away ten kilometres when all she wanted to do was curl up on the couch.

She spends five minutes outside the apartment block, stretching. Her muscles are warm and pliant.

'Howdy, Katy.'

It's Jim, her next-door neighbour. The porch lights glare down on him.

She smiles. 'Hi, Jim. What're you up to?'

Jim is one of those red-haired men who're hard to put an age to, maybe because most men of his generation have gone grey a long time ago. His face is deeply weather-beaten and yet strangely youthful. He's always keen for a chat.

'Just had to duck out to the shops for some bread.' He frowns as he looks her up and down. 'Bit late at night to be out on your own.'

'I know.' She balances herself on one leg, using the wall as support. 'Just the way things happened tonight. But I'm pleased with myself for making the effort.'

'Good on ya, love. No more strange notes?'

Jim was the neighbour who came around the night she found the note on her hallway floor. *You need a boyfriend, Katy, and better security in your apartment block …* Just thinking about it makes her shudder. Jim didn't mind being called on to search the apartment. Quite the opposite, in fact.

'Nope,' she assures him. 'All's quiet.'

Katy has been trying not to give in to her fears, constantly reminding herself that trespassing or breaking-and-entering aren't the only possible scenarios. Someone could have asked another resident to deliver the note, perhaps one of the kids who live in the block. Likewise, someone could have used a series of intelligent guesses, rather than her browsing history, to figure out her plans regarding Luke's sperm. She's putting her faith in these other scenarios. How else can she keep coming home to her suddenly vulnerable apartment? How else can she fall asleep at night?

Jim ambles off and Katy does a final stretch of her ankles before going inside. Her flat is silent and lonely. It always has a desolate air when she comes home late.

She has a shower and dinner in record time. Then she settles in front of the television with her laptop. She has fallen behind with the yearbook and reunion preparations because she's been so busy at work. Time to send out another appeal for RSVPs and a last-chance for the yearbook updates.

From: admin@yearbook.com.au
Subject: Reunion menu

Hi everyone,

New venue has been booked and would love to know your thoughts on attached menu for finger food. The new yearbook isn't going as well. Come on, people. Aren't you interested in where everyone has ended up? Entries by end of week, please.

Thanks,

K

Katy spends the next few minutes working through the list of people she still hasn't made contact with. Only five names; she's slowly getting there. David Hooper is the only one she can remember clearly. An introverted boy who excelled at French and spent lunchtimes in the library, playing chess. Katy used to talk to him on occasion, but conversation wasn't his strong point and sooner or later she would give up.

Remnants of one such aborted conversation.

Katy enquiring, 'Why do you spend so much time in the library?'

David replying, 'Why do you want to know?'

Katy blushing violently. 'No reason.'

Another memory: David helping Robbie up from the ground, shepherding him towards the bathroom to get cleaned up, a job that used to be Nick's but Robbie's brother had graduated by then and Katy could no longer run to fetch him.

Katy gushing to David, 'Thank you so much for helping.'

A rebuking stare. 'Just give us some space, okay?'

She's interested to know what became of David. Whether that brusqueness softened over time. Whether his social skills improved. Where he found his niche in the world. But nobody seems to have the first idea where David is today. Nobody knows anything about his family either. How can someone disappear without a trace? Did the family move overseas? Relocate to some country town that's off the grid? Is David one of those rare people who doesn't use Facebook or social media? Is he alive and well and oblivious to the fact that she's trying to track him down, or has he – like poor Brigette Saunders – succumbed to some illness or tragic accident and had his life cut short?

Katy is mulling this over when – with uncanny timing – a new message pops up in her inbox. It's from Mike, Brigette's husband.

Great to hear you've found another venue. I'm looking forward to meeting everyone. I'll bring lots of photos of Brigette and Toby.

There's no need to answer, but Katy does so anyway. It's nice to have someone to talk to, even if it's only via email.

I wish everyone was as enthusiastic as you! Still waiting on RSVPs. Don't know what to do about the yearbook. People are still getting nasty messages and the whole thing seems like a bad idea now.

Katy hits send and waits for his reply. She pictures him sitting at his desk, or maybe stretched out on the couch, like she is. Lonely. Wanting to talk to someone. Even a virtual stranger.

She has to wait only a few moments for his response.

Did I mention that I work in security? I might be able to figure out who's behind this. My number is below if you want to talk.

Does she want to talk?

She doesn't even know him.

She knows him better than the men on those dating sites that Nina makes her fish through.

What is the harm in calling him and having an amicable discussion about the yearbook and whatever else might come up in conversation?

Come on, Katy. This isn't really about the yearbook or the fact that he works in security. This is a man who's obviously lonely and vulnerable after the death of his wife. Stay clear.

What would Nina say?

Nina would roll her eyes and declare that Mike would have to be an improvement on William's dull devotion and Rickie's drunken booty call.

What would Luke say?

Luke isn't risk averse, far from it, but at the same time he's savvy and has a sixth sense when it comes to trouble. Is this the very reason why he's refusing to discuss the idea of having a baby together? Does he see the arrangement as being nothing but trouble? Even last night, when he was drunk and excited about coming home for the reunion, he skilfully diverted Katy every time she got close to raising the subject.

Katy makes up her mind and picks up her phone.

'Hi, Mike. This is Katy.'

'Hello, Katy.' His voice is warm, deep and instantly attractive. 'I'm so glad you called.'

26
ROBBIE

Robbie forces himself through the gate and up the mottled pathway. The lawn needs mowing, and he wonders if his father is still up to the job. Robbie and Nick used to fight over whose turn it was. The mower was temperamental to start, black smoke billowing in their faces when it eventually got going. He assumes his father bought a new one, or maybe he gets someone in to do the lawn for him. The thought of his father being afforded this small luxury – even though the current state of the grass disproves it – pleases Robbie.

'Hasn't changed a bit, has it?' Celia says.

Her arm is hooked through his. If it wasn't for her grip and determined stride towards the house, he doubts he could go through with it. Every fibre of his being wants to turn and run. The front door – shabby and in need of a paint – appears in front of him. Celia turns the handle, and suddenly they're ensnared in the hallway. Robbie stops dead. Celia pushes him forward.

'It's all right. There's nothing to be afraid of here.'

A glance into the front room: same floral carpet, new couch and curtains. His parents' bedroom is on the opposite side, door closed. His mother and father are waiting in the kitchen. Once again, Robbie is struck by how old they are. How white – both their hair and their skin – and frail. Mum steps forward, as though to hug him. He flinches. She looks hurt and fills the kettle instead. Dad is sitting at the table, fingers laced, as though bracing himself for bad news.

'We're here.' Celia states the obvious before pushing him towards the rear extension. 'Come on, Robbie. Keep going. We'll come back for tea when the tour is over.'

She was insistent about doing this. About facing his demons, which are here, within the walls of this tired suburban house. And at the school, of course. But the school is gone now, demolished. There's satisfaction in that image: a wrecking ball smashing through those grim brown-brick walls. Flattening the hall, the science labs, the changing rooms, and filling the maze of corridors with rubble. It was the corridors that were the worst. Too narrow to pass by unnoticed. No escaping without turning back the way you came and hearing their mockery behind you.

Celia opens the door to his bedroom and memories

slap him in the face. He recoils. Makes a sound that's not unlike a child's cry.

She steadies him. 'Come on, you've got to do this. It's not as bad as you think.'

He looks around with slitted eyes. Same posters on the wall. Parallel single beds, neatly made, as though waiting for Nick and him to return. Robbie almost laughs at the thought of the two of them, grown men, being restored to those beds.

Celia whips open the wardrobe doors. 'Some of your clothes are still here.' She looks him up and down. 'They might even fit you!'

Robbie stares into the gloom. His school uniforms, a couple of shirts that were trendy at the time, some jackets. He can actually smell his teenage self from the clothes, but that can't be possible, not after all this time. Now he feels like he might faint. He pushes past Celia, sits down heavily on the bed. The room is swimming. The posters – Coldplay, Red Hot Chili Peppers, Foo Fighters – whirring round and round, mocking him.

Celia is crouched down in front of him. 'Are you okay?'

'No.' He's angry with her. For bringing him here. 'Can you open the window at least?'

She pulls back the net curtains and a disproportionate amount of light pours in. The window slides upwards, and suddenly there is air, scented with gardenias from the garden.

'Can you leave me alone for a while?'

'Sure.' She squeezes his shoulder as she leaves. His sister is a good, kind person. He doesn't deserve her. Doesn't deserve his parents either, who're waiting for him with mugs of tea and a plate of 'good' biscuits that are usually reserved for visitors. That's what he is now: a visitor. Or a ghost. They're all scared he'll disappear again.

Celia said coming here would be closure. 'You need to see there's nothing to be afraid of. What happened was more about your state of mind than the actual place.'

She fancies herself as a psychologist. She's wrong, though. Doesn't know what the fuck she's talking about. It *is* the place. Just being here weakens him. His shame is almost part of the furnishings.

Pull yourself together. Pull yourself together, you weak fuck.

He opens the top drawer of the bedside cabinet. Stray pens and paperclips. His student ID. A birthday card. *Dear Robbie, Hope you have a wonderful day. Xx Katy*

She was the only one who remembered, other than his family. Every year she'd decorate his locker and leave a card. She did it because she had a kind heart, not because she actually cared. She had no idea how much it meant to him, her kindness. How it kept him going.

He opens the bottom drawer, which is deeper and filled with old exercise books. It smells of school: a mix of lead, sweat and boredom. He flicks through an

221

English book. Sees his teenage handwriting, reads some of it and thinks it's decent: at least he was able to string sentences together and use some fancy words. There are drawings on the inside cover, as he knew there'd be. Elaborate depictions of daggers, pistols and nooses. He poured a lot of detail and time into those drawings. It was all he could think about: how to end it.

He goes back to the wardrobe. Slides his hand along the top shelf. His fingers come away with a thick layer of dust. He tries again, going on his tiptoes, reaching back further. His heart stops. It's gone. How can that be?

His eyes are drawn to the bookshelf, over by the window. There it is, its spine tattered and readily identifiable, propped up by smaller, thicker volumes. His mother must have put it there, or maybe Nick or one of the kids when they've come to stay. Robbie pulls it out.

You don't need to do this. You don't need to torture yourself.

But he still does it. Sits on the floor with it cradled in his arms. Dares to read the front cover: *Yearbook of Macquarie High, Class of 2000*. Forces himself to scrutinise the photo beneath, taken outside the gym, everyone's arms in the air: school's out.

His heart is beating again, erratically, painfully. The book opens on Zach Latham's page, and Robbie's handwriting – deeper and better formed than the writing in his exercise book – fills the right-hand margin.

Fucking bastard. Hope bad things happen to you and you have a miserable life. Fucking bastard.

Stop, he implores himself. *Stop. This isn't doing you any good.*

He can't stop. It's like scratching a scab. He's bleeding but he has to keep gouging.

Grace's page. Cute ponytail and smile. More notes etched in the margin. *Vacuous bitch. No thoughts of your own. You're just as bad as them.*

Melissa. Luke. Annabel. Faces plump with youth and self-confidence. *So, you think I'm disgusting, do you? Well, I think the same about you and worse!*

Katy's page is the only departure. A love-heart with an arrow through its centre. *You'll never know how much you mean to me.*

Finally, Jarrod's page, near the front. Sports captain. Grinning at the camera. Holding up a large trophy, probably for rugby or cricket. The same phrase engraved a hundred times over, on the margins, amid spaces in the text, even across the photograph. *Leave me alone. Leave me alone. Leave me alone. Leave me alone...*

Oh God. Oh God.

Robbie wants to hide. He can't go back out there and face his parents. Doesn't matter how much it means to them. He can't do it. He wants to – *needs to* – hide.

He crawls inside the wardrobe, shuts the door. Blackness. Nothingness. Just the sound of his own sobs.

27
GRACE

Grace is sick to her stomach. She recognises this feeling from long ago. It's how she felt when she found out an ex-boyfriend had been openly cheating on her. All the evidence was there, right in front of her nose, but she was the last to know.

Melissa had pulled her aside in the end. 'Look, I know we aren't friends any more, but I think you deserve to know the truth. He's been cheating on you, Grace. You need to dump him. Pronto.'

Grace can't remember if she thanked Melissa. All she can remember is being utterly mortified, and feeling let down by Annabel because *she* should have been the one pulling her aside.

Now those same feelings: a nauseating suspicion in the pit of her belly, the vague threat of complete mortification.

Tom knew about Daniel all along. Is it possible he sent that email to Annabel to force her to take action? And because he'd sent Annabel an email, did he feel compelled to send Grace one too, in order not to arouse suspicion? But what about the others? Why target Zach, Melissa, Luke and Katy? People he hasn't even met? And why bother to tie it in with the yearbook? If he had something to say to Annabel, surely he could have said it face to face?

Grace thinks about her own email. The detail about the miscarriage. Her fears about Lauren. The photo that was temporarily missing from the fridge. The same photo that Tom 'found' and returned to its rightful place. Her head is spinning. She has barely slept these last few nights. The idea has taken hold and now she can't stop thinking about it. She can hardly look her husband in the eye, flinches every time he comes close to touching her. One minute she's almost certain that he's responsible, the next minute she's just as certain he's not. The problem is that deep down she knows it's not beyond the realm of possibility. Tom's always had a vigilante side, an ingrained righteousness and, at times, intolerance. He might be lenient with parking tickets and other small misdemeanours, but he has a completely different attitude to what he regards as reckless behaviour. Drug users, in particular, have always infuriated him.

An old conversation plays back in her head.

'Throwing away all the privileges they've been given.

No respect for themselves, their families or society. Sucking up police and medical resources. It's a crime.'

'They can't help it, Tom.'

'It's self-inflicted. A mockery of all the poor kids who don't have a home or good health. It drives me insane.'

There's no doubt he would have been furious to find Daniel in the park smoking weed. But was he infuriated enough to send that email? Did Annabel's hush-hush approach prompt him to go to such extremes?

'Mum, I need help.' It's Tahlia. She's sitting at the kitchen table, chewing the top of her pen. Her teacher has been piling on homework, in an attempt to prepare the class for high school next year. Poppy is sitting opposite, industriously colouring in one of her own creations. 'It's algebra. It's so *hard*.'

Grace's brain is muddled enough as it is. She sighs and sits down next to her oldest. Pulls across the workbook so she can read the question. Suddenly, she can see herself doing this alone: helping with homework and school projects, ferrying the children to parties and sport, putting them to bed at night. She can actually *see* herself as a single parent. Now she's panicking. Jumping to all sorts of crazy conclusions.

'Look, all you have to do is move this figure over to the opposite side of the equation. Do you know what happens when you move it across?'

'It becomes negative.'

'Exactly.'

Grace leaves Tahlia to it and goes to check on Lauren.

The bedroom door is closed. She knocks and sticks her head inside.

'What're you up to in here?'

'Reading my book. We had library today.'

What would happen to Lauren if she and Tom were to split up? Lauren adores her father. She trusts him, even more than she trusts Grace. He's the preferred parent when she's scared or upset. He's the one who can talk her around, calm her down. Trust is such a big thing for Lauren; it would be heartbreaking to see it broken.

Next Grace checks on Billy, who's playing Lego in the playroom-cum-study. Billy is the most like Tom. Same physique: shortish, stocky, that proud tilt to his head. How would it feel with Tom gone and still seeing his image in her youngest child? Would some of the children eventually choose to live with their father? She must stop catastrophising like this. There is no proof. All she has is a niggle. And the knowledge that if Tom is indeed responsible, she'll never be able to feel the same way about him. Their marriage will be over.

Grace sits down at the home computer while Billy constructs his Lego uncomfortably close to her feet. She opens her inbox, deletes some junk mail, then sorts the messages by sender. There are half a dozen messages from Katy, most of which are addressed to the entire year group, with all the individual email addresses plain to see.

Did she leave her inbox open on the computer? Would it have been that easy for Tom? It's not as if she's security conscious; she's never had anything to hide from her husband or he from her. Tom's email account is linked to hers. She switches accounts and it asks for a password. She types *Grace123*, which has been Tom's password for as long as she can remember. *Password incorrect.*

She hears the front door open and shut again.

'I'm home,' her husband calls out cheerily.

Billy drops the Lego and sprints to greet his father. Lauren will have dropped her book and rushed to meet him too. Tahlia and Poppy are getting too old for the rock-star reception, but they'll happily succumb to Tom's bear hugs when he eventually makes it to the kitchen.

Grace closes down the screen. Stands up slowly. Composes herself.

How can she face him?

Stop. You're acting crazy. You know this man. He doesn't have a bad bone in his body.

Except when it comes to being righteous. At times, zealously so.

She walks into the kitchen, smiling brightly. She plans her route so that she's giving him a wide berth. There's no opportunity for him to pull her close for a kiss or hug.

'I haven't even started dinner. There's time for a shower, if you want.'

'Is that a polite way of telling me I'm sweaty?'

She tries to return his grin. Her face hurts from the effort.

He heads towards the bedroom, whistling. Lauren returns to her book and Billy to his Lego. Tahlia is doggedly working through the algebra: her persistence will get her far in high school. Poppy is bent over her colouring, frowning with concentration. Tom's keys and phone are where he left them on the kitchen counter. Is there enough time? She picks up his phone, shielding it from Tahlia and Poppy's line of sight. The screen is still open, as are his emails. She scrolls down. Nothing untoward. She goes to his sent messages. Nothing there either. Of course, there wouldn't be. The fake yearbook entries were sent from a different email account. She checks his internet history: breaking news; sports results; an online menu for a restaurant. Then she checks his text messages. Mostly to work colleagues and herself. Squeaky clean.

She puts the phone back down where she found it and tries to gather her wits. Dinner. What's on tonight's menu?

She's half-heartedly chopping vegetables when Tom reappears. Hair glistening. Smelling of aftershave. Wearing a favourite old T-shirt. Her heart constricts. She's not sure if it's from love or grief.

'Anything I can do to help?' he asks, nodding towards the chopping board.

He is a good man. She knows this in her heart. *She*

chose a good man; she has reminded herself of this fact every day since they've been together.

'Can you have a look over Tahlia's algebra?'

Why doesn't she ask him outright? *Did you send that email to Annabel? And then to me and all the others so it wouldn't be obvious?*

She can't. She can't ask the question. This is her family at stake. Everything she holds dear. She has been smug. About her cosy little family and perfect husband. Now it could all implode. She would never think of him in the same way again. Never.

Tom was there, right next to her on the couch, the night Katy phoned, fresh with panic and terror. But he'd been out earlier in the evening, on his usual patrol, and Katy said she couldn't be sure when the note had been slipped under her door.

There's no proof. None whatsoever. Only a horrible niggle. The very same niggle she had about that scumbag ex-boyfriend and chose to ignore.

28
ANNABEL

Annabel is in Daniel's room when there's a loud knock on the front door. She has been checking his drawers and other potential hiding places. She doesn't exactly know what she's looking for: syringes, suspicious-looking tablets or maybe another bong? She can't find anything. She suspects it's because he's become better at hiding the evidence.

She hurries down the stairs and whips open the door, expecting it to be a parcel delivery or perhaps a neighbour. Instead she finds two police officers standing on her doorstep.

'Mrs Harris?'

Oh God, oh God, oh God. Is it Daniel? She can't bring herself to ask. She's not brave enough. He *should* be at school – it's not yet lunchtime – but that's no guarantee of anything these days. One of the officers is female and the other male. They don't look much older than Jemma.

'Mrs Harris?' the female checks again.

'Yes. Please tell me what's happened.' Resignation underscores the panic in her voice.

'I'm Constable Jaegar and this is Constable Walsh … It's about your husband.'

Annabel is momentarily stunned. She was so sure it was Daniel. Now her brain is scrambling, struggling to change direction. Jarrod? How can it be Jarrod? Her mouth is open but no words are coming out. Has Jarrod been in an accident in the van? Or had an electric shock from some dodgy wiring? It wouldn't be the first time.

'Your husband has been in an altercation.' The constable's voice is both soft and grave. 'He's been taken to Northern Beaches Hospital. He's in a serious condition.'

Serious condition: does that mean his life is at risk? No, they would say 'critical condition' if that was the case, wouldn't they? But what does 'serious' actually mean? Does he have broken bones? Is he conscious? And what does the police officer mean by an 'altercation'? Has Jarrod hit someone, been in a fight?

Annabel can't think straight. She has so many questions to ask and yet all that comes out of her mouth is, 'Oh my God.'

Think. *Think.* The hospital. She must go there. Handbag and car keys.

'We can drive you to the hospital, Mrs Harris,' the female offers gently. 'You've had a nasty shock.'

It's tempting. But how will she get back in time for school pick-up if she doesn't have the car? After school there's ballet, and after that music lessons. Then it hits her. Jarrod's in a serious condition. There will be no school pick-up or music or ballet lessons today.

'Thank you,' she says, her voice cracking. 'I just need a minute to get my stuff.'

She runs into the rear of the house, looks around wildly, before spotting her handbag on the floor. She picks it up, flies out to the hall, only to remember that the back door needs locking. Then realises she has no shoes on. And that her phone is upstairs in Daniel's room. With each delay, she becomes more and more frantic.

Finally, she's in the back of the police car and they're on the way. She takes deep breaths and tries to clear her head. She texts one of the school mums to see if she can help with Mia after school. Then she texts Daniel to let him know the house will be empty when he gets home. It's a struggle to find the right words. She doesn't want to unduly alarm him. He's erratic enough as it is.

Dad is in hospital. I am on my way there now. Try not to worry. I'll text you when I have news.

Now Jemma. Her timetable is patchy; there's a good chance she'll be able to answer her phone. Annabel visualises her oldest daughter, walking through the university campus, wearing one of those long flowy skirts she favours. Jemma doesn't answer and Annabel resorts to another text, with slightly more detail than the one to Daniel.

Jarrod's parents are next on the list. His father, Bernard, is distraught and has a thousand questions she can't answer. Was it an argument about money owing for a job? Has someone been charged by the police?

Annabel is still talking to Bernard when they pull up outside the hospital.

'Look, we're here now … I'll phone you back when I find out what's going on.'

Accident and Emergency has a handful of waiting people and a sleepy air. Maybe this is the aftermath of a busy period, a lull before everything becomes hectic again.

'You'll need to report to the triage desk,' the female police officer says. Her colleague has stayed in the car. 'We'll be back in touch when Jarrod is able to talk and tell us what happened.'

She departs before Annabel has the chance to thank her for her kindness.

Annabel is required to fill in some paperwork at the desk. Her handwriting is all over the place. Her trembling fingers struggle to extract her Medicare and health insurance cards from her wallet. Her phone rings as the triage nurse takes her through to the treatment rooms.

'We discourage the use of phones in this part of the hospital,' the nurse says kindly.

'Sorry,' she mumbles, turning the phone off. 'It's my daughter. She'll be beside herself.'

'Things like this are hard on the kids,' the nurse concurs.

Another image of Jemma, her face creased with worry, tears threatening her clear grey eyes. Then Daniel, vulnerability breaking through his façade of loathing. Finally, Mia. Sitting dreamily in class, doodling in her book instead of listening to the teacher. Sweet Mia. Daddy's girl. She'll be hit the hardest.

The nurse has stopped at one of the curtained cubicles. There's a gap for them to walk through and Annabel sees another nurse bending over the patient in the bed, shielding him from view.

'This is Annabel, Jarrod's wife,' the triage nurse announces to her colleague. Then she squeezes Annabel's shoulder. 'Good luck.'

Annabel will never forget that first view of her husband. The dark swollen eyelids. The puffed-up lips, leading her to suspect that he has lost some teeth. The left side of his head, where the hair is matted with blood. But the worst thing by far is his utter lack of response. He does not lift or turn his head on her arrival. He does not smile or grimace or do anything that Jarrod would normally do by way of greeting. He could be dead.

'Oh my God.' Annabel can feel her legs going from under her. 'Oh my God. What have they done to you?'

The A&E nurse catches her and guides her to the visitor's seat. 'Here, take the weight off your feet. Deep breaths now. Deep breaths. That's it, love …' She has a northern English accent and a capable air. 'It's not a pretty sight, is it? I bet you've seen him look a lot better than this.'

The deep breathing works. Annabel comes back to herself. The nurse's face is close to her own. Concerned. Kind.

'Was he unconscious when he came in?'

She nods. 'There's some swelling on the brain that we're concerned about.'

Swelling on the brain. What does that actually mean? What's the bottom line here? How is she to summarise this for Jemma, Daniel, Mia, Jarrod's parents and everyone else?

'Is my husband going to be okay? Is he going to wake up? Will he be *the same* when he wakes up?'

'His vital signs are positive. Heart rate, pulse, blood pressure, all good … He has some fractures on his face and the left eye socket, but it's mainly the swelling we're worried about. A small bleed showed up on the MRI. We're moving him to ICU shortly and he'll be monitored very carefully. Dr Chan will come and see you. He'll be able to tell you more than me.'

Annabel takes another despairing look at her husband, his bloody distorted face, his lifeless form under the blankets, the tubes and various machines he has been connected to. The nurse goes back to what she was doing when Annabel came in. Rolling back his eyelids. Shining a torch into his eyes. Checking his pupils? Annabel scrapes her seat closer. Leans across to take his limp hand in hers. There's blood creased on the skin of his hand and underneath his fingernails. She can only assume it's his own blood, not someone else's.

'Who did this to you?' she whispers. 'Who would do such a terrible thing?'

29
MELISSA

'What have you done? Are you *insane*?' Henry is furious. Melissa's husband is usually mild-mannered to a fault. 'What about your long hours? Who's going to take care of it?'

The puppy, the cause of Henry's consternation, has wiggled out of her arms and is bounding around the rug. Floppy ears, tan-coloured fluffy coat, brown human-like eyes. From the corner of his vision, he catches sight of the tip of his tail, and barks. Melissa laughs. He lunges, trying to catch it, resulting in circles of dizzying speed. It's hilarious and adorable but Henry is too busy ranting to notice.

'It will ruin the apartment. Chew everything it can get its teeth into. Pee on your carpet.'

The puppy has had a few 'accidents' since she

brought him home yesterday. On the tiles, luckily, and easy enough to clean up.

'Why didn't you consult me?' Henry whines.

Finally, she deigns to answer him. 'You don't even live here. Why on earth would I consult *you*?'

He is visibly hurt and she feels guilty. The idea of the puppy was to bring joy and some welcome unpredictability, not to be the cause of more arguments.

She tries to explain further. 'Look, Cassie's friend is a breeder. Someone was due to buy PJ.' This is what she decided to name the dog after making a long list of potential names and trying them out as the puppy darted around her feet last night. 'They'd paid a deposit, but there was an illness in the family and they couldn't take him after all.'

'Buy why should *you* need to be involved? Doesn't the breeder have a waiting list?'

'Because Cassie thought I needed a dog.'

'How is Cassie such an expert on what you need? Last time I checked, she was in human resources, not psychology.'

It's tempting to answer his sarcasm with more of her own. She tries honesty instead. 'Cassie's my friend, she knows how much I've been struggling … I need something to change, Henry. And this is definitely outside my comfort zone.'

'You're not even a dog person,' he points out.

True. Melissa has never been one to seek out dogs for cuddles. But there has been a loneliness in her life, an emptiness, and something living and breathing – and furry – seemed like a way to fill it. Definitely better than re-establishing a relationship with Jarrod Harris. Their messages have progressed from brief and jokey to lengthy and more serious. Jarrod has indicated that things are tough at home. Melissa admitted that she and Henry are at a crossroads. She hasn't answered Jarrod's last message, a text sent two days ago: *Want to meet up for a drink?*

'Jesus Christ, he's peeing on your floor.'

This is also true, Melissa establishes as she follows Henry's horrified gaze.

'It's no big deal. I just lift him up when he does that and take him outside to the loo.'

Melissa scoops up the dog, holding him in front of her so she doesn't get caught by the wee.

'You're leaving a trail,' Henry points out unhelpfully.

'Clean it up, then.'

Out on the balcony, Melissa deposits PJ on the 'loo' (a piece of synthetic grass on top of a waste container) even though they both know there is nothing left to come out. He gives her hand a lick. She gives his head a scratch.

'Henry is not normally so cranky,' she says. 'You need to give him time.'

Henry, when they go back inside, is making a show of cleaning up, using paper towel, disinfectant and lots of muttered swear words. Melissa smiles. There is something very normal about the scene. It has to be said that having her husband irritated and put out is so much better than having him contained and distant.

'Morning, Samantha ...' Melissa has been up for hours when she calls her personal assistant. PJ woke her at 5 a.m. – an improvement on yesterday morning – crying to get out of his crate. She took him straight outside to the loo, and he actually did a wee; she felt inordinately proud of him. Then she played with him, fed him and cleaned the crate before putting him back inside for another nap.

'How's PJ doing?' Samantha coos on the other end of the line.

'Oh, he's wonderful. He did a wee in the pet loo this morning.' Melissa cannot believe she just said that.

'What a clever boy ... When are you going to send photos?'

'I have hundreds already but most are out of focus. Trying to keep him still is harder than getting Pharma Direct to sign on the dotted line.' Pharma Direct is one of her most difficult clients, which brings her back to the reason for her call. 'Look, I'm going to work from home again today. He's so tiny, I just can't leave him alone all day.'

It's a dog, not a child, but who would have thought it would be so hard to leave him? If only her working day wasn't so unforgivingly long. If only the office was closer, and she could duck home for playtime and toilet breaks.

Melissa works solidly for the next few hours. Her doorbell buzzes in the early afternoon. She checks the video screen, which is part of the security system, and is surprised to see a group of schoolgirls gathered outside the main door of the building.

'Can I help you?' she enquires into the intercom.

One of them steps forward. Tucks her hair awkwardly behind one ear. Melissa realises it's Tessa, Henry's daughter.

'Err … I was wondering if I could see the puppy.'

Melissa buzzes them in. She can't remember the last time Tessa was here. Not since the early days with Henry, before they decided to get married and the battle lines were drawn. The same applies for Christopher, her brother.

Tessa and her friends tumble through the door, their hair in ponytails, their faces soft and unknowingly gorgeous. Melissa is sharply reminded of her own school years.

'Sorry,' Tessa says breathlessly. 'I wanted to see the puppy, and then everyone else invited themselves along. We have a free period … Oh my God. *Look at him*. He is *so cute*. Can I hold him?'

'Sure.' Melissa hands over the squirming ball of fur.

PJ is passed from arm to arm and clucked over like a newborn baby. With a strange out-of-body feeling – maybe getting up at the crack of dawn is taking its toll – Melissa puts some chocolate-chip cookies on a plate. She recently read something about food being a sure-fire way to impress teenagers. She suspects it's not that simple.

The girls devour the biscuits and Melissa puts out some more. In the meantime, PJ manages to escape their arms, jumping down and launching into his party trick: a spot of tail chasing before running around the place at top speed.

'Oh look, he has the zooms,' says one the girls.

Round and round he goes. Up on the couch. Vaulting over the back. Skidding round the kitchen island. The girls are laughing hysterically and half-heartedly trying to catch him. It seems that pets work just as well as food when it comes to dismantling teenage cynicism.

'Tessa,' Melissa says quietly amid all the shrieking and laughing.

'What?' Ah, there's the suspicion and negativity she knows of old.

'I need someone to check on PJ during the day, while I'm at work.'

Tessa's face is deadpan. She doesn't give much away. She should think about a career in law.

'I'm willing to pay,' Melissa adds, aiming to sound matter-of-fact rather than needy.

The school is within walking distance. Tessa is a senior student and allowed to leave the premises at lunchtime and during free periods.

'How much?'

'Fifteen dollars a visit ... That's seventy-five a week.'

Tessa's eyes – her lashes spiky with mascara that's

surely against school rules? – narrow as she weighs it up. It's easy money and if it were anyone else making the offer, they both know she would snap it up. Melissa is left with the sense that she's shown her hand too soon. She should have waited. Her intuition, which is perfect when dealing with difficult clients, has consistently let her down when it comes to Henry's children.

'Okay,' Tessa says slowly. 'But only if my friends can come too.'

'Of course,' Melissa agrees, struggling to disguise how pleased she is. 'That goes without saying.'

Melissa works for another few hours after the girls leave. Then she attempts another photo shoot.

'Good boy ... Now look this way.'

PJ looks everywhere but the camera. Nevertheless, she proudly sends the blurry photos to Samantha, Cassie and Henry.

After dinner, she watches TV with PJ's warm body curled up in her lap. She's bemused that she already loves this puppy so completely and uncomplicatedly. It's starting to get dark outside. She moves him to the rug and goes around the apartment, pulling shut the blinds, something she was never pedantic about before. She hasn't been able to shake the feeling that someone has been watching her apartment, cataloguing Henry's visits, connecting the dots of her private life.

'How are you at being a guard dog?' she asks as she carries PJ to his crate.

Pretty useless, going by his enthusiastic response to today's visitors. But for some reason, his very presence makes her feel considerably less alone and vulnerable.

'Night night,' she says, giving him one last cuddle.

Time for bed for Melissa too. It has been an extremely long day. Tomorrow will be another early start. But there is one more thing to do, to close out. She owes Jarrod an answer to his question.

Want to meet up for a drink?

What to say? How to say it? She scrolls through the photos she took earlier, selects a particularly cute one and forwards it to him.

Sorry I haven't been in touch. This is the reason why. His name is PJ.

He has his answer from the delay in her response, as well as the blatant change of subject. It's a no. It has to be a no. They're both married, and probably incapable of being platonic with each other.

Satisfied, she removes her jewellery and clothes. She goes for a shower, squeezing her eyes shut under the gushing water, forcing herself to look forward, not back.

Her phone screen is blank when she returns to the bedroom. No response. This is good, this is what she wants.

It's over. Extinguished. They've both heeded the warning signs: dangerous territory, keep back.

30
ZACH

Zach's on the late shift. This means he gets the feverish babies who can't fall asleep, the ailments that have suddenly got worse with the onset of dark, and the jaded working population who have to wait until after hours for a doctor's appointment.

He picks up the phone and punches in Sandy's extension. 'I'd like a second opinion on something, if you can manage the time.'

Sandy can't manage the time. It's evident from her reluctant tone and the queues in the waiting room. 'Give me a few minutes.'

Zach's patient is a man in his thirties who has been feeling 'under the weather' for a few days. 'Hey, mate, should I be worried about something?'

'Your symptoms are a little inconsistent. Sandy has

more clinical experience than me … it's worth her having a look.'

The man has dark skin, which is not helping in terms of identifying the rash across his torso.

'Are the lights bothering you?' Zach asks for the second time.

The man squints at the downlights inset in the ceiling. 'Nope.'

'Do you feel confused?'

'No more than normal, mate.'

They both laugh.

'Sleepy? Nauseous?'

'Not specifically … Just unwell.'

If it wasn't for the rash, Zach would be writing him a medical certificate and recommending that he spend the next few days in bed, shaking off the virus.

Sandy comes in ten minutes later, stethoscope draped around her neck. Her eyes are as weary as his own.

Zach gives her the run-down. 'Patient has been feeling unwell since Wednesday. Temperature 40.8, stiff neck, bad headache, and this rash … But no photophobia, confusion or drowsiness.'

Sandy presses her fingers against the rash, and then a glass, which is exactly the process Zach followed. The rash does not appear to fade with the pressure.

'I don't like this rash. Even though the other symptoms all appear to be within the range of a normal virus.'

'That's what's making me hesitate, too.'

'No point in hesitating if the question is there.'

'Yes, agreed … Thank you.'

Zach shoots Sandy an appreciative smile as she slips out of the room. He doesn't know why he's second-guessing himself tonight.

He turns his attention back to his patient. 'I'm going to organise an ambulance. Meningitis can be a very serious illness and we—'

'Meningitis? Fucking hell! Are you serious?'

Zach summons a tone of calm authority, the best anti-dote for panic. 'This is precautionary because of your inconsistent symptoms. Let me make the call, and then we'll inform your family—'

'The wife's at home putting the kids to bed. She thinks I have a bad case of man flu.'

It's after 10 p.m. when Zach finishes up, an hour behind schedule. He hasn't called Izzy. She's a doctor herself, she knows what can happen. Gloria and Sandy have already left and it's Zach's job to lock up. Unplug the sterilisers, instrument dryers and the television in reception. Lock all the windows and doors. Set the security system. Everything seems to take longer than it usually does.

The surgery has half a dozen car spaces at the rear that the doctors don't reserve: they're all fit, healthy and perfectly capable of a short walk, unlike many of their patients. Zach always enjoys the walk, finds it rejuvenating, especially tonight as he is out of sorts for some reason.

He texts Izzy as he walks.

On my way.

He can see her in his mind, pillows propped behind her back as she reads and yawns, reads and yawns. She's an early-to-bed and early-riser type, but she tries to wait up until he comes in. It's one of her mainstays – being there to greet him, no matter how sleepily – and he loves her for the sentiment.

Zach unlocks his car as soon as it comes into sight. He steps on to the road, waits for a car to pass. He's inside the vehicle, the engine running, before he notices the paper wedged under the wiper. And then he knows. He knows this – the prospect of a follow-up note – has been the cause of his disquiet. He knows this time he will have to tell Izzy the truth.

He sits back inside the car. Takes a shaky breath. Unfolds the paper.

For the last twenty years, I've thought of nothing else but killing you. I've fantasised about circling your throat with my hands. Blocking the air to your windpipe. Seeing you gasp for words. I've fantasised about plunging a knife into your skin. Blood spurting like a fountain. I've seen myself shoot you, heard the bang and smelt gunpowder in the air. I've seen myself push you in front of a bus, an articulated truck, a train, anything that would obliterate you from this world.

Bottom line is that you don't deserve to live. And she deserves someone much better than you.

Are you going to tell her what a scumbag you are, or will I?

Jesus Christ. Zach looks around wildly. Is the person who left this note lurking somewhere, watching his reaction? He presses the central-lock button of the car, then swings around to make sure there is no one in the back seat. Jesus Christ. His heart is thumping, hands shaking so much they're hopping off the steering wheel. Is he okay to drive?

Who is doing this? This is serious. All pretence of joking is gone.

It's Robbie. It has to be Robbie. Who else could hate him this much?

31
KATY

Katy is the first to arrive at the tapas bar where she and Mike agreed to meet. It's a small place and immediately obvious that her date – although she shouldn't really be using that term – isn't here. She sits down at one of the tables, and a waiter who reminds her of Luke – same height and build – takes her drinks order.

It doesn't matter if he stands me up, she tells herself. *I've nothing to lose.*

She has been stood up more times than she cares to remember. Nowadays she has a policy of waiting for no longer than twenty minutes. Time enough to allow for transport problems or other genuine reasons for being late. Time enough to finish one drink and look as though she is the kind of girl who regularly goes out on her own.

The waiter arrives with a large glass of sangria. She takes a long gulp. Checks the time on her phone, then notices a movement by the door. He's here. Relief.

'Sorry I'm late,' he says, even before he reaches her table. 'Babysitter problems.'

Katy is attracted to him straight away. Average height. Dark hair. Pale skin. An athletic body from working out at the gym or some other regular sport. She stands up. Offers him her hand.

'I always allow my students one chance,' she says, only half joking.

'What happens if they're late a second time?' Even his smile is attractive, encompassing his whole face, shining through his dark brown eyes; she could get lost in his eyes if she looked for too long.

'Detention. Or clean-up duties. As well as being in my bad books for the rest of the year.'

He laughs and pulls out a seat to sit down. 'I'll keep that in mind.'

The waiter reappears and Katy thinks of Luke again. If her calculations are correct, Luke and Aaron should be getting on a plane quite soon. She offered them the use of her spare bedroom during their visit but Luke declined. Apparently, Aaron wants to stay in the family home, which is admirable but potentially disastrous.

'Can I get you something to drink, sir? A beer or some wine?'

Mike nods at Katy's sangria. 'I'll have some of that.'

'How about a jug to share?'

Katy and Mike exchange a quick look. They both know that they'll be here for more than one drink.

'Sounds good,' Mike confirms. He begins to talk about his sister, who is the babysitter tonight (and ninety per cent of the time). According to Mike, she's the flakiest babysitter in the world, so chances are he'll end up in Katy's bad books again sometime in the future.

Sometime in the future.

The casual assumption that they'll meet again makes her feel disproportionately happy. She tells herself to get a grip.

She asks him about his son, who was in some of the photos he sent for the yearbook. He promptly shows her more photos on his phone: Toby on a scooter, Toby at the beach, Toby with a soccer ball in his hands.

'I'm a big believer in recording everything. Photos. Videos. Writing down the funny moments as well as the not-so-funny moments. It can be gone so quickly.'

Katy's heart aches. For Mike. For four-year-old Toby, who will grow up without his mother. For Brigette, who will miss out on all his milestones, and even the everyday things like nagging him to clean his room and brush his teeth.

They both realise how hungry they are and order some tapas. She learns that he doesn't like chorizo, and he discovers her weakness for pork flatbread. He asks her a million questions about school, her students, her timetable, her colleagues. She asks him about his work: the security firm that he owns, the type of security they provide (building security solutions) and what he likes and dislikes about it.

'I like that it's so broad. Every building is different, every client is unique, no two jobs are the same. What I don't like is when there's an after-hours incident. It's difficult with Toby, especially if it's the dead of night.'

Katy can see Toby curled up in bed, his dark head resting on his pillow, a soft toy held loosely in his arms. 'What do you do if that happens?'

'Drop him at Mum and Dad's. Or a neighbour's house.'

'Not your sister?'

'Emergencies aren't her thing. I've told you, she's flaky.'

They both laugh and then order another jug of sangria.

Mike becomes serious after that. 'So what's the latest about the yearbook and the mysterious messages?'

Katy almost forgot the reason they're here in the first place: to see if he can get to the bottom of what's going on. 'I had a missed call from Zach Latham earlier today. It sounds like he got another note, a really nasty one.'

'So has everyone in the year group received messages?' His question is slow and thoughtful. He comes across as someone who doesn't rush in, someone who'd be calm and measured in a crisis.

'Not everyone. A certain group. What we used to call the popular group … And, quite strangely, me.'

'You weren't part of the popular group?' He seems to find this hard to believe.

'I had bright orange hair and loved science,' she says drily. 'What do *you* think?'

He laughs, deep grooves forming at the sides of his mouth.

'As far as I know, six people have received messages,' she continues. 'Annabel, Grace, Luke, Zach, Melissa and me.'

As Katy calls out the names, she realises that Jarrod is missing from the list. Does this mean something?

'Can you get me copies?' Mike asks. 'Sometimes there are obvious clues when all the evidence is seen together.'

'I think so ... I'll ask everyone. Some of the content is sensitive – both Annabel and Grace were quite upset – but hopefully that won't stop them from sharing.'

Should she mention Jarrod? Jarrod would hardly send his own wife a nasty email, would he? But it's odd that he hasn't received anything. Maybe he did and decided to keep quiet?

'Some of the messages are emails, others are physical notes,' she says instead. 'I don't know if that's important.'

Mike stares at her. 'Seems important to me. A note means they know where to find you.'

Her eyes widen. 'Now you're scaring me.'

'Sorry.' He reaches across the table and briefly squeezes her hand. 'I don't mean to freak you out.'

Katy is distracted by the sound of a chair scraping on the floor. She looks over her shoulder and sees that the staff are stacking chairs on tables and casting meaningful glances in their direction.

Mike seems just as surprised as she is. 'I didn't realise the time.'

He calls for the bill, and offers his credit card without giving her the chance to see what's owed.

She puts fifty dollars on the table. 'This is for me. I pay my own way.'

It's one of her rules. Just like the waiting thing. Always pay your share, because you don't know the financial status of your date, and you don't want to create any false expectations about some form of 'payback'.

He looks at the money, then looks at her face, no doubt seeing the determination there. 'Can't you pay next time?'

Once again, the suggestion of the future makes her heart miss a beat.

'No, thanks.' Then she grins to take the edge off things. 'Besides, next time could be somewhere more expensive.'

He takes the money and the awkward moment passes.

Outside the restaurant is surprisingly busy for a Thursday night. Pedestrians and revellers walking past, cars whizzing by on the main road, a police presence outside the pub a few doors up.

What now?

Even as she is thinking the question, he draws her close. His lips are soft and questioning. She melts into the kiss, answering the question: *yes, yes, yes.*

'Your place isn't far from here?'

'A few minutes.'

'Let's go. I'll walk you.'

'You should get home to Toby.' She doesn't know why she is dissuading him. She would love him to walk her home.

'I can spare a few minutes.'

He takes her hand in his and they cross the road. For the first time they're quiet. Katy is absorbing details that she didn't notice at the restaurant: the slightly rough skin of his hand, the smell of his aftershave, the upright manner in which he walks.

It's over far too soon.

'This is me. Thanks for seeing me home.'

There seems no point in inviting him in. He must get home to Toby. And she has a rule – something about not letting strange men into her apartment – although she is sorely tempted to throw her rulebook in the gutter.

He kisses her again. A deeper, more intimate kiss. A kiss that makes Katy feel both weak and strong. They're both breathing heavily when they finally stop.

'Gotta go,' Mike says reluctantly. Then he adds, promises, 'I'll call you. Don't forget to get those copies for me.'

'Goodnight.' Her voice doesn't sound like her own. It's squeaky, feeble. 'I won't forget.'

She watches him retrace his steps down the street. He turns to give a last wave before disappearing from sight. She swings around to go inside and nearly jumps out of her skin.

'Howdy, Katy.' It's Jim, her neighbour.

'Jesus, Jim. You gave me a fright. What are you doing there?' He's standing half in the shadows. Was he watching her and Mike?

'Sorry, love. Didn't mean to startle you. Just taking out the rubbish. Did you have a good night?'

Katy can see he's keen to chat but she desperately wants to get inside, to be alone, to examine everything that has happened tonight and rejoice over it.

'Yes, thanks.'

'No more strange notes under the door?'

'Nope. Night, Jim.'

She turns on all the lights when she gets inside. Pours herself a glass of water. Sits on the couch with a smile that will not be suppressed.

He likes you as much as you like him. Unless you've got your signals mixed up.

It wouldn't be the first time she's got it wrong. A wonderful, promising first date followed by … nothing.

No, this is different. Sometime in the future.

She realises that she hasn't checked her phone for hours and retrieves it from her handbag. Dead. She sets it to charge and begins to get ready for bed. Her phone has come back to life by the time she emerges from the bathroom. There are several missed calls from Zach and another voice message.

'Hi, Katy. Zach Latham again. We've been playing phone tag. Give me a call when you get this message.'

It's almost midnight. Obviously too late to call now. And too late to text Nina, to tell her about the incredible night she's just had.

Sometime in the future.

Katy climbs into bed, lies in the dark replaying every moment, and falls asleep with a smile on her face.

32
LUKE

Luke belts himself in and a female flight attendant snaps shut the locker overhead. 'Jesus, this is weird ...'

Aaron laughs. 'Planning on being one of those difficult customers?'

Luke grins back. 'I'll give them shit from start to end.'

The flight is full. Passengers sandwiched together. Strangers manoeuvring to keep their elbows and legs to themselves. There's a baby crying somewhere up the front. Poor thing, its misery has just started. Thirteen hours to Singapore, a quick stop to refuel, then another eight hours to Sydney. It's been a while since Luke's been a passenger on a plane. Before Aaron, holidays were in far-flung places – Nepal, Russia, Iceland – taking advantage of generous staff discounts. In recent years he has favoured other forms of transport. Meandering car trips to Wales to see Aaron's parents. Trains north to Edinburgh and Glasgow. A ferry over to Ireland.

He has written to his father to let him know he's coming. A card with the cartoon image of an aeroplane on the front; flight numbers, times and dates written inside. An old-fashioned means of communication for an old-fashioned sort of man. A dinosaur who hasn't embraced the convenience of technology. No computer or email or internet. No mobile phone or texts. None of that gay stuff either, thank you very much. Nonsense, the lot of it.

I'm bringing a friend, Luke wrote below the travel details.

What will his father make of that? What kind of reception will Aaron get? Civil, is the most Luke can hope for. Scornful is what he expects. Hostile is what he's most afraid of.

They're in the air, thick cloud obscuring the view of London. The drinks trolley seems to take for ever. Luke and Aaron order a wine each, on the understanding that Aaron will only drink half his and surrender the remainder to Luke. Luke needs the alcohol to numb his sense of foreboding. Duty calls him back to Sydney every three or four years: usually friends or extended family celebrating weddings or significant birthdays. He stays with Katy and other friends during these trips, calling on his father only a handful of times – the minimum he can get away with – every minute an endurance. The house is depressingly male. Everything clean and neat but woefully dated and drab. His father puts the kettle on and they try to talk about what's happened in the years since they've last spoken.

'How's the job going?'

'Still in the same flat?'

'Living the same *lifestyle*?'

This is his way of asking if Luke is still gay. As though Luke might wake up one morning and suddenly decide he is not homosexual after all.

'Dad, you should really redecorate in here. Make it brighter …'

'Why don't you let me set you up with a computer or even an iPad?'

'Have you met anyone special, Dad?'

Luke's mother died when he was eight. He was shielded from the gravity of her illness, her chemotherapy sessions scheduled for when he was at school, her long periods in bed put down to the simple need to rest. He remembers her making light of it, patting her scarfed head and laughing, 'Like my new hairstyle, Lukey? It's all the rage.' He didn't understand that she was bald under the scarf until she was long dead.

Later on, when she was gravely sick, she still made a supreme effort in his presence, cuddling him on the hospital bed, sometimes entangling him in her drips and wires. Acting like she wasn't dying and those wires weren't pumping her with drugs to make her last a little bit longer.

'Tell me about your day, Lukey. What's going on at school?'

He really thought she was going to get better. That she would be home any day. Then the morning his father told him she'd passed away in her sleep. Profound shock. Crushing grief. Feeling stupid for not 'getting it'. Later, as a young teenager who was quite certain about his sexuality, and just as certain about his father's opinion of it, he liked to think that his mother's presence would have softened things, made it easier for his father to accept. As an adult, having seen first-hand how obstinate and immovable human beings can be, he isn't so sure.

He has thought a lot about his mother in the days leading up to this trip. She's the one who comes to mind whenever he thinks about home. Her laughter, her light, her loss. Luke has surpassed her age by two years; she was only thirty-five. So fucking unfair. *Why her?* Why the fun-loving kind-hearted parent instead of the miserable, bigoted one? He often imagines her alive, healthy and happy in a parallel life. Visiting him in London. Shrieking in delight at the sights and shopping. Linking his arm, calling him 'Lukey', loving Aaron to bits. His father doesn't feature in this parallel life. She would have divorced him long ago.

Aaron reaches across and squeezes his hand. 'How're you feeling?'

Luke grimaces. 'Like I need to be perpetually drunk to get through the next few weeks.'

Aaron rolls his eyes. 'Don't be a moron.'

Luke's doing this for Aaron. Because Aaron is desperate to meet his family, to see where he comes from, to get to know that part of him. Luke has tried to explain what his father's like – aeons from Aaron's liberal-minded welcoming parents – but Aaron remains convinced he'll be able to charm him. Aaron is not often wrong but this time he is. Is it too late to change their arrangements and stay with Katy instead? Oh God, some fucking holiday this will be.

Now it's the food trolley, an unappetising smell preceding it. Aaron has fallen asleep, his head on Luke's shoulder. Luke bypasses the food and orders two more wines, on the pretence that one's for Aaron. The flight attendant gives him a knowing look. Then her eyes flick to Aaron, snuggled into Luke's side, and she smiles.

Sometimes acceptance throws Luke just as much as bigotry does.

His thoughts reverse to Katy, who has always accepted him, who never had an agenda other than to be his friend – until now. He loves Katy, he wants her to be happy, but even she must understand that it isn't just sperm they're talking about here. Luke would be a *father*. How involved would Katy want him to be? Doesn't she realise how inept he is, and how scarred from his own experience? It's not like he's had a good role model, for fuck's sake.

Luke finishes the wine, goes to the bathroom, checks his watch: another eleven hours before the first leg is done. Jesus Christ. Time drags when you're sitting there, doing nothing but thinking (and drinking). He'd much rather be busy cleaning up meal trays, or tending to passengers who need water, tissues or sick bags. He contemplates sticking his head around the galley, saying hello, striking up a conversation. No, this isn't his shift. Back to his seat where he unwraps a blanket from its cellophane and tucks it around Aaron. Unwraps another for himself. Reclines his seat. Drifts off sooner than he expected.

He dreams of Katy. The young Katy with her sunset hair and her heart on her sleeve. He's kissing her. Her lips are soft and luscious. He's enjoying himself. Getting into it. One hand on her breast, the other entangled in her hair. His father is there. Grinning from ear to ear. 'I knew you weren't a faggot,' he declares.

Luke wakes with a start. Takes a moment to determine where he is: mid-air somewhere over Eastern Europe, his whole left side numb from Aaron's weight. He manoeuvres Aaron off him, ignoring the sudden temptation to rouse him, to blurt out what's been plaguing him for months: *Let's get married.*

Gay marriage has become legal since Luke's last visit home. He didn't ask his father how he voted in the postal survey. He didn't need to.

He presses the button for the attendant.

He needs another drink.

33
ZACH

Zach looks up and down the street when he gets out of the car. Robbie knows where he works. Does he know where he lives, too? Has he watched the house, seen Izzy and Carson go about their daily routine? The thought makes Zach feel sick.

The house is in darkness, except for the light in their bedroom. He sees Izzy in his head. Hair in a long plait down her back. A book propped on her knees. She'll be tired, gently affectionate, oblivious to what's coming. Zach hates himself for the upset he is about to cause.

He slips off his shoes and socks at the door.

'Dadda?'

'Coming.'

He pads into his son's bedroom. 'Hey, mate, what are you doing awake?'

'Waiting for you,' Carson replies, his voice overly

loud; whispering is something he finds difficult to do. 'To tell you about my day.'

This is part of their routine, when time permits. Carson recounts the minutiae of his day and usually falls asleep well before he gets to the end.

'Well, I'd be happier if you got your beauty sleep,' Zach says, kissing his son's forehead. 'You need all the help you can get.'

Carson giggles – his sense of humour is more sophisticated than many of his other cognitive skills.

Zach puts a finger to his lips. 'Shush. Now, tell me a short version of what you did today.'

Carson snuggles under the sheets, sighing contentedly. He's at his happiest when everyone in the family is present and accounted for. 'I wrote story about kitten … His name Scratchy … He black and white … He go on bus and get lost … and … and…'

Carson's eyes are drooping. He manages another disjointed sentence or two. Zach waits a few minutes, absorbing the purity of those closed eyelids.

'Hey.' Izzy smiles when he walks into their room, directly next door. 'Long day, huh?'

Zach nods a reply. The toll of two late shifts in a row, dealing with ill patients and medical emergencies while those words – *For the last twenty years, I've thought of nothing else but killing you* – tumbled round in his head. He needs to tell Izzy. He should have done so last night, but she was complaining of a headache and he put it off.

The mattress sinks as he sits down. She reaches to put her hand on his arm.

'Everything okay?'

'No.' He feels a surge of self-loathing as he extracts the note from his pocket. 'This was left on my car last night.'

Her fingers brush his as she takes the piece of paper into her possession. Is this a moment he will look back on? A line in time, distinguishing between 'before' and 'after'? 'Before' signifying love, trust and closeness. 'After' being the disintegration of their marriage.

She reads. Her eyebrows – fine and with a natural arch – rise until they almost reach her hairline. 'This is scary … Is this person mentally ill?'

'Perhaps, I don't know.'

'You need to tell me something … What is it you need to say?'

Zach forces himself to meet her eyes. 'I need to tell you two things, actually.'

She takes a sharp breath. '*Two things?*'

'The first goes back to my school days. There was this kid, Robbie McGrath. I was a shit to him.'

Her expression is guarded. 'What did you do, Zach?'

'Poor kid had epilepsy. Had a few seizures at school. I am ashamed to say it, Izzy, but my party piece was to mimic him.'

'Mimic him?'

'Having the seizure. Jerking and moaning on the ground. Then getting up and walking as though I'd wet my pants.' Every part of Zach is cringing. He's mortified and utterly perplexed by the cruelty of his teenage self. How had he thought it was even remotely funny? Why hadn't someone punched him in the face and made him stop?

'You did this "party piece" at school?' Izzy's voice drips with disdain. 'In front of this unfortunate boy?'

'Sometimes at school. Mostly at someone's house, when we were bored or drunk.'

At school Robbie would've seen snippets. Zach contorting his eyes and mouth, or pretend-shuddering, clutching his crotch. Nothing longer than a few seconds, but enough. The 'full performance' was reserved for parties, and Robbie was spared because he wasn't part of that scene. Except for one memorable occasion, when someone actually thought to invite him. It was a big party; Zach hadn't even noticed Robbie was there. He launched himself on to the ground, writhing his body, lurching his head from side to side, hysterical laughter prompting him to exaggerate his movements even further. Then the laughter stopped dead and someone said, 'For fuck's sake, Zach. Cut it out. He's here.'

By the time Zach got unsteadily to his feet, Robbie was gone. There were a few awkward minutes, when nobody knew where to look or what to say, then someone turned up the music, and the party resumed with as much gusto as before: Robbie's feelings were no reason to stop enjoying themselves. The party was shortly after the HSC. Zach hasn't set eyes on Robbie since that night.

'And you think this boy, this *man*, left you this note on your car?' Izzy asks now.

Zach shrugs. 'Whoever it is has been waiting twenty years, which means it's someone from school.'

'Maybe there are other people who hated you. *I* would have hated you.'

Izzy has a point. There were other victims, other students and even some of the teachers: Mr Collins with his nervous facial tics; Mrs Romford with her masculine voice. He can't recall wanting to deliberately embarrass or belittle anyone: his actions were prompted by the need to elicit laughter from his friends, nothing more. Does that mean that underneath all the bravado he was as insecure as everyone else? Or is that just looking for excuses?

What appals him the most is the thought of Carson being subjected to the same kind of treatment, his clunky movements and speech providing comic material for some smart-arse kid. Zach now understands the irreparable hurt that can be inflicted by mockery, especially when it's targeted at something that can't be controlled. One minute, Robbie would be walking to his locker. The next he'd be on the floor, body shaking violently, saliva frothing from his mouth, urine spreading across the crotch of his school shorts.

'What's the other thing you need to tell me?'

Zach stalls. Does he really need to tell her? He's

270

vacillated since last night, changing his mind every five minutes.

Tell her. You should have told her years ago.

Don't. She'll never trust you again.

Izzy is strong and incredibly forgiving. She can recover.

Some things can't be recovered from.

His wife is his closest confidante. This confession is long, long overdue. He has hated himself, for the deception as much as the act itself. His relief at getting it off his chest is almost as great as his shame.

Nobody knows. Whoever wrote this note can't know about this.

A few people know. And they could have told others. When someone says they want to kill you, doesn't it make sense to be fully honest?

'It happened about a month after Carson's birth. I tried to be strong, like you were, but every time someone looked at him or said something ... I guess I underestimated how it would impact our family and friends. Their pity derailed me ... You remember I had a medical conference around then?'

Her expression hardens. She's guessed. Bed-hopping is common at these conferences. If you're the cheating type.

He forces himself to go on. 'I cried and cried that weekend. All the tears I felt I couldn't shed in front of you. I couldn't understand it ... Why was I so deeply affected by the change in expression every time someone peeked into his pram? It wasn't as though

271

I was scared of having a disabled child. It wasn't as though I hadn't adjusted my expectations … But every one of those pitying glances broke something in me. I got drunk on the second night of the conference. Outrageously drunk. And I was unfaithful to you …'

Silence. He searches her face, her eyes, for the disgust, for the hurt, but she's unreadable: everything about her is closed off.

'Who? Who did you sleep with? Do I know her?' Her accent is the only clue to her feelings: it always becomes stronger when she's upset. Even though she has never been the kind of woman to scream or act out, Zach would welcome a torrent of abuse or even a slap across the face. He deserves it.

'No. She was from Melbourne. I've never seen her since. I'm so sorry.'

'And you think the person who sent this note – Robbie – knows about this affair?'

It was a one-night stand, hardly an affair, but correcting her would not serve any purpose. 'I honestly don't think so … But I've wanted to tell you since the moment it happened. The secret has been eating away at me. This might seem a strange time to tell you but I want full disclosure, no more secrets, so I never have to disappoint you like this again.'

He needs her. With her by his side, he is a good man, a compassionate man, a loving man. Without her, he can be cruel, selfish, ugly. She knows this. She knows that she has been transformative for him.

'You will take this note and its …' She pauses while she searches for the correct word. 'Its … *threats* … to the police tomorrow?'

'Yes. I will.'

Zach has no idea what the police will make of it. Maybe it needs to be combined with the other messages to see the full picture. He has phoned Katy to let her know. He should call Annabel too.

'I need time to think about this.' Izzy turns around and throws a pillow at him. 'You can sleep on the sofa tonight.'

Tears blur his eyes. As a young man, he never cried. It was Izzy who taught him it was okay.

'I'm so ashamed of myself. I'm not worthy of you.'

She replies by turning off the bedside lamp.

34
ANNABEL

Annabel wakes dozens of times during the night. Every time a nurse comes in, a shadowy figure at the end of Jarrod's bed updating his charts. The times when his monitors beep, and she wakes with a jolt of terror, certain that he has stopped breathing or is going into cardiac arrest. Then the usual hospital noises: the squeal of trollies as they pass outside, the trill of the phone at the ICU reception desk, and intermittent sirens, as ambulances arrive with new emergencies.

At 7 a.m., as the hospital bustles into full operation, she folds away her pull-out bed for the third consecutive morning.

'Don't feel you have to stay here,' the nurses have said gently. 'We'll call you if something changes.'

But she doesn't want to go home to sleep in a bed

without Jarrod. She wants to be by his side for this ordeal. She owes it to him.

'It's time you woke up,' she says, kissing his cheek. 'I haven't been this tired since Jemma was a newborn.'

Unfortunately, waking up is not within his control. He's in a drug-induced coma. Yesterday, they shaved some of his hair and drilled a hole in his skull to drain the fluid. Just looking at that vulnerable patch of white scalp is enough to make her cry.

She leaves to use the bathroom, taking her toiletries and a change of clothes with her. The morning sun streams through the bathroom window, and the mirror is unforgiving. Blue-black circles around her eyes. Dark roots coming through her hair. Beneath the carnage, she can see a new hard-fought wisdom. The last few days have given her clarity. About Daniel: she and Jarrod have been divided, blaming each other instead of pulling together. About the business: Jarrod has been killing himself keeping up with its demands, and she has punished rather than supported him.

Her thoughts keep returning to the night she told him she was pregnant. They were on 'a break' at the time. They'd had numerous breaks, kissed and dated other people, before finding themselves drawn back together again. But that particular split lasted eight weeks, longer than any of the others. Jarrod began dating Melissa, and Annabel see-sawed between being quietly heartbroken and violently jealous. She was in denial about what was happening to her body, passing off the nausea as a stomach bug, attributing her missing periods to stress, blaming everything – illogically – on Melissa.

She was four months' gone before she confronted the truth, and Jarrod. They stayed up all night. Crying. Consoling. Blaming. Beseeching. Finally, coming together. It was far from ideal but they'd do the best they could. Jarrod would split with Melissa and commit to Annabel and their unborn baby. And here they are. Twenty years and three children later. A home and mortgage, a thriving business, and a drug-addicted son. When she thinks back to 'that night', the overriding image is of herself and Jarrod holding hands. Gripping each other, bracing for the onslaught of their parents' wrath and a future neither of them had imagined. They had unity and not much else. Somewhere along the line, they've lost that unity.

'I'm sorry,' she says to her reflection, to him. 'We'll get it back. I promise.'

Later in the day, carrying through with her resolve to be more supportive, Annabel takes Jarrod's phone and leaves the sterile confines of the hospital room. ICU is strictly technology free, which is why she hasn't attended to the growing number of unanswered voice and text messages on his phone. She sits on one of the benches outside the main foyer.

'My husband has been in an accident … I know, I apologise … Have you got a pen and paper handy?'

She returns the calls and texts one by one, apologising for the inconvenience and providing the number of another electrician whom Jarrod is friendly with. Until she comes across a message that has nothing to do with the business.

Sorry I haven't been in touch. This is the reason why. His name is PJ.

Jealousy rears up Annabel's throat. PJ, going by the photo, is a very young puppy; Mia would go wild for him. But why is Melissa sending this photograph to Jarrod? What does she mean about not being 'in touch'? There appear to be no earlier messages between the two. Has Jarrod deleted them? Is this a renewed friendship or something more threatening?

Annabel takes a moment to gather herself. She can't deal with this right now. Doesn't have the emotional capacity, the brain space or the strength. She'll ask Jarrod for an explanation when he is well enough. For now, she has no choice but to trust him. That doesn't stop her from wanting to gouge Melissa's eyes out.

She takes a deep breath, rallies herself. Picks up the phone again, this time to call home. Jemma answers; she's taken some time off university to help out.

'Hey, Mum.' Her voice is girlish. She sounds barely older than Mia. 'How's Dad doing?'

'They're still worried about the swelling. They've popped in a tube to drain the fluid.'

Annabel is being deliberately casual. The tube was not something that was 'popped in'; surgery was required, a hole drilled, the catheter placed in the ventricle and then tunnelled under his skin to his abdomen, where the extra fluid is to be absorbed.

'When are they going to wake him up?'

'As soon as they get the intracranial pressure within a normal range.'

Annabel has tried to press the consultant for specifics. She has been told that every brain injury is different.

'We don't predict too far ahead,' Dr Chan said. 'We see what each day brings.'

It's been especially hard for the children. Allowed into ICU for one brief visit. Seeing their father in that battered comatose state. Shepherded away before they had the chance to get their bearings or process how they felt. Their ongoing questions met with vagueness that makes them even more upset.

'How are things there?' Annabel asks. 'Everyone arrive home from school in one piece?'

She has barely been home since the accident. A couple of hours here and there to pack fresh clothes, have a proper shower and instruct Jemma on what groceries to buy.

'Mia needs some stuff signed by you for the end-of-year excursion. I've put the paperwork on the hall table.'

'And Daniel?'

'Ah ... Daniel isn't home yet.'

Annabel closes her eyes. It's Friday, isn't it? It's hard to keep track in the hospital. Days and nights meld into each other. Yes, definitely Friday. He's probably at a friend's house.

'Can you find out who he's with?'

This is not strictly fair: making Jemma the policeman. But Daniel responds to his older sister better than to anyone else.

'Okay ... Mia's here. She wants to talk to you.'

Jemma hands over the phone and Annabel is greeted with a breathless gush of information: the upcoming excursion at school, and how *everyone* got kept back for ten minutes at lunchtime just because a few were being noisy. Any moment now Mia will remember her father. It's like her brain needs to unload the day's minutiae before she can contemplate the unfathomable.

'Is Daddy getting better? Can I come and see him again?'

'Yes, he's getting better. Maybe tomorrow or the day after.'

'Will he be awake?'

'I'm not sure ... The doctor says we have to wait and see.'

'I've drawn him a picture.'

Annabel smiles. Jarrod is often presented with Mia's prolific well-meant art. 'Daddy will love that.'

She finishes the call, stands up too quickly and has to grip the bench to counteract a spell of dizziness. It's catching up with her. The all-consuming worry about if there'll be any long-term damage to Jarrod's health. The stress of not knowing what to expect, today, tomorrow, next week. The broken sleep on the uncomfortable pull-out bed. She missed lunch, deterred by the queues at the café. It should be quieter there now. Some food might make her feel better. She's on her way inside when someone grabs her by the arm roughly.

'Annabel!'

It takes a moment or two to recognise that it's Zach. He looks more dishevelled than when they last met. Bleary eyes. At least a day's worth of stubble. She shakes his hand off her. He rushes in with an apology.

'Sorry, sorry, I didn't mean to manhandle you. I've been trying to call you—'

This is true. Annabel has seen some missed calls and a text asking her to phone. But whatever Zach wants to talk about is not a priority right now.

'Jarrod's been ill. A work accident.' She keeps saying that: an accident. But it wasn't, was it? It was an attack, an *assault*.

Zach is immediately sympathetic. 'I'm so sorry to hear that. What happened?'

Annabel tries to tell him but the words get stuck, clogging her throat, forming a painful lump. The only sound that gets through is a sob.

He takes her by the arm, gently this time. 'Let's get you a coffee and some food. I bet you haven't eaten.'

She allows him to guide her to a seat in the café, allows him to buy her food, which he orders at the counter without asking what she wants. Tears stream down her face, her veneer of coping cracked by his concern. She's been yearning for sympathy these last few days. From the kind yet too-busy-to-stop nurses. From Jarrod's parents, who've been leaning on her rather than the other way around.

Zach returns with a skinny white coffee – he must have remembered her order from when they bumped into each other at the drugs centre – and a toasted sandwich. It's exactly what she needs and within minutes she feels better. Able to properly speak again. Hold her composure. She tells him the bare facts of the last few days. Jarrod being found unconscious at a deserted warehouse in Warriewood. The security guard who came across him and probably saved his life. The police knocking on her door and turning her world upside down. He asks more questions than she's prepared for.

'Have the police told you anything about their investigation?'

'How do they know it's a disgruntled client? Is there specific evidence?'

'What if it's the person who's been sending us these messages?'

Zach seems paranoid. Reassessing his bloodshot eyes and oddly dishevelled appearance, it strikes Annabel that she hardly knows this man.

'There was nothing threatening about the email I got,' she says carefully.

He reaches into his pocket. Takes out a folded sheet of paper.

'Read this … I'd appreciate your opinion.'

281

Annabel takes it from him. Notices that it's a photo-copy. Reads the text with increasing alarm.

Circling your throat with my hands … plunging a knife into your skin …

'Oh my goodness.' Her hand flies to her mouth. 'This is frightening. Have you shown it to the police?'

Zach nods. 'They have the original note and are checking it for fingerprints. I spoke with a detective at Manly but he was pretty sceptical. Asked me dozens of questions about my movements that day and gave the strong impression that he thought I'd put the note there myself.' He shrugs. 'I'd probably react the same way if someone came into my clinic acting paranoid. The fact is that a lot of these kinds of complaints are prompted by mental illness. It's pretty obvious that the detective isn't going to look for a culprit until my story checks out.'

Annabel is incredulous. 'You're a GP, Zach. Surely he can assume that you're mentally stable?'

Zach laughs. 'GPs work in a high-pressure environ-ment and can snap, just like anyone else. Going back to the note, it's not against the law to have a fantasy. Nobody's threatened me with a weapon or demanded money. But now you're telling me that Jarrod's been beaten up, I can't help wondering if there's a connection.'

Annabel's phone beeps before she has the chance to answer. It's a text from Jemma.

Daniel's with Liam. Okay?

Annabel's heart sinks. It's not okay. Liam is a drug friend. Oh God, as if she doesn't have enough on her plate.

'I'm so sorry, Zach. It's my daughter. I need to call her about something urgent.'

'Of course.' They stand up simultaneously. He reaches across to kiss her cheek. The gesture feels overly intimate. 'Take care of yourself. Remember to eat. And let me know what happens with Jarrod.'

'I will,' she promises. She pauses before she walks away. 'What are you going to do now?'

He looks resigned. 'Confront Robbie. It has to be him ... Maybe an apology will make him stop.'

35
KATY

'Don't confront him,' Katy says. 'Mike doesn't recommend it.'

It's Monday-morning recess. The bell will go in five minutes. Katy has no time to beat around the bush.

'Who the hell is Mike?' Zach exclaims on the other end of the line.

'Brigette's husband.'

'Dead Brigette?'

Zach used to be like this at school. Inappropriately sardonic. Shockingly insensitive.

'Show some respect, Zach,' she says, using her teacher tone. 'Brigette left behind a little boy and a lot of people who cared about her.'

'Sorry. I didn't mean any disrespect to Brigette, I'm just confused about why her husband is offering his opinion.'

Katy supposes that's fair enough. 'I've told Mike about what's going on. He works in security, knows all about surveillance techniques, and even the type of personality that would do something like this.'

'Someone with a grudge,' Zach supplies.

'Yes, someone who's held a grudge for a long, long time. And, going by your latest note, someone who at least *thinks* about being violent.'

One thing has become blatantly clear: the reunion must be cancelled. Katy will send out a message when she gets home tonight. She notices some female students heading towards the toilet block, checking over their shoulders, looking like they're up to no good. She's about to tell Zach she has to go when he suggests, 'Why don't you come with me? Might be better if there are two of us.'

Katy's first reaction is no. Mike – who has read all the messages with the exception of this latest one to Zach – is concerned that this person poses a real danger.

'Either way, I'm going there,' Zach declares without waiting for her answer. 'I'm not sitting on this for any longer.'

The truth is, Katy is curious. She wants to see the man that Robbie has become and struggles to believe he would be capable of this: being so devious and vindictive, sabotaging the reunion and all her work to date, making Zach feel unsafe enough to talk to a detective. Her instincts tell her Zach's wrong: it's not Robbie. It doesn't fit with the boy she remembers as being so gravely insecure. Katy herself was awkward and self-conscious, but she blossomed outside the constraints of high school. Maybe Robbie has too.

'Let me think about it,' she says, striding towards the girls' toilets. What is she going to find? Cigarettes? Drugs? Some inappropriate content on someone's phone? 'As far as I know, Robbie's staying with his sister. Maybe it would be better to speak to her instead.'

Mike leans forward and kisses her on the mouth as soon as she opens the door. Then he hands her an expensive-looking bottle of wine.

'Come in,' Katy says, indicating the way with a flourish of her hand. 'It's pretty small.'

It's his first time coming around to her apartment, and soon – going by the intensity of that kiss – it will be their first time sleeping together. Things have been progressing quickly. Four dates in five days. That first time at the tapas bar. A couple of days later, a few drinks at her local pub. Then yesterday, a walk in the park and an ice cream with Toby, his son. Katy is nervous. Scared of being disappointed. Trying hard not to think of all the times she's got to this stage only to be let down. Sex is such an intimate, revealing act. Someone's skin on your skin. Their hands touching every inch of your body. There are so many ways to be turned off. Their breath, their smell, the noises they make.

Stop. Keep thinking like that and you'll be celibate for the rest of your life.

Katy has made a light dinner. Cajun chicken, green salad and crusty bread. Dessert is a store-bought lemon meringue pie.

'Who's babysitting? Fiona?'

Fiona is the flaky sister. According to Mike, she allows Toby to eat unquantified amounts of lollies and biscuits, and blithely ignores his bedtime.

'Toby's at a sleepover with Mum and Dad.'

This means it's happening: Mike is staying the night. Katy's body responds positively to the certainty. A tensing between her legs. She wants this. She wants him.

Conversation over dinner is not as free-flowing as usual. The atmosphere is heavy with anticipation. She hasn't finished her dessert when he lays his hand over hers on the table. She feels a jolt of attraction, of longing. She gravitates towards him, their lips meet, and suddenly they're kissing fervently. He manoeuvres her on to his lap. His hands are inside her top. Cutlery goes rattling to the floor.

'Let's go to bed,' she murmurs into his neck.

They slow down once they reach her room. Undress little by little. Kiss deeply. Explore each other. Everything is right. His smell. The weight of him on top of her. The fact that he barely makes any noise – she hates the grunters. He is good at this. Expertly brings her to the most exquisite orgasm.

She falls asleep afterwards. Wakes up feeling disoriented. The room is shadowy and smells of sex. She checks her watch: 9.36 p.m. Where has Mike gone?

She gets up, throws on a dressing gown and pads into the living room. There he is. Sitting at her desk. Tapping on her keyboard.

'What are you doing?'

He turns his head. Seems taken aback at the sharpness of her tone. 'Running some diagnostics on your laptop.'

She comes closer and peers over his shoulder. A scan of some sort is fifty per cent complete. Apparently, four threats have been found.

'You mentioned that you were concerned about spyware,' he says. 'It looks like you were right to be worried.'

This is true. It was on their second date, at the pub. When she'd handed him copies of all the notes and emails and felt compelled to elaborate on Luke's in particular. 'I still can't figure it out. Either it's an educated guess that I'd like to have a child or they have some way of seeing my online activity.'

At the time Mike suggested she run some diagnostics. Now he has taken matters into his own hands. The night has lost its sheen of perfection. He did everything right over dinner and in the bedroom. But now this, a blatant invasion of her privacy. The assumption that she can't sort it out herself.

'Don't go on my laptop again without asking, okay?'

His face fills with remorse and embarrassment. He stands up, moves away from the laptop, which seems to have identified another threat. 'I'm sorry, you're right. I didn't want to wake you up ... but that's no excuse.'

They stand facing each other. Katy unconsciously squares her shoulders.

'I don't like men thinking they can waltz in here and take over. I'm perfectly capable of sorting out my own shit.'

'I don't doubt it.' He risks a smile. 'Does this mean I'm in your bad books, Ms Buckley?'

'Consider yourself on a warning,' she says, not even joking.

She flicks on the television and offers him a drink. They watch a travel show and finish a bottle of wine. Mike nuzzles her neck, plays with her hair, drops kisses on random parts of her face. They go back to bed, where he proceeds to do everything exactly right, as before. When she wakes the next morning, she's relieved that he's beside her, not off doing something on her laptop.

'I need to get going,' he sighs. 'Toby wakes early. Mum and Dad will have had enough by now.'

She needs to get going too; it's a school day. She stays in bed, watching him get dressed: last night's jeans and shirt, slightly wrinkled. She doesn't offer him breakfast.

He kisses her before he leaves. 'Do you want to come over to my place on Wednesday night?'

She shakes her head. Has an excuse ready. 'Sorry, I'm meeting some friends.'

Luke sent a text when he touched down Saturday, suggesting they meet up for drinks. Katy is slightly apprehensive about seeing him but is confident any awkwardness will quickly dissipate. She's still surprised that he chose to stay with his father. Luke and his father have never seen eye to eye.

Mike lets himself out. Katy stays in bed for another few minutes, dissecting the night. She should be happy. It went well, very well in some respects.

She finally gets up, showers. Her body feels good after the sex: alive, womanly. She washes her hair, exfoliates, moisturises, gets dressed. Emerging into the living room, the first thing she glances at is the laptop. There's a Post-it stuck to its screen.

Dear Katy. I don't want to upset you again, but you really do need to put a password on your network. X Mike

She immediately bristles. He means well, that's obvious, but still. He's having the last word. Asserting himself in her business, her life, her right to do whatever the hell she wants with her internet security.

She sighs. This is what happens. They always, *always* do something to disappoint.

36
ROBBIE

The kids fight over him. Sienna is particularly possessive.

'I asked him first.'

'Uncle Robbie said he'd help *me*.'

'Go away, Charlie. Leave us alone.'

She is forever grabbing Robbie's hand, dragging him places. 'Come on. Let's go.'

Sienna will not take no for an answer. She will not be deterred by a grumpy face or a harsh tone of voice. It's obvious that she regards him as someone special, someone worthy of her possessiveness. She is so very wrong.

Robbie's last seizure was two months ago. It was a bad one, the full shebang. Some people have warning signs, an aura that gives them the chance to get to a safe place. All Robbie feels is his body going rigid, and nothing after that.

He came around on the floor of the local Centrelink office.

'There's an ambulance on its way,' someone said. 'You've had some kind of fit.'

Apparently, it's very confronting. Onlookers are terrified they're about to witness a death. Some of them mistake the seizure for a heart attack or a drug-related reaction. Pissing or shitting himself, which happened that day in Centrelink, takes it to a whole new level. He was there to fill in some forms for his disability pension. If they needed any proof, here it was in all its humiliating glory.

Even though he was fuzzy and weak, he got to his feet and stumbled out of there as quickly as he could. His trousers were wet and sticky. The stench was reaching his nostrils. The embarrassment sat heavily in his gut.

'Wait,' someone called. 'The ambulance will be here any minute.'

He was waiting for no fucking ambulance. Outside on the road, he paused for a moment and regarded the traffic. Three lanes, dense with cars and trucks. A bus came into view. That would do the job. He wasn't brave enough, though. Didn't have the balls to step out and put an end to his shame. Instead he went home, cleaned himself up, packed his bag, and caught the next Greyhound bus out of there. Next city, please.

Sienna has her hands on her hips. 'Okay, Uncle Robbie. You're the teacher, I'm the kid. I'm being naughty today.'

Robbie finds it amusing that Sienna wants to play school after spending all day in the classroom. But he goes along with it. Gives a good impression of being stern – the teachers in Sienna's imaginary school are the old-fashioned cranky kind. He gives her detention. Makes her write lines: *I am very naughty and annoying.*

His niece has got under his skin. Forged a fondness, a tenderness he didn't know he was capable of. Robbie can't bear her to see one of his seizures. Can't bear her to see the truth of him: as far from special as one can get. It could happen any day now. He can go for long stretches of time – his record is three months – and then have two in quick succession. The frequency means he's categorised as having 'uncontrolled seizures', the result being he can't drive, or effectively work, or even play contact sports. The medication has come a long way since he was first diagnosed as an adolescent, having a couple of seizures a month. Some were minor: strange lapses in time, speaking weirdly, blinking a lot. It was the serious ones that petrified him, and that fear – of losing control and dignity in public – led to his anxiety problems and depression. To make matters worse, anti-epileptic medications are known to affect mood. Robbie's struggle with depression has often been as intense as his struggle with epilepsy.

*

Robbie's watching television when there's a knock on the door. Sienna flies to answer it. Charlie is upstairs on his Xbox, and Celia is getting dinner ready.

Robbie hears the door open, then his niece's voice, 'Hello?'

He can tell by her tone that she doesn't know who it is. He stands up, comes out to the hallway and stops dead. Fucking hell, it's *her*. She's with a man. Longish light brown hair, shirt and tie. A new boyfriend?

'Robbie?' She sees him and smiles. 'It's Katy Buckley and Zach Latham … from school.'

She offers him her hand. He takes it. Then Zach holds his out. Fuck, that's a hand he doesn't particularly want to shake, but he does it anyway. Are they a couple? No. Katy's not wearing a wedding band and Zach is. Besides, they seem quite separate from each other.

'Can we come in?' she asks.

Robbie pauses. He doesn't want them inside, doesn't want to hear whatever they're here to say. Because it can't be good. Katy must have seen him following her and she's here to ask him to stop. Fair enough. She has every right. But why Zach? Is he some sort of reinforcement?

Celia appears and issues the invitation he doesn't want to impart. 'Come in, come in.' She opens the door to the sitting room, flicks on the lights. 'You can sit in here. Can I get you a drink? Tea, coffee, something stronger?'

Katy is smiling again. It's a genuine smile, reaching

all the way to her eyes. A smile that warms you on the inside. 'Tea would be lovely, thank you.'

'Come on, Sienna,' Celia says, steering her daughter out of the room.

'Why can't I stay?' Sienna objects.

'Because you can't.'

They sit down. Katy and Zach on the sofa, and Robbie in one of the armchairs. The room has a bare, disused feel to it: it doesn't have a television and so doesn't attract the children. Katy is looking at him closely and Robbie feels exposed and terribly ashamed of himself. Has she recognised him from the bus? Or the times he pretended to be working in the school gardens? Why did he do that? He's never done anything like it before.

'Why are you here?' he asks, resting his hands on his knees.

Katy and Zach exchange a glance and seem to agree that Katy will be the spokesperson.

'Because of the school reunion,' she says, 'and some … upsetting … emails and notes that were sent.'

Robbie is taken aback. The answer is nothing remotely like what he was expecting.

'What do you mean? What emails?'

Katy opens her bag and takes out a sheaf of papers. 'These.'

Robbie begins to read. Annabel, Luke, Grace … he knows these names. Daniel, Lauren, Carson … those are foreign to him. When he gets to the last note – the one that talks about knives and guns and choking – he finally understands.

'You think I sent these?'

Zach clears his throat. 'Well, you came to mind … because we – me in particular – were such shits to you back then.'

Robbie stares at him. Zach has the same clean-cut good looks he had at school. The kind of looks that attracted people. Didn't matter what damage he was causing, who he was hurting or belittling or sneering at. He was the kid who got warned a thousand times but never got expelled. He was the kid who never tried hard, yet had opportunities handed to him on a plate.

'I'm an epileptic who suffers from depression, not a psychopath.' Robbie enunciates his words clearly. 'You need to find someone else who you treated like shit. There would be a long list to choose from, wouldn't there?'

Zach's face darkens. Is he blushing? 'I'm sorry … I'm *deeply* sorry for the distress I caused you.'

Celia chooses this moment to arrive with tea and biscuits. Can she feel the tension? The vestiges of twenty-year-old hatred? Sienna tries to sidle in unnoticed but fails. Her mother grabs her hand, hauls her away.

'Fuck off,' Robbie says, as soon as the door closes. 'You can take your apology and fuck yourself.'

Zach shrugs. 'I deserve that. I deserve for you to be angry with me … But what I can't understand is Jarrod, why you'd be angry with him.'

'Jarrod?' Robbie is blindsided. 'Jarrod Harris? Where does he come into all this?'

Zach's eyes are locked with his. 'Someone attacked him. Was that you, Robbie?'

'What the fuck are you taking about?'

Zach raises his hands. 'I know what *I* did to you. I just want to know what Jarrod did … Whether he needs to say sorry too.'

Robbie gasps. How can Zach be so wrong and so right at the same time?

'Shut up, Zach,' Katy says, standing up. 'It's obvious Robbie has no idea what we're talking about.' She crouches in front of him. Now she has one of his hands held in her own. 'Sorry, Robbie. Sorry for coming here and upsetting you. Of course it isn't you sending these messages.'

Robbie remembers her kindness, her compassion. He remembers it as vividly as he remembers Zach's cruelty and Jarrod's thoughtless sabotage. Katy will never know how much her kindness meant to him. Her smiles when they passed each other in the corridor. A few words here and there, sometimes the only conversation he'd had all day. He'd been more than a little in love with her. Maybe that's what he was trying to recreate by stalking her: an emotional connection.

But look at her now. Glossy hair. Trendy clothes. Still kind and caring, but *normal*, something he's not and never will be. Katy can drive; Robbie has seen her behind the wheel, her car disappearing down the ramp into the car park of her apartment block. Katy has a career, work colleagues and future prospects. She enjoys a glass of wine and a varied social life.

Robbie can do none of these things. His illness and depression have rendered any kind of long-term employment or social life too difficult to pursue.

He is defective. Not good enough. Never has been.

He pulls his hand away from her grasp. 'You should go … I'll see you out.'

37
GRACE

The reunion has been called off. Grace is both relieved and disappointed on receiving Katy's email.

From: admin@yearbook.com.au
Subject: Reunion cancelled

Sorry, everyone. People are still being sent threatening notes and so the reunion is off. Maybe another year. Let's stay in touch. Use the Facebook group to post old photos and news. Xxx Katy

There will be no night out in Manly, no overnight stay in a hotel, no complicated babysitting arrangements. Their budget will be the better for it. She was so looking forward to it, though. Seeing how everyone has changed, if they've transformed themselves – like

Katy – or are essentially the same – like Annabel. Grace likes to think that she falls into the former category. She has changed, grown, become a better, stronger person. Not as easily influenced as she once was.

Tom sticks his head around the study door. 'Are you coming to bed?'

'Just finishing off a few things,' she says vaguely. 'I'll be a few minutes.'

Most nights she waits until he's asleep before slipping carefully between the sheets, keeping a safe distance when before she would have cocooned her body in his. She can tell he's puzzled by her behaviour this past week, which has been see-sawing between avoidance and sudden interrogations.

'Have you come across Daniel recently?'

'Are you sure you've never met Zach Latham? He's a well-known GP in Manly.'

She brings up Luke's name, Katy's name and Melissa's name, and searches his face for recognition: not a glimmer. Unless he's a very good actor. *It makes no sense*, she tells herself. There is nothing linking Tom to these people. And not only is there no link, there is no *reason*: other than the flimsy theory of Tom wanting to force Annabel's hand with Daniel, and then – because he had sent Annabel an email – convincing himself he needed to send others. Flimsy being an understatement. Grace has been inside her head far too much. She needs to talk this through with someone who knows both Tom and the intricacies of what's been going on. Someone who can tell her, in her usual brusque manner, to stop being daft: Annabel. But that's not going to happen anytime soon; her poor friend has barely left Jarrod's side. Grace's details about the accident are sketchy. Annabel's not allowed to have her phone switched on in ICU, and Grace has spoken to her only a couple of times, their conversation centred around practical ways in which Grace can help.

Her thoughts revert to her husband, and the disturbing truth that he knew all along about Daniel's dabbling with drugs.

Tom is a good man. He would never threaten or upset people. Yes, he can be a bit judgemental and zealous at times, but he would never do anything as extreme as this.

The reunion has been *cancelled* because of these messages. All of Katy's planning and organisation come to nothing. Grace's anticipation and nostalgia left with no outlet. But wait! Is that the point? Is that what she's been missing?

Maybe Tom doesn't want you to go, Grace.

Maybe it's that simple. For some bizarre reason known only to himself, her husband does not want her at this reunion and is prepared to go to crazy lengths to have it called off.

No, no, no. If Tom didn't want her to go, he would come out and say it. Wouldn't he?

Grace spends the following day in the kitchen, making a lasagne, a shepherd's pie and a pasta bake: crisis food.

She takes the meals around to Annabel's house in the evening, hoping to catch her friend on one of her quick trips home from the hospital.

Jemma answers the door. She seems pleased to have a visitor, and even more pleased when she sees the food. 'Hey, Grace. Oh, thank you *so much* … Come in.'

Grace steps inside the cavernous hallway with its glossy white tiles. Everything in Annabel's house is ridiculously oversized: the master suite, the his-and-hers bathrooms, even the utility room seems unnecessarily large. Mia comes skipping from the back of the house and launches herself forward for a hug. There's no sign of either Daniel or Annabel.

'How's your father doing?' Grace asks, sitting down on a kitchen stool.

'The same,' Jemma says, shooting Mia a wary glance and leading Grace to the assumption that the young girl is being protected from the gravity of her father's condition. 'Do you want some tea?'

Grace smiles. 'That would be lovely.'

Poor Jemma. Having to hold everything together at home while missing out on her university course and social life. But she's always been the kind of child who gets on with things without much fuss. Mia is the same: low maintenance. Daniel, of course, is a different story.

'Is your brother home?'

Jemma shakes her head, grimaces. 'He's been taking advantage of Mum not being here …'

Grace feels a flare of anger towards Daniel. For his

colossal selfishness. For giving his mother and sister something extra to worry about, as if the situation with Jarrod wasn't enough.

Jemma pours boiled water into two matching mugs. 'Milk? Sugar?'

Everything in Annabel's kitchen is colour matched and ultra-modern. Polar opposite to Grace's kitchen, which is more than forty years old and looks every day of it. Every time Grace comes here, she resolves to buy some new crockery at the very least, but she never does.

Grace sips her tea, chats to Jemma about university, gives feedback on a story Mia is writing for homework, before tucking her god-daughter into bed. The clock is edging towards 9 p.m. and still no sign of Daniel. It's a school night, for heaven's sake. Where is he? Just as she is about to say something to Jemma, that perhaps they should try phoning him, she hears the front door open and close.

'Daniel?' Jemma calls out, worry etched in her voice.

A grunt in response. Then the sound of another door opening and closing. His bedroom? The bathroom? Grace waits, wondering if Daniel is going to appear at any point. Ten minutes pass. Fifteen minutes. Twenty minutes. Apparently not.

'I'd better go,' she says to Jemma. 'Thanks for the tea. Tell your mum to call me if she needs anything at all.'

'I will,' Jemma promises.

Grace smells it as soon as she steps into the hall. Earthy. Woody. Unmistakable. 'That's weed.'

Jemma sighs. 'He's been smoking every day since Mum's been at the hospital.'

What an awful, awful mess. What kind of state will Daniel wake up in tomorrow? How can he pay attention at school? Have the motivation to learn and do well? What is even the point of school if this is all he cares about?

'Has he been going to school?'

'No. But Mum doesn't know that.'

'I should try to knock some sense into him,' Grace says, moving towards the stairs.

Jemma sticks an arm out, stopping her. 'There's no point when he's off his face. Trust me.'

Her argument is valid. Nevertheless, Grace finds it difficult not to barge into Daniel's room, demanding he not cause his family this extra worry. She is uneasy as she hugs Jemma goodbye.

Her own house is silent and mostly in darkness. She looks in on each of the children. Tahlia is lying on her side, facing the far side of the room. Lauren is on her back, her face illuminated by her bedside lamp. Poppy likes to burrow down: her head is barely visible. Billy's in a tangle of sheets. She says a quick prayer for each child, that they'll make the right choices and not end up like Daniel. She looks in on Tom, too, who obviously went to bed early because of his 6 a.m. shift. Or maybe he's avoiding her now. Playing her at her own game.

Grace pours herself a glass of water and begins to process her thoughts, which are as tangled as Billy's sheets. What if Jarrod ends up with some long-term brain damage or some other debilitating problem? Annabel said there's strictly no visitors, so all Grace can do is offer support on the home front. She can't help feeling she failed tonight. That she should have done something more. For a moment, while she and Jemma were at a stand-off in the hallway, she'd briefly thought about phoning Tom and asking his advice. This last thought brings her back to all the horrible doubts she's had about her husband and the aborted reunion.

She sighs. She should go to bed. She hasn't been sleeping well.

She rinses her glass, turns out the lights, and then something prompts her to return to Lauren's room. At the time it's an automatic thing, she's turning the door-knob without understanding why. Later she thinks she might have subconsciously wanted to turn off Lauren's lamp. Or perhaps she felt a draught, or an increase in noise, or sensed some other change in the atmosphere.

There's no denying what she notices as soon as she looks into the room. The window is open. The curtains are blowing. And Grace is very sure that the window was *not* open when she looked in fifteen minutes ago.

'Lauren, what on earth are you up to now?' she whispers to her sleeping daughter.

Grace pulls the window shut, trying not to make too much noise. Something goes floating to the ground. A folded piece of paper. Grace opens it.

I have one question for you. If it was one of your kids being harmed, would you still look the other way?

Grace screams. Lauren jumps up in bed and starts screaming too. Moments later Tom comes stumbling into the room. He finds his wife and daughter clutching each other, whimpering in terror.

38
MELISSA

Melissa's head aches. Today she delivered three client presentations. One of her sales team threatened to resign, and another found a significant error in his commission payment. She got a step closer to signing Pharma Direct, but a long-term client – one she has bent over backwards to keep happy – is making noises about going elsewhere.

PJ, of course, knows none of this. All he knows is that she is finally home, and he is really, really pleased to see her. First comes the jumping and pirouetting. Then the zooming, skidding out of control on the corners. Finally, he collapses on his belly and puts his face between his paws, as though to say, *Boy, I'm exhausted.*

'I know exactly how you feel,' Melissa laughs. She opens the balcony door to let him out.

Tessa has left a note on the counter. *PJ has been very scratchy today. Should we take him to the vet?*

Melissa notices the 'we' and smiles. PJ has been to the vet and was prescribed a special cream, which seems to be working.

'You're perfectly fine, aren't you?' Melissa says when he comes back inside. 'Tessa's just being a helicopter parent.'

She changes his water, gives him dinner, starts to make something for herself to eat, all the while keeping up a steady conversation with the dog, who cocks his head and gives the impression he understands.

'I'm becoming one of those weird dog ladies,' she said to Cassie today. 'I talk to PJ like he's a human being.'

Cassie laughed. 'They love the sound of your voice. That's not the case with a lot of human beings.'

After dinner, Melissa flicks on the television while she answers emails; it's a constant battle to keep up with them, no matter the time of day. She sends Henry a text to say hello but doesn't expect an answer. It's open night at Tessa's dance school. Parents are invited to come and watch the class perform. Phones would be switched off, no doubt. Melissa wouldn't have minded going – things have defrosted with Tessa and she would have enjoyed watching her dance – but neither Henry nor Tessa suggested it.

At 9 p.m., Melissa lets PJ out for his final toilet, and then locks up. She realises afterwards, when she goes through the chronology of the night, that this is her first time entering the bedroom since getting home. She notices it immediately, the instant she turns on the light: a white envelope propped against her dusky-pink pillowcase. She assumes it's another note from Tessa. Until she opens the envelope and reads what's inside.

You make me sick, Snow White. People like you who care so much about animals but don't give a shit about real people.

The police officers are male; similar in build, age and levels of cynicism.

'So, nothing has been taken?' asks the one with the darker hair.

'Not that I'm aware of.'

Melissa has checked her jewellery, the safe where she keeps her passport and other important documents, and the drawer next to her bed where she tends to keep extra cash. Everything seems to be accounted for.

'Any laptops or other devices missing?'

'No. I had them with me.'

'Clothes, shoes, handbags?'

She is the owner of two designer handbags and has already determined that both are where they should be.

'So, the only indication that someone has been here is this letter?'

'Yes.'

'Was anyone home today?'

'My stepdaughter, Tessa. She comes every afternoon to check on the dog.'

'Where's Tessa now?'

'At dance class. With Henry, my husband.'

Melissa doesn't mention that Henry and Tessa don't actually live here. She doesn't want to see those expressions become any more dubious.

'Was Tessa alone when she dropped in this afternoon?'

'I don't know. Sometimes she has friends with her. I can't contact her at the moment to ask.'

One of the officers – the one with the lighter-coloured hair – leaves the bedroom.

'He's just going to collect some fingerprints off the door and other hard surfaces,' the remaining one explains.

Melissa assumes that the fingerprinting will only yield a result if the perpetrator is someone with an existing criminal record.

'There are security cameras,' she says. 'We should be able to see who has come in and out of the building from the footage.'

'We'll check with the building manager,' he promises. 'Your balcony door was locked when you came home?'

Melissa casts her mind back to when she let PJ out. She flicked the lock before she slid open the door. Didn't she?

'I think so.'

The officer checks the bedroom window, which is locked, and proceeds to check the other windows in the apartment. Finally, he examines the lock on the front door. 'No sign of forced entry.'

Did Tessa leave the door on the latch? The intruder wasn't in the apartment at the same time as Tessa, was he? Melissa's heart freezes.

'Look, can we sit down and talk?' she says to the darker-haired officer, his counterpart busy with dusting paraphernalia. 'There's a bigger picture here. Other people have been getting notes too.'

They sit, and she proceeds to tell him about the reunion, the yearbook, and what she knows about the emails and notes. She has him over the line by the time she's finished; his scepticism has been replaced with concern.

'It sounds like we need to get a detective out to see you. Probably be tomorrow before we can organise that. Do you feel comfortable staying here in the meantime?'

Melissa does not feel comfortable staying here. Someone has been in her apartment, in her *bedroom*. She feels violated, more scared than ever in her life. *Dying alone. And you will.* Those words have taken on a heightened level of threat.

She shakes her head. 'No … but I have somewhere else I can stay.'

She goes back to the bedroom and quickly packs some essentials. PJ has been sitting out all the drama in his crate. She gives him a cuddle before attaching his lead. 'Come on, boy. We're going on an adventure.'

The police officers walk out with her, one of them offering to carry her bag. The car park is deserted, menace lurking in every shadow; she is extremely glad of their presence.

'We'll be in touch.' They shake her hand and depart.

Melissa throws her bag in the boot and hurriedly secures PJ's lead around one of the headrests. She turns on the ignition and doesn't exhale again until all the car doors are locked.

'Let's get the hell out of here,' she says. The tyres screech when she turns the steering wheel, causing another surge in her heart rate.

It's 10 p.m. Henry and Tessa will be home by now. Should she phone? Warn them that she and PJ are on their way?

'Oh, whatever! Henry will just have to deal with it. Tessa and Christopher, too. We're coming to stay and there's not a single thing they can do to stop us.'

It's a fifteen-minute drive to Henry's house. Melissa grips the steering wheel and repeatedly checks her rear-view mirror. Someone could be following her. How would she even know it if they were? All she can see is the blur of headlights. She presses down on the accelerator. She's well over the speed limit, doesn't care, can't get to Henry's house fast enough.

39
ANNABEL

'Mrs Harris?'

Annabel looks up from her magazine. Takes a moment to focus. It's a woman. Short hair, freckles. Late twenties or early thirties, perhaps? Her clothes look more suited to an office than a hospital: fitted black trouser suit, white shirt with a frill down the front, flat stylish shoes.

'Sorry,' she mumbles, quickly putting down the magazine. 'I didn't hear the door. Must have been half asleep.'

It's been a week now. A haze of sleep deprivation and too much time spent in this room.

'Detective Sergeant Brien,' the woman says, holding out her hand. 'I was wondering if I could have a word?'

'Of course.' Annabel stands up to make the

handshake. 'Actually, I could do with a change of scene ... Should we try the café downstairs?'

While they're in the lift together, the detective makes enquiries about Jarrod's condition and Annabel wearily relays what Dr Chan has said: it's a matter of waiting, being patient, taking each day on its own merits.

The café is full, so they order take-away coffees and sit on one of the garden benches.

'Mrs Harris, I'm here today to give you an update on our investigation,' the detective begins. 'We assumed that your husband received what he thought was a call-out to the warehouse. We've checked his phone history for the days prior, focusing on incoming calls. Next we looked at location data to see which of those numbers were in the vicinity of the warehouse at the approximate time of the assault.'

Annabel listens carefully. The coffee has made her feel less sluggish. 'You mean you've used GPS?'

'Not all phones have GPS enabled, but we can usually establish an approximate location by looking at signals from the handset to the local base station.'

'And did you find any suspicious calls?'

'We believe we've identified the relevant phone number, yes. A ten-dollar prepaid sim that looks like it was used for one single phone call. We're currently tracking down the paperwork at time of purchase.' She anticipates Annabel's next question and expands, 'Evidence of identity is required, unless paying by credit or debit card.'

'So you're saying we should be able to find out who did this? We just need to find out who bought the sim?'

The detective smiles ruefully. 'It's rarely that straightforward. There are ways of getting around the identification process: false IDs, et cetera. But the fact that the call was made from a prepaid is a warning bell. It implies the assault wasn't something that happened in the heat of the moment ...'

Annabel's stomach lurches. 'You're saying someone *planned* to hurt Jarrod?'

'What I need to know from you, Mrs Harris, is who Jarrod's enemies are. Does he have any clients who're engaged in illegal activities? Has he recently fallen out with any circumspect friends? Has there been anything *unusual* about the past few weeks?' The detective's eyes are earnest. 'I need total honesty here. If you know something, or even have a slight suspicion, I want to hear about it.'

Annabel leaves the hospital shortly afterwards. Her head is spinning. *Someone planned to do this to Jarrod.*

The traffic is relatively light and she is home in less than ten minutes. The house is quiet; Jemma must have gone out. Mia and Daniel aren't due home from school for another hour. Annabel should have a shower, a decent meal, even a nap ... but the same urgency that drove her out of the hospital propels her to the study, where Jarrod keeps his business paperwork.

'Did someone owe you money?' she mutters, opening

315

the drawers of the filing cabinet. 'Or was it you who owed them?'

She scans each file, paying particular attention to recent correspondence, finding nothing. Some overdue amounts, yes, but nothing significant enough to warrant this kind of action.

If this wasn't about the business, then what was it about? Annabel moves to the bedroom. She checks the pockets of Jarrod's jeans and jackets, then his bedside drawer, where he tends to throw loose change and receipts.

The detective made blunt enquiries about Jarrod's – and Annabel's own – fidelity.

'Is it possible this is a love affair gone wrong?'

'No!' Annabel cried. 'I know he works long hours, but I'm pretty sure that's all he's been doing.'

She didn't mention the message from Melissa. It was a photograph of a puppy, for God's sake, hardly evidence of a raging love affair.

Then she remembered Zach, dishevelled and shaken, convinced that Jarrod's accident was related in some way to the reunion.

'There is something. A twenty-year school reunion. It's been getting rather nasty …'

The detective asked a torrent of questions: who was organising the reunion, had Jarrod been acting strangely about it, and the names and phone numbers of everyone who'd received messages.

But if this is really about the reunion, why didn't

Jarrod get an email or a note? He'd been the epicentre of all the boys at school, just like Annabel had been the epicentre of the girls. It sounds vain to say that everything revolved around both of them, but it's true.

Annabel shuts the bedside drawer. She's drawn to the window. The sky is blue and cloudless, yet something about the lighting makes the day seem overcast. Lack of sleep is tinting everything, even the sunlight. Jarrod's van is parked on the grass verge, the front wheels turned slightly out, as though waiting for its owner to jump on board. Tom was kind enough to drive it back from the warehouse after the accident. Annabel wonders if the police will want to have a closer look at it, given their recent suspicions. Then she remembers: sometimes Jarrod leaves paperwork in the van.

She hurries downstairs, locates the keys, and almost runs outside, having no idea why she is suddenly in such a rush. She opens the passenger door and finds a considerable amount of paperwork lying on the seat. Invoices payable. Receipts. Electrical plans. Some of Mia's drawings. Then a sheet of paper typed in an all-too-familiar format.

Name: Jarrod Harris

Highest achievement at school: Sports captain.

What you do now: Electrician. Self-employed.

Highlights of last twenty years: Been a hard slog, hasn't it? Ever wondered if there would have been more 'highlights' with Melissa?

Lowlights: The day your own son punched you in the face? Or maybe it was the night he got wasted and beaten up in Manly?

Deepest fears: That Daniel will be the undoing of everything.

So, Jarrod received a note too and neglected to tell her about it. Annabel's knees are shaking; she needs to sit down. She pulls herself into the van and curls forward, her head in her hands.

How on earth does this person know about the row in the restaurant? How do they know about Daniel getting beaten up? Everyone in school knew about Jarrod and Melissa, so no mystery there, yet this is where Annabel's thoughts become snagged. Fucking Melissa. Why did she send Jarrod a photograph of her dog? What has been going on? Is Melissa, or Jarrod, trying to rewrite their story? Jarrod committed himself to Annabel and their unborn baby. He never once, in any argument or disagreement since, implied that he regretted his choice. But Annabel can't help wondering if he would have been happier with Melissa. And would Annabel herself have been happier with someone else? How can she even ask these questions sitting outside their home, a house they built together, the place where they've reared their children?

Annabel wipes away her tears with the heel of her hand. She is overwrought and exhausted to the point of feeling ill. This is why she is sitting in her husband's van having a breakdown, in full view of the neighbours. She will take a photo of the note and send it to the detective. First, she'll go inside and at least have a shower before the children get home from school.

She turns to open the door and is startled by the sight of a face pressed against the glass.

'Mum?' It's Jemma. She's holding some grocery bags.

Annabel opens the door and swings herself down to the ground. She turns her head so Jemma won't see her tear-streaked face.

'What are you doing in Dad's van?' her daughter asks suspiciously.

Annabel waves the sheet of paper. 'Finding evidence for the detective … They suspect that the assault on your father was planned in advance.'

Jemma is visibly taken aback. 'What? Can I see?'

Annabel hesitates, unsure if she should share this burden with her daughter, and even more unsure if she can cope with Jemma asking questions about Melissa. Jemma is aware that her conception wasn't planned but has been led to believe it was a pleasant surprise, something her parents were thrilled about – once they'd got over the shock! Jemma may be technically an adult, but that doesn't mean she wouldn't be deeply upset by the

319

knowledge that Jarrod had been in a different relation-ship at the time, and the obvious truth that there had been no 'pleasant surprise'.

'Sorry, love. The police will probably want to take fingerprints. Best not to touch.'

'I can read it without touching,' she insists.

'I'd rather you didn't,' Annabel says, more harshly than intended.

She takes a few steps towards the house, in the hope that Jemma will follow and drop the issue. No such luck. The shopping bags are on the ground, her arms are folded; Jemma's not budging.

'Why can't you tell me what's going on?'

Annabel pauses and reconsiders. Jemma is nineteen going on twenty. She deserves some sort of explanation.

'It's to do with the reunion. You know how we were planning on having an updated yearbook?' Jemma nods. Annabel has mentioned it before on several occa-sions. 'Well, some of us had updates written for us, containing quite sensitive information. At the start it seemed like someone was playing a joke, but the mes-sages got nastier and nastier. One of the avenues being investigated by the police is if your father's assault has anything to do with the person writing the fake year-book entries ...'

Jemma looks stunned, her mouth agape, and Annabel immediately regrets being so candid. Jemma is at that weird stage of life, an adult by law but still incredibly vulnerable and easily upset. Annabel was mother to a toddler at the age Jemma is now. Her heart breaks a little every time she thinks about her teenage self and how quickly her youth and vulnerability got left behind.

'What happened to Dad has nothing to do with the yearbook entries … The police need to look for the real culprit.'

Annabel takes a moment to process what her daughter has said, and another moment to hear – and question – the certainty in her tone.

'The police are investigating a number of avenues, the reunion being one of them,' she reiterates. 'Come on, let's go inside and have a cup of tea.'

But once again, Jemma isn't budging. She looks Annabel squarely in the face.

'It was us, Mum. Me and Daniel.'

'What?'

'We were stoned one night and thought it would be funny. You're always harping on about your school days, how you were school captain and super popular, so we thought we'd send you an "update" on how you're doing today, bring you down to size … It was incredibly immature, I'm sorry …'

Annabel can feel her legs go from under her. Jemma's words repeat themselves. *Stoned. Popular. Immature.* She grabs at the porch wall to steady herself.

'No … You couldn't … It's not …'

'We did.' Jemma is adamant. 'It was us. Daniel and me.'

40
LUKE

Luke wakes to the sound of a child's laughter. He has no idea where he is. It takes a few moments to find his bearings. Floral wallpaper. Light flooding through sheer yellow-tinged curtains. He's in his childhood bedroom. He doesn't have a hangover. The bed next to him is empty, which means Aaron is up and about. Downstairs having a natter with his father? Jesus, time to get up and rescue him before something unforgivable is said.

Luke stumbles to the bathroom, brushes his teeth, runs a rough hand through his hair. He looks like he has been out on the town, which couldn't be further from the truth. The last few nights have followed the same pattern: a quiet dinner with his father before his eyes begin to droop, unable to fight the pull of sleep, and having to excuse himself for 'an early night'. Luke can't understand it. Never before has he so fully succumbed to jet lag. Must be years and years of it, catching up with him all at once. Or maybe it's exactly what Aaron suggested when he convinced him to take this holiday: the toll of all those exhausting shifts without taking enough leave to recuperate. Whatever it is, jet lag or burnout, Luke has never slept so long or so soundly. What's odd is that it's happening here, in his father's house, a place he associates with unrest and agitation.

There's a strange woman in the kitchen when Luke goes downstairs. She has short hair and a familiar manner with his father, standing close to him as she sips from a mug. She says something and his father chuckles. If that's not startling enough, there's *a child* sitting under the kitchen table – a boy of about three or four years old – playing with toy cars, manoeuvring the vehicles around the legs of the chairs.

'Luke.' Tony spots him standing by the doorway. 'Thought you might be dead up there. This is Maxine and Jed.'

Jed regards him curiously from underneath the table while his mother's face creases with warmth. She puts down the mug, comes forward to greet Luke, grasping his hand in both of hers.

'It's so lovely to meet you at last.'

At last? How long has this woman featured in his father's life, and in what capacity? She's significantly younger than him, at least twenty years. She's obviously a very nice woman. What the hell is she doing here, with the King of Grumps?

'Your father is always talking about Luke this and Luke that ...'

Luke doubts this very much but is too polite to pull her up on it. Where's Aaron? Luke needs him here to share in his incredulity.

'Aaron's gone for a walk,' Tony says, anticipating the question. 'He's been up since the crack of dawn.'

Poor Aaron. While Luke has been clearing fourteen hours' sleep, Aaron has been lucky to get six. Then again, he has plenty of sleep reserves to draw on, unlike Luke.

'Cuppa?' his father enquires, already on his way to refill the kettle.

'Sure.' Luke turns to Maxine and tries to make a joke of his confusion. 'So, do you come here often?'

She throws back her head and laughs. 'Often enough to be a nuisance.' She points at Jed, who's clambering out from under the table, presumably to take a closer look at Luke. 'The problem is that this little fella has taken a strong liking to your father, and nags me all day long. Can we go and see Mr Willis? *When* can we go? Are we going *now*? I eventually give in, otherwise he'd drive me insane. We've tried to keep away the last few days, to give you all some space, but Jed has been pining, so here we are ...'

Since when has his father held such appeal for small children? Luke looks from Maxine to Jed, wondering if he's still asleep and they're the product of some weird dream that subverts reality.

'Maxine and her partner moved into the Murphys' place,' Tony says, which explains a lot. It's obvious that Maxine has made it her mission to befriend the cranky old man next door. She's using Jed as a ruse, pretending that the child wants to come here.

Jed holds out one of his toy cars to Luke. 'You can have the blue one,' he declares solemnly.

Next he goes to Tony, and slips another car into the old man's hand. 'You can have the green one. It's my favourite, but you can play with it today.'

His father reaches down to ruffle the child's hair. There is such genuine affection in the gesture that Luke feels tears spring to his eyes.

'It's like he's had a fucking personality transplant,' Luke exclaims in disbelief. 'Since when has he been so fucking welcoming to the neighbours? Since when is he someone who ruffles hair, for fuck's sake?'

Luke and Aaron are at Dee Why Beach, towels spread out on the sand, their skin white from the European winter. Aaron turns over on to his side and gives him an amused stare through his sunglasses.

'What are you complaining about, exactly? That your dad has become a nicer person? That he's making new friendships with people of different ages? Would you prefer the grumpy, intolerant version, just so you can feel justified hating him?'

Aaron's right. Luke's been blindsided by this softer version of his father. He's wary of him in the same way he'd be wary of a stranger. He doesn't understand how he has materialised. And he sure as hell doesn't know how to feel about him.

'It's too fucking late for him to become nice,' he says petulantly.

Aaron laughs. 'Now you're being a moron!'

'Fuck off,' Luke retorts, and Aaron laughs again because he knows that's what Luke says when he's beaten.

Aaron turns on his back again, propping himself on his elbows, admiring the view. 'Some panorama, eh?'

Once again, he's right. The navy-coloured ocean. The whitewash from the waves. The tint of orange in the sand. Luke has travelled the world and nothing compares to this coastline. Beach after beach, headland after headland, all the way to the tip of the peninsula.

Aaron's staring at the horizon now. 'So Tony wasn't a great dad. So he was harsh and a bit of a bastard at times. So he wasn't cool about you being gay ... But that was over twenty years ago. It was a different world then, and he was a different man. He's mellowed. The question is: are you willing to mellow too?'

'I have a voicemail from a detective. What the fuck is going on?'

Luke is back at home, boxed in by the floral wallpaper of his bedroom, sunburnt after spending too long

326

on the beach, and perplexed to have a missed call from a Detective Brien at Manly Police Station.

Katy sighs on the other end of the phone. 'Yeah, I got a call too. Apparently, things have got more serious. The detective wants to talk to all of us together. I can pick you up, if you like. We could go for a drink afterwards?'

Luke still hasn't seen Katy. They were meant to meet up on Wednesday night but he was too tired and texted her to cancel. He knows she would have been disappointed, hurt even, and so he grasps the chance to make it up to her.

'Yeah, that'd be great. Aaron can hang out in Manly while we're at the station.' Aaron is presently having a shower and taking his time about it. Luke has a few more minutes to chat while he waits his turn. 'So what's been going on? How serious is it?'

Katy's explanation is jumbled. Jarrod in a coma. Zach being threatened. Both Melissa and Grace have had intruders? Luke finds it all rather fantastical and hard to follow. Maybe because he and Aaron went for some beers after the beach.

'So, you're basically saying I've come back for a reunion that's been fucking cancelled?'

'Sorry. You were in transit when this all blew up. Besides, you were overdue a visit home. How is Aaron enjoying it?'

'Loving every minute.' Luke yawns. 'What time can you swing by and pick us up?'

'About five thirty.' Her voice catches. 'I can't wait to see you ...'

'Me too ... See you then.'

As though on cue, Aaron walks into the bedroom, towel around his waist. His hair is wet and beads of water glisten on his shoulders. He has the beginnings of a tan.

'It's all yours,' he says.

'About fucking time,' Luke grumbles, flouncing out of the room.

The bathroom is like his bedroom: a time warp. Cream tiles with a floral border. An old-fashioned shower, complete with plastic base and mildewy shower curtain. Pale pink enamel toilet and sink. The height of chic in its day, a long time ago, before Luke was born.

'I love the house,' Aaron declared this afternoon, at one of the trendy new bars on the promenade. 'It's very retro.'

Aaron seems determined to love everything about Sydney. The beaches, the lifestyle, even the fucking house. His enthusiasm is downright irritating.

Luke runs the shower on the cool side, in an attempt to wake himself up. That damned tiredness again. The house is sapping him. He's drying off when he hears it for the second time that day. The sound of a child's laughter. He goes to the frosted window, its top panel propped open to let out steam. Jed is playing in the garden next door, running along, pulling some sort of basic kite. Maxine is standing on the deck watching him, smiling, calling out, 'Careful … Don't tangle it.'

Someone joins her on the deck. Another woman, maybe a few years younger. She puts her arm around Maxine and draws her close. Kisses her on the lips in an unmistakably sensual manner. Luke does a double take.

Fucking hell. He's in a dream. This whole day has been one long weird fucking dream.

41
KATY

Katy pulls Luke into her arms. The dimensions of his body feel achingly familiar. The curve of his neck. The shape of his shoulders. Even the smell of him. She doesn't want to let go.

'It is *so good* to see you,' she says, when she finally pulls away. Then she opens her arms to Aaron. 'You too, buddy.'

Luke slams the front door behind him, as though he is putting an end to an argument.

'Is your dad home?'

'Nope.' His response is terse and Katy assumes it's the usual friction between father and son. 'Come on, let's get this police thing over with so we can go for a drink.'

She rolls her eyes and murmurs, 'Some things never change.'

Aaron laughs. 'You're telling me.'

Katy treats herself to a closer examination of Luke's profile as they walk towards the car. She discovers new lines in the corners of his eyes and around his mouth. He looks drawn, tired, and she forgives him for cancelling the other night, although she was cross about it at the time. He opens the passenger door and flings himself on to the seat. She's immediately reminded of their senior year of school, when she was like his personal taxi service.

'Looks like you're relegated to the back,' she says to Aaron.

She starts the car and does a U-turn. Luke has an attitude shift as soon as the house is out of sight. He angles himself in the passenger seat, so he can see both Katy and Aaron, and begins an animated account of the last few days.

'Aaron's been dragging me up and down the beaches, and all over the bloody city. He fucking loves it here.'

'What's not to love?' Aaron pipes up from the back seat. 'You people have no idea how good you have it.'

Luke ignores him. 'What about you, Katy? What have you been up to recently?'

'Oh, just writing reports and trying to come up with nice ways of saying "your child is crap at science".'

Luke laughs at this, as she knew he would. 'Are you seeing anyone?'

She hasn't seen Mike since she slept with him. He has texted, called and made all the right signs to indicate

331

he wants a relationship, but something is holding her back. She sees him sitting at her laptop and something inside her says 'no, no, no'.

Luke is waiting for a response. A quick glance in the rear-view mirror shows that Aaron is too. Katy settles for, 'Sort of.'

They're in Manly now. Traffic is slow along the beachfront. Katy turns off the main drag and scouts the side streets for a parking space. There. She puts the gearstick into reverse and moments later they're alighting from the car.

'I'll take a walk around the wharf,' Aaron says, obviously keen to explore. 'Text me when you're finished.'

He darts across the road before either Katy or Luke can offer further suggestions.

'Bloody tourist,' Luke says and they both laugh.

'It's going well?' Katy asks in a more serious tone.

'Extremely well. I want to ask him to marry me but I keep chickening out.'

Katy is happy for him, she really is, but the teenage part of her remains heartbroken. He was her first love and she has spent the last twenty years trying to find the same intensity of feeling, the same close connection, the same wry sense of humour and everything else that makes him who he is. She wants a heterosexual version of Luke, and it doesn't exist. This is why Mike and all the rest of them always fall short.

'Hey, don't cheat me out of a wedding. Stop being a

wuss and ask him.' She links her arm with his. 'Come on, time for a trip down memory lane.'

It's a surreal experience. Zach, Melissa, Annabel, Grace, Luke and Katy sitting round a table in one of the meeting rooms at the back of the police station. Here they are, all together again, just not in the way anyone imagined: the strangest reunion ever.

The detective looks around the table. 'Thank you all for coming here today. My name is Detective Sergeant Brien, and I became involved in this case when Jarrod Harris was assaulted last week. At the time we believed Jarrod's assault was an isolated crime, but a more detailed investigation led us to the reunion and the realisation that other crimes have been committed which may be connected. When police see a common thread across crimes we sometimes coordinate our efforts by forming a taskforce.' She pauses, her brown eyes looking at each of them in turn. 'From now on I'll be the first point of contact for any concerns you have, any further mysterious or threatening notes or emails, or any other crimes that appear to be connected to the reunion.'

The room is deathly silent. Katy finds her eyes drawn to Melissa and Annabel, the only two people in the group whom she hasn't recently seen. It seems appropriate that they're sitting on opposite sides of the table. Jet-black hair versus blonde. White skin versus tanned. Both attractive, even glamorous, but in vastly different ways. There was a time at school when they were close friends, but towards the end they became known enemies. How do they feel about each other today?

Annabel clears her throat. 'Shouldn't we tell them about Jemma and Daniel?'

'What about Jemma and Daniel?' Zach asks immediately. 'What've your kids got to do with this?'

The detective answers his question. 'We've established that the first two emails were sent independently of the others. They were sent by Annabel's children.'

Katy is completely blindsided. Annabel's *children*? What on earth? She sees Grace take hold of Annabel's hand and it's obvious, from her wordless support, that she's already aware of this development. Everyone else appears to be as staggered as Katy is.

Annabel waits a few moments. Looks down at the table. Then a quick anguished glance at Grace before she admits, 'They thought it would be "funny" to send an update on my life. Mocking me about how I haven't achieved anything since school, and what they saw as my unnecessary worry about Daniel's drug-taking. Later on, they decided to send a second email to Grace, in order to make mine seem more authentic ... Their story stands up, I'm mortified to say. The photo of Grace was taken from the family picture she included in our Christmas card. Jemma knew about Grace's miscarriage and her concerns about Lauren, and she admits to setting up a special email account. Both Jemma and Daniel are adamant they didn't send any other emails or notes, and Detective Brien and I believe they're telling the truth. It looks like someone else decided to get on the bandwagon and continue what they started … I'm so embarrassed and so very sorry.'

Annabel finishes to complete silence. Katy flits back through the chronology of events and remembers her own email asking whoever was sending the fake year-book updates to stop. Did her email inadvertently give someone the idea to continue? Annabel's head is bowed and Katy suspects that she is fighting back tears. Katy can't help feeling sorry for her. She knows all too well how cruel young adults can be. How mocking and derisive of their parents. How quick to inflict hurt without thinking through the consequences of their actions.

The detective opens the file in front of her, breaking the silence. 'Okay, next steps … We're reviewing CCTV footage outside a restaurant where Annabel's family ate after Mia's communion. The author of the notes seems to be aware of a family altercation that occurred, and hopefully the footage will show us who was in the vicinity at the time. We're also reviewing footage from outside Melissa's apartment block and have put an urgency on fingerprints taken from her apartment, as well as the hard-copy notes we have in our possession. We're looking through CCTV of the arterial road closest to the warehouse where Jarrod was found, and talking to homeowners in the street where Zach's car was parked. I'm asking you all to think hard about who in your cohort had a grievance, who would have the motivation and personality type to go to these lengths—'

'Robbie McGrath,' Zach cuts in quietly. Then he looks in Katy's direction and shrugs. 'I'm sorry, but I keep coming back to him.'

'It's not Robbie,' Katy says through gritted teeth. 'He wouldn't do something like this. We've been over this, Zach. Robbie's spent the last twenty years doing his best to disappear. It doesn't make sense that he would suddenly decide to return and get revenge. Besides, he was never someone to draw attention to himself or play games.'

'People do all manner of things that make no sense,' the detective says. She flicks through the file and extracts a page, her eyes quickly scanning the contents. 'I see you mention Robbie here, Zach, when you made your initial statement to the police. It looks like you gave him a hard time at school ...'

Zach adjusts his position in his seat. 'It's not something I'm proud of.'

The detective nods. 'Actions like yours can leave a deep psychological impact. I'll call on Robbie and have a chat.'

Katy thinks back to that day in Robbie's house, herself and Zach having a heated discussion afterwards in the car, when Celia, his sister, rapped on the passenger window. Zach stopped mid-sentence and rolled down the window. Celia's pale eyes were tearful and pleading. 'I've only just got my brother back after twenty years. Please don't scare him away again. You really upset him just now. Leave him alone. Please.'

Katy felt so ashamed of herself. Now a detective is about to turn up at his door making more accusations. Robbie deserves an apology, not their suspicion. But she supposes that the detective must do her job, and Zach can't help how he feels. All his instincts are pointing to Robbie, in the same way that Katy's instincts are pointing away from him.

The detective looks around the table again. 'Now, before we finish up, is there anything anyone wants to add? Anything you feel might be relevant? Sometimes it's the smallest things that are the most important.'

At first Katy thinks, no, she has nothing to add. She checks her watch; Aaron must be getting fed up waiting for them. Luke is reaching in his pocket for his phone and Melissa has put her handbag strap on her shoulder. Everyone is keen to leave. For some reason Katy's thoughts propel to Mike. There he is again, sitting at her laptop, tapping on her keyboard, running diagnostics without her permission.

She puts her hand up and immediately feels foolish. Why is she suddenly behaving like a school student? Even worse, her face is hot: she's blushing.

'I've been told there was spyware on my laptop … Maybe that's how this person got access to everyone's email addresses and other personal information. I was collating data for the new yearbook.'

Her laptop also contains browsing history relating

to fertility clinics, sperm donation, gay dads and single parenting. Oh God!

The detective nods slowly. 'It's possible, depending on the sophistication of the spyware ... We'll organise for forensics to take a look at your laptop.'

Might be too late for that. Mike removed all the spyware, didn't he? Has he helped the situation by removing the 'threats' or made things more difficult, perhaps wiping out important evidence? Oh God!

'Now, some housekeeping rules,' the detective continues. 'I've been quite candid today about the steps we're taking because I know you're all worried and I want to assure you that we're doing everything we can to get to the bottom of this. I won't be so candid going forward. You will be aware, from high-profile cases in the media, that information management is crucial to any investigation. To this end, I would ask that you don't discuss this among yourselves. If you feel the need to talk to someone, pick up the phone and talk to me.'

This gets a reaction, with several murmurs of dissent. 'What about our spouses?' Zach queries. 'Surely, we can speak to them? I mean, they're impacted too.'

'Minimal information is to be shared with family members.' The detective is firm. She closes the file in front of her and stands up. She is surprisingly short in stature. 'In the meantime, I want you all to exercise appropriate caution. Be alert. Be vigilant. Keep your homes secure. Try not to be alone.'

Outside the sun has fallen in the sky and the group stands uncertainly on the pavement. What now?

'Does anyone want to go for a drink?' Katy asks, looking around to gauge reactions. She wanted it to be just herself, Luke and Aaron tonight, but now it seems churlish not to extend the invitation.

'Good idea,' Melissa says and Katy realises it's the first time she's spoken all evening. 'I'm in.'

Luke takes Katy's hand in his as they walk towards the Corso. 'Bloody hell, Aaron's not going to believe this. It's like something from a novel, not real life.'

Katy is about to remind him that they're meant to keep the specific details confidential. The reprimand dies in her mouth. Mike's back in her head again; he will not go away today. She sees herself handing him copies of the messages. She sees herself discussing all the people involved and divulging all sorts of other details. In a moment of true horror, she realises that Mike knows almost everything about this investigation … thanks to her.

Oh, Katy, you fool.

What does she really know about him other than the fact that he was married to Brigette and supposedly works in security? He's a man who initially made contact with her through Facebook, for God's sake. He's a man who suggested they 'meet up' and was suspiciously quick to offer his help and experience. A man who she found on her laptop, breaching her privacy at best, and at worst deleting evidence that would've been useful to the police. A man who has slept in her bed, who has made love to her, but who is really, to all intents and purposes, a complete stranger.

Oh, Katy, you fool.

42
GRACE

Grace sticks close to Annabel in the pub even though part of her would have relished the chance to talk to Katy. She's surprised that Annabel agreed to come. She has so much to deal with. Jarrod showing no outward signs of improvement. Daniel, self-destructive and self-absorbed as ever. Now Jemma, the last person Annabel was expecting trouble from. Poor Annabel has been left reeling.

The pub is busier than expected. Melissa and Katy manage to secure a couple of stools but the rest of them remain standing.

'You all right?' Grace whispers, looking closely at her friend's face.

Annabel shudders. 'I keep having to redefine what rock bottom means.'

On hearing Jemma's confession, Annabel phoned the detective first and Grace second, so upset that Grace could hardly decipher what she was saying. That's how she ended up in Annabel's kitchen that afternoon, consoling both mother and daughter.

'I'm sorry, Mum,' Jemma wailed. 'I didn't think Daniel would become so addicted. I didn't think he'd be like *this*. Now I'm here every day, I can see what a problem he is and I feel so bad I had a part in it ...'

'I thought I could count on you, Jemma,' Annabel wailed back. 'I can't believe you would be so *irresponsible* with Daniel, and so *cruel* to both me and Grace!'

Grace refrained from adding her viewpoint, which took a lot of self-control. Jemma had violated the lines between adult and minor, getting stoned with her under-age brother. And why all this unwarranted vindictiveness towards her mother and Grace?

'Sorry, Grace, I know you tell me off only because you love me. Sorry, Mum, I'm so sorry. Now I can imagine what it's like to be a mother at my age, how daunting and constant it is ...'

Grace made them both tea that they didn't drink. She arranged for Mia to go to a friend's house after school. She didn't know what to do about Daniel but suspected he wasn't at school anyway. Later that night, she relayed everything to Tom. Everything but the fact that she'd actually suspected *him*. She will never tell him. Never admit that she lost faith in his goodness. He would be so hurt and bewildered. When she found that note in Lauren's room, Tom was her only solace; there was no doubt left in her mind.

Annabel has already finished her glass of wine. She takes her purse from her handbag. 'I'll get another … then it's back to the hospital for me.'

Grace declines Annabel's offer of a second drink. She wants to get home soon. To the kids. To Tom. She feels safer when they're both in the house. Two sets of eyes to watch the children. Next week they're having an alarm system fitted to the windows and doors. She is worried about the extra cost and what it will do to their precarious finances but at the same time counting down the days. She never wants to walk into a child's bedroom again and see an open window, a rectangle of darkness through which anything could have happened. She never wants to experience that sense of violation, that sheer terror. Fear about one's own safety is one thing. Fear for your children – so vulnerable and innocent – is quite another.

Katy comes over while Annabel is at the bar, giving the impression that she waited for the coast to clear.

'Hey, Grace.' She flits her eyes to the rest of the group. 'Well, this isn't what any of us expected.'

'No. It's quite the nightmare.'

'How is Annabel holding up?'

'She's doing her best.' Grace takes a sip of wine, reaches a decision. 'Listen, while you're here, there's something that's been on my mind.'

Katy cocks her head, smiles a little warily. 'That sounds serious.'

'It is ... I owe you a long-overdue apology. For pathetically standing by and allowing Annabel to be so awful to you at school. My loss, really, because I think you and I would have made great friends.'

Katy's smile changes to one of surprise and embarrassment. 'Well, thank you, but no apology required. What happened was nothing I don't see at work every day. For every kid who is lacking in empathy, there's another who's lacking in resilience. They're all emotionally underdeveloped and categorically self-absorbed, but that's part of their journey and most of them turn out okay.' Her eyes veer to Annabel, who is in the process of handing over cash to the barman. 'I get a lot of mums who see me because their child is being bullied or excluded. Some of them think it's payback, because *they* used to be the mean girl in their day, now the shoe's on the other foot. They are perfectly nice women, devoted mothers, as I am sure Annabel is.'

Now Grace wants to be friends with her all the more. How wise she is. Motherhood *is* a great antidote for meanness, as well as many other failings.

'Oh, look, there's Aaron.' Katy waves to catch someone's attention. 'He can't see us. Excuse me.'

She moves through the crowd, continuing to wave. Moments later Annabel returns with a fresh glass of wine. The timing is almost too perfect.

Melissa is next to make an approach. Grace tenses as she sees her coming. Another victim of Annabel's. Another apology owed.

Melissa holds out her hand to Annabel. 'I'm so sorry about what has happened to Jarrod.'

Annabel accepts her handshake and murmurs, 'Thank you … Everyone's concern means a lot.'

Twenty years of estrangement stand between them. It's hard to imagine what common ground they might have today. Grace is contemplating saying something, alleviating the awkwardness, when Melissa speaks again.

'I have teenage step-children. They're incredibly difficult at times …'

Grace thinks that 'difficult' is a diplomatic word to describe Jemma and Daniel's behaviour.

Annabel nods. Takes a large gulp of her drink. Grace knows her well enough to tell that she's planning her exit: the awkwardness is excruciating.

Melissa also senses Annabel's imminent departure. 'Stay,' she urges. Both Annabel and Grace are equally taken aback by the firmness in her tone, the authority. 'Stay a minute and listen. I've just realised something that doesn't add up … Some of us don't belong here. Me and Katy, for example. We were not part of your core group.'

Grace inhales sharply. Melissa has a point. Why didn't anyone think of this before now?

The question on Annabel's face transforms into a frown. 'So, what are you saying, exactly?'

Melissa's gaze swerves to Katy, who is now chatting to Luke, Zach and another, unfamiliar, man. 'I'm saying that our cohort – Robbie McGrath included – would not put me or Katy in this "group". They would've known I was blacklisted, and that Katy was never cool enough in our eyes to be granted entry.'

Melissa has Grace's full attention, Annabel's too. She stands in an erect and confident manner. Grace can imagine her on a stage, giving a presentation to hundreds of people, not one bit afraid of the limelight.

Her stare is quite piercing. 'I'm saying that whoever is doing this, whoever is sending these notes, is someone *outside our year group*. Someone close enough to know who's who and think they have a handle on the dynamics, but not close enough to get it fully right.'

43
ZACH

Zach's had three beers. He spent most of the time talking to Luke and his partner, Aaron, a sociology professor. He enjoyed their company, shook Luke's hand and asked him to keep in touch, even though he's fairly sure neither of them will make the effort.

It's raining when he gets outside, a summer storm that's come out of nowhere. Thunder, lightning, the works. Zach pauses, contemplating where he'll have the best chance of getting a taxi. The wharf or the beachfront? He jogs towards the beachfront, one of the few idiots braving the deluge.

He reaches The Steyne, looks left and right: not a taxi light to be seen. Lightning streaks the sky, illuminating the ocean. A deafening crack of thunder overhead. Then a miracle: a taxi pulls in a short distance up the road to drop off passengers, two women who giggle as they run for cover in their high heels. Zach sprints towards it, jumps in the back seat, slams shut the door.

'Forestville,' he instructs the driver, wiping water from his face.

As the taxi edges into the traffic, Zach notices a man standing close to the edge of the pavement. The man has a baseball cap pulled down over his eyes. He's obviously frustrated, his leg kicking out in temper. Zach wonders if he inadvertently pushed ahead of him. Maybe he had his eye on the taxi too?

Too late now, mate. Sorry.

Carson is awake when he gets home. No surprises there.

'Dadda?' he calls, as soon as Zach shuts the front door behind him.

'Coming,' Zach calls back, slipping out of his shoes and leaving them to dry on the mat.

He bounds up the stairs and sticks his head around his son's door, which he likes to leave slightly ajar.

'I'm soaked through, mate. Just give me a minute to get out of these wet clothes and I'll be back.'

'Okay,' Carson replies from the shadows. 'Hurry.'

Zach has to laugh. Carson has a funny concept of speed and when it's required. Izzy is not in their bedroom even though the light is on. She must be reading somewhere downstairs. Zach changes into jeans and a T-shirt, then doubles back to Carson's room.

He sits down on the side of the bed, strokes his son's hair back from his eyes. 'Tell me all about your day.'

Carson starts with vigour. A speech he had to deliver at school. Falling over at lunchtime and scraping his knee. He drifts off in the middle of telling Zach about his art project, something that undoubtedly involves copious amounts of glitter and enthusiasm. Zach kisses his son on the head and straightens the bedclothes. He never knew it was possible to love someone as much as he loves Carson.

He finds Izzy downstairs, sitting in the semi-dark, a book on her lap. Things remain strained between them. Zach has been sleeping in the study and of course Carson's deeply concerned about the change in the status quo. Zach explained that he'd been snoring – the first excuse he could think of – and had to sleep downstairs so he wouldn't keep Mumma awake.

Izzy turns down the corner of the page she was reading and snaps the book shut. 'We should talk.'

Zach closes his eyes, says a quick prayer: *Don't end it. Please don't end it.*

He sits down next to her, clasps his hands together, waits for her verdict.

'I hate what you did,' she opens.

'Me too,' he says, searching her face, her dark inscrutable eyes, for clues. He knows her better than he knows himself, but she folds into herself when she's upset. She becomes steely and aloof. Totally unlike her usual warm nature.

'The boy at school ... I understand you were a differ-ent person then, a selfish, shallow teenager.' Zach nods. That just about sums up his younger self. 'But cheating on Carson and me, that's been harder to rationalise. You were a grown man. You were a husband and a father—'

'I'm sorry,' Zach interjects. 'I'll be sorry till the day I die.'

'It was a difficult time,' she concedes. 'Such a diffi-cult time. Making an effort to be happy and proud like other new parents. Modelling excitement and positiv-ity in the face of all that pity ... But Carson loves you so much, Zach.'

Tears spring to his eyes. 'I love him, too. More than words can say.'

She nods. 'I love Carson more than I love you ... which is why I must forgive you. I must see your infi-delity as part of the struggle we were going through at the time, and try not to let it hurt me today.'

She's going to forgive him. For Carson's sake. He's crying in earnest now.

'I won't let you down again. I won't ever let either of you down again.'

'Please don't,' she says plainly, then takes him in her arms.

Sometime later, when Zach's emotions are back under control, he tells her about the group meeting with the detective. No more secrets. Besides, he knows she can be relied on to keep the details to herself and not compromise the investigation in any way.

'Do I need to worry about Carson and me?' she asks. 'Do I need to be careful when we go out?'

'I think you should be more vigilant than usual,' he says slowly. 'Keep the house locked when you're at home. Nothing has been proved but when you add up all the separate instances …'

'And the police are going to pay a visit to this man, Robbie?'

'Yes. I'm adamant it's him but Katy's just as adamant it isn't. I guess we'll see what the detective thinks.'

Izzy accepts this. She stands up, stretches. 'I'm ready for bed. Will you lock up?'

'Sure.'

Zach checks all the windows and doors, taking extra care to make sure everything's locked and secure. The curtains in the study are open. Rain slashes the window. Thunder is a far-off rumble. The storm is on its way somewhere else. Zach closes the curtains, gets his pillow from the sofa bed and goes upstairs.

A terrible burden has been lifted. He's both lighter and stronger. At peace with himself. He's just like Carson in that regard: happy only when the status quo has been re-established.

44
ROBBIE

Robbie is in the garden playing football with Sienna and Charlie when Celia comes out. There's a stranger with her, a youngish woman wearing a suit. Something about her makes Robbie feel breathless.

'Sienna, Charlie, go inside, please,' Celia commands.

'But we're *playing*,' Sienna protests.

'Now!' Celia uses her do-not-argue-with-me-or-you'll-regret-it tone.

The children go inside with great reluctance. Robbie kicks the ball away and tries to act nonchalant.

'This is Detective Brien,' Celia says. There's a quiver in her voice. 'She wants to speak to you about Jarrod Harris.'

Not this again. First Zach and Katy. Now a detective pointing the finger at him. For fuck's sake.

'I wasn't the one who attacked him.' His voice has a quiver too. He sounds guilty as hell. 'I haven't set eyes on him since I've been back.'

'How do you know he was attacked?' the detective asks with a scrutinising stare.

'Zach.' Robbie is sure Zach told him but suddenly doubts himself.

She nods as though she's accepting this, but only for now. 'Can you tell me where you were Tuesday last week? Around midday?'

Fuck. Robbie looks from the detective to Celia and back to the detective again. Colour floods his face. *Oh fuck.*

'It's important we know your whereabouts,' the detective says, her voice hardening. She knows guilt when she sees it. 'So we can eliminate you from our investigations.'

Robbie needs to sit down. His knees are shaking. Every part of him is shaking. He's ashamed, so ashamed. He jerks his head towards the outside table setting.

'Can we do this sitting down?'

He doesn't wait for a reply. The seat is damp from last night's rain, moisture spreading on the seat of his shorts. Fuck! The detective sits across from him, clasping her hands on the table and leaning forward, interview style.

'I was at Newtown,' he blurts out.

'Where in Newtown?'

'A school ... Where Katy Buckley works.' It's no better sitting down. He's trembling just as hard.

The detective's face registers surprise. 'Did you meet Katy for lunch? Can she corroborate your whereabouts?'

'Katy didn't know I was there,' he admits hoarsely. 'I've gone to the school some days when I've been at a loose end …' He can't bring himself to look at Celia, can't face her dismay and disappointment. 'I've pretended to be one of the maintenance staff, even done some gardening … I don't know why. Maybe because Katy was always kind to me and I wanted to feel that connection again.' Robbie forces himself to continue. His stomach churns with self-disgust. 'I've followed her home on the bus and to her apartment. I've been *stalking* her.'

Will they charge him for this? For trespassing on school grounds? For following and watching Katy without her knowledge? He risks a glance at Celia. His sister's expression is rightfully appalled.

The detective reads his thoughts. 'It's all right, Robbie. Don't worry about the technicalities. If you meant Katy no physical or mental harm, it will count in your favour.' She pauses, her eyes holding his, making it impossible to look away. 'I just want your honesty for now, we can deal with the other stuff later. We know about your history with Zach. He's admitted to the terrible humiliations he inflicted upon you and is deeply regretful. Did you have a history with Jarrod, too?'

Robbie closes his eyes. Jarrod's face is there. Cocky. Forceful. Refusing to back down.

'You're in a safe place, Robbie.' The detective's voice

sounds far away. 'You can be completely honest and I'll protect you as best I can. I need your help to understand who Jarrod was back then. Was he as cruel as Zach?'

Yes. And his actions had much longer lasting ramifications.

'He stopped me,' Robbie whispers.

'Stopped you from what?' The detective's voice is so distant it could be entirely in his head.

'From killing myself.'

Celia yelps. Presses her knuckles to her mouth. *'Don't say that!'*

Robbie is back in time. Running down the street, away from that awful party, away from the image of Zach writhing on the ground and everyone sniggering. There's shouting behind him, the thud of feet in pursuit.

'Stop! Hold on!'

Robbie didn't stop. He didn't hold on. Every breath felt like fire in his throat. His sneakers had thin soles, unsuitable for running, and pain reverberated from his feet to his shins. He knew only what he was running from, had no idea where he was actually going. Then it came to him. The playing fields. The rock face on the eastern end, remnants of an old quarry.

'Zach's a dickhead! Don't pay any attention to him!'

Jarrod was gaining ground, faster and fitter from all the sport he played. He caught up at the fields, lunge-ing at Robbie from behind, both of them rolling on to the dewy grass.

'Zach's a dickhead,' he repeated. 'Don't listen to him.'

'Fuck off.' Robbie pushed Jarrod away and jumped back on his feet. He began to half-walk, half-run across the grass; it was hard to see very far ahead. No street lights up here. No moon or stars. Just blackness.

'Wait,' Jarrod panted, a few steps behind. 'Just wait.'

Robbie ignored him. Plunged ahead. Reaching the far side, he started to climb the embankment, then the overgrown track to the summit.

'What the fuck are you doing?' Jarrod stopped at the bottom. He sounded both annoyed and incredulous.

Robbie didn't answer. He stumbled, almost fell flat on his face. Brambles and scrub scratched his legs but he didn't care. He had a purpose. He was going to do it. Right here and now. He was going to end his defective existence, put his fucked-up, seizure-prone brain out of its misery.

'Stop!' Jarrod commanded. 'It's pitch-black. We could fall and kill ourselves.'

'Result,' Robbie shouted from above.

Jarrod finally understood. 'Fucking hell. You can't be serious?'

Robbie reached the summit and negotiated the last few metres to the sheerest section of the rock face. He peered over. Was it far down enough? Was there enough clearance to make a clean jump to the bottom? There was a slight wind. He liked the feeling of it on his face, imagined himself being buffeted on the way down. He could hear Jarrod scrambling up the track, thrashing through the undergrowth and straggly trees.

'Go home,' Robbie instructed him. 'You don't want to see this.'

Jarrod's voice projected through the dark, husky, panicky. 'I'm not going to "see" anything because you're not fucking doing it.'

He reached the top. A standoff: they both stood there, barely able to see each other.

A few steps forward, that's all it would take. Robbie felt strong enough to do it.

'Let's just sit down and talk things through,' Jarrod pleaded. 'Come on. What's the rush?'

Jarrod sat on the ground, his voice dropping with him. Then he started blabbering. About Annabel being pregnant. About both sets of parents being aghast. About how they hadn't planned it – obviously – but they would try to do their best. He talked until Robbie, becoming distracted, sat down too. He talked until Robbie's intensity and resolve dissipated, and all that was left was weariness and a desire to curl up in bed. Sometime in the early hours of the morning, by mutual agreement, they made their way back down the hill. Jarrod escorted him to the door of his house.

'I'll be checking up on you, mate,' he threatened.

And he did. Every fucking day he would come to the house and knock on the door, asking for Robbie. They would have a short one-sided conversation.

'You okay?'

'Not planning any more rock-climbing?'

'Want to talk?'

Celia, Nick and his parents were perplexed by Jarrod's bizarrely brief visits.

'Is he blackmailing you or something?' Nick asked one night.

Robbie laughed off his brother's question. Nick was closer to the truth than he realised. Jarrod *was* blackmailing him. Making it impossible to try again, not giving him enough time with his own thoughts to work himself up to it.

A couple of weeks later Robbie packed his rucksack and got on that early-morning bus out of town.

'I hate Jarrod Harris,' he finishes now, tears streaming down his face. Celia is bawling too, and even the detective looks shaken. 'He stopped me, and even though I've wanted – many, many times – to try again, I've never worked up the courage. I've never felt as determined or as strong-willed as I did that night.'

45
ANNABEL

Annabel gets the call around 7 p.m. She's in the hospital foyer, taking a short break. It's Daniel's phone number but an unfamiliar voice.

'Mrs Harris?'

'Yes,' she replies cautiously.

'It's Liam, Daniel's friend.'

Annabel freezes. She knows who Liam is. He uses drugs with Daniel. That does not, by any definition, qualify him as a friend.

'Is something wrong?' she asks, even though she already knows the answer. Why else would Liam be calling from her son's phone? Why else would he sound so scared?

'There's an ambulance here ... Daniel's unconscious ... The ambos told me to phone his family ...'

So here it is. The phone call she's been waiting for since the last time. The phone call she's been dreading and fully expecting.

'Is he breathing? Does he have a pulse?' she croaks. She wants to shout and scream but her voice is like the rest of her: sapped of strength.

'The ambos said his vital signs are good but he's unresponsive ... He's out cold, Mrs Harris.'

She sees her son in her head. Pale, lifeless, oblivious to everything: the panic he's caused his 'friend', the weary resignation of the attending paramedics, the helpless terror of his mother at the end of the phone.

'Find out where they're taking him,' she says.

She hears a muffled exchange in the background. One of the paramedics mentions 'Northern Beaches' before Liam comes back on the line to confirm it.

Annabel almost has to pinch herself. Her husband is in ICU on the first floor of the hospital, and her son is about to be brought into A&E.

'This can't be happening,' she sobs. 'This can't be real. It's too much.'

Liam is still on the line. 'I'm sorry, Mrs Harris. I'm really sorry. I hope he'll be okay.'

If he wasn't the prolific drug user she knows him to be, she could easily mistake him for a responsible and empathetic young man.

Daniel regains consciousness just after 8.30 p.m. He opens his eyes abruptly. Squints into the bright lights of the emergency room. Blinks in surprise when he notices his mother. Stares down at his hand, which is grasped in hers. His face fills with confusion.

'Hello,' Annabel whispers. 'You're in hospital.'

'What happened?' He sounds remarkably lucid. Must be whatever they've pumped through his system, washing out the toxins.

'You overdosed. You've been unconscious for almost two hours. Apparently, you were vomiting and unable to move your head. Liam put you into the recovery position and called an ambulance. It was very fortunate you were with someone responsible.'

She can't believe she's making Liam sound like a hero. Things have become that surreal. Standards have become *that low*.

'Sorry,' Daniel mutters, his eyes cast downwards.

'Here you are,' Annabel says sadly. 'And your father is upstairs. What am I to do, Daniel? What am I to do with you both?'

The irony is, she had a serious chat with Daniel only last night. They were both home at the same time – a miracle! – and she took the opportunity to sit him down. She explained the gravity of his father's condition, how she felt compelled to be by his side, and how much she needed Daniel to stay on the straight and narrow and not cause problems at home.

Now this. Less than twenty-four hours later. She had obviously been wasting her breath.

*

361

Daniel is to be kept in for observation overnight. He's given a bed on the third floor.

'You don't need to come with me, Mum, I just want to sleep. You should go back to Dad.'

She doesn't put up a fight, which immediately makes her question what kind of mother she is. She watches the orderly wheel him away and tries to comprehend her mixed-up feelings: detachment, defeat, a reluctant acceptance of the situation. More than anything she feels a need for space, to be away from him in order to get her head together and work out what to do from here.

'Annabel?'

She swings around when she hears her name. Zach. Again?

He grins as he comes closer. 'Hey, I thought it was you. We must stop meeting like this.'

That's twice in the space of a week. In addition to the time in the alcohol and drugs centre. How can it be possible to have so many 'accidental' encounters after twenty-odd years of practically nothing?

'One of my elderly patients had a fall,' he says, obviously noticing the quizzical look on her face. 'Thought I'd check on her on my way home.'

He's a GP and this hospital is the closest major hospital to his practice. Of course, she's a lot more likely to run into him here than anywhere else.

'How's Jarrod? Any improvement?'

He asked the same question last night, as soon as

362

she arrived at the police station. The answer hasn't changed.

'He's the same. There's still a lot of pressure on his brain. They can't wake him up until the pressure is within a normal range.'

The doors to the department swing open and a stretcher is pushed through. A teenage girl, circled by doctors and nurses, trailed by paramedics and shell-shocked parents. The scene radiates urgency and Annabel is revisited by the terror she felt when Daniel was wheeled through. She needs to get out of here. She doesn't like this part of the hospital. The terse instructions from the emergency doctors, the palpable distress of the families and friends, the agitation and obvious pain of some of the patients. She much prefers the calm orderliness of the ICU.

She hurries to catch the doors before they shut. Zach falls into step beside her.

'How's your son? I meant to ask at the pub but couldn't get you alone.'

Now she's suspicious again. If he's here to see a patient, why stick around asking questions about Daniel? It's so odd he has turned up again. Is he too concerned about Jarrod and Daniel? Are all these 'meetings' accidental or staged? Then she has a thought out of nowhere. The note he showed her – the one where the author was fantasising about killing him – what if he wrote that note himself? What a perfect way to throw them all off the scent.

Stop being so paranoid. Zach is an old friend of Jarrod's. Of course, he cares about both Jarrod and Daniel.

Annabel walks through the waiting room, keeping her eyes trained ahead. Finally, she's outside, away from all the disinfectant and despair. Zach stands next to her, his hands in his pockets, waiting for her to answer his question. Now that she's out in the fresh air she realises her imagination has run away with her. Zach has no ulterior motive other than concern.

'My son overdosed,' she confesses, her voice overly harsh from her efforts not to break down. 'He's being kept in for observation …'

Zach rests his hand on her shoulder. 'I'm so sorry to hear that.'

'He could have died. His friend called an ambulance. He saved him. I should be grateful.'

Zach is embracing her now. Her cheek comes to rest against the thin cotton of his shirt, warmed by his skin beneath. His aftershave smells nice and she wonders how she can notice such things while being so distressed.

She tilts her head back so she can look at his face. 'I don't know what to do, Zach. I am all out of ideas.'

He stares down at her, his grey-green eyes narrow and pensive.

'I'll ask Izzy if she can see Daniel before he's discharged,' he says eventually. 'She has a way with teenage boys. For some reason they seem to listen to her … You just concentrate on Jarrod.'

46
KATY

Katy is setting chemistry homework when a runner knocks on the classroom door. Runners are Year 8 students who get a day off school in return for delivering paperwork around the campus. Usually the paperwork relates to permission notes for debating, sports or drama. On this occasion the note is addressed to Katy.

Detective Brien in the foyer waiting to speak to you.
Will send a sub teacher to cover your next class.
Jenny

Jenny is the school office manager, known for her strictness with students and teachers alike. Katy is slightly alarmed that a sub teacher has been organised so promptly. Is Jenny using her intuition or has Detective Brien inferred that their discussion will not be brief?

The bell goes and the students rise from their seats. Chair legs scrape the floor, bags are hoisted on to shoulders, and chatter and laughter erupt as they escape the confines of the laboratory. Katy wipes the whiteboard clean and packs her books away. What does the detective want? Surely, it could have waited until lunchtime or after school?

She runs into William on her way to the foyer. He's wearing an unflattering maroon-coloured shirt and a hopeful look on his face.

'Katy, I was wondering—'

'Sorry,' she cuts in breathlessly. 'Can't stop.'

One of these days she'll have to tell him the truth: *Nothing is ever, ever going to happen between us. I'll never be that desperate. Look somewhere else for your future wife.*

Detective Brien is studying the student artwork displayed on the walls of the foyer. She's in plain clothes.

She smiles and sticks out her hand. 'Katy, nice to see you again. Let's go and have a chat … The vice principal has offered the use of his office.'

The vice principal? What has any of this got to do with the vice principal? Katy catches Jenny's eye as she passes the front office. Jenny's expression is a mix of curiosity and knowing. Does she believe that Katy's in some sort of trouble with the police? How long has the detective been in the building? It's evident that she's spoken to both the vice principal and Jenny. Who else has she spoken to? And why?

The vice principal's office is lacking in both air and

366

natural light and there's no sign of its usual occupant. The detective waits until Katy is inside before shutting the door behind them. They sit down at the small circular table that's usually used for student conferences.

'Has something happened?' Katy asks with concern.

'There's been a development.'

'What's happened? Is everyone safe?'

'Everyone's fine. I'm here because Robbie McGrath admitted to trespassing on school grounds. CCTV footage corroborates that he was here Tuesday two weeks ago.'

Katy's breath catches in surprise. Well, that explains the vice principal's involvement; CCTV and grounds security are part of his remit.

'What on earth was he doing *here*? Was he lost or something?'

The detective's brown eyes lock with hers. 'He was watching you, Katy. He also admits to following you home on the bus and back to your apartment.'

Katy shivers. She pictures herself on the bus, busy on her phone or gazing sightlessly out the window. She sees herself walking through the all-but-deserted side streets of Neutral Bay, pondering what she'll have for dinner, or perhaps gearing herself up for a run. She shivers again, goose pimples on her bare arms. Why would Robbie do such a thing? Does this mean Zach was right all along?

'Are you saying that Robbie's behind the notes?'

The detective shrugs. 'We don't know. What we *do*

know is that the school's CCTV footage removes him from our inquiries about Jarrod's assault. But at the same time, it raises new concerns … about your personal safety.'

What were Robbie's words the day she and Zach went to see him? *I'm an epileptic who suffers from depression, not a psychopath.* But how can he justify stalking someone? Surely that's approaching psychopath territory? She remembers taking his hand in hers. The overwhelming sympathy she felt for him. The urge to help him in some way, although she couldn't for the life of her think how.

'I don't think Robbie would actually hurt me.' Even as she's saying these words, Katy is asking herself how she knows this for sure. She has no idea what he is capable of. 'Has he been following anyone else in the group?'

Once again, the detective shrugs. 'He claims that it's you only. Says he wanted to reconnect … It's obvious he has unrequited feelings for you.'

Katy's face floods with colour. It's not as if this news is a shock. She suspected that Robbie had romantic feelings for her at school, although she never encouraged him. 'I was kind to him when no one else was.'

It's obvious that he's still hanging on to that kindness today, attaching meaning to it. How sad!

'There is one other matter of concern,' the detective continues. 'We've noticed that the note you received is markedly different to the others, both in structure and tone.' She pulls a notebook from her jacket pocket and reads the words that Katy knows verbatim: '*You need a boyfriend, Katy, and better security in your apartment block. Great idea to have a new yearbook, though. Hope you're enjoying my contributions!*'

The detective has an expectant look on her face, as though she is waiting for Katy to suddenly cotton on to something. Katy frowns and concentrates. Yes, she supposes it could be Robbie. It's definitely less hostile than the other notes, and could even be interpreted – in a very warped way – as being protective. It fits with the stalking and the unrequited feelings, but it doesn't fit with what she saw when she held his hand in hers: the honesty in his eyes when he denied his involvement.

'I don't know why, but all my instincts are *still* telling me it isn't him. He may have the motivation, but he doesn't have the vindictiveness, or the slyness, or even the cleverness to orchestrate something like this.'

The detective nods, as though she has the same doubts. 'The author of this note seems to like you more than the others. Is there anyone else, either in the group or on the peripheries, who may have especially liked you? Any old boyfriends who come to mind?'

Katy blushes again. The detective seems to have the impression she was some sort of femme fatale, which is almost laughable. She sees herself in her school uniform going between classes, clutching her books like an armour: neither popular nor unpopular, one of those plain girls who boys never noticed – except for

Robbie. Then her thoughts jump forward, to today, and latch on to Mike.

'There is someone.'

She tells the detective all about Brigette Saunders's husband, who negotiated his way into her apartment and into her bed and who – through her naivety and poor internet controls – had access to all sorts of confidential information.

The detective takes reams of notes and follows with some hard-hitting questions.

'How do you know that Mike was actually married to Brigette?'

Good question. Katy took his word for it, which now seems rather lame. He sent some photos but, really, it could have been any woman in those photos.

'And you say that he works in security? Do you know the name of his firm?'

No, she does not.

'When did you last see or hear from Mike?'

At least this she can answer.

'Last night.' He phoned while she was out running. She didn't pick up.

The detective snaps her notebook shut. Her tone is urgent. 'Avoid seeing Mike or even speaking to him until we run some inquiries and forensics finish having a look at your laptop. Be careful, Katy. Don't be alone if you can help it … I'll be in touch soon.'

47
LUKE

'Hands on the wheel at ten to two ... Now move your foot from brake to accelerator ... Gently, gently ...'

Luke tries to be gentle, he really does, but the car surges forward, startling both him and his father. He immediately jams on the brake pedal, almost sending the two of them through the windscreen.

'Okay,' Tony breathes. 'Okay.'

They're in the car park at the local aquatic centre, a popular location for learner drivers. It's reassuringly deserted at this time of day.

'Let's try again. Gently, gently, that's good ...'

This is difficult for both of them. Luke is twenty years too late learning these skills. His father is an old man who might be a lot more patient than he used to be, but whose heart may not be able to withstand too many frights.

'Corner coming up … Ease off your foot. Easy … *Easy* …'

Luke makes a mess of it, Tony having to eventually reach across and guide the wheel around. Luckily, there's lots of space; they need it.

'Sorry, that was crap,' Luke apologises.

'You're all right,' Tony says, and something about his tone makes it seem as though it's meant in a much broader context than the driving lesson.

'I can take you out in the car today, if you like,' he had blurted out over breakfast.

Initially, Luke thought his father was suggesting they go for a drive somewhere.

'We could go up to the aquatic centre. There's nobody up there this time of day.'

Luke finally understood. His father was offering a driving lesson. He wanted to say, 'No, thanks, too fucking late,' but Aaron kicked him in the shin and chirped, 'Great idea. You guys can do that while I catch the ferry to the city.'

So here they are. Stopping and starting, again and again. Turning the wheel, then straightening it. Stopping, starting, turning, straightening, going round in circles. Luke hardly notices the time – more than an hour has passed. By the end of it, he can move off relatively smoothly. He can turn the wheel, although his hands are not always quick enough to complete the arc satisfactorily, and he can brake and come to a stop without inflicting whiplash.

'It's a start,' Tony says, when they swap seats for the drive home.

Luke has two weeks left of his holiday. If they do this every day, he might be someway competent going back to the UK. He'll at least have the basics. A start.

Maxine and Jed are coming out of their house when Tony pulls up at the kerb. Jed is on his tricycle and is so distracted by the sight of Luke and Tony, he almost crashes into the gatepost.

'Easy,' Tony says, averting Jed's crossbar to avoid the collision. Luke laughs inwardly. Tony has gone from one crap driver to another.

'This one needs to learn to keep his eyes on the road,' Maxine says with a grin.

Tony jerks his head towards Luke. 'Tell me about it.'

Something about the exchange makes Luke suspect that they've spoken about this before. About the fact that Luke – at the grand old age of thirty-seven – can't drive, has never been taught. Did his father admit to Maxine that he used his son's sexuality as leverage for lessons?

Stop being such a faggot and I might teach you.

Luke's been called a faggot many times since, but none that rendered him so powerless because driving, when it came down to it, equated to independence. Did flying become his substitute? All those kilometres clocked up in the air, all those long distances between countries and continents. Who needs wheels when wings can have the same effect, and better?

What made Tony change his mind? About the lessons. About his son's sexuality. Because it's very evident – from this morning's events, from how accepting he has been of Aaron – that something fundamental has changed. Has it been a gradual shift in attitude over the years, so slight that Luke failed to notice on his previous trips home? Or was it Maxine and her partner moving in next door, proving beyond doubt that non-heterosexual people are perfectly nice and normal, and in fact make excellent neighbours and friends.

Maxine and Jed continue on their way, Jed veering all over the footpath and Maxine jogging to keep up with him. His father bends down to get the post and the newspaper from the mailbox. They walk side by side up the driveway, their feet crunching on the gravel. Tony parks on the street because he's afraid the pebbles will damage the car's paintwork; he's pedantic about things like that.

'When did you find out they were a same-sex couple?' Luke asks quietly.

A pause. Laden with everything that has remained unspoken, unresolved, unforgiven between them.

Then Tony answers: 'I met Maxine and Jed first because they're home during the day. Jed took a liking to me and the three of us became friends. It was a few weeks before I realised that Jed had two mums.'

'How did you feel about that?'

Tony shrugs. 'I felt okay about it … I've come a long way, son.'

Luke swallows a lump in his throat. Jesus, why is he feeling so fucking emotional all of a sudden?

'I never asked what you voted.' Then he expands, even though his father knows exactly what he's referring to, 'In the same-sex marriage survey.'

Tony's stare is unflinching. 'I voted yes.'

Luke has to blink away tears. His throat feels like there's a golf ball wedged in it. He voted *yes*. He actually voted *yes*. The King of Grumps. Despiser of Faggots. Wait till Aaron hears about this turn of events! Luke wants to retort with something sarcastic but the words can't get past the damned golf ball. His father is staring. Tony seems sad, oddly vulnerable, his hair grey and thin, his face lined and full of regret.

Then the moment is over. Tony strides towards the door, sticks the key in. The kitchen, with its seventies fittings, is bright, almost cheerful.

Tony deposits the newspaper on to the table, and flicks through the post.

'There's something here for you,' he says, then looks confused. 'Must have been hand delivered.'

The envelope has Luke's name but no address or stamp. He opens it warily.

It should have been you they were fucking mocking, with your girlie clothes and prancing. Faggot.

Jesus. That word again. That hateful, belittling, hurtful fucking word. Far too early in the day to numb its effect with alcohol. Unfortunately.

'Are you making a cuppa, Dad?'

Tony refills the kettle as Luke sits at the kitchen table, re-examining his memories of Robbie McGrath and what he might have done to elicit such hatred. Robbie's locker had been situated directly below his and there was one occasion when Luke dropped a heavy textbook on his head. A genuine accident, followed by a laughing apology, because it was kind of funny. Another memory from cross country, the year when it rained heavily and the course was like a mud bath. Luke lurched over the finish line, lost his footing, and accidentally took down another competitor with him. He and Robbie ended up caked from head to toe. Another laughing – hysterical, actually – apology.

Neither incident warranted more than a fleeting grudge, if even that. Surely, Robbie would have seen the funny side? Maybe he didn't. Or couldn't. It can be hard to shake off the mantle of persecution in order to view someone or something through a softer lens. Luke knows this because he's been having the same trouble.

Tony sets down a steaming mug in front of him. 'Here you are, son.'

48
MELISSA

Melissa is sitting at the kitchen table with the original yearbook and a pen and paper. PJ is asleep at her feet. Henry and Christopher are at cricket practice and Tessa is somewhere in the house. The children are adjusting to the fact that she has been living here. PJ has helped enormously.

'You like it here, don't you?' Melissa murmurs, leaning down to give him a pat. 'It's much more exciting than my boring apartment.'

She has been back to the apartment only once, to collect more clothes. The police phoned the morning after the break-in: they'd found some slight damage to the front-door lock, dents on the pins consistent with the use of a 'bump' key. Melissa – after a quick, extremely alarming google on the mechanics of bump keys – immediately organised for a locksmith to install a more sophisticated high-security lock. The security footage hasn't yielded anything definitive from the traffic in and out of the building. Each resident has to be identified before being eliminated: not a quick process.

Henry accompanied Melissa when she went back to get her clothes but she still felt on edge. Would the sense of violation ever go away?

'I don't know if I'll ever feel safe in here again,' she said sadly.

Henry gave her a hug and then went to examine the shiny new lock while she gathered her things.

'Can you get that box down for me?' she asked, pointing to the top shelf of the linen cupboard.

Henry needed a chair to reach it. It came down in a billow of dust that made him sneeze.

'What's in it?'

'Some mementos from school.'

Melissa wasn't after the old school photographs or award certificates. The yearbook was what she wanted.

'Come on. Let's get out of here.'

Now, the yearbook is open next to her on the table. She's concentrating on the teachers, many of whom are profiled towards the rear of the book. Mr Collins, from the science faculty, who was mocked mercilessly because of his nervous tics. Mrs Romford, with her masculine voice and physique, who – quite incongruously – taught drama and dance. Miss Hicks, Year

Adviser with a hatred of chewing gum and a single-minded mission to eradicate it from the schoolyard. At the top of the pecking order was Mr Rowland, the rigid humourless school principal. Did any of the teachers have a grudge, an axe to grind? Where are they today? Retired? Travelling? Perhaps still doing some casual teaching or tutoring?

'What's that?' It's Tessa. She has come looking for PJ and found him curled up at Melissa's feet.

'It's my yearbook. All the way back in 2000. Ancient history.'

'Can I see your page?'

'Sure.'

It's not only the kids who've made adjustments. Melissa has learned to pause what she's doing when they appear, to give them her time – it's never for very long – and attention. If they don't converse with her of their own accord, she lures them with an offering of food, or funny stories about PJ. Now she flicks to her page in the yearbook and Tessa leans over her shoulder. Her eyes with their spiky mascara scan the photograph and then the accompanying text.

'You'll be remembered for being smart and a bit too serious? And your best memory of high school was awards night? *Really?*'

Melissa laughs. 'I was a bit full of myself, wasn't I?'

'Just a bit,' she agrees drily. Then her eyes turn back to the photograph. 'You were pretty.'

Melissa tries not to be offended by her use of the past

tense. She shows her Annabel's page. 'She was the prettiest. She was school captain, too.'

Tessa picks up PJ and hugs him close, like a baby. She seems in no rush to leave.

'Who was the best-looking boy?'

Melissa laughs again and turns the pages until she gets to Jarrod. 'I dated him for a few months. But he married Annabel and now they have three children.'

She doesn't tell Tessa that Jarrod is in hospital, or that his assault may be connected with the reunion. Tessa is aware there was a break-in at the apartment, but that's the extent of what she knows.

'Show me your friends,' she asks, curiosity piqued. 'Who you hung out with.'

Melissa complies. 'That's Zach Latham. Thought he was hilarious and God's gift to women. Happily married now, though. This is Grace, who was a close friend until I dated Jarrod, at which point I became enemy number one.' She gives Tessa a stare. 'Please don't fall out with your friends over boys. They aren't worth it. Not ever. Girls need to stick together.'

Tessa rolls her eyes. PJ has woken up and scrambles to get down. Tessa lets him go and begins to turn the pages herself, asking about anyone who catches her eye.

'Who's he?'

'Robbie McGrath. Bit of a sad story. We were awful to him. I wish I had stood up for him at the time.'

'And him?'

'David Hooper. Pretty introverted, kept largely to himself. As far as I know, Katy hasn't been able to track him down. Disappeared into thin air …'

Tessa seems shocked by this. 'No one knows where he is?'

'No one.'

Melissa thoughtfully makes a note in her pad: *David Hooper*. Does it mean something that Katy has found no trace of him at all? Who were David's friends at school? Are his memories of the good or bad variety?

PJ has made his way to the door; he wants to go out. Tessa notices at the same time as Melissa and goes to open it. Then she follows him outside, squealing with laughter as he zooms around the garden at full speed.

Melissa smiles and returns her attention to the teachers. She gets her laptop and opens up Google and Facebook. It's not long before she finds a picture of Mr Collins and his grandchildren, and asks herself if a kindly grandfather would do something like this? Then she sees a grey-haired Mrs Romford photographed on the Inca Trail. Is it possible for someone who's adventurous and well travelled to be hung up on some grievance in the far-distant past? On Melissa goes, methodically working her way through each name, and by the time she's done, she's satisfied in her own mind that it's not one of the teaching staff.

Without knowing why, she flicks back to Robbie's page. Looking at the photo, you would never guess. He's smiling, albeit shyly, because that's what people do when they're photographed. Slight curl in his hair, gentle eyes, he's nice enough looking, although she never noticed it at the time. It doesn't matter how hard she scrutinises it, the photograph offers no clue about the misery Robbie endured at their hands. Her eyes veer to the text.

Name: Robbie McGrath

What you will be remembered for: Just forget me.

Best memories of high school: None.

Worst memories of high school: Everything.

What will you be doing ten years from now: Living far away from here.

Poor Robbie: his memories of high school contained nothing positive whatsoever. He wanted to get away, and who could blame him? *Just forget me.* Melissa could never forget him, and she's sure the same is true for the others. She'll never be able to eradicate the image of him shuddering on the ground, foaming at the mouth, or the horror and helplessness as she looked on. It's a confronting thing to see at any age, but especially so for teens, who're so vulnerable beneath those faux-tough exteriors. *Just forget me.* Robbie was her first exposure to epilepsy, to malfunction in the human body, to the notion that invincibility was not a guarantee for any of them.

A repressed memory is swimming to the surface. Robbie sitting down next to her in class one day, Melissa promptly standing up and moving to another seat. It wasn't because of him, but he wasn't to know that. Annabel was sitting directly behind, and Melissa could not endure a full hour of hatred boring through her shoulder blades. She imagines how Robbie might have perceived the incident. If only she'd taken the trouble to explain to him afterwards.

Another memory. Annabel holding her stomach, gagging.

'He's *disgusting*. I'm going to be *sick*.'

The smell was unpleasant, but that was no justification for such callousness or theatrics. Melissa will never forget the misery in Robbie's face as he scrambled to his feet. A few weeks later an explanation materialised for Annabel's overreaction: she was queasy and highly strung because she was pregnant. Robbie would never have thought to connect the dots, and Annabel would never have thought to apologise.

It's funny how Zach keeps coming back to Robbie and now Melissa is too. If there is one thing she has learned from all her years in the corporate world, it's that the answer is often the most obvious one.

Robbie McGrath is the only person between these pages who had a genuine grievance. A reason for hating them all. For wanting revenge.

49
ANNABEL

A harsh and repetitive noise pierces Annabel's consciousness; it sounds like something one might hear at an airport, going through security. She is sluggish to wake up and then confused about where she is. She is not at the airport, she is at the hospital. But who is she with? Jarrod or Daniel? Jarrod, of course; Daniel was discharged earlier in the day. Annabel sits up in the pull-out bed. How could she forget where she is? She's been in this same room, sleeping on this same thin mattress, for two long weeks. What's different is that she has never found it so difficult to wake up. The beeping is coming from Jarrod's monitors, red lights flashing to the same insistent beat. She rushes to him, the floor cool beneath her bare feet. His hand twitches when she takes it in hers.

'You're coming back to us,' she whispers, her other hand reaching to stroke his face.

The door flies open and two nurses rush in. Annabel steps back to allow them access.

'I think he's waking up,' she murmurs.

One of them lifts Jarrod's hand to take his pulse, the other rolls back his eyelids and shines her torch into his pupils. Neither of them acknowledges that Annabel has spoken. She realises that they didn't even hear her. They press buttons on the monitors, their movements quick, their voices urgent as they relay various readings. Annabel feels the beginnings of fear.

'Paging Dr Chan. Paging Dr Chan.'

Dr Chan is the neurosurgeon who inserted the tube into Jarrod's ventricle, to drain fluid and relieve the pressure. Has something gone wrong with the tube? Is more surgery required? She needs to sit down; she can no longer trust her legs to bear her weight. She half falls on to the pull-out bed, the bedclothes thrown back from when she scrambled out only moments before.

'What's happening?' she rasps. 'Can someone please tell me what's happening?'

Finally, they hear her. They glance at each other – wordlessly deciding who will answer – before the older one approaches, crouching down so she's at Annabel's level. She's about Annabel's age, hair scraped into a bun, her face compassionate.

'I'm so sorry, Mrs Harris. We think he's having another bleed. Help is on the way.'

Before she has finished speaking, the door bursts open again. Two more staff in green scrubs, doctors of some description. Terse questions and replies. More fiddling with the monitors. Now they're doing something to the bed.

'We're just taking him down for an MRI so we can see what's happening,' the nurse explains breathlessly. She has left Annabel on her own again and now she is unplugging equipment from the sockets behind the bed. 'Dr Chan is on his way.'

The wobble in her voice gives her away; she is scared that Dr Chan will not get here in time.

'One, two, three.'

On 'three' the bed and associated equipment are mobilised and manoeuvred out of the room. Annabel goes to follow them. Then realises she has no shoes on her feet. Echoes of the day when Jarrod was admitted, and she was about to hop into the police car barefoot. Have they come full circle? Is this the end of what started that day two weeks ago?

She searches the floor for the sandals she was wearing before going to bed. Slips them on her feet and – quite bizarrely – decides to straighten the bed-clothes and plump the pillow. She stifles a sob. The rattle in the nurse's voice, the haste at which Jarrod was wheeled from the room, the fact that Dr Chan would only have stumbled out of bed minutes ago and would be in transit, at best – all of these things, as well as her own gut instinct, are telling her this may be her last time sleeping on this pull-out bed, in this room.

The MRI is undertaken in the medical imaging department on the ground floor, and the emergency surgery that follows happens in one of the theatres on the fifth floor. Between Jarrod and Daniel, she is an expert on all the different floors and facilities at the hospital. Annabel sits rigidly in her seat while she waits for news. She doesn't look at her phone or the pile of dated magazines that are within reach on the coffee table. The only thing she checks is the time. 2.17 a.m.: she imagines Jemma, Daniel and Mia sleeping in their beds at home, blissfully oblivious to what's unfolding. 2.34 a.m.: she's reliving those early, heady days with Jarrod. Feeling the heat of his eyes as they rest on her during class. Standing close together at the lockers, breath mingling, fireworks going off in her chest. 2.51 a.m.: she is back in the ICU room, visualising an entirely different scenario, one where Jarrod wakes up and gazes lovingly into her eyes. 3.02 a.m.: over an hour has passed since the monitors went crazy, indicating an increase in intracranial pressure and possibly another bleed. 3.17 a.m.: someone familiar is coming towards her. He's wearing scrubs and his sallow skin is pale and etched with exhaustion: Dr Chan.

He sits down next to her and takes both her hands in his. 'I'm so sorry, Mrs Harris. I'm so very sorry.'

50
KATY

Katy hears the news at lunchtime, when she checks her phone.

So sad to let you all know that Jarrod passed away in the early hours of the morning. He had a massive brain haemorrhage. Unfortunately, nothing could be done to save his life. I'll send funeral details as soon as I know.

Xx Grace

Jarrod is *dead*? Tears of shock prick her eyes and the screen blurs. She rushes from the staffroom, down the long corridor to the closest exit. Outside, students swill around her as she gulps warm air: it's well over thirty degrees today.

Jarrod is dead. She never imagined this outcome,

never imagined a scenario where he wouldn't wake up and be perfectly fine, because isn't that what generally happens with people like him? The attractive and popular people, who invariably bounce back from whatever misfortune befalls them, luck and fate unreservedly on their side. Oh God, is she somehow responsible for this? Did it happen because of her stupid notions about having a reunion and an updated yearbook? Did she unwittingly spark something in someone, a vicious desire for revenge? Would Jarrod still be alive if she hadn't been so fixated on having this reunion and proving to everyone just how much she's changed?

No, no, no. The assault on Jarrod could have been the result of a business dispute. Nothing has been proved. But, oh God, what a terrible thing to happen. Annabel and the children ... Katy can imagine their horror and shock. The father of one of her students died suddenly last year. The family was devastated, still are. The effect on the whole school community was profound.

'There you are!' It's Nina. She must be on supervising duty. Her eyes narrow in scrutiny. 'Is something wrong?'

Katy tries to tell her. About Jarrod. About Robbie, Mike and the detective. About her sneaking suspicion that she's somehow responsible for this awful, awful tragedy. Everything comes out in a wail that causes students to pause and stare.

'I think you need to go home,' Nina says, taking her firmly by the arm. 'You've had a bad shock. Come on, let's get a substitute sorted.'

It's worse at home, not better. There's more time to think. More time to blame herself. More time to feel scared. Mike has called twice since her chat with the detective. He seems to be extraordinarily persistent. Has the detective checked him out? *Was* he married to Brigette? What about his son, Toby, whom she met so briefly? Is he Brigette's child, or the child of some other woman? Is Mike genuine or fake?

How could you be so stupid, Katy? So trusting of someone who contacted you through Facebook?

But what about Robbie? What's his part in all this? Has he been motivated by unrequited love, as the detective suggested, or something altogether more sinister?

He followed you, Katy. Stood outside your home.

Now she has gone from scared to petrified. She jumps up, runs to the window, and frantically scans the street outside. The only person out there is a woman with a pram. Would Robbie stand in full view of her window? Wouldn't he be more discreet? She yanks up the lower section of the window and sticks her head out, scouring potential screening offered by trees or bushes. No one there. At least not that she can see.

She slams the window shut and her thoughts jerk around before randomly settling on David Hooper, one of the few students she couldn't track down. Why has *he* come into her head so suddenly? Is her subconscious trying to tell her something? Did David have some personal issues that she can't remember? Were his school years unhappy? Did they leave behind a residue of bitterness and a desire for revenge? All Katy can recall is that he was very good at French and used to spend lunchtimes in the library.

She's on her way to the bedroom, to look up David in the yearbook, when there's a loud knock on the door, rattling her nerves even further. Who would be calling this time of day, when she's not even meant to be home? How did they get through the security door downstairs? She tiptoes to the door and peers through the peekhole to see a magnified image of Jim's weather-beaten face.

'Just me,' he says as she opens the door. 'Noticed you were home early. Just popping down to the shops and wondered if you wanted anything?'

Katy knows she is losing her grip then because she experiences a dart of pure, electrifying fear. Jim, her next-door neighbour. The man who knows her exact movements, day in and out. The man who has a spare key to her apartment, who could have easily used her laptop and accessed all sorts of information. It makes no sense why he would send terrifying notes to people he hasn't met, but that logic does absolutely nothing to curb her terror.

'I'm fine,' she yelps and closes the door in his face.

She doesn't know how to stop the fear now it has taken hold. Jim, Mike, Robbie, David Hooper: their faces rotate in her head, their expressions increasingly menacing. She hates feeling like this. The fear is a mockery of her coveted independence, of what she preaches to her students about being brave and taking on the world.

It's 5 p.m. The evening stretches out in front of her, full of unspecified terror. What if Mike phones again? Or Jim knocks on the door for the second time? Robbie could be on his way here to take up watch. She can't be alone tonight. She picks up her phone.

'Hey, Luke, it's me …'

Luke comes with a bottle of wine in each hand and Aaron carries a plastic bag filled with take-away containers. Katy has never been so happy to see them.

They sit at the kitchen table, devouring the food, slugging the wine, talking about Jarrod. How deeply shocked they are, even though it's been twenty-odd years since he's been part of their lives. Jarrod was the first to get his driver's licence, driving his father's Toyota Camry to school every day, skidding into the unsealed car park in a billow of dust. One afternoon, Luke decided to sit on the bonnet as Jarrod reversed out of his space, and they were spotted by Mr Rowland, the principal.

'We got detention and had to write an eight-hundred-word essay on road safety. Jarrod was furious because he missed rugby training.'

Both of Luke's bottles are empty. The alcohol has done its job. Katy feels fuzzy, affectionate, quite sheepish.

'I'm so glad you're both here,' she blurts out, cutting Luke off mid-sentence. 'I was so scared. Seems so silly now.'

Luke's face is flushed; his glass has been refilled more often than hers. The truth is, he drinks too much. Another truth is that he can be incredibly selfish at times. Luke is far from perfect and yet she still loves him and has never felt the urge to catalogue his faults the way she does with other men. *Why is that?*

'I love you,' she says, then turns to Aaron. 'You too, buddy.'

Luke and Aaron share an indecipherable look.

'Tell her,' Aaron says quietly.

'Tell me what?' she demands, looking from one to the other.

Luke takes her hand in his. 'Aaron and I have talked about it …'

'Talked about what? *Are you getting married?*'

He laughs and throws another enigmatic glance at Aaron. 'No, not that. But I'll do it … I'll have a baby with you.'

51
MELISSA

Melissa bawls her eyes out when she reads the email from Grace. She cries in the same unabandoned way she cried when Jarrod broke up with her all those years ago. She cries for the loyal caring boy who existed beneath the confident competitive exterior. She cries for the man he became, the husband and father, and for Annabel and the children. She cries until her nose begins to run and her stomach feels hollow.

She becomes aware of her assistant hovering by the door to her office, unsure what to say or do in the face of such an outpouring of raw emotion.

'Sorry.' Melissa blows her nose loudly. 'I've had some bad news.'

'Is it Henry or the kids?' Samantha asks worriedly.

'No, no … Just a boy I went to school with.'

That makes him sound like nothing, a nobody. Jarrod was her first love and she fell hard and fast. Impulsive, adventurous, physical: he was so very different from her. He opened up her narrow existence, made her realise there was more to life than exams and academic achievement. She likes to think that she also opened up new possibilities to him, stoked his ambitions for the future, caused him to aim a little higher. For many years she compared her subsequent boyfriends to Jarrod; they always fell woefully short. Until Henry, who's so starkly different it actually works.

Melissa finds she is unable to refocus her attention on work. She is too deeply shaken to deal with either clients or staff.

'I'm going home,' she informs Samantha. 'My head's all over the place … I'm no use here.'

The next morning, after a few additional bouts of crying, followed by a surprisingly good night's sleep, Melissa's head is a lot clearer. She feels strong enough to go into the office today. But first she must follow up on something. A question that's been nagging at the back of her mind the past few days.

She phones Zach because he seems to be on the same page as her.

'Morning, Zach. It's Melissa Andrews … What are you doing right now?'

His response is wary. 'Getting ready for work. Why?'

'Can you spare a half-hour?'

'That depends ... What are you up to, Melissa?' Undisguised suspicion now.

'I want to go to Robbie's house. I want to talk to his sister.'

'Celia?' His tone sharpens. 'Look, she wasn't exactly thrilled with Katy and me the last time we went there ... She asked us in no uncertain terms to leave Robbie alone.'

'No problem then,' she states. 'I want to talk to her, not Robbie. Can you give me the address?'

A pause punctuated by a sigh from Zach. 'Didn't the detective ask that we call her directly if we have any concerns? Why are you taking this on yourself, Melissa?'

Good question. Her only answer is that she feels compelled. Jarrod is dead, and someone out there is guilty of manslaughter or even murder. Is that not a call to action?

'This isn't a concern, as yet,' she placates. 'Just following my instincts. If anything eventuates, I'll call the detective immediately ... promise.'

'Melissa, I—'

'Oh, whatever! I'll go on my own.'

'No, no ...' Zach sighs again, more heavily. 'I'll come, okay? Even though it's against my better judgement.'

'Great, thank you ... The address?'

She types it into her phone as he calls it out. She knows the street. That should make things faster.

'I'll meet you outside,' she says, grabbing her car keys. 'Hopefully, we can catch her before she leaves for work.'

52
ZACH

Zach gets there before Melissa. His house is considerably closer, just a few suburbs away, whereas Melissa needs to cross the bridge. He parks a few houses down and turns off the engine. Why has he allowed her to talk him into this? Why is it imperative that it happens now, at 8.30 in the morning? He is due at the surgery in forty minutes. It seems inevitable that he's going to be late.

No doubt Melissa is reacting to the same emotions he had when he heard the news about Jarrod. His medical knowledge didn't ease either the shock or the sadness. Poor Annabel. He should call to the house, see how she's holding up and check on Daniel, too. Izzy managed to have a chat with Daniel before he was discharged from the hospital. A long honest conversation while Zach waited outside in the corridor. At certain points he could hear his wife's soft laughter as well as sniggering from the teen, although he couldn't imagine what was funny about the situation.

Izzy came out about a half-hour later.

'How was it?' Zach wanted to be able to give Annabel a full account and some degree of hope.

'You know teenagers … they simply can't imagine what it's like in their parents' shoes, can't understand what all the fuss and worry are about. So I focused on his friend, Liam, and the upset he caused him. It was easier for him to understand that … I also asked Daniel to pop in to see me every now and then at the centre. The good news is he didn't say no.'

This is the miracle of Izzy. Teenagers rarely say no to her. They may be obstinate, belligerent and defiant with their parents, but become oddly malleable around his wife.

Zach kissed her on the lips. 'You are extraordinary.'

Now everything has turned on its head. Daniel is without a father. The grief could drive him in one direction or the other. Izzy's magic might not be enough to save him.

Melissa is here, her blue Mercedes coupé hard to miss as it turns into the street. She gets out of the car and smooths down her skirt. Zach jumps out to join her.

'Can you explain again what we're doing here?'

She nods. 'Like you, I keep coming back to Robbie. He's the only one who had a legitimate reason to hate us all.'

'Robbie has an alibi for the afternoon Jarrod was assaulted,' Zach supplies. He heard this from Katy, who called him after the detective came to the school. Nobody has complied with the directive not to talk about the case. Zach's guilty too: he has told Izzy every last detail.

Melissa purses her lips. 'Robbie may have an alibi … But let's see if his sister does.'

Zach forgot about Melissa's intellect, her ability to see things from an entirely different angle. Of course, Celia would feel aggrieved about what happened to Robbie. She watched her brother go through hell at school, and then had to cope with him disappearing from her life, not knowing where he was, if he was safe or even alive. *Celia would hate them as much as Robbie does.*

Great theory. Surely deserving of at least a phone call to the person in charge of the investigation?

'Shouldn't you be relaying your suspicions to the detective?' he asks once again.

She tucks a strand of jet-black hair behind her ear. 'I will … once I've convinced myself there's something worth relaying.'

As though by mutual agreement, they turn to walk towards the front door. Melissa lifts the knocker and clangs it down twice. The door swings open remarkably fast. Celia is right in front of them, bag and car keys in hand, obviously on the verge of leaving for work.

She stares at Zach. 'Oh, for God's sake, I thought I asked you to leave him alone? Anyway, he's not here, he's walking my son and daughter to school—'

Melissa quickly introduces herself. 'Actually, we were hoping to chat to you.'

'Me?' Celia holds up her keys and jangles them. 'I'm in a rush, okay? This is not a good time. Actually, no time is a good time, I don't want to talk to any of you.'

'We're sorry,' Melissa cuts in. 'We're sorry about how Robbie was treated. We're sorry that our actions drove him away from his family, from *you* …'

Celia is visibly unimpressed with the apology. She steps out of the house and forcefully shuts the door.

'Are your parents still alive?' Melissa falls into step next to her as she walks towards her car, a hatchback that looks like it'll have trouble passing its next road-worthiness check.

Celia's profile is set in a frown. 'My parents are frail and elderly. Please don't go bothering them.'

'Was it just you and Robbie growing up?' Melissa is persistent, Zach has to give her that.

'And Nick. He lives in Melbourne with his wife and children.'

'I'm often in Melbourne with work. Which suburb?'

Celia frowns again. Zach can tell she's conflicted. She doesn't want to continue the conversation but finds it difficult not to answer such a simple question. 'Bentleigh.'

'Do you see him often?'

'Every few months.'

Celia unlocks her car door, goes to get inside and then changes her mind. Her expression changes, becomes beseeching. 'Please … I'm begging you, please leave my brother alone. He's feeling hounded, and when he gets like this he runs away … If you're really *genuinely* sorry, you would do the decent thing and leave him be.'

She slips into the car, clicks on her seatbelt, and looks over her shoulder as she reverses out of the driveway. Where does she work? Going by her clothes – department-store trousers and blouse – probably an office. Going by the battered state of her car and the slightly rundown air of the house, it's not a particularly well-paid job. Would a woman like this – with two young children, a full-time job and struggling to make ends meet – have the time and energy to orchestrate revenge on behalf of her brother? Zach recognises her demeanour from patients he sees at his surgery. People who hobble from day to day, doing the best they can in difficult circumstances. People who take each day as it comes, who rarely have the luxury of looking too far forward or too far back.

'Still think it's her?' he asks quietly.

Melissa shakes her head, obviously coming to the same conclusion. 'No … But I'd like to find out more about the parents and the brother.'

53

The house is full. Half the people are strangers. Friends and acquaintances of Jarrod's parents. Tradesmen of all descriptions – plumbers, builders, tilers, carpenters – who look ill at ease in shirt and tie. Daniel's gang from school. Jemma's crowd from university. At first Annabel was appalled by the idea of holding a wake and having her grief, as well as her home, invaded. Bernard, Jarrod's father, talked her round.

'It's a chance to make sense of something that makes no sense, love. It will bring you great comfort. Being in the midst of people rather than being on your own. Realising what Jarrod meant to them. Hearing their stories and memories. Seeing them laugh and cry.'

Bernard convinced her and now she is glad that he did. Food and drink had to be organised. The house prepared and cleaned. Jemma, Daniel and Mia pitched in to help and Bernard was right: the process has given them something to focus on, a degree of comfort as well as a reluctant acceptance that this is really happening. Jarrod is dead. His body has been buried in the local cemetery. Everyone is here to pay their respects.

'Mia and I are going to make a few more sandwiches.'

Jemma's wearing a black dress that belongs to Annabel. The black is harsh on her fair colouring, making her look washed out. Mia has cried so much the skin under her eyes has become flaky and red. Her innocence has been shattered. Her childish belief that mummies and daddies are invincible and will live for ever. Poor, poor Mia.

Jemma and Mia head towards the kitchen. Annabel looks around to determine Daniel's whereabouts. There he is, clearing away empty glasses with Tom, who has been a constant fixture over the last couple of days. Tom has taken Daniel out in his ute to buy supplies for the wake. They've moved furniture around, borrowed extra chairs from neighbours. It's obvious that Tom is watching out for Daniel. He is a good man. Grace chose well when she married him.

Jarrod, too, was a good man. A loyal husband, a loving father, a hard worker. She and Jarrod grew up together, fast-tracked from carefree teenagers to young parents shackled with responsibilities. They learned how to nurture, how to be selfless, how to weather the storms of family life. They grew up together ... but they won't grow old together.

She gasps. She is having one of those moments. When the shock hits her full pelt in the stomach.

I'm alone. He's gone. I'm a widow.

Someone is comforting her. Squeezing her shoulders. It's Tom. Annabel is confused about how he got here so fast, how he noticed from the other side of the room that she needed help to stay on her feet.

'You're all right,' he says. 'You're all right ... I have you.'

Grace has kept herself busy. Watching children, food supplies and whose drinks need to be replenished. It's getting noisy. People are on their second or third drink by now, voices are quite animated, considering the occasion. If she didn't know better, she could be at a party. A party where everyone wears dark colours and the only music is the rise and fall of voices. A party where tears and laughter are interchangeable and shock binds everyone together.

The children seem remarkably resilient. Billy is playing out in the garden with another boy of similar age. Lauren is reading a book in one of the bedrooms – she can't cope with the noise levels. Tahlia and Poppy have been helping Jemma and Mia serve food. Even Daniel seems to be behaving himself. He shakily delivered a reading at the service and was one of the pallbearers who carried the coffin out to the waiting hearse.

'Are you okay, Grace? Anything I can do to help?'

404

It's Katy. Zach, Melissa and Luke are here too. Grace has spoken to them intermittently; they've all offered to help.

'No thanks. Everything's fine for now.'

'It's hard to believe, isn't it?' Katy murmurs.

Grace goes to say something but her throat is suddenly blocked. It's the image of Daniel carrying his father's coffin. Is there anything more tragic, more irredeemable, more final than that?

There's an ache in her cheeks. Oh no, she's going to cry.

'I …' She sobs. 'I …'

She wanted to stay strong, for Annabel's sake, for the children's sake. Now here she is, unravelling.

Daniel's image is replaced with one of Jarrod in his rugby jersey, sweaty, passionate, shouting, '*Come on*, we can win this.'

Then Jarrod cradling the new-born Jemma, a look of puzzled wonder on his face. 'She cries all night. Every minute of the day is spent changing her, feeding her, settling her. I love her to bits.'

Grace has known Jarrod for as long as Annabel has. She is only beginning to realise her own loss.

'I … I …'

'Oh, Grace. Of course you're upset. You're all such close friends.'

Katy gives her a quick hug, as though she understands that Grace can't succumb for long, that she must stay strong.

405

Grace pulls away. 'Thank you … Sorry … Excuse me.'

Keep busy. Keep busy. She drifts towards the open-plan kitchen, collecting dirty glasses and discarded plates along the way. The dishwasher is long full; nothing for it but a sink of hot water.

Keep busy. Don't think about Jarrod on his wedding day: stoic, hopeful, tender towards Annabel. Don't think about him at the communion dinner: weary, withdrawn, at his wits' end.

A glass slips through Grace's wet fingers, shattering on the glossy floor tiles.

'Damn.'

She bends down and picks up the larger pieces; the rest will have to be swept. One of the shards nicks her finger. It's a superficial cut, causing a surprising amount of blood. It's quite mesmerising, watching the blood spurt and bloom. It brings her back in time, to the food tech room. She stands up, her eyes automatically seeking out Melissa. *Look what I've done. Silly me.*

Melissa isn't with Luke and Zach, where she has been stationed all evening. There she is, zigzagging through the crowd, heading towards the doors that lead outside to the patio.

Melissa's phone has been buzzing in her handbag and she's ignored it for as long as she can. She weaves in and out of people until she's outside. The rear of the house is as tastefully styled as the rest: sandstone paving, modern outdoor furniture, a generously sized

406

pool. Two women are standing at the far end of the patio, talking quietly and smoking. Children are tearing around the garden, playing some form of chase in the dusk.

There are four voice messages on Melissa's voicemail. One from Samantha, who needs help locating an urgent file. One from Cassie about an HR issue that has blown up late this afternoon. One from Henry – pretending to sound inconvenienced – wanting to know what time she'll be home, and if he should feed PJ. The last one is from Megan McGrath.

'Hello, Melissa. You left a voice message yesterday for my husband, Nick. Just letting you know he doesn't live at this address – he moved out a few months ago. I'd give you a mobile number if I had it. Sorry, his old number seems to be disconnected.'

So Nick doesn't live with his wife and family. Where does he live, then? Is it possible he's not in Melbourne, but here in Sydney? Quite suddenly, his whereabouts seem vitally important.

Should she call Megan back? Ask some further questions? When did Nick leave the family home? Why doesn't Megan have a contact number for her estranged husband? Why does Celia seem unaware of the separation? Does Nick hate their cohort because of what they did to his younger brother? Is he the type of man to hold on to grudges?

Stop, Melissa chides herself. *You're at a wake. You should not be on your phone. Deal with this later.*

Another part of her is arguing back, urging her to make the call. *You owe this to Jarrod. His family deserve to know who did this and if it has anything to do with the reunion.*

The decision is made. She makes the call.

'Hello?' Megan sounds as though she has run to get the phone.

'Oh, hello, Megan, this is Melissa Andrews again. Sorry I missed you earlier. Look, this might sound odd, but is there a possibility Nick has been living in Sydney?'

Silence. Megan seems to be weighing something up. 'I don't care where he lives, so long as he isn't near me or the kids.'

Melissa's heart does a little jump, like it sometimes does when she solves a tricky problem at work.

'Megan, something awful has happened and I'm trying to figure out if Nick had any involvement. I'm sorry if this causes offence ... Is he capable of being violent?'

Another, more ominous, silence.

'We've all learned to keep out of the way when he's in one of his rages ...' Melissa hears embarrassment, sadness and the quiver of tears. 'Look, I've got to go. Sorry.'

The women have finished their cigarettes and give her disapproving looks on their way back inside. Yes, she knows it's exceptionally rude to be on one's phone at a wake, especially for an extended period of time.

She should be inside, paying her respects, but her good manners have been overtaken by gut instinct.

Melissa dials another number.

'Detective Brien? Hello, this is Melissa Andrews. I'm ringing with some information about Nick McGrath ...'

54
ZACH

Zach has left his suit jacket on the back of one of the chairs. His phone is tucked away in the inside pocket. He extracts it and sees there are several missed calls from Izzy. He's about to call her back when he receives an incoming text.

Outside. Hurry.

He finds Annabel in the kitchen and waits until she puts down a tray of food before giving her a hug.

'Izzy is outside with Carson … I'll call you during the week.'

She pushes a tendril of blonde hair back from her eyes. 'Thanks for everything. And please thank Izzy for talking to Daniel at the hospital. I haven't had the chance to say how grateful I am.'

Izzy is not someone who seeks gratitude. Every day

she sees mothers like Annabel in her clinic. She deals with their disappointment, their fears, their grief, their desperation. Her reward is the kids she manages to save.

Zach is in the hallway when Daniel catches up with him.

'Are you going home already?' the boy asks tremulously.

Daniel has managed to hold himself together all day. Now it looks as though reality has caught up with him. His father is dead. When everyone goes home today, an incomplete family will be left behind. They will have to learn how to navigate life without Jarrod, resume school and university, everyday tasks and chores, while at the same time contending with the fact that there's an enormous, unfillable void in their lives.

'Izzy is waiting,' Zach explains. 'She's outside with my son, Carson. Come and say hello.'

This is how Daniel is standing a short distance behind him when he opens the front door. And Tom, who has been watching Daniel like a hawk, is also nearby, although Zach is unaware of this fact until later. Izzy is directly outside. She must have been knocking and no one heard.

'Hi, love.' Zach bends down to kiss her cheek. 'Sorry I didn't hear the phone. Where's Carson? Daniel's come to say hello.'

Izzy's silence is his first alert that something's wrong. Then her face: her skin is drained of all colour. She is afraid. No, not afraid: she is petrified. Her eyes are

411

enlarged, her mouth is trembling. She is trying to tell him something.

Behind me, she mouths.

Behind her there's the curved front path and some shadowy garden on either side. It takes him a few moments to pick them out. There's Carson's silhouette. Someone is with him, someone considerably larger. A man, going by the breadth and height. His elbow is bent. He appears to be holding something. It's hard to see; they're standing against a large bush and it's almost fully dark now.

'Carson?' He steps across the threshold, towards his son.

'Dadda? He gonna cut me. He gonna cut me.'

Zach's heart clenches with love and terror. This is some horrible nightmare, it can't be real. His terror is mirrored on Izzy's face. *It is real*. Someone has their beloved son. Someone is threatening to harm him. But why? *Why?* Then Zach remembers. *Bottom line is that you don't deserve to live.* It's him this person is after. It's him they want to hurt. Carson is the most sure-fire way to do that.

'Dadda's coming and we'll sort this out,' he says, trying to keep his tone light but there's a tremor that can't be disguised. 'Don't move a muscle.'

'Close the door.' The command comes from a mature-sounding voice. The man would only have a partial view of the door from where he's standing. Is Daniel within his line of sight? Zach complies and turns to shut the door. Daniel is still there, standing slightly

412

back. How much has he seen, heard, understood? Zach forms a silent shush with his lips, and then – holding his hand close to his chest so no one but the two of them can see – he opens and shuts his thumb and middle finger to form three zeros. A moment later he is closing the door in a very deliberate manner, one that says, *Do not, under any circumstances, come out here.* He prays that Daniel will understand and call the police.

'Come here ... Come closer ... I want to talk to you ...'

Zach follows the voice. Izzy too. He wants to tell his wife to stay back but knows it's pointless. It's obvious now that this man coerced her into phoning him repeatedly, luring him outside. Izzy will be feeling responsible, though none of this is her fault. Her brain will be in overdrive, trying to establish the best way to protect her son. Carson is her life, her world.

'That's enough!' the man yells when they're within a couple of metres. Zach is close enough now to establish that he's holding some sort of butcher's knife. The blade glints in the dark; it's being held in front of Carson's face. Oh God. Oh God. He needs to get that knife away from his son. A man of this bulk could be expected to have slow reflexes. How long would it take him to react if Zach lunged? No, lungeing is a bad idea. His medical training recommends talking in scenarios like these. Conversing with the man until he feels listened to, until he becomes less heated and calms down. Until he sees sense and realises this stand-off will achieve nothing.

'We're here,' Zach breathes. 'Now, tell us your name and what you want.'

Carson is sobbing and muttering 'Dadda, Mumma, Dadda,' but at least he's staying relatively still. It's hard for any child to achieve perfect stillness but it's especially hard for him.

'What I want?' The man laughs sarcastically. 'What I want is my brother to reclaim the last fucking twenty years. What I want is for me and Celia and our parents not to have been out of our minds with worry. Always believing the worst had happened, imagining him lying dead in the street, or his body being dredged from a river … Do you know what that does to a man? The guilt that you've let someone down, the person who was closest to you, who you shared a fucking bedroom with, who you should have been watching out for above everyone else?'

This man is Robbie McGrath's brother. Melissa's instincts were right.

'I've said sorry to Robbie,' Zach enunciates each word carefully. 'I've tried to live a better life since then. I'm a doctor now … I help people every day, many like Robbie, who're doing it tough.'

He's met with silence. Robbie's brother – he cannot remember his name, although he's sure Celia mentioned it yesterday – seems to be listening at least. Izzy moves a tiny step closer, her voice bridging the dark.

'I'm Izzy and that's Carson, my son, although I think you already know our names … What's your name?'

Her tone is friendly, reasonable, hard to resist.

'Nick …' he says reluctantly.

'Where do you work Nick?'

'I lost my job a couple of months ago.'

'That's a shame … Were you in retail?'

He clears his throat. 'I worked in a technology company.'

Izzy is doing her magic. Nick is talking even though he doesn't want to. Zach's head scrambles to assimilate the information. Technology. That fits. The know-how to gain access to Katy's computer and install spyware or some other sort of monitoring program. The ability to set up an untraceable email address.

Izzy tuts sympathetically. 'Some of my patients work in the technology sector. I've heard there have been a lot of cutbacks …'

Carson has begun to sway from foot to foot. He does this when he's trying to soothe himself. 'Dadda, Mumma, Dadda, Mumma.'

'Stay still,' Nick barks. 'Stop moving around.'

'He has Down's syndrome,' Izzy says with supreme calmness; she would normally fly into a rage if someone spoke to her son in that manner. 'He's not like other kids.' She takes another indiscernible step forward. 'Do you have children, Nick?'

A pause. A sore point? 'Shut up. Just … shut … up.'

Zach notices a movement out of the corner of his eye. Someone is crouched down in the shadows on the right-hand side of the garden. The figure is slowly inching closer. His heart sinks when he realises it's Daniel. He must have come through the side gate. Oh God, if things weren't bad enough! Has he at least called triple zero? Is help on the way?

'Why don't you put down the knife and we'll talk this through,' Izzy murmurs. 'Maybe you can think of a way Zach can make it up to Robbie and your family …'

This suggestion makes Nick shout in fury. 'Are you mad? Nothing he can do can make up for *twenty years*. We didn't know where Robbie was. Do you know what that feels like? It's worse than someone dying.'

'I know, I know,' Izzy soothes, edging closer again. 'I can only imagine what it was like for you all … But you feel guilty too, Nick. You feel guilty because you didn't know what Robbie was going through …'

Zach hears him sob. Izzy has hit home. 'I was his big brother. It was my job to watch out for him. I knew he wasn't happy but I didn't know how bad it was till I found that stupid yearbook. He hated you, Zach. He wrote in there how much he hated you and Jarrod and the rest of them.'

Zach understands then. How they have got to this point. Nick finding the old yearbook and seeing written evidence of Robbie's torture. His hatred festering and festering until something – perhaps losing his job or perhaps learning there was a reunion coming up – made him feel compelled to act. He sees another movement, this time on the left periphery of the garden. There is someone else out here, not just Daniel. Two of them, coming from either side, melding with the shadows, edging closer and closer. Has Izzy noticed too? How long before Nick does? Keep him talking. Keep him looking in this direction.

'I'm incredibly sorry for what I put Robbie through,' he says. 'I'm ashamed of what I did, of who I was back then—'

'You lot and your fucking reunion, you all make me sick. All happy, happy, happy, pretending there was nothing but good times when it was all *so fucked up*. Nobody cared what happened to Robbie, what became of him.'

Zach identifies the second shape as Tom, Grace's husband. Today was Zach's first time meeting him and now here he is, crouched in the darkness. His head is turned in Zach's direction; he's obviously waiting for some kind of signal. What if Nick's reflexes are faster than they think? What if the knife goes through Carson's throat or one of his arteries or vital organs before they can wrench it from Nick's hand? What if Daniel, Tom or Izzy get hurt too?

Zach says another quick prayer then nods his head in a signal that can't be mistaken. Nick doesn't see them until they're upon him. Tom goes directly for Nick's arm, twisting it down and away from Carson. Daniel launches himself on to Nick's back, closing his hands around his neck, trying to cut off his airway. Carson is free within moments, screaming in terror as he runs into the safety of his father's arms.

417

'Dadda, Dadda, Dadda!'

Zach attempts to hand him over to Izzy so he can help restrain Nick but his son won't let go; he can be surprisingly strong at times. Nick has already managed to dislodge Daniel, the teenager falling awkwardly against the retaining wall on one of the garden beds. Nick's arms – thick, muscled, capable of untold damage – swing into action. A punch connects with Tom's shoulder, bone crunching on impact. Then, before Tom can recover and retaliate, a blow to the midriff, or maybe the lower ribcage, which leaves him doubled over in pain.

'Carson, go to Mumma, go to Mumma ...'

Carson has no such intention. He hangs on to Zach with all his might, screaming and sobbing hysterically. Zach tries to forcibly put him down, but Carson clutches at his clothes, somehow holding on.

Nick looms over Tom's crooked figure, pummelling at whatever parts of him he can reach. Fists powered by twenty years of pent-up fury.

'Stop!' Izzy implores, dangerously close to those pummelling fists. 'Please, Nick, let's talk!'

Nick is deaf to her pleas, deaf to Tom's groans of pain, to Daniel's shouts and attempts to pull him off, to Carson's sobbing and wailing. It strikes Zach that he's the only one who is silent, who is slightly apart from the scene, rendered helpless by Carson. He's thinking about the steps he *should* be taking.

Put Carson down ... Restrain Nick ... Get help.

Tom tries to straighten up, to defend himself, but it's

obvious he's hurt – possibly suffering from a cracked rib or two – and is in no fit state to fight back. Another flurry of blows, some of which he fends off. He loses balance, stumbles to the ground, and Nick comes at him with his legs, kicking viciously.

'Stop, Nick. You're hurting him. *Stop*.'

Izzy's magic has lost its effect. Nick's in a place where he can't be reached or reasoned with. Zach hears far-off sirens and breathes a sigh of relief: Daniel *did* call for help. The question is if it will get here in time.

'The police are on their way,' Izzy cries. 'Come on, Nick. Don't make this worse than it already is!'

Nick is oblivious to Izzy's voice, oblivious to the sirens. One kick to the head and that could be it for Grace's husband. One kick to the head and there could be another funeral, another family left devastated.

Put Carson down … Find the knife … Find the knife …

Zach frantically scans the grass and the shadows at the base of the retaining wall. He can't see it. Too dark. Too many people in the way.

'Leave him alone!' Daniel throws himself between the men in an attempt to protect Tom. 'Leave him alone!'

Nick's pounding Daniel now. He's twice the girth; the kid doesn't stand a chance.

Zach prises his son's fingers from his shoulders. 'Let go … Let go … Dadda needs to help …'

Carson will not let go. Sirens sing in the background, sounding no nearer than before. A powerful undercut sends blood gushing from Daniel's nose.

'Look what you've done!' Izzy is beside herself. 'He's just a boy, *a child*!'

Nick is not going to stop. He can't hear or feel anything other than his own rage. Where is the knife? Where is the goddam knife? Just as Zach is asking this question, he sees his wife bend down and pick something up from the grass. He knows from the way she is gripping it in her hand. He knows from the way she is standing, that outward poise of hers, so contrary to the fierceness surging beneath. She cannot bear to see a child at risk: her whole existence is about steering kids out of trouble, safeguarding their future.

'Nick. Look at me.'

Her quiet command penetrates his frenzy. He reels around, absorbs the knife in her white-knuckled fist ... and grins in a deranged fashion. He thinks she is not a serious threat. He thinks she doesn't have it in her. Izzy is so easy to underestimate.

Daniel groans in pain, inadvertently drawing attention back to himself. Nick lashes out, striking the boy full force in the face. The teenager's scream melds with Izzy's war cry.

All Zach has time to do is bury Carson's head in his chest, so their son doesn't bear witness to what happens next.

The knife plunges into Nick's abdomen, directly under the ribcage, the blade angled upwards towards his heart. She is a doctor. Her aim is perfect.

55
KATY

One year later

It's there when Katy gets home from work. Propped against her apartment door. A white A4 envelope, weighty, DO NOT BEND stamped in red ink. Jim would have put it there; he's been bringing in her post, taking out her rubbish, offering to do her groceries; he seems to think she is invalided rather than pregnant.

Katy stoops to pick up the envelope – she can still bend over, just about – and brings it inside. She kicks off her shoes, swings her feet with their ballooned ankles on to the couch, and impatiently tears the seal.

Yearbook of Macquarie High, Class of 2000.
21st anniversary edition

The cover is glossy and much better quality than the

original. Annabel has done a good job. This was her idea, her project, her way of coming to terms with what happened and marking the first anniversary of Jarrod's death. There is a page dedicated to him, photos with his kids and Annabel. At the beach, at an amusement park, and Mia's first communion. Below the photographs, an epitaph: *Jarrod Harris. Beloved father and husband. Sorely missed*. The doctors told Annabel that her husband wouldn't have felt any pain beyond the initial blow to his head. Nick McGrath hadn't used a weapon, just his fists and the element of surprise. Jarrod believed he'd been called to the warehouse to change a fuse: he had no idea that the caller had an age-old vendetta against him, no hint that he was walking into danger, no chance to explain to Nick that his anger was based on a mis-understanding. Jarrod had never harmed Robbie. The only crime he'd committed was to talk him back from the brink of suicide. Robbie hated him for that, not for the reasons Nick conjured up in his head.

The next page Katy turns to is Brigette's, which is also a dedication. Brigette and Mike on their wedding day. Brigette cradling a newborn baby – Toby – in her arms. Brigette crossing the finish line of yet another marathon. In each photograph she radiates vitality; it seems unbelievable that her life was cut so short. Katy keeps in touch with Mike. He's dating a woman he met at Toby's school. He is a nice man with good intentions, albeit not the right man for her.

Luke's page is a few after Brigette's. There's a picture

of Luke and Aaron on their wedding day in London, both of them looking extremely debonair and happy. Katy was suffering from severe morning sickness at the time and couldn't travel but Tony, Luke's father, made the journey and, by all accounts, gave a very touching speech at the reception. Other photos show Luke beaming alongside a famous soap star who was on one of his flights, and standing in front of a white Ford Focus, his first car. The caption says: *London watch out. Luke's driving skills are still very much a work in progress.*

Katy flicks back through the pages until she gets to Grace, who has become a very dear friend over the past year. Along with being a warm and lovely human being, Grace is a fount of information on pregnancy and what equipment is required in order to be 'baby-ready', as she calls it. There's a gorgeous photo of Grace, Tom and their four children, who all look like mini versions of their father. Then Grace with her youngest, Billy, on his first day of 'big' school back in January. Finally, Grace on her own, proudly standing outside Sydney University on *her* first day. The caption reads: *Back to school for Grace. Good luck with your Bachelor of Education, Early Childhood.*

Melissa's page is towards the beginning of the book. There she is, with Henry, his children and the family dog. The dog is propped in Melissa's arms and everyone is gazing at him instead of the camera. Another shot of Melissa shaking the hand of the NSW Premier, and another in evening dress, holding an enormous framed certificate: 2020 Business Woman of the Year. On hearing about the award – which was reported in all the major newspapers – Katy invited Melissa to talk to her Year 11 and 12 students. Melissa accepted the invitation and delivered an engaging and empowering speech that was also, in parts, extremely witty and entertaining. Katy and Melissa had lunch together afterwards – gourmet sandwiches from a nearby deli, which soon had them reminiscing about the less-than-gourmet offerings from the old canteen at Macquarie High.

Katy turns the pages until she reaches Zach. Another lovely family photo: Zach, Izzy and Carson at a school event, one of Carson's socks endearingly half-mast. What a year they've all been through. Izzy detained, questioned and charged with manslaughter before being released on bail. Waiting for the court case, the exact events of the night, and the weeks preceding, dissected by lawyers and a jury. Megan McGrath's statement was pivotal: her ex-husband was a violent man, a man given to vicious vendettas, a man capable of harming Carson, Daniel or any of the others at the scene. Daniel also made a significant statement: Nick had been there the night he was beaten up by the gang in Manly. He remembers Nick pushing into him, saying, 'This is him', immediately before the youths descended with thumping fists and kicking legs. It seems that Nick instigated the beating by either offering money to the youths or saying something to incite their anger towards Daniel, but this couldn't be proved. What was proven, via CCTV, was that Nick McGrath had loitered outside the restaurant on the evening of Mia's communion, corroborating the theory that he'd followed Jarrod and his family for some weeks before staging his final revenge at the warehouse. Police also confirmed that Nick had been receiving reports on Katy's online activity via a system-monitoring program installed on her laptop, with traces of his DNA found on both the laptop and her desk. All this evidence came down heavily in favour of Izzy, proving that her fear for Daniel's life was warranted. She was acquitted of all charges. The whole group is so much closer as a result of the ordeal. Daniel helps out in Izzy's clinic, talking to other youths about the risks of using drugs and how important it is to have good friends. Both Tom and Grace have been constant in their support for Annabel and her family. Tom mows the lawn, does any maintenance work that's required around the house, and continues to be a father figure for all the children. Luke and Zach are back in contact after all these years, exchanging regular texts and messages. And everyone is immensely proud of Melissa, who was always destined for great things.

Of course, one person is missing from the anniversary yearbook: Robbie. He is the only one without a page, without family photographs, without any account of where he is or what he's doing today. None of what happened was his fault, and yet he was deeply implicated. Katy bumped into Celia a few months ago down at the beachfront. Katy was walking along, or rather waddling along, when she noticed a vaguely familiar woman jogging towards her. The woman's children were on bikes and at the last moment her eyes swung from the kids to Katy and there was a sickening moment of recognition. They passed each other and it took Katy a few moments to collect herself and turn around.

'Wait, wait,' she called. 'It's Celia, isn't it?'

The woman had also stopped. 'Hello, Katy.'

Katy took a few steps closer. 'How's Robbie? Has he stayed in touch?'

She'd heard that Robbie left town immediately after his brother's funeral. She thinks about him often. Glancing over her shoulder when she's on the bus or walking home, half expecting to see him, ready to speak to him if he does materialise.

Celia indicated her daughter, who was pedalling vigorously and was some distance away now. 'He formed a close bond with Sienna. She writes to him constantly and sometimes he writes back. Last I heard he was in Byron Bay ... Look, I'd better catch up with the kids ...'

Katy's last image of her was running along the beachfront, ponytail swinging, in pursuit of her children. She wanted to tell her not to feel responsible but there was no opportunity, unless she was willing to yell it at her back. Celia had sent a message to Zach in the weeks after her brother's death. Zach had shared the message with Katy and the others.

I feel responsible. I was so busy defending Robbie I didn't even entertain the possibility of Nick. Both my brothers are at the heart of this tragedy, one of them seeking revenge on behalf of the other, and I had no clue. Neither did I know that Nick was violent to Megan and the kids. This is my family. I feel I failed you all because I didn't know things that I should have known. To make matters worse, I was the one who initially told Nick about the reunion, and that Katy Buckley had been trying to get in contact with Robbie. I have a horrible feeling I had a part in setting him upon this path. I am so very sorry.

By all accounts, Nick was a complex man with a propensity for both fierce loyalty and vicious rages. A man who'd been close to his brother when they were young, who drifted apart from him at high school, and who was devastated (and enraged) to find that old yearbook and see evidence of his brother's torture written in the margins. What were his plans that evening in Annabel's front garden? To genuinely harm Carson, or to merely frighten the hell out of Zach? What were his intentions with Jarrod? To land a blow that would teach him a lesson, or one that would ultimately take his life? Katy doesn't know. All she knows is that nobody blames either Celia or Robbie for what happened. All she knows is that she wishes Robbie had a page of happy photographs in this 21st anniversary edition, just like everyone else.

Katy hears a key in the door. David. He's home early.

He smiles when he sees her on the couch. 'There you are.'

She still has to pinch herself to believe it. The email she received from David Hooper this time last year, apologising for the delay in responding and asking if the reunion was still going ahead. Her response that, no, it wasn't, but it was good to hear from him at last and what had he been doing with his life? David had been living overseas for sixteen of the last twenty years, working as a translator. His parents' declining health and the break-up of a long-term relationship had brought him back to Sydney. They exchanged more warm, chatty emails, which led to David suggesting they meet for a drink. The pregnancy was a complete accident. In her mind, she was going down the sperm donation route with Luke, when the time was right for both of them. But then David happened. Everything about him felt 'right' from that first meeting in the pub. A couple of months later, the pregnancy – a profound shock but welcome news once they got used to the idea.

Luke laughed when she told him. 'You're saying my sperm is no longer required?'

She'd thought Luke had ruined her for other men. That she would never find someone like him, someone who could evoke the same intensity of feeling, someone who could make her laugh and who – albeit being imperfect in many ways – never disappointed her. All the men she rejected over the years, all the men who rejected her, who let her down or who weren't right for one reason or another, they were all leading to David. She knew the moment he walked into the pub.

She suddenly remembered him. Tall. Shy smile. Hard worker. His slightly brusque manner, which confused her at school but is actually very endearing.

They embraced and the sense of knowing him was even more acute. Who he was then, who he is now, the boy and the man, the whole of him. The surprise of it and yet the utter certainty.

Now she closes the yearbook and puts it carefully down on the coffee table.

She beams at him. 'There *you* are.'

ACKNOWLEDGEMENTS

First up, a big thank you to Ashling Carroll for giving me the idea for this novel (sorry that your Year 6 year-book was such a disaster, but silver linings, etc.). Thank you Nic Herrmann and Merran Harte for dusting off your high-school yearbooks and giving the idea legs!

Thank you to my early readers, Petronella McGovern, Rob Carroll, Conor Carroll, Erin Downey, Kimberley Atkins and Ann Riordan, whose excellent feedback helped shape the novel into what it is.

Thank you to my last-minute readers, John Newson and Christina Chipman, who read the edited manuscript at lightning speed to reassure me it all still made sense (my brain was so muddled at that point, I couldn't really tell!).

A particularly heartfelt thank you to Helen Watson, Jess Wootten, Donna Heagney, Melissa Millar and

Aaron O'Driscoll for your technical assistance and for answering my annoying questions. (Confession: there are a few instances where I have stretched the truth with regard to police, medical and legal procedures for the sake of the story.)

Thank you to fellow authors and wonderful friends Dianne Blacklock and Liane Moriarty, whose advice and support have been constant throughout all the ups and downs of writing this novel.

Thank you to my agent Brian Cook, from The Author's Agent. It's been eighteen years and nine novels since our first phone call! As always, your support has been phenomenal.

Thank you to everyone at Profile Books and Viper, in particular Miranda Jewess for believing in this novel and making such insightful editing suggestions (and for not laughing at my colour-coded spreadsheet!).

Thank you to my family (Rob, Conor and Ash) and the extended Downey and Carroll clans for your unwavering support and for providing endless writing material over the years (life is never boring in big families!).

Finally, but most of all, thank you to my readers. I am just like you – I'm always talking about books, swapping books with friends (although I get very annoyed when they don't return them), and I can't think of anything worse than not having a book to read. Words cannot express how grateful I am to have my books read, swapped and talked about by fellow book lovers.

ABOUT THE AUTHOR

Ber Carroll was born in Blarney, a small village in Ireland. The third child of six, reading was her favourite pastime (and still is!). Ber moved to Sydney in 1995 and spent her early career working in finance. Her work colleagues were speechless when she revealed that she had written a novel that was soon to be published. Ber now writes full-time and is the author of nine novels. *The Missing Pieces of Sophie McCarthy* and *Who We Were* are published under B.M. Carroll.